THE HOLLAND FAMILY SAGA

THE HOLLAND FAMILY SAGA

PART SEVEN

NO ROOM FOR MERCY
BY
CLEVER BLACK

THE HOLLAND FAMILY SAGA

All rights reserved. No part of this book may be reproduced in any form, or by any means without the prior consent of the Author and publisher. Except for brief quotes used in reviews.

ISBN:978-0-9892445-2-7

This is strictly a work of fiction. Any references to actual events, real people, living or dead, or actual localities, is to enhance the realism of the story. Events within the novel that coincide with actual events id purely coincidental.

All material copy-written and filed on site at The Library of Congress.

THE HOLLAND FAMILY SAGA

I would like to thank God for blessing me with the talent He has bestowed upon me, from Him derives my love of writing and telling stories that reflect all but a small portion of life's grand scale.

So many people to thank, but I first have to send so much love to Black Faithful Sister and Brothers Book Club. My first home. What Dama Cargle, Zaneta Powell, Gabrielle Dotson, Carla Towns, Arabia Dover and Sandy Barrett-Sims did for a brother will never be forgotten. Much love ladies!

Treasure Blue, thank you for your kindness and thoughtfulness, brother. Another highlight on my journey that I will never forget. I look forward to networking with you more in the near future.

To all the readers throughout the nation, across the pond, (hi Saima) and those soldiers over in the Middle East, thank you very much for giving me a chance. I was just a man with a story, still am, but now I write with you all in mind every time I pull up to my computer. Knook Barrow, Pat Rice, Renee Gallman-Jones, Rosalyn and Rosalind, (I mix those names up sometimes, lol) Gina Lucas is bananas with it, Denise Stokes and Sharon Blount in Building Relationships Around Books Book Club, Florida, California, Georgia, Alabama, Louisiana, (I see you Amanda, got you covered cuz-in-law), Mississippi, Arkansas, Wisconsin, Oklahoma, Nevada, Arizona, Missouri, much love. East Coast! So many to name, but I send my heartfelt thanks to everyone aboard The Holland Express. Thank you all very much.

I have come into contact with some interesting people in some groups on line, one in particular is the rowdy bunch inside Just Read Book Club, "The Looney Bin", and it is said with affection. Shout out to Mary, Monica, and Natoya, Nikkieshia, Blaque Thetwistedauthoress, Wilkinson, Tajauna—that is one of the most happening clubs on the internet in my humble opinion.

The list of those I know and have had communications with runs long, but you know who you are. If anyone has ever had a convo with me at length, I thank you. I wrote one book, now moving into my seventh and have several more projects in store that I hope you all will enjoy. Today? Right now, though? Let us see what No Room for Mercy entails. Tickets, please!

THE HOLLAND FAMILY SAGA

Dynamic (of a process or system) characterized by constant change, activity or progress.

Greetings, family, may you all be in the best of health and ready for another ride aboard The Holland Express. The definition above is the word that best fits this installment of The Holland Family Saga. Here, as you will discover, transformations will take place, the new will mix with the old and plenty ground will be covered. Excuse the bloodshed.

It is my every intent to keep the train rolling. The last ride was across wide open pastures, this go around? We enter into dangerous terrain. The Holland family is prepared for the rough road ahead; you all, however, are asked to hold onto to your seats. Excuse the bloodshed.

The places I went in my mind to pull up this story, to create this plot and these new characters that will be joining us, are innumerable. I hope I have done you all justice, enough justice to keep the train rolling. All aboard!

Clever Black.

THE HOLLAND FAMILY SAGA

CHAPTER ONE
LA FAMILIA

They look like small piles of Lego blocks from afar. White, dusty roofs of houses compressed together and tucked in amongst irrigation ponds and warehouses surrounded by chain link fences. Churches with pointed steeples rose above every other structure on the town's southwest side, and cars, moving objects that looked like ants from the sky, scurried up and down the town's roads in silence.

The rundown soccer field with small dots identifiable as children jetting about brought a smile to her face, but also brought about a touch of sorrow. Her brothers were supposed to rebuild it and other structures, but they never got the chance, having had their lives taken at the hands of another inside an airport in the city of New Orleans while she lay comatose in an intensive care unit in Denver, Colorado. All those things and more was on her mind as the Learjet she flew in cruised over the city in a slow and steady descent, touching down on a dirt runway on the city's far southwest side and rolling to a complete halt.

The doors opened slowly and twenty-two year-old Carmella Lapiente` laid eyes upon her homeland for the first time in just under three years. She'd never planned on staying away for such a long period, but a home invasion in Memphis, Tennessee back in March of 1999, where she'd taken two bullets to the skull and had three of her soldiers murdered, had placed her on the road to recovery. Now, in August of 2001, just over two years after that fateful night, she was back where she was strongest and the love was the greatest—her home town of Valle Hermoso, in the state of Tamaulipas in the country of Mexico.

Valle Hermoso was a small town roughly thirty-five miles south of Brownsville, Texas. It was a poor town. With a population of 49,000, its citizens were primarily laborers and farm hands, or soldiers working for various drug cartels based further south. Valle Hermoso was a smuggler's paradise. Corrupt politicians catered to the will of drug traffickers and went to the highest bidder or did their bidding willingly under the threat of reprise. The desert town was the last Mexican outpost for drug traffickers looking to ship their merchandise into the United States at the Brownsville, Texas crossing, which lay just a half hour drive north. Christ was in the hearts of many of the town's citizens as was evident by its numerous Catholic houses of worship, but many others worshiped another god—the god of money—and those who possessed it were treated as such.

When the doors on the plane opened completely, Carmella Lapiente` emerged from the belly of the luxurious metal bird just as three silver Hummer H-1s came into view. "Volvamos a lo nuestro, DeAngelo." (Back to business, DeAngelo.) she said as she scanned the entire area while slowly descending the stairs.

The Hummers slowed to a roll and paused in front of Carmella and DeAngelo and the front passenger side and rear doors on the lead vehicle opened slowly and out stepped twenty year-old Kathryn 'Toodie' Perez and her sister, eighteen year-old Phoebe Perez. Toodie and Phoebe were Valle Hermoso natives that had dual citizenship. They could travel back and forth to America freely just like Carmella and DeAngelo. They were under Carmella in Memphis and had been sent to the city of Saint Louis to expand the business just weeks before Carmella was hit.

Toodie and Phoebe were identical in looks; tall, slender,

light-skinned females with shiny black hair, long, curvy legs, wide mouths and pretty faces. They should've been on the cover of someone's magazine instead of pushing weight and holding down the streets of Saint Louis for Carmella; but gangster was all the Perez sisters knew how to be and do—and the Perez sisters did gangster very well. They'd decapitated two rivals in Mexico and had murdered four potential rivals in America since Carmella's absence. They were doing their best to hold the city of Saint Louis down for Lapiente`, but they had to cut a few deals to maintain their status.

Toodie walked up and hugged Carmella tightly, backed away and said, "*Estamos listos para volver al trabajo, jefe. Todo lo que necesitas hacer para llegar a esto hacer estallar otra vez darle nosotros la palabra.*" (We ready to get back to work, boss. Whatever you need done to get this thing poppin' again just give us the word.)

"*Cuál es nuestra situación en el medio oeste, Toodie?*" (What's our status in the Midwest, Toodie?) Carmella asked as she gave Phoebe a hug.

"We got a connect outta Minneapolis with some Somalis that allow us to move ounces, but the price we payin' is holding us back from pushing the kilo. How soon before you get back to business? Because if we get things back up and running here, we can flip it back in America and have everybody buying weight from us." Toodie replied.

"Not long. I have to get some people in line here in Valle Hermoso first, but it won't be long in doing," Carmella responded as she greeted several more female soldiers, many from her neighborhood.

"Good. We need to get back to moving big weight as soon as possible. We doing good selling ounces, but we can't sell the kilogram because of what the Somalis charge."

"How much are they charging?"

"Twenty-four for a key of yao." Toodie answered.

"Why are we dealin' with 'em at such a high rate?"

"Because they some muscle. We buy from them and they do

hits for us. I know it's not the best deal around, but when you went down in Memphis buyers started flexing and coming short."

"Why didn't you go see Dead Eye and Big Bounce up in Texas, Toodie?" Carmella inquired.

"We did see Texas," Phoebe chimed in. "But Dead Eye and Big Bounce had their own problems down in Houston. Nobody out the crew had muscle to loan. The Somalis came on the scene at the right time and we made it work as best we could."

"Everybody was tryin' to maintain, boss," Toodie added. "Besides Saint Louis, we had to hold off other clicks in Cincinnati and Kansas City. We got spread too thin, so I let the Somalis handle that for us."

"The Somalis are willing to kill for us in America. We can use them," Carmella said as she looked to the ground in deep thought. "But we will supply our own product now. I want to meet with these Somalis so we can discuss a new arrangement. If they're willing to help us kill our enemies and reestablish our position I'll cut them in on a deal at a fair price. If they don't agree to that deal and are unwilling to negotiate we'll kill them all."

"Si, boss. One other thing," Toodie said as she snapped her fingers, "they got a crew over in Saint Charles pushing major weight and they seem strong."

"Who are they?"

"Coban Benito and Humphrey Gaggi are the lead men. They some Italians bringing weight in through Chicago is the word on the street. And they got a strong crew of Italian and Black gangsters from Illinois supplying their muscle. Don't know who they are all yet, but they gone be a problem."

"So they our competition in Saint Louis, huh?" Carmella said matter-of factly as she checked her nails. "We'll get 'em," she responded casually. "Top priority in America for you when you get back is to set up that meeting. From there we'll deal with this organization in Saint Charles."

"Done deal," Toodie answered.

THE HOLLAND FAMILY SAGA

The Lapiente` Cartel, which primarily consisted of Mexican females, had a method of operation much different from their American rivals; their methods were centered on the complete removal of the competition through outright murder. Having a closer tie to the drug trade south of the border, coupled with dual connections in America and Mexico gave the Lapiente` Cartel an edge that made them a formidable opponent on U.S. soil. No questions or compromises from these drug traffickers, any crew that sold kilograms where the Lapiente` Cartel set up operation either closed shop or boarded ship. The Somalis in Minneapolis were already willing to climb aboard, and all need be done was for Carmella to institute the rules on the new arrangement of things.

This other crew over in Saint Charles were some unknowns to Carmella; but if they were selling kilograms wholesale, then it was a good chance they had their own connect somewhere south of the border and they weren't going to go away so easily. Carmella understood she would probably have to go up against a strong crew and take them down if she were to corner the market in Saint Louis, but it was nothing new in her line of work. She'd helped her brothers take down some of the best crews in the Midwest from Kansas City to Cincinnati—and they'd taken those cities by force by annihilating the competition.

The crew from Saint Charles was unknowingly up against a major player aiming to take back the drug trade in the city of Saint Louis entirely. The city was Carmella's biggest money making set and she wasn't willing to share. Coban Benito and Humphrey Gaggi, counterparts to Mendoza Cernigliaro and the rest of the Chicago Gang, were now on the Lapiente` Cartel's radar.

Carmella and her crew piled into the Hummers and headed for an old warehouse a few miles to the north just inside the city limits of Valle Hermoso. As Carmella rode in the back seat, she scanned the town scenery. Valle Hermoso hadn't changed much in her eyes. Rundown homes bordered by rusted chain link fences or rotting wood reminded her of some of the poorest sections of Saint Louis where she ran her dope houses. And the town still seemed weighted down by corrupt government officials and drug traffickers who used its citizens to do their bidding before discarding them back onto the streets, back into abject poverty in order to prey on their own. Carmella was no different, but there was a method to her madness that the town's people could appreciate.

"Who's the major player here in Valle Hermoso, DeAngelo?" Carmella asked from the back seat.

"These guys that work for a dealer from Venezuela moved in when we grew weak here. Nine guys on the north side of town are controlling traffic."

"They must be removed. Before Toodie and Phoebe leave for America I want them taken care of. Only one cartel will move cocaine through Valle Hermoso from now on."

DeAngelo paused for a minute, and thought. He was about to speak out in protest, but he decided against it for the moment. "Si, Carmella," he said lowly as he stared out the window in deep thought.

After a short drive through the southeast portion of town, the warehouse the Lapiente` family owned came into view. The main building to *The Valle Hermoso Tomato Company* sat off in the distance with three black jaguars parked out front in the dirt parking lot and two container trailers that were backed into the dock with their doors open. A soldier walked over and unlocked the gate and Carmella was taken into the tomato factory, which was actually a cocaine packaging plant, where she greeted a few workers and was brought up to date by DeAngelo.

"From our supplier," DeAngelo said as Carmella walked alongside him eyeing the pristine facility, "from our supplier the cocaine will be flown to a small airstrip outside of Mexico City. It will be unloaded, trucked here and repackaged inside this warehouse for transport to America. Our driver will drop it inside the port of entry in the city of Brownsville, Texas, and another driver will take it to our warehouse over in Houston, Texas to be distributed."

"How will we hide it?" Carmella asked as she listened intently to DeAngelo.

DeAngelo led Carmella, Toodie and Phoebe through the 50,000 square foot warehouse with its numerous tomato bins that were filled with the freshest tomatoes in northeastern Mexico, along with its high tech conveyor belts, labeling machines and packaging processors, towards a pristine room about half the size of an NBA basketball court that was filled with stainless steel tables stacked with shiny tin cans.

"Here," DeAngelo said as he picked up an empty container, "here inside this room the cocaine will be placed inside one of these tin cans and loaded onto pallets." DeAngelo then led the crew back out into the warehouse where the machines were and stood at the foot of a slow moving conveyor belt. He stuffed a two and a half pound bag of wrapped sugar inside the tin can he held and placed a sunken tin cap on top and sat the can down and the crew began walking beside the conveyor until they approached a large spicket. A pile of tomato sauce was released and the can moved down the line where a vacuum sealed lid was clamped down. The can moved further down the conveyor belt and was wrapped with colorful labeling with *The Valle Hermoso Tomato Company* in small lettering across the top side.

DeAngelo went and grabbed the can as it approached the end of the line and held it out before Carmella. "A pallet and two loaders will be here," he said as he pointed to floor. "Eight kilograms on each pallet, but it all depends on how much we move. The entire pallet is then wrapped in plastic and loaded inside the containers. Then we fill the rest with actual cans of tomato sauce all the way to fill out the trailer."

"How much are we paying per kilogram?"

"Eight thousand dollars."

"Not a bad price. Who will supply us?" Carmella asked as she eyed the trailer being loaded, impressed with the overall process.

"We have a guy out of the state of Sinaloa supplying us our product, boss."

"Sinaloa? That arrangement places everything here in Mexico where we're the strongest. There's nothing in our way down here, DeAngelo." Carmella calmly spoke as she and DeAngelo resumed walking through the pristine facility.

"Now would be a good time to grasp power in Valle Hermoso," DeAngelo remarked as he and Carmella emerged onto the loading dock, "but the things is, if we kill those nine guys on the north side of town? That will agitate their supplier. He operates out of the Margarita Islands in Venezuela and he has friends in high places there and friends in America as well."

"What is this supplier's name?"

"His name is Rafael Gacha."

"Oh, that guy." Carmella sighed as she and DeAngelo walked down a flight of stairs where the two began walking amongst the three luxurious Jaguars that were out front. "The guy that killed my brothers is an American. His name is Benjamin Holland and he's locked away in Florence, Colorado is what you told me, right, DeAngelo?"

"Si."

"So we can't touch him right now," Carmella remarked casually as she walked around the three 2002 Jaguars wiping dust off the windows and inspecting the insides of the cars. "My Ma-Ma and my brothers all went and asked Rafael could they kill Mister Holland for shooting me long before he was captured and Rafael denied their request. Did you know that, DeAngelo?" Carmella asked as she opened the back door of one of the bullet proof Jaguars and sat in the back seat and began fumbling through the console.

"Of course, Carmella. I was there in New Orleans on that day and was a part of the hit. Your brothers wanted to split up after that job. I drove back to Houston, they caught a flight."

"I know that, DeAngelo, but somebody must have tipped Mister Holland off. No way would he just risk running into an airport and kill my brothers if he weren't certain they were going to be there."

"The men that tipped Mister Holland off are two ex-narcotics agents that worked for him down in New Orleans once upon a time. They are wanted in America now and are on the run." DeAngelo remarked as he went and sat in the driver's seat.

"I now understand why Rafael didn't allow my brothers to kill the guy. He was a major player in the business we once shared. But if Gacha has said fuck my family? I say the same, about him, and anybody that is affiliated with him. These nine guys here in town work for Gacha, right?" Carmella reconfirmed as she picked up a finger nail file and began filing her nails.

"Si, boss."

"Good. Being that I can't touch Rafael Gacha or Benjamin Holland right now, these nine guys that work for Gacha will have to suffice." Carmella stated as she moved the file back and forth over her nails. "Mexico City isn't going to work either," she then added. "Our pilot has a plane that can fly from Sinaloa straight here to Valle Hermoso. This is my gift to them for supplying us so cheaply—I will guarantee delivery from Sinaloa all the way to America after I am allowed to eliminate Gacha's crew here."

"We will anger a lot of people, boss."

"Not a lot of people, just Gacha," Carmella smirked as she blew dust from her nails. "He is our only competition here in town. This hit will work."

"What makes you so certain there won't be any retaliation from Gacha?" DeAngelo wondered as he turned around and stared at Carmella.

"Gacha will surely want to avenge the hit, but he can't leave Venezuela unless the DEA pluck him up from the streets. That I know is for certain. He can try and send his body guards here to get me, but I will smell them coming long before they arrive. The hit on Gacha's men still stands and the Sinaloas will back me without fail."

"What about the American border? We cut out Mexico City we lose our connections with the politicians who have ties to the U.S. Border Patrol."

"Politicians in Mexico City won't interfere in our plans.

Their water's just been cut off that's all, they'll understand. And to get our shipments into America, we'll just do here what we did there in Mexico City. Nearly everyone in government in this town has somebody on the payroll inside the U.S. Border Patrol. People we can make do our bidding."

"Si, boss. Who do you want us to kidnap?"

"I want you to kidnap the mayor's youngest child the same night we hit Gacha's men. When you do, you give the mayor a message from Carmella Lapiente`. Tell the mayor that if he refuses to give me access to those agents on the U.S. side of the border and let me do my thing, I will personally kill everyone in his family one at a time before his very eyes and then I will cut off his head." Carmella said before exiting the car.

"Si, boss," DeAngelo followed.

****

After spending a little more time with her soldiers, Carmella headed to town; but before she left, she was presented with a gold-plated .50 caliber handgun by one of her truck drivers and it was love at first sight.

"Your brother Damenga, he was planning on giving this very gun to you upon the day of your arrival back here in Mexico. Of course he and Alphonso aren't here to do so, so we held on to it because we always knew you would return, Carmella," the old Mexican driver said proudly.

"*Gracias, viejo leal.*" (Thank you, loyal old man.) Carmella said as she eyed the weapon. "*Voy a matar a mi primer Italiano con esta arma.*" (I will kill my first Italian with this gun.) she told him before hopping into one of the Jaguars and she and her crew drove to her neighborhood.

Word had spread quickly that Carmella was back in town. People in her neighborhood had deep affection for her and her family because when business was good for the Lapiente` family, nearly every other family in the neighborhood did well. Before the Jaguars could stop completely, people were surrounding the vehicles, looking through the dark tinted glass trying to figure out which vehicle held Carmella. When she'd finally exited the third car, Carmella was holding onto a stack of hundred dollar bills over six inches thick. A crowd of at least thirty people swarmed her and began telling her their problems. A sick child, eviction deadlines, car troubles. Carmella walked amongst the people from her old neighborhood where she grew up dirt poor, and asked each of them how much money they needed after hearing their problems. A couple of thousand here, a few hundred there; it was like a holiday as many people from the neighborhood received the monies needed to have their problems rectified.

One woman approached Carmella with a child about age ten or eleven and asked for a very special favor. "Miss Lapiente`," she said, tugging on Carmella's tight-fitting beige tank top, "this is my daughter, Peppi Vargas. She needs a simple operation for a heart murmur. I have money to pay for her surgery in America, but I can't afford to pay someone to take me there. Can you help?"

"We can get you and your daughter to America," Carmella said as she eyed the little girl. "But I will be here for some days. Is she real sick?"

"No, ma'am. And she isn't any trouble."

"Most children aren't. When I leave I'll come for you both. Be looking for me at this house."

"Gracias, Carmella."

"Sure," Carmella responded as she patiently listened to the problems of several more people from her neighborhood.

After an hour or so of mingling with the people, Carmella climbed back into her Jaguar and she and left the area. "Time to see my Ma-Ma, DeAngelo," Carmella remarked. "Take me home."

The Lapiente` family's home sat on six hundred acres of land south of the airport where Carmella had landed earlier. Tomatoes were grown and cattle were raised here along with the grooming of horses. The land was lush and pristine, a far cry from the rundown neighborhood where Carmella had grown up when she was a toddler. Upon reaching the family's nine thousand square foot two story villa, Carmella was waved through a brick overhang by a soldier holding an AK-47 in his arms. There were at least a score of bodyguards along the dirt road leading up to the villa. Some men sat inside pick-up trucks, others rode horses across the land off in the distance.

Carmella exited the car and walked under the breezeway, looking through the windows on the first floor into the luxurious interior of the home as she strolled by. The home was empty, except for a couple of maids who were dusting the furniture. Nearing the center of the villa, Carmella emerged from under the breezeway and entered the courtyard and the open garden area which featured a huge water fountain surrounded by colorful flowers in the center of the garden. A single goat was gorging itself on the grass in the square that was surrounded by the home, and several dogs lay relaxing under a shade tree.

Carmella walked past the fountain and stood before a stone bench that was tucked in a corner of the garden and somewhat hidden by a large rose bush. She stomped down into the grass and heard a hollow sound. *"Ma-Ma still has it here,"* she said to herself as she looked around, making sure she was alone in the garden.

Carmella knelt down and felt around in the grass until she found the small handle and pulled up on the hidden door and quickly climbed down the stairs and entered a narrow tunnel. She reminisced about her days as a child when she and her brothers used to play hide and go seek as she walked, slightly crouched over. The tunnel, with its concrete flooring, walls and ceiling with its dangling light fixtures that flickered on and off, seemed much bigger, but she was a mere child the last time she'd walked this secret passage.

Damenga and Alphonso always seemed to disappear whenever she had to find them during a game of hide and seek. Carmella never knew where they were hiding until Damenga pulled open a door inside a horse stable, climbed down inside and led her down a tunnel towards another set of stairs on the opposite end one summer morning.

THE HOLLAND FAMILY SAGA

Carmella climbed the ladder and opened the door and saw her mother pouring water onto flowers beside her newly erected water fountain on that day and realized that their home had a secret passageway. Only members of her family knew of the tunnel, which was to be used during a raid or other unforeseeable danger, and Carmella was sworn to secrecy by her mother and father that very same day.

That was the summer of 1984, Carmella was only five years-old at the time, but she remember those days as if they were yesterday. She missed her brothers dearly; and wished that they'd waited for her to recover fully in Denver before they went after Ben Holland because she just knew they would've killed the man and gotten away. Smiling while reflecting upon greater days long gone, Carmella reached the opposite end of the tunnel and climbed the ladder, opened the door and stepped up into the last stable inside the family's barn.

Quintessa Lapiente` was brushing the mane on a brown mustang and talking calmly to the animal when she heard the movement in the stable next to her. She slowly turned and looked towards the floor, and when she saw those stylish boots her daughter were known to wear appear before her eyes, she sat the large brush down, turned around and faced Carmella and said, *"Casi lo mataron, tus hermanos con a una muerte prematura en Estados Unidos, pero debe continuar el negocio, Carmella."* (You were nearly killed, your brothers met an untimely death in America, but business must go on, Carmella.)

Fifty-eight year-old Quintessa Lapiente` and her husband, Fabricio Lapiente`, who'd been killed shortly after Carmella was shot in Memphis, were among the first to set up a pipeline directly from Colombia to America. Many other smugglers used planes and boats to transport their drugs. The Lapiente` family, however, drove their product into America from Valle Hermoso on their own trucks. For nearly two decades they'd been funneling drugs into the United States. They were an infamously violent family with roots that spread all the way back to Colombia, the country where they'd originated.

"Yes, Ma-Ma. Business must go on and I'm ready." Carmella

said as she walked over and hugged her mother tightly.

"You look very beautiful, Carmella. Your brothers would be proud." Quintessa said as she removed her gloves and ran the back of her hands across her daughter's face.

"We have a lot to make up for in America, Ma-Ma."

"I know everything you know and more. DeAngelo has been keeping me well-informed. Mister Holland can't be reached for now and he hasn't any children. Until we can touch him, we focus on the things we can control."

"I visited the factory and the old neighborhood before I come here."

"I know. DeAngelo showed you the operation and I trust you know of our new arrangement in Sinaloa?"

"Si, Ma-Ma."

"We have enemies who have grown strong on the north side of town. They're friends of a man we once did business with, so that makes them our enemy," Quintessa said as she grabbed Carmella's arm, the two beginning a leisurely walk out of the barn into the openness of their land.

"I have everything under control, Ma-Ma. We're going to hit all of Gacha's men on the north side and kidnap the mayor's youngest child and bring him here until we can negotiate a deal that will allow us to begin shipping our product back to Houston."

"You know as I got older, as I got older, I believed that the dark side of the business would be a thing of the past, but for twenty years now we've been a part of a cycle that grows more violent year after year. The only thing that ever changes is the names of the dead and dying."

Carmella said nothing as she walked beside her mother, who wore a tight-fitting white jockey uniform, black knee-length leather boots and a small, black felt fedora-style hat. Quintessa had a certain grace about herself. She was an educated woman, having attended college in Mexico City and earning a degree in agriculture. It was fair to say that Quintessa, who was the older version of Carmella, with her shapely figure, auburn hair, tan skin and brown eyes, was the driving-force behind the Lapiente` family's business endeavors in Mexico.

Good living had aged Quintessa Lapiente` well; she looked years younger than fifty-eight. She continued talking about days long passed as she and Carmella approached the man-made lake on the property where they walked along the shore towards a medium-sized two story second home on the property that lay on the opposite bank.

"Again you are going to have take lives here, and in America," Quintessa said as she stared at a few ducks floating by near the shore. "You need to be careful how you move in America. Don't stay in one place too long, Carmella. Use the homes your brothers had there and remain behind the scenes as much as possible."

"Si, Ma-Ma. This is nothing new for us. We'll be fine."

"Hit those that stand in our way where it hurts," Quintessa said as she hugged her daughter, the two of them remaining silent as they approached Damenga and Alphonso's graves. "Where it hurts, my child." she ended as she and Carmella knelt before their family's tombstones and entered into a deep prayer.

THE HOLLAND FAMILY SAGA

CHAPTER TWO

A DAY IN THE LIFE

"No hang ups out there, baby?" Naomi asked as she poured Doss an afternoon glass of wine.

Doss and the big three had arrived on the ranch a couple of hours earlier, fresh off their job from Las Vegas and he and Naomi were now discussing the intricacies of the family's latest hit in the comfort and security of Ponderosa inside Doss's private room.

"T-top," Doss said as he looked to the floor and rubbed his chin in deep thought, "one of the marks asked Tiva out on a date and she accepted."

"What happened?" Naomi asked as she peeked inside the duffel bag Doss had sat atop his bar counter and eyed rubber-banded stacks of hundred dollar bills.

"She went out and had dinner with the boy and handled things okay, but those guys were small time. Wiser marks would have picked up on what was going down. And 'the lure' isn't a move I like to make. Haven't done that since ninety-four. Overall, the kids did well, but we stayed longer than I felt needed. The second phase went off without a hinge, though."

"You need me to talk to Tiva?"

"I handled it on the ride home, baby. I think they understand."

"Okay. Doss? Martha came and questioned me about what we talked about may happen the day you and the kids left."

"Whether we were actually going to Chicago or not?" Doss asked as he sat down on his main bar stool.

"Yes. She asked me what was going on exactly and I told her what we agreed to—that you all were going to Chicago and that was all to it."

"You think she believes you, baby?"

"She's taking me at my word at best, but I think she'll figure it out." Naomi replied as she slid into her husband's arms.

"If she does? I think she'll be okay with it given her resume`. What about Twiggy?"

"Those two are close so it's a chance Twiggy knows what Martha knows," Naomi replied as she rubbed Doss's muscular biceps. "But Irene has never asked about things and I don't think she ever will. All she wants is to be able to drive for the family. She wants us to buy her a truck so she could run freight for us. I suggested she train Martha so the two could drive together."

"Slick," Doss said with a grin on his face.

"What?" Naomi asked as she leaned back and smiled.

"It's good you don't want your sister involved, and it was slick to get her to drive trucks. She'll be gone for a while."

"I don't want Martha involved. Not now anyway, because if she learns now she would want in and she's just coming home from doing seven years. It's too soon and I'm not even sure I want to tell her, Doss. She can learn to drive and make money legitimately for now."

"Sounds like a real good plan. You think Martha will go for it?"

"She's already agreed," Naomi said through a proud smile. "I'm looking into trucks in Des Moines through Zell's old connect. This will be a good diversion for Martha. It'll keep her and Irene busy and away from our other business right now."

"If Martha and Irene want to work for the family in a legit fashion I say give them jobs. Let's make it happen. Our cut on this job is a quarter million dollars. The family back in Chicago gets a hundred large and ten kilos at no charge on the next delivery. Can you wash all this money clean for everybody in a timely fashion?" Doss asked as he scanned the money, which totaled $350,000 dollars.

"I left the books clear to cover a third for now. I'll put the rest in the safe. It'll take about two months."

"Well, let our family up north eat first, okay? You the best, baby," Doss ended as he kissed his wife's lips before he and Naomi toasted towards another successful job completed.

****

The bulk of the family was out on the patio having just eaten grilled ribs, steak and chicken to celebrate Doss and the big three's return while Doss and Naomi were inside talking. Martha was sitting on the brick wall bordering the patio watching things unfold. Doss and the big three had been back for a couple of hours now and things seemed okay; but it was something about Dawk, Bay and T-top. Their demeanor had changed entirely upon their return. They seemed more serious in Martha's eyes; and they were always together, talking lowly amongst themselves and growing silent whenever a family member approached. They would then resume talking when they knew they were out of earshot.

Martha was dying to know what was going on with her oldest nieces and nephew because it just looked as if a trip to a warehouse in Chicago was not what was actually going down when they left the ranch with their father. Something inside was telling Martha that there was much more to the story.

Whatever Naomi, Doss and the big three were involved in, they were obviously getting away with it and had been doing so for a while in Martha's eyes. She bit into her rib and then eyed Mary and Regina, who were engaged in their own conversation, totally unaware of the changed behavior in Dawk, Bay and T-top. Naomi and Doss reemerged on the patio, and Martha at that moment, not wanting to let on that she was suspicious of the conduct of certain family members, got up and walked over and sat down at Mary and Regina's table and joined the conversation.

"And then Ne`Ne` said, 'Dimples you can take my English two test and I can take your Biology quiz!'" Regina remarked as she laughed aloud. She then went silent and eyed her mother, awaiting a response.

Mary didn't say anything, however; she only smiled as she stacked her fork with lettuce and cucumber and dipped it into a dish of ranch dressing.

"You not gone say nothing, momma? You not mad we was doing that?" Regina asked.

"Girl," Mary said once she swallowed her food, "me and Martha used to do that all the time in Tuscaloosa. Martha, remember when we used to take each tests in high school?"

"I remember them days," Martha responded as she peeked over towards Doss and Naomi, who went and sat at a table a ways off.

Dimples grew quiet and eyed her mother meekly.

"What?" Mary asked. "I know that look. What's on your mind, Regina?"

"I been wondering about my daddy lately."

"I bet he ain't wondering about you, Regina!" Martha snapped.

Mary looked over to Martha and sniggled slightly before she turned back to her daughter and said, "Your daddy is God knows where doing God knows what, Dimples. It's been twenty-five years now since I last seen him. And in that span of time he's lost one daughter, has a grandson he doesn't know exists and a step sister who hates his guts."

"I never been nothing to that, boy. Reynard was a punk!" Martha said as she waved Mary off.

"People change, Auntie."

Martha curled her lips and stared at Dimples. "If that man

cared, he would not have done what he did to your momma. Remember that, okay?" she said as she stared her niece in the eyes.

"But, I'm just saying he might not be the same person, Auntie."

"So what are you getting at, Regina?" Mary asked.

"I don't know." Regina sighed as she shifted her plate around on the table nervously. "Sometimes I just wonder if I have other sisters or brothers, maybe nephews or nieces out there in the world. That is my daddy and I just wonder about him sometimes that's all."

"I always told you I would never talk bad about your father and I'm holding true to that statement, Regina—but if you're thinking about looking for that man ever? Please leave me out of it."

"Okay, momma."

"And definitely keep me out of it. Nobody ain't studdin' your punk ass daddy," Martha ended as she watched the big three's reaction as Kimi and Koko approached their table.

****

"I think we took too long down there like daddy said," Dawk stated in a near whisper.

"I know," T-top responded. "That was on me, but we got the job the done. We have to get faster when we out there, too."

"Here they come," Bay said as she eyed thirteen year-olds Kimi and Koko approaching.

The big three went silent as their younger siblings approached, each holding open shoe boxes in their hands.

"Umm, what is this?" Kimi asked as she placed one hand on her hip and held out the box.

"What's what?" Dawk inquired.

Koko rolled her eyes. "The straps are missing on these sandals and this is not the brand we asked for! Did anybody, I mean did *anybody* check the merchandise before it was

27

purchased? We can't wear these without the straps!"

"Talk to your sisters about that there," Dawk remarked as she shifted in his seat and eyed Bay and Tiva. "I was supposed to get a couple of video games for Walee 'nem while we was out there."

"You got the games they asked for?" Kimi asked.

"Yeah, they inside playing it now," Dawk answered casually as he smiled over at Bay and T-top.

"Walee 'nem do the same thing to you, yeah?" Bay scoffed as she cut her eyes at Dawk.

"I might shop for 'em, but all I gotta do is find a toy store and I'm good. Y'all went from store to store for Kimi and Koko, wasting time," Dawk chided as he shook his head from side to side, trying to hold back his laughter.

Dawk, Bay and Tiva knew Kimi and Koko didn't know that they weren't really going to Chicago, but when their siblings asked for gifts it was no big deal. Right away, Dawk, knowing his five youngest siblings, offered to get Walee, Spoonie and Tyke a gift. They were easy to please and he knew everything they asked for would be found in a toy store.

Kimi and Koko, however, when they asked for something, they wanted that specific item and Dawk knew it; Kimi and Koko always sent items back by UPS or FedEx if it wasn't the right color or size. Bay and Tiva thought they could just throw the most expensive pair of sandals they could find from the mall they'd stopped at down in Albuquerque, New Mexico in front of their middle sisters and they would be satisfied. Their plan didn't work, however, now Bay and Tiva had Kimi and Koko all up in their face asking them about some sandals and Dawk wanted to hear what they would say. He was getting his kicks out of the situation.

Bay turned to her sisters and stared at them both. "What's wrong with the sandals, y'all?" she asked flatly.

Kimi and Koko stared at one another with their arms extended, eyes wide and mouths hanging open in disbelief like, *"Did she just ask us that?"*

Naomi and Doss's middle daughters were borderline prima donnas. Everything had to be the best for thirteen year-olds Kimi and Koko Dawkins. They were the divas of the family, but they were also the most studious. Kimi and Koko would spend hours in one of the family's libraries studying arithmetic, their favorite subject, and looking up fashions on the home computer. They were the typical teenagers who listened to the latest music, talked to boys on the phone and hung out at Kaw Lake Park with some of their friends from town.

"This is mauve," Kimi said out loud as she and Koko stared down at Bay and T-top while holding onto their sandals.

"What is mauve, Kimi," Bay questioned, shaking her from side to side and wishing Kimi and Koko would just let the matter die.

"Mauve is a lighter shade of purple, Bay. I got these, I mean me and Koko both have these silk tennis skirts with the matching tops in our closets. We couldn't find the right color shoe when we ordered the outfits, but I laid the sandals on top and they match perfectly so y'all get an A for effort this time."

"So, y'all happy with the sandals?" Tiva asked.

"We ain't saying all that now," Koko responded as she threw up a hand and looked Tiva up and down. "But we can make them work."

"Bay? You and Tiva are going to have to come correct next time we put in an order." Kimi followed, eyeing Bay with mocked disappointment.

"You got the sandals, already," Bay said in near aggravation. "What is the problem?"

"What is the problem? What is the problem? First of all this isn't tangerine, Bay." Kimi said. "This is like, like a mauve or lavender as we've said already. We specifically asked for tangerine Gucci sandals with the calf straps. Instead we get some knock off imitation beach bum flip-flops that matches nothing in our repertoire except for one outfit we almost sent back to Neiman Marcus."

"Nothing in your repertoire? A thank you would be nice,"

Tiva said as she laughed lightly.

"We couldn't find those tangerine sandals." Bay remarked as she crossed her legs and looked out over the land.

Kimi and Koko both rolled their eyes simultaneously in disbelief.

"That's the best you can come up with?" Dawk asked as he leaned back in his chair and rubbed his hands together.

"It's the truth, though. You thought we was gone lie," Tiva said as she smiled and cut her eyes at Dawk.

"In Chicago?" Kimi asked with one hand on her hip while staring Bena and Tiva up and down, stirring the big three from their private conversation.

"What is it now, Kimi?" Bay asked in an annoyed manner as she tapped the table lightly. "Dammit, man!"

"The Magnificent Mile did not have tangerine Gucci sandals with the calf straps," Kimi asked in disbelief. "The Gucci shop, which is the brand we asked for and is practically headquartered there in Chicago? The Gucci shop did not have tangerine Gucci sandals?"

"That's our story and we stickin' to it," Tiva remarked as the big three sniggled. The oldest three siblings soon excused themselves from the family's presence, Dawk grabbing his twelve gauge automatic while Bay and T-top grabbed their Dragunov rifles and slid the straps across the backs of their shoulders.

"We going walk through the stockyards and practice shooting for a while." Bay told Kimi and Koko. "Enough of this, already."

"We gotta feed the chickens. We gone be down in a minute. Thank you, though Bay and T-top. We'll make it work, y'all," Kimi replied as she and Koko headed back inside to place their sandals in their bedroom.

Just then, Walee, Spoonie and Tyke ran out the middle patio doors. "Now when you ask for something and the person you ask for something make something happen for real? You workin' with a winner, already! Madden is ridiculous on the PlayStation!"

"And MLB, too!" Tyke quipped.

"Where my main man Dawk?" Walee asked as he danced out into the patio opening with Spoonie and Tyke on his heels.

"He going through the stockyards to go shooting with—"

"They right there I see 'em!" Walee said, cutting Koko's remark short. "Come on Spoonie and Tyke! We going catch up with 'em."

"They too far! Don't you three go down there by that stockyard." Naomi yelled.

"Never mind, momma! We just gone go feed my turtle!" Walee yelled back as he, Spoonie and Tyke jumped down the stairs and ran out into the open field, trailing behind their oldest siblings.

****

The big three had crossed over into the lush pasture on the eastern portion of the ranch and walked across the field with their guns strapped across their shoulders. They were dressed in Wrangler denim jeans and flannel shirts wearing $1000 dollar custom-made boots, $100 dollar ten gallon hats with $400 dollar sunshades covering their eyes. They approached the stockyard loading docks about twenty minutes into their walk.

It was a busy day on the Holland ranch. Livestock was being shipped to meat processing plants so there was more traffic than normal in the family's huge stockyard. Big rigs were backing in and pulling out of the family's three loading docks constantly and ranch hands were scattered all about tagging cattle ears, weighing hogs and washing them down with disinfectant in preparation for transport to slaughterhouses in Kansas and Iowa. It was a good time for the big three to practice because their gunshots amidst the constant noise wouldn't disturb the land or the animals.

Numerous tractor trailers and a couple of bulldozers kept the dust in a constantly whipped-up state and the smell was unbearable at times. On days like this, however, when livestock was being transported, all many members of the Holland family who knew the deal were able to smell was money because they knew thousands upon thousands of dollars were in the process of being made.

A long concrete sidewalk split the loading area in half. It was a walkway used by all to cross the loading docks and head into the stockyard, which bordered a small forest the big three used to set up a target range. Dawk, Bay and T-top were waiting for a truck to back in over the sidewalk towards a loading dock when thirty year-old Flacco approached holding a clipboard.

"Okay, mi amigos. Contamos con un camion cargado. What did I just say?" Flacco asked as he rubbed his chin slyly.

"We have one truck loaded," Dawk, Bay and T-top replied in unison.

"Si! You are learning to speak Spanish very well from ole Flacco. And today is my lucky day because you three have saved me a trip across the land back to Ponderosa." Flacco sang as he extended a clipboard and ran the tips of his fingers over his neatly trimmed goatee.

"What you need a signature?" Dawk asked.

"Someone to sign the bill of lading and we'll have one down and four to go."

After signing the bills to release a trailer load of cattle, Dawk, Bay and T-top chatted with Flacco for several more minutes and continued on down the sidewalk towards the cattle pens and out into the forest where their shooting range lay.

****

Walee, Spoonie and Tyke were now out in the open field, Walee jogging backwards and Spoonie and Tyke skipping happily as the three made their way to another portion of the forest.

"Walee," nine year-old Tyke said as she skipped behind her brother, "before we go and see your turtle, let's go see Mister Spots."

"We're not supposed to go over there by ourselves. We should just go this way," ten year-old Walee said as he pointed to his right, where the worn trail broke off in another direction.

"Us three together can cross the yard." Tyke said as she pointed left towards the stockyards.

"I don't know, Tyke. It's dangerous because of all the big heavy equipment that moves about over there."

"But I wanna see Mister Spots! I haven't seen him none this week and I'm sure he misses me and Shima both," Tyke yelled as she jumped up and down.

"Let's go another day. Today isn't a good day."

Spoonie folded her arms and frowned at Walee. "If we don't go see Mister Spots, we're not going see your turtle. And we'll tell momma you be sneaking and playing the games at night and boiling wieners while everyone else is asleep," she demanded.

"Would ya' really do that to me, Spoonie?" Walee asked as she bumped his fists together while smiling and licking his lips.

"We sure will!" Tyke snapped as she skipped around Walee. "Mister Spots! Mister Spots! Mister Spots!" she sang happily.

"Okay," Walee replied matter-of-factly as he gave in and led the way towards the stockyards with Spoonie and Tyke trailing happily.

At age nine, Spoonie and Tyke were the hearts of the family. They were small for their age, but they were strong and very athletic. They loved the game of baseball, courtesy of their grandfather DeeDee, and Mendoza, who'd started playing with them when they were just toddlers, and they were now the stars on their little league softball team.

The youngest set of twins in the family could best be described as inquisitive. Petite frames with smooth, brown skin and big, round, dark eyes gave way to the most beautiful smile ever. Their crown was a thick, jet black Afro. Spoonie and Tyke never wore their hair in braids or platted. They sported a natural at all times, or wore two Afro puffs like the ones they sported on this day. That was their only style and it fit the two perfectly.

The three prodded along and before long the dusty stockyards were upon them with all its noises, odors, and hustle and bustle. Walee stopped just before the sidewalk and waited to see if there were any adults walking down the pavement, which would let him know it was safe to cross. Trucks were everywhere, some idling with drivers standing out front talking, a large bulldozer shoving hay into piles and pickup trucks cruising by slowly.

While the three kids were waiting for a clearing to walk out onto the sidewalk, Flacco approached. "Walee," he exclaimed. "What are you and your sisters doing down here alone?"

"I was going feed my turtle but these two wanted to come and visit Mister Spots before we did so."

Flacco took off his ten gallon hat and scratched his thick head of black hair over the circumstances. He knew Mister Spots was Spoonie and Tyke's favorite calf. They'd known him for almost a year now and loved to feed the white cow with tan spots all over his body at least twice a week while petting him. The only problem with Mister Spots was the fact that he was headed to a meat processing plant so today would be his last day on the ranch.

"Okay, Mister, umm, Mister Spots is, he's—"

"He's over there in the first pen I can see from here, Flacco!" Tyke yelled excitedly as she clutched Flacco's hands. "I wanna go and see Mister Spots!"

Flacco looked at Walee, who only shrugged his shoulders, and pulled him over to the side and knelt down. "Did you tell them what goes on on a day like today, Senor Walee?"

"I ain't say nothin'. I tried not to bring them over here but, they got some dirt on me so I had to compromise."

"Well, today is not a happy day for Mister Spots."

Walee smiled down at Flacco. "I know that—but they don't know that," he said with a grin as he eyed his sisters standing just out of earshot.

"They may question why Mister Spots is not here next time, no? Just like the other two calves? And the little piggies they used to play with?"

"If they do? I'm gonna tell them the truth."

"No, no. It'll break their little hearts. Don't say nothing about what will happen to Mister Spots, okay, Walee?"

"Hey? They wanna threaten to expose my late night happy hour? I'll hit 'em where it hurts." Walee said as he folded his arms and stuck out his chest.

"You're going to regret doing that, Senor Walee," Flacco warned as he stood up and grabbed Spoonie and Tyke's hands. He walked the twins across the loading area to the loading pen that held Mister Spots and eleven other cattle that were destined to become someone's dinner. Flacco said nothing as he opened the gate and led Spoonie and Tyke inside, handing them fresh straw to feed their favorite bovine.

Spoonie and Tyke loved the animals on the ranch. The bigger ones they avoided, but the smaller ones that they knew to be friendly, they would take a liking to. The twins would often visit their 'pets' to feed and water them, and to just be around creatures who constantly amazed them both. From the ponies to the many goats, chickens and calves, Spoonie and Tyke's world was one of exploration and fascination. Little did they know, however, that their entire understanding of the world around them would change before day's end.

"You two ready to go see the turtle now?" Walee asked a few minutes later, having grown tired of watching his sisters tend to an animal that was about to go away and never be seen again.

"Yes," Spoonie said as she gently stoked Mister Spots's side. "Bye, Mister Spots! See you next time!"

Tyke hugged the calf and ran her hands across his head before she got up and said, "Next time we'll stay longer."

Flacco made sure that the kids cleared the stockyard after their hands were sanitized and he watched them walk down to the edge of the forest where Walee scooped up his turtle and began leading the way back to the horse field where he was met by Siloam and Twiggy, who'd just finished riding horses and were now driving a golf cart back to Ponderosa. Certain that the family's youngest three were now safe and in good hands, Flacco returned to the stockyard and resumed his previous duties.

****

The sun was beginning to set a few hours later and the family had been outside for nearly the entire day. Everyone was exhausted as they began making their way back to Ponderosa and washing up for dinner. Walee had placed his turtle back into its cage beside a pond at the edge of the forest and he, Spoonie and Tyke were now walking back to the patio.

"We should go and see Mister Spots again before dinner. We played with your turtle all day, Walee. Me and Spoonie could've stayed with Mister Spots if we knew we were going to be back here the whole day."

"Mister Spots is gone, Tyke." Walee said matter-of-factly.

"Gone? Gone where?"

"Oh!" Spoonie chimed in. "Remember the last calf we had and that little pig? Momma said they went to a new home. Maybe Mister Spots went to the new home where our other calf and our pig went."

"They went home alright," Walee chuckled.

"What's that supposed to mean?" Tyke asked.

"Mister Spots and ya' little pig friend's new home will be in the meat department at the grocery store."

Spoonie and Tyke couldn't make sense of what Walee was telling them; they looked at one another briefly before running up behind Walee.

"I'm not understanding this," Spoonie said as she walked beside her brother. "What does the meat department in a grocery store have to do with Mister Spots?"

"You know them ribs we was eating earlier today?"

"Yeah," the twins answered simultaneously.

"Well, that's what happens when Mister Spots goes to his new home. They chop off his head, take off all his skin and cut him up into tiny pieces so we can eat him and his friends."

Spoonie and Tyke paused in their tracks and covered their lower faces. "They gone kill Mister Spots?" Tyke asked through trembling lips.

"They gone kill Mister Spots, ya' favorite chickens and even those little pigs who y'all be calling the stinky beasts. They gone kill all of 'em. Every time you see those big trucks back there that mean one of ya' little animal friends is about to die."

"They gone kill Mister Spots?" Tyke cried again in disbelief.

"What I said? As of now," Walee said as he looked at his bare wrist as if he were wearing a watch, "as of now my Rolex is telling me that Mister Spots is on somebody's meat hook being skinned alive and ready to go to the meat market."

"Mister Spots," Spoonie and Tyke gasped in shock as they two took off running towards Ponderosa, crying their little hearts out in disbelief.

Walee was surprised at his sisters' reaction. He ran and caught up with Spoonie and Tyke and stood before them, stopping them in their tracks just beyond the patio. "Move out the way," Tyke snapped as she walked around Walee. "Me and Spoonie have something to ask momma."

"We have to wash our hands first." Walee said as the three climbed the patio stairs and walked amongst the family.

"Okay," Spoonie remarked as she and Tyke followed Walee into the home. "But we're still gonna ask momma what we have to ask her."

"Spoonie? You and Tyke can't say nothing about this to no one. You can't say nothing, okay?"

"But Mister Spots was—"

"Listen to me!" Walee said under his breath as he led his sisters into the bathroom and closed the door. "After we play softball tomorrow we can go pick out another calf and y'all can keep it alive until it dies. They can live twenty years or more on their own."

"And twenty years is how long?" Spoonie asked as she went and grabbed three towels out of the spacious walk-in cabinet.

"You two would be around twenty eight or twenty-nine years old. Does that help you to understand how long twenty years is?" Walee asked as he dabbed liquid soap into his sisters' towels.

"That is a long time," Spoonie replied as she turned on the water. "But I still want Mister Spots back! He was our pet, just like you have your turtle!" she snapped.

"And we're still going to have ask momma if what you said is really true." Tyke chimed in as the three began washing their hands and faces at the four light-grey marble sinks inside the spacious bathroom.

When Spoonie and Tyke left the bathroom, Walee began to get nervous. His sisters were really hung up over Mister Spots. He never thought they would react the way they did once he'd told them the truth. He only wanted to get back at them for threatening to expose him playing video games and boiling wieners at night, but things had spun out of control all of a sudden. He tucked his hands into his jean pockets and walked out onto the patio to await his fate because he just knew Spoonie and Tyke were going to let everybody in the family know what they'd learned from him.

When Walee walked out onto the patio, he saw Spoonie and Tyke sitting in between Koko and Kimi with Mary and Regina sitting on the opposite side of the table.

Martha, Bena and Tiva were sitting at another table talking with Siloam, and Dawk was sitting at a table with his mother and father.

Walee walked over and sat beside Mary and looked over to his sisters. He was now sorry he'd hurt them, and whatever came of the situation he would deal with it and accept it as he felt he deserved it because he truly felt bad about himself. Spoonie and Tyke both had a disheartened look on their face as they eyed some of the steaks and ribs in the baskets sitting atop the cart near the grill pit. The family all held hands and Naomi said prayer before getting up and walking over to the grill.

"They have some new chicks back there, y'all" Koko said as she got up to help her mother and father serve dinner.

"I knew they were going to hatch soon. Did you two separate them and their mother from the rest of the bunch?" Naomi asked as she wheeled a cart around the patio, Doss sitting baskets of ribs and steaks out each table and Koko following with another cart filled dinnerware.

"Yes, ma'am," Koko replied as she handed Regina a stack of dinner plates. "And we locked the roosters up before we left, too, momma," she added.

Spoonie was sitting beside Kimi with her arms folded in silence. When Kimi placed two ribs onto a plate and handed it to her, she yelled aloud, "I'm not eating that! You're tryna feed me Mister Spots!"

"Mister who?" Kimi asked in a perplexed manner as she sat the plate down before Spoonie.

"Mister Spots," Tyke said while shoving the plate away from her and her sister.

"Who is Mister Spots, Sinopa?" Kimi asked as she bit into a rib. *"These ribs are really good,"* she said to herself.

"He was our animal friend!" Tyke snapped. "Everybody always says that the animals were going to a new home, but today we learned something new! Mister Spots and the rest of his friends are being made into food and we don't like it! We're some bad people because we're killing animals and eating them alive!" she yelled aloud, getting everyone's attention.

"How you gone kill 'em and eat 'em alive, Tyke?" Kimi asked as she sniggled.

"You know what I mean!"

"Lord, here we go with another jaunt," Naomi sighed. "Where'd you here that, Tyke?"

When Tyke pointed over to Walee, the entire family eyed him, some shaking their heads in disbelief.

"What? What did I do now?" Walee asked, pretending to be unaware of what a stir he'd caused.

"Why did you tell them that, Walee," Bay sighed before she bit into her rib. "You could have explained it much better and you know that," she then said as she wiped her mouth with a napkin.

"Mister Spots sure taste good, already," T-top said to herself, caring not to indulge in the conversation.

"They was like, 'let's go see Mister Spots', yada, yada, ya. So I told them the truth about the animals." Walee finally admitted, careful not to reveal the real reason for his upsetting his sisters.

"You went down to them stockyards after I told you not to, young man?" Naomi asked from her table.

"Flacco walked us across. They really wanted to see their pet so we just went for a few minutes and then Flacco walked us back to the open field.

"Walee said Mister Spots head gets cut off and he's skinned alive." Spoonie cut in.

Kimi looked over to Spoonie and shook her head as she chuckled. "If his head is cut off he can't be skinned alive because he's dead already," she said through light laughter.

"Momma," Tyke chimed in. "Do Mister Spots and his friends go to the meat department at a grocery store?"

"Sometimes, Tyke. Yes they do. But they aren't harmed." Naomi said as she crossed her legs and stared at her daughters.

"How are they not harmed if they're dead?" Tyke inquired.

"Because it's done quick, babies." Naomi remarked softly.

"How is it done quickly, momma?" Spoonie asked.

"They put them to sleep first with sleeping pills. They don't feel a thing."

"Sleeping pills?" Tyke wondered aloud.

"Yes. And Mister Spots and animals like him is happy to do their part for us humans. The animals know what they're doing, my loves."

"Sleeping pills," Walee said through laughter. "They don't use—" he immediately went silent when he saw his mother eyeing him harshly.

"However they do it—me and Spoonie is not eating meat ever again! It's Mister Spots and his friends and we're not touchin' any meat ever again!" Tyke said loudly as she folded her arms and tucked her chin in. "And I'm hungry!"

"Well, what you want," Naomi asked as got up and walked over towards her youngest daughters. "Would you two like a salad?"

"No, momma," Spoonie answered on behalf of her and her twin. "We want corn on the cob. Is there any corn?"

"I'll get it," Doss said as he wiped his hands with a wet towel. He returned with four corn on the cob and grilled them while the family chatted and ate.

Koko whispered something to Kimi and for several lingering minutes, the two couldn't stop laughing and sniggling.

"I'm gone say it," Kimi finally blurted out.

"Girl, shut up!" Koko giggled.

"No. Because I bet I'm not the only one thinking it," Kimi laughed.

"Thinkin' what?" Doss asked as he sat the grilled corn on the table for Spoonie and Tyke.

"That Mister Spots and his friends sure are delicious!" Kimi blurted out before she and Koko laughed aloud.

Some in the family laughed openly as Spoonie brushed up against Koko, who lovingly grabbed her little sister.

"I'm sorry, Shima, but I couldn't let that one slide. So you and Sinopa are vegetarians now that you know the truth?" Kimi asked through light laughter.

"Yes we are."

"For how long?" Naomi inquired. She was surprised over her youngest daughters' reaction to learning the truth about some of the animals on the farm.

"Forever!" Spoonie and Tyke replied in unison.

"Thank you, Walee, for letting me and Spoonie all know about Mister Spots and his friends," Tyke added.

"Glad to help out," Walee responded as he himself bit into a rib, satisfied that he wasn't going to get into trouble for revealing to Spoonie and Tyke what every other family member had being knowing for years now.

On top of that, his sneaking to boil a couple of wieners and eat hot dogs while he played his Playstation would remain intact. This was a typical day on the ranch for the Holland-Dawkins family, each day was different, but it was always interesting.

CHAPTER THREE
OUT THE GATE

A black, stretched Mercedes Benz AMG limousine with mirror tint sat beside a hangar off the runway of Loveland Municipal airport just, south of Fort Collins, Colorado, as a black Gulfstream G200 Corporate jet rolled to a halt. The door opened and forty-three year-old JunJie Maruyama exited the plane followed by his son Phillip Tran, his godson Grover Kobayashi, and his associate from Illinois. The men, fresh off a flight from Seattle, were all dressed in $4,000 dollar custom made silk suits and matching $2,500 dollar shoes and all were holding either a briefcase or a duffel bag.

When he saw the men riding towards him in a golf cart, thirty-one year-old Montoya Spencer, A.K.A. Asa Spade, stepped out the back of the limousine with the cousins, Percy and Douglas 'Dougie' Hunt following his lead. Asa Spade and his crew were decked out in the finest silk linens and leather shoes also; they waited patiently beside the limousine for the men to arrive.

"Mister Spade," JunJie said through a smile as he and his clan exited the golf cart a couple of minutes later, "it's nice to meet you under much better circumstances. It wasn't long ago, my friend, that you were under the care of my doctor."

"The wounds are still healing, but I'm far better than I was a few months ago."

"I want you to meet someone," JunJie said as he stepped aside to let his associate come into view. "This is the man that will be behind your transport. His name is Finland Xavier."

Forty-six year-old Finland Xavier's first impression of Asa Spade was that of a petty criminal, but it wasn't a slight against the man. He'd just seen Asa's kind too many times to count inside Cook County Courthouse. Asa's associates, who appeared to be in their early twenties, seemed to be from the streets, too; but it was what Fin was expecting to see because he knew he would be encountering drug dealers who were at least three levels beneath him and JunJie; but if he was being introduced to these people by JunJie himself, Finland knew these men were to be some major players in the trafficking operation that was beginning to expand into Colorado.

"Mister Spade, I've heard nothing but good things about you, sir." Finland remarked as he extended his hand.

"Can't say the same, but it's good to meet you," Asa Spade responded in kind.

Asa's first impression of Finland Xavier was that of a somewhat shady character. He was a square in his eyes; a man that would possibly cave under pressure. He was JunJie's guy, though, so Asa didn't let on that he really didn't like Finland Xavier from the outset.

"Shall we ride and talk? Denver is about an hour's drive or so south of here." Asa stated as he extended his hand towards the limousine.

Once inside the car, the group immediately got down to business. Twenty-five year-old Grover Kobayashi, a husky Japanese with a head full of stringy black hair and a thin mustache, opened his briefcase and turned it around and put ten kilograms of uncut white powder on display. "One hundred percent pure," he said sternly. "Our suggested retail price is twenty-eight thousand dollars per kilo with an even split for starters."

"Twenty-eight is kinda high." Asa remarked as he eyed the product.

"We figured you would say that," Phillip Tran, a short, well-fit twenty-five year-old, smooth-faced Japanese spoke on Grover's behalf. "We've done our homework, Asa. The going rate is twenty-five in this area, but it's stepped on. By all accounts we should be charging no lower than thirty-two because our merchandise is the best thing going. You can cut this shit two times if you want and still compete. We're giving you leeway for the time being to allow you to establish yourself. We wanted to show just how serious we are about this venture."

JunJie leaned forward at that moment. "You want to open a night club," he told Asa. "You need wheels, and a place to stay. This here is our gift to you to help you and your crew make the necessary moves you all need to make."

"I have a base set up in Shorter Arms Apartment near downtown," Asa remarked as he rubbed his chin. "We're set to go on this end. I just need more fire power. Two AK forty-sevens and a couple of handguns ain't gone cut it."

Phillip unzipped the duffel bag between his feet at that moment and pulled out a black Mini-14 submachine Uzi. "Will five of these help?" he asked.

The Asians were dead serious in Asa's mind. They'd flown into Colorado with ten kilograms of cocaine and six Ruger Mini-14 Uzis and where ready to make a power move. It was an offer and a role Asa Spade would gladly take on and ride for as long and as far as he could.

"Logistics is your crew's need, Asa," Finland stated, removing Asa from his thoughts. "We can make this kind of trip maybe one or two more times, but after that we can't just fly into town with a suitcase full of cocaine and a bag full of machine guns. I'm gonna set you up a small warehouse. A rental space so my driver can have a place to drop off. The driver is out of the loop by the way, so whoever unloads the merchandise should be aware not to discuss shipment?"

"My guys never discuss business with outsiders," Asa told Finland as he turned towards JunJie. "I figure I can move these in a week. How often you talking about dropping off and in what amounts?"

"We're looking at sending you forty kilograms a month for starters on an even split with the anticipation that you will move the merchandise in a month's time," JunJie answered. "You stand to make over a half a million dollars a month out the gate, my friend."

"We got ourselves a deal." Asa Spade said as he shook JunJie's hand.

****

"You don't say? And now Spoonie and Tyke are vegetarians, son?" DeeDee asked through laughter as he sat talking on his cellphone inside a sparsely-filled *Eastside Bar* over in Cicero, Illinois. "And this happened yesterday?" he asked as Mendoza, Lucky, Coban Benito and Humphrey Gaggi entered the bar. "That's funny there. I wonder if they'll still be vegetarians come Thanksgiving. I'd put money on the fact that they wouldn't be come Thanksgiving. Look son, I have company. We'll talk later," DeeDee said before he hung up the phone with Doss, still laughing over Spoonie and Tyke's decision.

"These guys here are priceless let me tell ya'," Mendoza said as he led the men through the bar towards DeeDee's booth.

"What's the deal?" DeeDee asked as he eyed the men approaching the table.

"They wanted Eddie and his crew to wait on them while they come inside and have a drink with us," Lucky said as he eyed Benito and Gaggi and shook his head in disbelief.

"With twenty-two?" DeeDee asked dumbfounded as he made a small square with his hands.

"Twenty-two." Mendoza said as he eyed DeeDee and through his hands up like 'what the hell'.

"Where's Eddie?" DeeDee questioned.

"Eddie looked at 'em like they were wearing big red noses before him and his brothers pulled off." Mendoza answered as he grabbed a bottle of scotch from behind the bar.

"I didn't see the problem," Gaggi said as he removed his

fedora and suit jacket and sat it on the back of the chair. "We always have a drink before we leave Cicero. Eddie knows that," he added as he pulled out a comb and ran it through his thinning white hair.

Lucky sat across from Gaggi staring him down, amazed that he and Benito would actually sit and have a drink knowing they'd just scored twenty-two kilograms of cocaine. "Not under the circumstances. You two should not be having a drink under the circumstances," Lucky stressed the two aging mobsters before leaning back in his chair. "The best thing to do is to get on the road immediately after a score. You guys should know that all the years you been around."

"I know how you feel about it, Lucky but it's an old Italian tradition. If you can't spend time with life long friends in this business who can you spend time with?" Gaggi asked as he lit a cigar.

"They is right about that I give the guys credit." Mendoza said as he approached the table with the bottle of scotch. "Junior and a couple of guys from Saint Charles is tailing Eddie so everything's okay, son. I made sure of that. Somebody has to make sure these two lushes are safe. How's the streets down there in the Gateway City, you guys," he asked while pouring drinks for Benito and Gaggi.

"It's been amazingly quiet. A couple of homicides back in the city, but nothing that affects us directly, though. Business is good." Gaggi said as he downed his shot of liquor.

"Anybody hear from Finland over in Colorado?" Lucky asked.

DeeDee crossed his legs and said, "He called me an hour ago just after our guy on the force had the bar swept for bugs. He's looking into some real estate is what he told me. Those Asians ain't fuckin' around. They're expanding into Colorado now," he ended as he dipped his hand into a bowl of pistachios.

"I tell ya'," Mendoza said, "I never seen so much money flowing through this place. If Zell were still alive I think he'd have to change his thinking about not gettin' involved in the business."

"I beg to differ," Lucky said. "Zell was every bit like these two bums sitting across from me," he chided. "Old Mafioso 'til the death of 'em."

"The Egan's Rats made Twenty Third legendary, you know?" Gaggi said as he slid his glass forward, signaling for another shot of scotch. "They started out with baseball bats, you know?"

"Who?" Lucky asked as he eyed Gaggi.

"Twenty Third. They were playing baseball when my great grandfather asked these four Italian guys who used to play baseball together at the park up the street could they do him a favor. That was back in the twenties." Gaggi responded while Mendoza was pouring him another drink.

"I heard that story," Mendoza said, pointing at Gaggi and nodding to confirm. "They beat a gun dealer to death with a baseball bat and stole three guns he had stashed, and went and killed their marks. Got paid five thousand dollars for that job. A lot of money back then. That's how this outfit got started in the contracting business."

"Frank Knitty, Tony Arlito and Sam Giancana all came later," Gaggi added. "After Capone died, those guys netted millions. But the Egan's Rats basically started this thing of ours in the Midwest and were the first ones to go extinct."

"That didn't have to be. The thing that keeps us afloat here in Cicero is that we know how to recycle." Mendoza said proudly.

"And we're equal opportunity employers," DeeDee added as he laughed slightly.

"What does that mean, il mio amico? You all know how to recycle?" Benito asked curiously as he slid his glass forth for another drink.

"Recycling means we train the ones coming behind us and we welcome all kinds." Lucky answered as he poured Benito another shot of scotch.

Benito gulped downed his drink. "We're equal employment opportunists ourselves," he laughed. "Our guys just can't get made."

"None of our associates who aren't Italian get made either," Mendoza remarked, "but they hold positions of power. The founders of the Egan's Rats never did that. They ran a lot of, damn near ran all others not their kind out of business. Killed plenty of men in the process, too."

"And they began feeding on themselves down in Saint Louis and there went the demise of the Egan's Rats," Gaggi remarked somberly.

"You know? Zell," Mendoza said as he coughed slightly, "Zell made sure everybody got to eat back in the day—no matter their race. And that has been the key to our longevity here in Cicero."

Lucky was the youngest of the five men sitting at the table at age forty-eight. Together these men had decades of mafia experience under their belt and many homicides to coincide. Telling gangster tales and reminiscing about days long passed was a time of bonding for the men, who'd been putting in work since the early fifties. Nearly five decades later, they were still in the business, only this time they were making money hand over fist while literally sitting on their asses. Twenty Third Street Mafia was now more affectionately called the Chicago Gang because many of their old Mafioso ways had waned and more and more non-Italians were taking on lead positions.

The one thing that remained intact, though, was the Chicago Gang's ability to go up against anyone who impeded upon their lucrative cocaine venture, now their main source of income. That went without saying as the men continued to reflect upon days of old, but the unsaid truth would soon be tested to a degree no one sitting inside *Eastside Bar* on this day in August of 2001 had ever seen in all their years of living life outside the law.

CHAPTER FOUR
SPILLED SANGRIA

"*Verla! Asegurese de que ve usted! Ella le ve a usted si! Si ella te ve she'll...*" (See her! Make sure she sees you! She will take you if she sees you! If she sees you she'll...") the bullet-riddled woman's voice went silent before she could finish her last remark as her daughter lay crying on her chest, staring her directly in the eyes and begging her to stay, but she slowly drifted off into eternal sleep anyways.

Only in town for a total of four days, Carmella Lapiente` was now putting her plan in motion. Toodie and Phoebe had completed the first phase of the organized hit by spraying a kids' birthday party in their own neighborhood with automatic gunfire to preoccupy police throughout the city in order to go after their main targets, which were nine drug traffickers on the northwest side of town.

"Who was that lady you shot, Toodie?" Phoebe asked as she looked back at the carnage.

"Who the fuck cares? She was an easy target. She kept me from having to shoot up the entire front of the home." Toodie answered while sliding another clip into her Heckler and Koch MP5 as the driver sped up the street.

The three silver Hummers cruised through town toting a dozen hired female killers through the streets of Valle

Hermoso shortly before midnight. It may have been late down in Mexico, but it was the middle of summer and the town's people often hung out into the wee hours of the night grilling, playing dominoes and listening to music, but what had just happened on the southeast side of town was only the beginning of a night of mayhem and massacre.

Toodie and Phoebe's crew wheeled into the northwest side of town and entered a neighborhood just east of Highway 53 where there were numerous two story bungalows with neatly trimmed front lawns and backyards. Custom-designed swimming pools and driveways containing Mercedes, BMWs and Ferraris belonging to the town's wealthiest were mainstays. The people here felt immune to the violence that often plagued the southeast side of the city, but some were about to receive a rude awakening—literally.

Turning down one dark street, the Perez sisters and company slowed to a creep as they came upon a house in the middle of the block whose occupants seemed to be settled in for the night. The Hummers hadn't stopped completely before Toodie, Phoebe, and several more soldiers hopped out and ran up to the front of the home where one of the soldiers aimed her twelve gauge and blew the double wooden doors wide open with a single gunshot blast. Screams began to be heard inside the home as the Perez sisters and their gang charged into the home.

"*Carmella Lapiente` dica hola! Carmella Lapiente` dica hola!*" (Carmella Lapiente` says hello! Carmella Lapiente` says hello!) was sung constantly amidst the gunfire as the agonizing screams of men, women and a couple of children slowly subsided. Amidst the smoke and gurgling sounds of the dead and dying, Toodie and Phoebe emerged a couple of minutes later with their soldiers trotting behind them and jumped back inside their rides and the crew rolled on towards their next destination about four miles away.

"*Qué horas son?*" (What time is it?) Toodie asked as she slid another clip into her MP5.

"*Doce cuarenta y cinco.*" (Twelve forty-five.) one of the soldiers responded as she grabbed two hand grenades and passed one to Phoebe.

"Tres abajo, seis más que ir." (Three down, six more to go.) Toodie said as she reached for the bottle of tequila once more.

Putting in work down in Mexico was nothing new for the Perez sisters. In fact, they preferred murdering here because they could use more crucial tactics and do things on a scale that would undoubtedly bring about a Congressional Hearing if they were ever perpetrated on American soil. An entire family consisting of a husband, a wife, two children and two other soldiers had been killed. Everybody in the house, with the exception of the kids, was key members of the Gacha Cartel, but they'd just been wiped out in a matter of minutes.

Entering another neighborhood just north of their previous locale several minutes later, Toodie noticed that a party was still underway out in of front the house they were planning on hitting. It wasn't a problem, however, because Toodie actually wanted people around for this third attack so as to strike terror in the hearts of those who may have wanted to aide Gacha; thereby deterring them from deciding to retaliate against the Lapiente` family in Valle Hermoso once they left for America.

The vehicles slowed to a halt a ways down from the celebration where Phoebe hopped out, pulled the pin on the grenade and lunged it into the belly of the crowd. The small, green metal ball bounced on the ground and rolled a few feet and paused in front of a Mexican man who was laughing and sipping Sangria wine and he quickly took notice.

"Bomba de mano! Bomba de mano!" (Grenade! Grenade!) the man yelled as he and the crowd scattered.

Several seconds later the grenade exploded and gunfire erupted. A couple of soldiers returned fire and Toodie saw one of her soldiers go down as a second grenade, thrown by one of the Perez sisters' soldiers exploded. Two Lieutenants belonging to the Gacha Cartel lost limbs in the blast and their shrapnel-filled corpses now lay sprawled out on the well-sculpted lawn.

Windows had shattered on cars and adults were shielding the young as the gun battle intensified. While running for cover, a second soldier belonging to the Perez sisters went down. The people here weren't going to go down easy, Toodie understood, but the crew still had managed to kill two more of the men on Carmella's hit list. When she saw the last four marks jump into a white Cadillac Escalade and speed off, Toodie yelled aloud, *"Vuelven a caer! Los cuatro en que jeep es que estamos! Let's go!"* (Fall back! The four in that jeep is who we're after! Let's go!)

The gang of seven ran back to their rides while steadily firing off rounds to keep their enemies pinned down. When Toodie and Phoebe reached their Hummer, they eyed their dead driver slumped over in the front seat, the top of her skull missing and her body trembling in rapid, jerking motions. Phoebe ran around to the driver's side and pulled the young woman out by her feet and hopped in behind the wheel. *"Que manera de escaper! Veamos!"* (They getting away! Let's move!) she said as she brushed shattered windshield glass off the dash.

Toodie and two of her soldiers hopped in and continued spraying the home's front lawn from the passenger side as Phoebe sped off in the direction of their intended victims. They left in their wake three dead men, a wounded woman, a dead little boy and a score or more of children and adults who would all be scarred for life after witnessing such carnage. It was a miracle more weren't killed at the hands of these vicious banditos.

Inside the Escalade, the last four survivors were in a state of confusion. They'd been hit on their home turf and were trying to put the pieces together as they headed east out of town down a dark and lonely four lane highway. The two men in the backseat were tending to their wounds while trying to reload their handguns while the two guys in the front passenger seat were on the phone with Rafael's bodyguards.

During the chaos, a silver Hummer pulled alongside and a grenade landed in the lap of the man in the back driver's side seat. *"Bomba de mano! Bomba de mano,"* he cried. *"Oh mi Dios detener el automovil!"* (Oh my God stop the car!)

The Escalade swerved violently from the right lane to the left lane and skidded out of control, going into a spiral spin that left if facing the three Hummers when it finally came to a halt. The man with the grenade in his lap had tossed it into the front seat in a state of panic as all four men hopped out of the Escalade upon its detonation. The driver's midsection was ripped open by shrapnel, but he continued running away from the chaos while holding onto his mangled entrails. The soldier in the passenger seat was decapitated by the explosion's shock, his head blasted off completely. The gang of nine emerged from their Hummers and surrounded the last two survivors and opened fire, riddling their bodies with hot lead.

"*Obtener los machetes.*" (Get the machetes.) Toodie commanded as she stood amongst the mangled corpses.

****

The following morning, Quintessa and Carmella were over to their villa milling around their kitchen. Carmella was scanning images of the gruesome shootings the night before and the decapitated bodies of four men along the highway on the east side of town that had been printed in the newspaper. "They've done just as I've asked, Ma-Ma," she said happily.

"Don't they always?" Quintessa smiled as she spoon fed a little girl a plate of eggs and sausage. The nine year-old child was undoubtedly terrified, having been snatched from her bed just before dawn while her mother and father and two sisters sat on the living room floor of their home handcuffed and blindfolded. She sat blindfolded and handcuffed while being spoon fed by her kidnappers, but she was so nervous, she'd vomited some of her food into her lap just as the spoon touched her lips.

Quintessa jumped up and kicked the little girl's legs. "*Usted descuidada puta!*" (You sloppy, whore!) she yelled aloud. "*Mira el desastre que has hecho en mi piso caro!*" (Look at the mess you've made on my expensive floor!)

The little girl was heaving uncontrollably with tears streaming down her face. "*Quiero ir a casa. Quiero ir a casa,*" she cried.

"You'll go home soon enough! So long as your father does as we say!" Quintessa snapped just as her daughter's cellphone rang.

"*Hola?*" Carmella said.

"The mayor says he will do as you ask, but he wants to make certain his child is still alive," DeAngelo remarked.

"Is he with you?"

"Si."

"Ma-Ma? We have the mayor," Carmella said.

"Put him on the speaker phone," Quintessa said as she sat down beside the little girl. "Your father wants to hear your voice," she told the child.

"Pa-Pa?" the little girl cried.

"*Rita, estoy aquí. Usted estará bien. Usted estará de acuerdo.*" (Rita, I'm here. You'll be okay. You'll be okay.) the mayor said as he sat at the kitchen table of his home surrounded by four women toting machine guns.

"*Estoy asustado, Pa-Pa.*" (I'm scared, Pa-Pa.)

"It'll be okay." the mayor told his daughter just before Quintessa's voice came across the phone.

"*Se me cruzan nunca ves a tu hija otra vez y vamos a matar a ella y al resto de su familia, entienden?*" (You cross me you never see your daughter again and we will kill her and the rest of your family, understand?) Quintessa asked calmly as she sat beside the mayor's daughter.

"You'll get whatever you ask. Just don't hurt her." the mayor pleaded.

"She'll be okay so long as you do what we ask. We hold her a week until we cross the border. If anybody comes near me your daughter will most certainly die. And then I'll have the rest of your family murdered before I kill you." Quintessa said in Spanish before she nodded towards Carmella, signaling her daughter to end the call.

****

A few hours after she and her mother conversed with the mayor of Valle Hermoso and stated their terms, Carmella was back in her old neighborhood where she'd met up with the

Perez sisters.

"Good job last night." Carmella told her girls as she entered the front yard of the small brick bungalow that was used as a safe house.

"That shit was fun actually," Toodie said through laughter. "We lost three of our own, but the job is done."

"I heard. I will pay their families for their troubles before I leave here. You and Phoebe need to go and cross the border now. I've paid our guys on both sides so while they are there you must go." Carmella told Toodie.

"Okay. You not coming? We were waiting on you, boss."

"I'm awaiting our first shipment, Toodie. DeAngelo is meeting our supplier later today and we still have the mayor's daughter in our possession. I'll be here about another week until our shipment crosses over. This business with your Somali friends is your next job in America, Toodie. I want you to set up a meeting a week from Sunday. Get that done before I get to Saint Louis."

"Si, boss," Toodie answered as she and Phoebe began making their way inside the house to prepare for their trip back to America.

"*Me dijo que nos vemos, Carmella!*" (She told me to see you, Carmella!) a little girl yelled aloud to Carmella just as she was about to climb back to her Jaguar.

How this little girl had gotten up close to her had left Carmella puzzled, but she had seen the child's face before and knew she wasn't a threat. She emerged from the backseat of her car and looked down at the little girl and asked, "*Dónde está tu madre?*" (Where's your mother?)

"*Estuvimos en una fiesta anoche.*" (We were at a party last night.) the little girl told Carmella as she pointed up the street to where yellow tape surrounded a house on the corner. "*Me dijo que asegurarme de que te veo bien antes de los ojos cerrados.*" (She told me to make sure I see you right before her eyes closed.)

Carmella eyed the corner and quickly realized that her crew

had killed the woman who'd asked her the same day that she'd first returned to the old neighborhood, if she could take her daughter to America to have surgery on a heart murmur. She'd actually forgotten about the promise she'd made to the little girl's mother, but she was going to see to it that the little girl and her mother made it to America to have the surgery and send them back home anyway had they reminded her, so Carmella went ahead with her promise. She had the little girl wait outside and she returned to the safe house in order to notify Toodie and Phoebe of the change in plans.

The Perez sisters remembered the little girl as well; they'd surmised what they'd done and what the conversation was about as they watched Carmella and the little girl converse from inside the home through the kitchen window just before Carmella reentered the front yard.

"Boss," Toodie said through light laughter as she and Phoebe stepped out of the house, "I swear on all I love I ain't know that was that girl momma out there last night."

"I take responsibility for this, Kathy. But we have to take care of her now because she hasn't a mother anymore," Carmella responded softly as she placed her hands on her hips and stared back at the little girl, who was kicking over rocks with her dirty sneakers as she clung onto the fence, staring pitifully down at the ground beneath her feet.

Toodie looked over to Phoebe, her eyebrows hanging low and her face wrinkled looking perplexed. She felt felt nothing over shooting the little girl's mother; it was all business as far as she was concerned.

Phoebe wouldn't have cared about the dead woman either had not the full scope of the shooting be thrown at her feet. She looked at the little girl standing outside the gate and felt pity. The Perez sisters' mother had died in a bus crash back in the city when Toodie was thirteen and Phoebe was eleven.

Phoebe and Toodie had grown up on their own. She understood how rough things were on the streets of Valle Hermoso. She and Toodie were lucky to have survived, having met Carmella and her brothers a year after losing their mother.

They were able to make their own money and raise themselves working in the tomato fields until they moved over into the Lapiente' family's cocaine operation. Phoebe, like Carmella, felt the least she could do was help the little girl out in her plight because it was a good chance she would not make it on her own.

"The boss wants us to bring the little girl with us, Toodie," Phoebe said a few seconds later as she eyed the little girl, feeling a little sorry that she'd lost her mother. "No big deal," she shrugged.

"What are we gonna do with that girl, boss?" Toodie asked, all the while wiping the constantly reemerging smirk on her face that was hard to suppress.

"We will look after her until she can fend for herself. We've killed her mother and it is the least we can do." Carmella said in a near whisper.

"Fuck her and her mutherfuckin' momma! They asses shouldna been out there!" Toodie snapped.

Carmella hauled off and punched Toodie in the mouth, knocking her to the ground. *No podemos hacer nada, de veras!"* (You don't run shit, I do!)

Toodie backed away from Carmella and leaned against the side of the house and wiped her bloody mouth. She was stunned by Carmella's reaction to her statements. "Carmella, I'm sorry. I never knew you to care about *shit*!" she said in shocked manner.

"I *don't* care about shit! But this isn't *shit*! She's a human being, Toodie," Carmella said under her breath as she pointed back at the little girl. "This is a child whose innocent mother we've killed. She was a woman I had promised to help. I'm going to keep that promise. If anything happens to this child during my absence you will have to answer, Toodie."

"I'll, I'll look after her, boss," Phoebe replied as she helped her sister up from the ground, trying to reinstate the peace.

"You both will look after her. She needs a surgery. Her Ma-Ma told me that a few days ago. Wait here," Carmella said as she walked back to her Jaguar and went up under her seat and opened a duffel bag. She reemerged a couple of minutes later and gave Phoebe thirty thousand dollars, all in hundred dollar bills. "Take her to a hospital in Saint Louis and get her the help she needs. Buy her clothes. Keep her fed and keep her safe until I get back up there to Saint Louis." Carmella ordered before turning and walking off.

"Si, boss," Toodie said lowly as she and Phoebe eased over to the front gate.

Carmella walked out onto the dirt sidewalk and knelt down before the little girl and put on a wide smile as she grabbed her hands. "What's your name again? I forget."

"Peppi Vargas."

"Okay, Pepper," Carmella said as she ran her hands through the yellow-skinned, dark-eyed, thin framed little girl's head of hair. "I will call you Pepper because you have such thick and shiny black hair on your head. You're very pretty, too. My girls Toodie and Phoebe over there will take you to America, but you have to stay here and leave with them today, okay?"

Ten year-old Peppi Vargas eyed Toodie and Phoebe with a hint of fear as they stood near the gate staring directly at her and Carmella. Peppi had witnessed the conversation between Carmella and the two sisters. She didn't know what they were discussing exactly, but she'd seen when Carmella hit Toodie and knocked her down before she pointed back at her.

Peppi wasn't sure, but she had a feeling Toodie was the one who'd shot her mother and she grew afraid. For all ten year-old Peppi Vargas knew, Toodie and Phoebe may just kill her and dump her body on side of the road before they even made it to the border, but if she didn't make it to America, she was as good as dead anyways so she might as well take her chances with the people who may have killed her mother the night before.

"*No quiero morir,*" (I don't want to die.) Pepper cried as she reached out and hugged Carmella tightly.

"Oh, my poor baby," Carmella said lovingly as she hugged

Pepper tightly and rubbed her back softly. "You will be okay in America, Pepper. Toodie and Phoebe will not let anything happen to you. You have my word that you will not be harmed, okay? You have my word, baby."

"Okay," Pepper said. "Will I ever see you again, Carmella?"

"As soon as I am done here," Carmella responded as she wiped subtle tears from her eyes. " When I'm done here I will come and see you, okay?" she assured as she opened the gate and welcomed Pepper inside. "Toodie? Somalis! Phoebe? Hospital for Peppi! Use the inside left lane crossing the border. They will know you are coming today," she then reiterated before jumping back into the Jaguar.

"Si, boss," Toodie and Phoebe ended in unison as they lead Peppi into the home.

CHAPTER FIVE
THEY COME FROM "THE AP"

"Mi papá siempre me sentaba al viejo campo de fútbol en el viejo barrio en Valle Hermoso y corría con mis brazos abiertos como un pájaro intentando volar." (And then my Pa-Pa used to always take me to the old soccer field in the old neighborhood back in Valle Hermoso and I would run around with my arms spread like a bird trying to fly.) Carmella said as she sat on Pepper's bed with her feet tucked under her body, telling her about her childhood.

True to her word, Carmella, after overseeing a shipment of fifty-six kilograms that had been delivered to Houston, Texas, had flown to Saint Louis and made her way over to SSM Cardinal Glennon Children's Hospital were Pepper was recovering with ease. The procedure Pepper had undergone was simple; doctors were skeptical as to whether she would need a catheter after hearing her story, so they evaluated her with an electrocardiogram before placing her under the knife. She was quickly diagnosed as having that of an innocent heart murmur, which required no medication or surgery. The condition was harmless and almost always went away once a child reached adulthood. Doctors in Valle Hermoso had merely misdiagnosed the child. Pepper was then given booster shots and placed under observation for a week.

When Carmella walked into the room, Pepper's eyes lit up.

She was surprise the woman had kept her promise. She now lay back in her bed licking an ice cream cone and listening to Carmella talk about her younger days.

"Are you good at soccer, Carmella?" Pepper asked.

"I hate that game, Pepper," Carmella said through laughter. "I never wanted to learn how to play. So, tell me, what is it that you like to do?"

"When my mother was alive she used to take me walking in the square back home. They had a band that used to play there and me and my mother would dance together. We painted pictures and baked bread. I had a good mother," Pepper sighed as her eyes filled with tears. "I wish she wasn't dead."

Carmella's heart really did go out to Peppi Vargas. What a twist of fate that things had unfolded the way they had back in Valle Hermoso.

"Toodie and Phoebe are not really nice, Carmella. Well, Phoebe is, but not Toodie. She yells at me a lot." Pepper said, shaking Carmella from her thoughts.

"I will talk to Toodie for you and tell her to stop yelling at you, okay? They don't know you, but they get along with children."

"What about you?"

"What? Do I get along with children?" Carmella asked as she pressed a finger to her heart.

"Si."

"Of course! I love children. I wouldn't be here with you if I didn't love children."

"I want to go to church and pray for my Ma-Ma that she's okay in heaven."

"Church?," Carmella smiled. "Okay. We'll go to the chapel here in the hospital before you leave, okay?"

"Thank you. Thank you for everything."

"It is all my pleasure. Oh, if the doctors ask you, I am your aunt and you're staying with me and your cousins here in Saint

THE HOLLAND FAMILY SAGA

Louis, alright?"

"Okay, Auntie." Pepper joked.

Carmella laughed and touched Pepper's face with the back of her hands. "You are such a darling," she said sweetly as she pictured Peppi Vargas years from now, all strong and healthy. "You will definitely be okay as long as I have a say so in the matter, baby," she said as her phone vibrated.

Carmella picked up her phone and looked at the text. *Old warehouse in East Saint Louis in one hour.*

"The Somalis. Good job, Toodie," she said lowly. "Pepper I must be going now. But I'll be back to have dinner with you tonight, mi amiga."

"I'll be here."

Carmella got up off the bed and kissed the top of Pepper's head before she left the room and told one of her workers, whose job it was to sit outside of Pepper's room, to notify her of DSS should they ever visit, and to make sure that Peppi received any and everything she asked for.

After leaving orders with her soldier, Carmella left the hospital and jumped into a yellow 2001 convertible Ferrari 360 Spider and hopped onto Interstate-70 and crossed the Mississippi River over into East Saint Louis and took Interstate-55 north for a few miles. She could see the old warehouse where she normally held meetings off in the distance to her left as she exited onto to Saint Clair Avenue and entered an abandoned warehouse district.

This part of East Saint Louis was a pure dump. Dilapidated multi-story brick buildings that should've been torn down years ago lined pot-hole filled streets that were littered with debris. Old abandoned rail lines with rusted out rail cars still perched on the tracks sat out front some buildings that once thrived with human activity. The new tenants were now the incalculable amount of pigeons, rodents and stray animals.

Carmella cruised under the pylons holding up the expressway and turned onto a service road and grabbed her .50 caliber and cocked it as she turned into the abandoned warehouse's back shipping dock which was hidden from the highway. She rounded the bend and saw Toodie and Phoebe, along with six other females from Fox Park sitting out on the concrete dock in the shade smoking blunts. She scanned the area briefly and noticed that only her girls' SUVs were parked in front of the building. Everybody was waiting patiently, but the soldier on the phone had caught Carmella's attention. She reached under her seat and grabbed a mini-Uzi and tucked her gold-plated handgun into the back of her waistband and stepped out the car door.

"Where are they, Toodie?" Carmella asked as she went and stood before the docks with her Uzi on display.

"Dumb asses got lost and rode way over to Saint Louis. One of the girls on the yap now guidin' 'nem in. They should be here in five minutes or so."

Carmella, for a brief moment, thought she was walking into a trap given the nature of the scene upon her arrival. Realizing she'd only had a brief case of paranoia, she walked over to the stairs. "Pepper tells me you that yell at her, Kathy. I'm a tell you once to not let it happen again. She's a child without a mother and on the strength of what she's going through she deserves to be treated better." Carmella said as she knelt down on one knee beside Toodie and reached for Toodie's blunt. She toke a few tokes before passing it back. "Do I make myself clear about Peppi?" she asked through a cough.

"We clear on that, boss. That little girl is a burden, though. She act like she can't do nothing on her own."

"Peppi can't do anything for herself right now, Toodie, and that is why we must look after her," Carmella said as she sat down on the edge of the concrete dock. "Peppi is only ten years old. She has lost her mother, believed she had a heart condition and was about to die, and she is in a strange place with people she doesn't even know. How could she be strong right now given her age and circumstances?"

Toodie reflected on Carmella's words as she blew smoke from her nostrils. It wasn't that she didn't like Peppi Vargas, she just didn't want to be bothered with tending to, what was in her eyes, a baby. The crew was about to get money and Toodie felt Pepper would only get in the way. "I'll make sure she's okay, but it's Phoebe here that is actually cool with her li'l ass." Toodie told Carmella as she passed her the blunt.

"I know. But remember, nothing happens to Pepper."

"Si, boss. We'll look after her," Phoebe said.

Carmella looked over to Toodie as she took a long toke off the blunt.

"What?" Toodie asked through a smile.

Carmella exhaled the smoke and said seriously, "I'm sorry about that thing in Valle Hermoso where I hit you. You know how I get, but that little girl means something to me, okay? She just means something to me, so look after her."

Toodie looked Carmella in the eyes and the two bumped fists. "Nothing happens to Pepper," she said as she looked down into her lap while nodding her head up and down.

Where are these guys? Carmella then wondered silently as she sat under the shade with her crew and checked the time on her Cartier watch.

****

"Bring it...we right here...we're not going anywhere...we right here...this is something we don't share...we right here... bring your crew 'cause we don't care...we right here..."

DMX's song *Bring It* was thumping hard from the interior of a black Range Rover on 23" inch chrome wheels as the vehicle turned off into the abandoned warehouse and paused beside Carmella's Ferrari a few minutes after Carmella's arrival. She and her crew watched as the four men, one whose name was Bahdoon LuQman, A.K.A. Q-man, slowly exited the ride on the front passenger side.

Carmella had never seen the Somalis before; she thought them to be a bunch of dark-skinned, thin men. To the contrary, Q-man and his goons looked every bit like a few of the fellas who balled on Fox Park with their brown skin and ripped biceps. They were all sporting either curly Afros or braids, baggy jeans, sparkling white tennis and ice white t-shirts with long platinum chains dangling down to their belt buckles. The Somalis were a handsome bunch, but they also had a certain style of ruggedness about themselves that Carmella could appreciate.

Q-man and his crew, all in their twenties, were from The Federal Republic of Somalia on Africa's northeastern slope. They'd immigrated to America with their respective parents in the early nineties to flee the country's civil war and were now fully adapted to the American way of life. They now called Minneapolis, Minnesota, which they affectionately referred to as "The Ap", their home.

It didn't take long for Q-man to click up with three other Somalis and form his own crew. They'd started out hanging together in middle school and began selling marijuana in their neighborhood by age fifteen. They soon graduated to robbing dope houses until they linked up with a supplier in New York City and started their own cocaine distributing operation.

Twenty-two year-old Q-man, a smooth-faced, tan-skinned curly-haired six-foot two, two hundred pound Somali with curly black hair, was holding down Minneapolis-Saint Paul on reputation alone. He and his crew were feared throughout the twin city area and were rumored to have had removed a rival Hispanic dealer from the game entirely, having made the man's body inexplicably disappear.

Carmella had gotten Q-man and his crew's street resumes` from Toodie and Phoebe early on and she was impressed. They'd killed before in the cities of Cincinnati and Kansas City on behalf of the Lapiente` Cartel. If they would all agree to the new deal, she knew she would have a formidable crew that would allow her to take over Saint Louis completely.

"You boys are late," Carmella said as she hopped off the dock and stood in front of her girls.

"Yeah," Q-man said nonchalantly as he stretched. "But we here now so what's up?"

"Toodie told you of my offer?"

"She mentioned it," Q-man said as he scratched his nose and looked off into the distance, never making eye contact with Carmella.

Carmella looked back at Toodie with a hint of apprehension. "What's with your people, Toodie? They act as if they would rather be somewhere else today."

"We would," Q-man said flatly.

"Q-man, get on with it, man," Toodie said as she and the rest of the crew jumped down from the dock. "You know the deal so it's yes or no."

"Why would we stop selling to you, so we can buy from you? We got our own thang going in the Ap. I'm not, I'm not feeling this shit here." Q-man said as he bumped his fists together and spat on the ground to his right.

"The hell you come down here for then," Carmella asked with a scowl on her face as she approached Q-man. "You knew the deal before you got here so what's up? You need me to say it again? We done buying from you and your people. And it can only be one supplier here in Saint Louis from this day forth."

"We ain't losing much if we concede to that. Just a few bricks here and there." Q-man said as he looked to the ground.

Carmella laughed to herself at that moment because she knew her crew was Q-man's top buyers. She understood fully that if she were to cut Q-man's water off like she was planning on doing, he'd be sitting on at least ten extra kilograms until he could find new buyers. It was a bargaining chip she could use to her advantage.

"Okay, let's talk numbers," Carmella said seriously. "You were selling to us for twenty-five, which means you probably paying seventeen or eighteen for your work. I give it to you for twelve g's flat, plus I give up the markets in Cincinnati and Kansas City. I'm done there in those places."

The number twelve thousand caught Q-man's attention. He now looked Carmella in the eyes. "Twelve on a brick?" he asked with raised eyebrows.

"You like that price, don't you?" Carmella reasoned with a sly grin. "See? Your work comes from here," she said as she pointed to the gravel beneath her feet.

"I don't get my work from nowhere near here," Q-man corrected.

"You're not understanding my point," Carmella chuckled. "If you deal with me, you will get your cocaine at a lower rate given my connections, but if you feel that you can outdo me here in Saint Louis? We will have to tool up and go to war because this city belongs to me and my girls."

Toodie and Phoebe, along with the rest of the females in the crew, all pulled out nickel-plated .9mm Beretta handguns with infrared beams and went and stood behind Carmella.

"Go to war, huh?" Q-man said as he looked back at his boys. "They some bad bitches, fellas," he remarked as his three goons nodded in agreement. Q-man and his squad were strapped too, but Carmella had the ups. He never had intentions on waging a war because he knew if he got in good with Toodie's connect, he and his boys would move up a notch in the game.

"Put your iron away and let's talk," Q-man requested.

"I prefer for us to hold on to them while we talk," Carmella replied as she spit on the ground. "What is your answer?" she asked as she clutched her Uzi, staring Q-man dead in the eyes.

Q-man understood that if he refused Carmella's deal on this day, he and his boys would have to shoot it out just to have a chance on making it out of the warehouse district alive. To refuse Carmella would be suicide no doubt, and the price she offered him per kilogram was an offer he couldn't resist. Rather than kick off beef with potential partners, Q-man opted for diplomacy. He stared Carmella in the eyes and said, "Me and my boys have mouths to feed back home in the Ap. Now, your numbers sound good and all, but what's the guarantee we gone get the price you quoting?"

"All I have is my word, which is law. If you buy from me, you will continue to kill for me and my girls like you've been doing whenever we need you to do so."

"See? You can't make all the stipulations because me and my dogs have just as much weight as you got in this deal."

"That weight being?"

"We done bodied niggas in Kansas City and Cincinnati for your family back in Mexico to keep y'all in power. We gone be partners in this shit, and we don't answer to no fuckin' body but ourselves. You give us bricks on the low and we will kill anybody you ask—but that's gone be extra. Taking out clicks is a high risk business that warrants extra compensation. That's our deal. If you don't agree with it? Then go 'head and handle your business."

"If you run your own crew and we have to pay you extra for contracts, then you don't sell where I say you can't sell. I'll give you bricks for twelve and connects in Kansas City and Cincinnati, but you will not sell in any other city we control. That's the deal. Take it or leave it."

"Final answer?" Q-man joked as he slowly reached into his baggy jeans pocket and pulled out a blunt and fired it up.

Carmella wasn't laughing. She was dead serious about the deal she was trying to forge and if Q-man didn't agree, she was thinking that she may just spray them all and get on with the rest of her plans.

"Twelve thousand does sound good. We can cut six off the top real quick and won't have to worry about transporting that shit from the Bronx. What you think, fam? Roll with it?" Q-man asked his boys.

"We keep our power and gain two more cities? And all we have to do is kill for Carmella and get paid for it?" one of Q-man's soldiers asked. "Q, jump on that A-S-A-P."

Q-man dapped his crew and turned to Carmella and nodded. "It's a deal," he said.

"Cool. You call Toodie for your first shipment. I expect to hear from you within a month."

With Q-man and his crew now on her team, Carmella began

making moves on the streets of Saint Louis in order to get up-close and personal to her rivals over in Saint Charles in order to hit them head on when the time was right.

CHAPTER SIX
FAMILY TIME

The O'Jays' song *Christmas Just ain't Christmas* was the first song played early Thanksgiving afternoon in 2001 down in Ponca City to kick off the holiday season. The friends and family from Chicago were in town and it was the usual festive familial atmosphere inside Ponderosa. Snow covered the ground outside and it was an usually cold day with temperatures in the low teens. Inside the mansion, however, the mood was warm and serene. Some of the family was busy cooking in the downstairs kitchen while Naomi, Francine and Mildred erected the family's Christmas tree on the second floor with the aide of the young five while the big three were all downstairs with their father and his friends in the living room putting up the second tree and wrapping gifts.

"You think Kimi and Koko will like these new laptops, Doss?" Lucky asked as he wrapped one of the gifts.

"The way they like to get online and shop I'd say absolutely."

"Cool beans. They fell offa truck so ain't no receipt on these bad boys."

"Always looking for a discount, huh? Cheap-skate." Mendoza said as he hung gold-plated bells onto the fresh pine branches.

"I wonder who taught me that, dad." Lucky replied as the men all chuckled.

"Dad," Dawk said, "before we left Chicago, me and granddad shipped some guns down to Saint Charles, but we never heard back from Eddie."

"Eddie called me," Doss responded. "They got 'em. Eddie thought it was an early Christmas gift."

"Well, it was, you guys," DeeDee chimed in. "Eddie put on some new soldiers outta Fox Park last month and he said they're good earners so we sent gifts for those youngsters."

"That's what we need—more soldiers. Benito and Gaggi running a smooth ship." Mendoza remarked.

"Umm, hmm. And Eddie's taking a lead role. You too, son." Lucky told Junior just as Martha and Twiggy entered the home.

"Okay! Now the holidays can really begin!" Martha yelled. "I want a drink, already!"

"I see the hams and turkeys is here already, Mar," Twiggy joked as she pointed to the men in the living room. "Not DeeDee, though! I like pimp daddy!"

"Girl, you is gone get what you looking for you keep flirtin' with this old man," DeeDee said through laughter as he poured Twiggy and Martha glasses of warm eggnog cut with brandy.

In September of 2001, Naomi had purchased Twiggy and Martha a brand new Peterbilt truck complete with bunk beds, refrigerator, TV, CB, six disc CD changer and radar detector. Twiggy was now training Martha to drive, but the two had come off the road for the winter and wouldn't start back up until the spring. Naomi would find the two freight and they would run the Midwest and West Coast. They'd been away for two months traveling the country and visiting various cities and had returned home for the holidays.

"The children will be glad to see you two," Doss said as he went and hugged the women.

"We been missing everybody," Martha said as she hugged

the men.

"How's life on the road been treating you two ladies?" Mendoza asked.

"We have been having the time of our lives, Mendoza," forty-three year-old Twiggy answered happily. "Me and Martha have seen so many beautiful cities and have been learning so much about this part of the country. It's really beautiful out on the road. It is a wonderful experience." Twiggy had turned her life around completely. The person she once was in Ghost Town was no more. She really saw no future for herself back the day. She always thought she would die violently like the rest of her family, but jail had saved her life. She had been welcomed into the family with open arms and given a brand new start. She had more to live for now than ever before and wouldn't change a thing about her life at this point in time.

"We took a lot of pictures," Martha said as she held out a scrap book. "We've visited Mount Rushmore, rode across the Golden Gate bridge, visited the Grand Canyon and a bunch of other places. We saw and we did a lot while we were out there. Check out the pictures, y'all."

The men stopped what they were doing and sat around and looked at the scrap book with Twiggy and Martha for a while before the women headed upstairs after greeting Mary, Regina and Siloam in the kitchen. When the two emerged from the grand staircase the young five went wild. They ran towards the two and were all over them as they entered the great room.

"Auntie Martha, we know dad 'nem down there wrapping gifts. Tell us what you saw!" Koko snapped.

"I ain't see no gifts down there!"

"What?" Koko asked in dismay as she headed towards the stairs. "Christmas—Christmas is around the corner and they ain't—they ain't got nothing going on down there?"

"Get back here!" Twiggy yelled. "Me and Martha is way more important than those gifts they wrappin'!"

"So they do have some stuff," Koko said through a smile.

"For everybody," Martha said. "Come on y'all. Let's help Naomi 'nem put up the tree."

A few hours later, the family had all dressed in formal wear; suits, wing tips and ties for the males, and dresses and high heels for the females. The family was seated at the two large formal dining room tables inside the caramel marble-floored formal dining room that featured a wood burning fireplace, two chandeliers and two white marble columns.

A turkey and ham was on each table inside the elegant room, along with all the trimmings, including dressing, collard greens, baked macaroni and cheese, chitterlings, green bean casserole, fresh baked bread, cakes and many more items. Naomi said prayer and the family immediately got down to business.

"Somebody looks hungry," DeeDee said as he cut the turkey at his table with an electric knife, eyeing Spoonie and Tyke, who sat on either side of him, the whole time.

"They sure do. That vegetarian couscous Francine made looks spectacular." Mendoza chuckled.

DeeDee stopped cutting the turkey upon hearing Mendoza's remark. "How you sound, old man? Couscous? Nobody won't even touch that mess."

"Okay," Mendoza laughed as he uncorked a bottle of red wine. "You have to be made into a believer I see. Go on and get to it."

"They gone prove you wrong today is what they gone do," DeeDee said matter-of-factly as he resumed cutting the deep-fried turkey.

Spoonie and Tyke hadn't eaten meat since the day they'd learned what actually happened to the animals, but their unbelieving grandfather was certain they would cave in on this day. He picked up a plate and pulled a wing off the turkey and placed dressing onto the dish and handed it to Tyke, who kindly passed the plate to Bay.

"Dad, put a pile of macaroni and cheese on here, please? And some cous—" Bay was about to be the first one to request some of the couscous, but the disappointed look on her grandfather's face had deterred her. "Just the macaroni and cheese, please." she said lowly as she eyed her grandfather. "*Sorry,*" she mouthed.

DeeDee loaded another plate and passed it to Spoonie, who kindly handed her plate to Lucky.

"Eh, mom. Dump some green bean casserole on here would ya' please," Lucky asked as he handed his mother a plate.

"Sure thing, son. Would you like some couscous as well?" Francine asked with a smirk on her face.

Lucky looked over to an obviously disheartened DeeDee. "Maybe later, mom," he said lowly. "Poor fella's about to lose some money pretty soon, eh, dad?"

"You don't know the half of it, son," Mendoza chuckled.

DeeDee repeated his routine, handing a plate of sliced turkey to Spoonie and Tyke, who only passed the plates along until they were the last two without a plate of food at the table. When DeeDee placed a slice of turkey on the plate with dressing and passed it to Spoonie, she folded her arms and said, "Me and Tyke only want the couscous, some macaroni and the collard greens that momma fixed for us without the meat in it!"

"Cous-damn-cous?" DeeDee said as he backed away from the table and placed his hands on his hips.

"Hey, watch it, dad!" Naomi laughed. "Now let me see you deny those two."

"I'm sorry, everybody. But this here? Are you two serious? I had money on you two!" DeeDee snapped.

"I want my thousand dollars," Mendoza said through laughter. "I want all hundreds too. Five each for Spoonie and Tyke."

Mendoza and DeeDee had bet that Spoonie and Tyke would eat meat on this day. They thanked Mendoza kindly, the two of them having earned an unexpected five hundred dollars on Thanksgiving. The bigger issue, however, was the fact that

Spoonie and Tyke were really sticking to their guns. To everyone inside the dining room, it seemed as if they truly were becoming flown-blown vegetarians.

"Wow," Junior said as he picked up a turkey drumstick, "never bet against family, DeeDee."

"These me and Doss's kids," Naomi chuckled while fixing Spoonie and Tyke's plate. "And ain't nothing fake about a Holland or a Dawkins."

"I know that's real," Martha chimed in. "Naomi pass me that bowl of turkey gravy, please? And the couscous when you're done fixing Spoonie and Tyke's plate," she added, bringing light laughter.

The bowls were passed around and when the food got to Twiggy, she handed Mary a brochure she was reading to free up her hands. Regina tried to grab the brochure, but it was too late.

"The Lost Orphan Committee," Mary said as she shifted her eyes over towards Regina.

"Twiggy, you weren't supposed to show her that." Regina stated, a little embarrassed having her mother learn of her intentions.

"Well, I ain't mean to. I think it's fine if you wanna find your daddy. These two here the ones with the problem," Twiggy said as she pointed to Mary and Martha. "And don't be you two be eyeing me like that! I been family since nineteen seventy-six, so I know I can speak what's on my mind."

"Mary told Dimples to leave her out of it. Ain't nobody interest in seeing that man." Martha said as she cut into a ham.

"Wasn't he your first love, Mary?" Takoda, Regina's husband asked.

"What makes you say that, Tak? I only had children for Reynard," Mary responded coyly as she ran her hands through hair.

Takoda smiled to himself at that moment and apologized. He and Regina got along real well most times in their marriage save for a few disagreements here and there, and he was like a son to Mary by all accounts. Takoda and Dimples were excellent parents, hard workers and could share just about anything. When Dimples started searching for her father a few months back, she'd told Tak, as was Takoda's nickname, and he'd offered to help and the two had been working on it ever since, but they hadn't made any progress.

Dimples was now considering using the same organization that had helped her aunt Naomi find Martha and Mary in order to attempt to find her father. She and Tak often talked about what that day would be like should it ever come to pass and they often questioned whether Mary would want to see the father of her kids again.

Dimples believed so, but Takoda didn't. Dimples came to her conclusion by watching her mother's reaction whenever she asked about her father. Mary would look away with this long gaze before telling her daughter that she had no interest in seeing the man. Other times she would respond like a shy little girl, just like she'd done seconds ago when Takoda posed his question. His wife was right it seems.

Mary never answered Takoda's question. "Can we not talk about that man on this day," she asked as she raised her hands in protest. "I don't want to talk about Reynard Jacobs. Here's your brochure, Dimples. Let's just talk about something else here at the table, please. Now is not the time."

"Okay, momma," Dimples replied softly as she got up and kissed her mother's temple. "I'm sorry."

"Come on," Mary said, getting back into family atmosphere, "my grandson say he wanna try some of that couscous," she joked, bringing a smile to her daughter's face.

Conversations soon began to unfold between all and the family went on sharing dinner before adjoining into the theater room to watch the Dallas Cowboys game while eating dessert. Thanksgiving of 2001 was turning out just fine for the family and friends down in Ponca City, Oklahoma.

****

"I never ate so much in my life," Asa Spade remarked as he pushed himself away from JunJie's table inside his spacious mansion and wiped his mouth with a cloth napkin.

JunJie had invited his closest friends from Denver and Chicago to his $10,000,000 dollar, nine thousand square foot two story mansion on Mercer Island, just west of Seattle, for a Thanksgiving feast. JunJie's was a classy affair, but more of an adult nature. Classical music was playing low in the background, liquor abounded and a small bowl of rolled up blunts sat in the center of the table amongst the food. Asian strippers from JunJie's night club served him, Grover, Phil, and Finland in tight-fitting, skimpy french maid outfits.

Asa Spade and Xiang had their own thing going, and Francesca and Ponita were kicking it with the cousins, the six of them unfazed by JunJie's explicit form of entertainment because they all knew how the man loved to be entertained when not conducting business.

JunJie beckoned a waitress and leaned over to his side and placed a thick, expensive cigar to his lips. He leaned back in his chair and took a few puffs once it was lit and closed his eyes and savored the piano style of Chopin's *Waltz in D-Flat*.

"So, Asa Spade," JunJie said after exhaling the thick cigar smoke, "business is good back in Colorado I take it?"

"We're doing real good. Looking in to a few things here and there," Asa replied as he stirred a glass of whiskey and coke.

"I've been tellin' you long before the death of Wayne Miller that we should do business. I'm glad everything is working out. Things are going along just as I had foreseen," JunJie remarked proudly.

"You always have been tellin' us," Asa said before he sipped his whiskey. "But had we done so back then I don't think it would've worked out. The timing was right when it happened."

Dougie was leaning back in his chair smoking a blunt listening to Asa and JunJie. The entire set up was on point. Dougie had never made this much money in his life. He was glad Asa had linked up JunJie because the man was the real deal. There was something about his method of operation that impressed Dougie tremendously: the way he handled conflict. The people he'd hired to deliver up Alvin weren't a bunch of amateurs. They were a team of professionals that did their job thoroughly.

"JunJie? Who were those people you had deliver Alvin?" Dougie finally asked.

"Just some friends from the Midwest." Finland replied on behalf of JunJie.

Asa Spade could respect Finland's secrecy, but he resented the man in spite of that fact. He just seemed like the type who would fold under pressure in his eyes and Asa couldn't shake that feeling no matter how hard he tried. "Whoever they are, make sure you thank them for me personally," Asa told Finland. "I been meaning to have you relay that message."

"Will do, brother. So what's your next move as far as legit revenue?" Finland asked while pouring a glass of red wine.

"By late spring of next year we'll have a night club up and running. It'll be a good front to wash dollars."

Finland nodded in appreciation. "That's a good move. It's all about washing dirty dollars clean at this point. We'll talk about more ventures later on because this is a holiday—and nobody that is worth their keep works on Thanksgiving," Finland said as he massaged a giggling waitress's ass. "You like how that feel, baby," he asked. The waitress only smiled and leaned forward more to allow Finland greater access to her most private area. "I think I'll turn in early, guys," Finland concluded as he picked up two stem glasses and a bottle of wine. He then grabbed three rolled blunts from the bowl and took the waitress by the hand and led her towards the stairs.

JunJie and company were preparing to go and relax in a specially designed sports bar deep inside the home's interior. They'd just left the dining room when JunJie received a phone call. He answered and listened for a few seconds as he stood in the wide hallway before ending the call.

"I must not be worth my keep on a day like today because I

suddenly have to go to work," JunJie quipped as he rejoined the group and turned on the lights inside the sports bar. "I seem to have some guests I wasn't expecting."

"Is everything okay?" Asa asked.

"Everything's fine. Getting ready to close another deal here. Son, you and Grover come with me. Everyone? Please, excuse us and make yourselves at home. The servers will be in shortly to fix drinks," JunJie said. The three men walked out of the room where JunJie led the way to his office. This day wasn't expected for at least another four months at the earliest, but it was welcomed nonetheless.

Hayate and Isao Onishi, brothers from JunJie's native homeland of Japan, were two shipping tycoons that owned a fleet of cargo ships and several warehouses on Seattle's shipping front. They were well-known and respected in the maritime business community and were looking for an investor to help renovate their port real estate and to expand their fleet of cargo ships, thereby earning the investor a share in the profits, and access to the eight state-of-the-art international cargo freighters the brothers owned.

JunJie was purportedly at the forefront of this fifteen million dollar proposal and was slated to make several million dollars annually off this deal. He was also planning to use the cargo ships to increase his cocaine shipments from Venezuela to accommodate the growing demand coming in from Asa's crew and the Chicago Gang. Things were lining up from JunJie's perspective, but the Onishi brothers had different plans.

The men greeted one another and JunJie walked around to the safe behind his desk. He was going for the contracts to close the deal, a smile on his face as he twisted the knob. "I never thought I'd hear from you guys so soon," he said happily as he pulled the safe open. "You must've really liked my proposal. We can go to work on renovating the warehouses here in America once I have a contractor in place. A new dock and a deeper channel will—"

"Mister Maruyama, I think you're getting ahead yourself," Hayate, a fifty year-old short and stout grey-haired man said as he went and stood before JunJie's desk.

"I am? Well, let's slow down to you guys' pace. What is it you have to say?" JunJie said as he casually took a seat and extended his hand, allowing Hayate to sit as he rested his arms on the desk top.

Hayate walked around the chair slowly and eased down into the seat. He sat upright and said, "We've come to tell you personally, before we leave for our flight back to Japan, that we've decided to go with an investor back home in Tokyo."

Tokyo?" JunJie questioned as he slowly rose from his seated position. His demeanor had changed from that of jubilation to seething anger in mere seconds. "How many more of us are you going to let gain a foothold over here? It's enough going around for us all to make money! The ones that are here already, dammit!" JunJie wasn't speaking of other Asians or anybody else for that matter; to the contrary, he was speaking on the drug business. The Onishi brothers were just as much into drug smuggling as was JunJie, the only difference was that the Onishi brothers pushed heroin whereas JunJie pushed cocaine.

Isao, the younger of the Onishi brothers at age forty-seven, sat in another chair before JunJie. "The deal from back home is too good to resist, Mister Maruyama," he remarked calmly. "We've looked at the numbers coming from your guy in Venezuela. They're excellent. But we don't think we can sustain moving thirty kilograms of cocaine a month. We have no legitimate market for cocaine outside of Seattle, which is your market, but we have a huge market with opium. Our network stretches from here to Philadelphia, but it is only an *opium* market for us."

"But we've already had blue prints drawn up for the new warehouse down at the port," Phillip said in frustration as he went and stood beside his father. "We were all set to go because you two had us under the impression that the deal was as sure as done. Everything that transpired from our meeting two months ago was supposed to be mere formality because you two said you needed time to set up the buyers."

"My godfather and Phil is right," Grover followed as he went and stood on the other side of JunJie and slid his hands into his silk suit jacket. "We've offered you in on our network at eighteen thousand per kilogram and are giving you unlimited access to our warehouses and trucking. That was the deal and you agreed to it in exchange for allowing us to use those ships you own. We had a deal in place. Honor it. Because now isn't the time to catch cold feet."

"We can reimburse you the fifty thousand dollars for the blue prints, JunJie," Hayate bargained. "But as far as shipping we can't help you there." he then stressed.

"We think it is best we all stay in our respective places so as not to step on one another's toes." Isao added as Grover and Phil looked over towards JunJie.

Hayate and Isao had grown hot under collar the moment they'd stop speaking because the look on the faces of JunJie, Phillip and Grover was neither pleasant nor inviting. Rage lay just beneath surface and the Onishi brothers knew it; the best thing for them to do, they both surmised, was to get up and excuse themselves. Before the men rose completely, however, Phillip walked from behind the desk and pinned Hayate's face to the top of it; Grover quickly grabbed Isao and forced him to sit once more.

"Stay a while longer," Grover said in a forceful tone.

JunJie, as his son held Hayate's face to the desk top, got up close to the struggling man and said in a low angry tone, "You double cross me for some people back home who have no interest in coming here to do business with us? You think that will stop me from getting what I want from you two? I need those boats you own."

"JunJie," Hayate called out. "This is not how business is done!"

"In this world these things are sometimes necessary," JunJie said calmly as he went and sat back behind his desk. "You can renege on the cocaine deal if you like, but you *will* give me access to those ships, and you will give me complete control of those docks or you will have no business to tend to."

"When hell freezes over you son-of-a-bitch! You kill us you lose everything, JunJie!" Hayate said as he struggled to free himself.

"Wrong," JunJie remarked as he leaned back and crossed his legs. "If I were kill you two I would have everything to gain, but let's not take things to such an extreme." he said as he nodded towards Grover and Phil, who released their grip on Hayate and Isao and calmly stepped back.

"We come here in peace and this is how you treat us? We are all men of *honor*! But this is *not honor*! This is savagery!" Hayate said as he straightened his suit.

"You're right. My apologies." JunJie said as he stood up to shake the brothers' hands. "We are men of honor. Although I wish you two would not be so hypocritical and honor the deal we've already made, Hayate," JunJie chuckled.

"Nothing is guaranteed until contracts are signed."

"We do not sign contracts. We shake on matters. And you two shook my hand with smiles across your faces. You can save face, though, because I have what is called a counter-offer."

"A counter-offer? What do you propose, JunJie" Hayate asked.

"I wasn't expecting word from you two for another five months. Let's take a breather, gentlemen. If we can't make a deal in a few months we will part ways."

"We have made up our minds, Mister Maruyama," Isao replied.

"Just think about it. I'll give you four months to think about it," JunJie suggested as he eyed the brothers seriously. "Just think about it," he reiterated as he extended his hands towards the doors. "Grover will see you two men out."

"What's your plan, dad?" Phillip asked as he closed the door behind Grover.

"I'll give this some time to let this incident blow over with those two. They won't go to the police because I have just as much on them as they have on me. All of their muscle is in Tokyo anyways. They're powerless here in America except for the heroin gangs they distribute to back east who could care less about them."

"How will you handle the situation? It's obvious things aren't going to turn in our favor in four months because they've made up their minds already, dad."

"I'll talk to them again and try and stall them, son. If they're not in agreement by March of next year we will just have to use another tactic," JunJie said as he eased up from his chair. "Come now, we've been rude to Asa Spade and we should rejoin the party. We'll deal with the Onishi brothers soon enough."

****

Carmella had just landed in Denver, Colorado fresh off a commercial flight from Houston, Texas. She'd been at her mansion down in Texas for a couple of weeks to oversee another shipment of cocaine and was now returning to Denver for the first time since she'd left the hospital there in the city. She had Pepper with her the whole time and she was actually growing quite fond of the ten year-old.

It was snowing in Colorado and that was the reason Carmella's flight was four hours late. She and Pepper, who was dressed neatly in a pink silk skirt and a white cashmere trench coat and pink knee-length leather boots, walked through the crowded concourse, Carmella searching for one person in particular.

"Over here, Carmella," a voice called out near the baggage claim.

Carmella turned around and eyed one of the most important people in her life—twenty-six year-old Desiree Abbadando.

Desiree was a five foot seven voluptuous woman with cropped black hair and slender, sexy lips. She had one of the widest, most gorgeous smiles ever. Curves in all the right places and big, dark, round eyes is what had drawn Carmella to Desiree, who ran the night club Carmella owned there in

Denver. She soon put Desiree on to help her move weight. Desiree was Carmella's personal informant, amongst several other things. She knew all the happenings in and around Denver and always kept Carmella abreast of what was going on in the streets of this western city.

A warm embrace brought the two together for the first time in nearly two years. The last time Desiree had seen Carmella, she was so doped up on morphine she didn't recognize her face, but she was still beautiful back then, but not as pleasing on the eye as she was on this Thanksgiving evening in her pink fur coat, matching hat and pink square-framed clear glasses.

"Carmella, I've missed you so much, baby." Desiree said as he stared her friend up and down in appreciation.

"I can't tell, Desiree. You haven't been to see me the whole time I lay here in the hospital." Carmella responded before turning towards the luggage carousel.

"I did go to see you," Desiree responded softly as she ran her hands across the sleeve of Carmella's mink coat. "You don't remember? I came often, but I didn't like seeing you like that. DeAngelo gave you my cards?"

"He did," Carmella replied as she grabbed her and Pepper's luggage. "You being there at the end would have meant a lot to me. And a card is not you."

"But those are my thoughts," Desiree said as she grabbed Carmella's suitcase. "I'll make it up to you, okay? You and your?"

"This here is my niece Peppi Vargas. We call her Pepper. Pepper say hello."

"Hola."

"Hola back! She's adorable, Carmella. In her little business attire," Desiree said as she smiled down at Pepper. "Damenga and Alphonso didn't have kids! Whose child have you stolen?" she whispered into Carmella's ear.

"Bitch, just go with it," Carmella said as she and Desiree laughed to themselves.

"Whatever. I got a surprise for you." Desiree remarked as the group made their way to the main entrance.

"Did you look after my brothers' home?"

"Paid the taxes and kept the lawn cut and the inside dusted. It's all set to go."

"Good. I may be here for a while. I really like this town," Carmella said as she and Pepper followed Desiree towards the out the main entrance doors where the trio hopped into an awaiting stretched Hummer limousine and headed over to Cherry Creek, a wealthy suburb on the southeast side of Denver.

Pepper was taking it all in. Ever since she'd left Valle Hermoso with Toodie and Phoebe, she'd been laying eyes on the finest of everything, save for the few trap houses she'd visited and the rundown apartment the Perez sisters often hung out in over to what she'd learned was a neighborhood called Fox Park.

The three females exited the limousine and Carmella grabbed Pepper's hand and walked with her through the blowing snow up a long winding flight of stairs to the front door of a home that to Pepper, looked like one of the huge churches back in Mexico. "This is where we'll live for a while, okay, Pepper?"

"This is really nice."

"Thank you, love. Come on in and make yourself at home." Carmella said as she held the door open for Pepper.

Once inside Pepper was amazed. It was as if she were standing on a stage atop snow white stone. There were four large white posts inside the home up ahead and and the ceiling sat high up. The home smelled brand new, and all the furniture around was covered in white sheets. Pepper walked down the stairs and entered the living room and stared at the large fish tank in the center of the room that was filled with numerous colorful fish. She then walked over to the furniture in the room and stared at the sheets, wondering what sort of pretty furniture lay underneath.

"Take them all off," Carmella said as she locked the door.

"We have to get this place up and running completely."

Desiree, meanwhile, had disappeared into the 6,700 square foot one story, six bedroom ranch-style brick home. She went into the kitchen, hoping the aroma wasn't going to give her surprise away. She put on an apron and pulled a warm turkey from the oven and sat it on the table inside the dining room, one of two places that had been specially prepared for Carmella's arrival besides the master bedroom. She'd just sat the baked bird on the table when Pepper and Carmella walked into the room.

"Surprise," Desiree said, smiling and extended her hands. "I fixed us dinner. Well, I started. I still have to make some corn bread dressing and warm up some string beans and bake the cake, but we can have wine and catch up while I do it."

"This is awesome, Desi," Carmella replied lowly. "This will be the first Thanksgiving I've had since ninety-eight. I wish my Ma-Ma could've come."

"Did you call her?"

"I did. She's fine. She's visiting Milan, Italy. Says she needs a new wardrobe."

"Your mother is a diva," Desiree laughed. "Check her out."

"She knows how to enjoy life," Carmella said as she tied on an apron.

The whole day was spent inside the plush mansion eating, drinking, watching football and talking. After a few blunts and several shots of tequila, Carmella went to her music collection and pulled out Los Angeles Negros's CD and put on the song *Tu y Tu Mirar*. Pepper, who'd been loving every minute of her stay with the two women, got up and began to dance to the bluesy-guitar Spanish tune ballerina-style. She also knew the lyrics to the song and sung them in Spanish as she danced.

Carmella and Desiree were floored. "She's great!" Desiree yelled over the music. "Go Pep! Go Pep! Go Pep!" she and Carmella sang as they sat side by side and watched the show unfold.

The day ended with all three females listening to numerous

Spanish tunes and dancing, Carmella and Desiree getting fuller by the hour. After another round of turkey and a bath, Pepper was taken to one of the bedrooms and tucked in by Carmella. She turned the TV on and turned the lamp light off and was about to walk out the room when Pepper asked, "Can I be like you when I grow up. Carmella?"

Carmella went and knelt before Pepper and said, "Peppi? What me and my girls do isn't fun and games. Many lives have been lost for what you see around you today. This life I live has consequences you can't even imagine."

"I heard you arguing with Toodie about my mother a while back."

"Your mother wanted me to take her and you here to America so you could be looked at by doctors. Remember the tests you took?"

"Yes. It didn't hurt at all."

"But it was needed. You are all well now. Had your mother not come to me before she died, you may be dead today. Your Ma-Ma loved you, Peppi. And I love you the same. I know I could never be her, but I'll do my best. I will make sure nothing happens to you."

"Will I ever have to go back to Saint Louis?"

"Someday, yes. But I'll be there with you most times. I have a home there too."

"Okay. I don't like Toodie." Pepper remarked as she sat up in the bed.

"Toodie is important to me. I need her to help me with you because some places I go, you can't, because it may be too dangerous, baby."

"I'd rather Phoebe be with me."

"You've told me all this already. Toodie and Phoebe are always together and they mean you no harm, Pepper," Carmella sighed, getting a little agitated with the discussion.

"So long as you're alive they won't hurt me. What if you were to die like my mother? Then what will happen to me?"

Carmella stood up at that moment and paced the floor. Pepper was asking some heavy questions, questions she hadn't pondered in a long time. She could die any day in her line of work and she knew it all-too-well given her recent tap dance with the Grim Reaper. She couldn't let those thoughts enter her mind, though; and if she were to die, then fuck it. Pepper would be the least of her worries if ever she were hit. While she was here, though, Carmella was trying her best to make certain that Peppi Vargas would be looked after as best she could.

"If I were to die, Peppi," Carmella said as she stood at the foot of the bed, "you go to a church and ask for help if you don't want to be with any of my crew, okay?"

"That's it? Go to church?"

"That's the best I can tell you! What is it you want from me?" Carmella screamed, having grown agitated because Pepper was forcing her to have an emotional conversation she was not prepared to have. "Haven't I treated you like family? Haven't I looked after you all this time," she asked in frustration. "Shit! I saved your," she toned it down at that moment, refusing to go off the deep end and read Pepper her rights. Disallowing herself to give this ten year-old little girl the hard truth—that she'd killed her mother by accident and was now feeling obligated to see to it that she made it into adulthood.

Carmella knew what she'd do under any other circumstance. Had this been any other person, helpless child or not, she would have killed her outright. She briefly envisioned herself walking around to the side of the bed and strangling Pepper to death. She could cut her up into pieces and burn her remains in the grill pit in the backyard, too. Nobody would know but her and Desiree. As heartless as she could be, however, Carmella couldn't find it in herself to murder an innocent child, especially one whose mother she'd taken out during a vicious takeover campaign and now had an affinity towards.

"I'm sorry I upset you," Pepper said lowly, interrupting Carmella's thoughts. "I just get scared sometimes."

"You don't have to be scared, baby," Carmella responded softly. "You don't understand fully, but you are in a good position. The boss loves you."

"Can I be a boss someday?"

"Being boss isn't easy. It is earned, Pepper. You have a long ways to go." Carmella said as she walked over and sat on the edge of the bed.

"But you can teach me." Pepper said lowly as she stared back at Carmella. The look in Pepper's eyes sent a chill down Carmella's spine. This little girl was more than serious. Whatever ideas she had formulating, Carmella didn't know, but one thing was certain—ten year-old Peppi Vargas had it in her to take on the world if that's what she wanted to do.

"I don't think you're cut out for this life," Carmella snapped as she jumped up from the mattress.

"I will prove you wrong someday if you teach me right," Pepper stated as she picked up the remote control and began flipping through the channels.

Carmella said nothing as she walked out the door. She liked what she saw in the child. It was never her intention to school Pepper on the business she was in, but she had seen enough in the little girl to train her and have her ready the day she came of age. This sparked conversation had oddly drawn the motley two closer, but only time would reveal what would become of their relationship and what would actually become of ten year-old Peppi Vargas.

Several hours later, Pepper, having awakened in the middle of the night, crept from her bed and was making her way back to the kitchen for another piece of turkey. She really liked being around Carmella, but she was conflicted over Toodie, and even Phoebe to an extent. The ten year-old's world was a confusing one that was filled with drug dealers and she was nearer violence more than she could ever imagine most times; and things would get even more confusing for the ten year-old as she grew nearer Carmella's bedroom.

Moaning sounds had slowed Pepper's stroll towards the

kitchen to a snail's pace and she began tiptoeing towards the open door where she peeked in and caught an eyeful. There, lying on the bed on her back with her legs spread wide, was Carmella. Her arms were at her side and her head was drawn back as her waist moved up and down, seemingly in slow motion. The person between Carmella's legs, Pepper knew, was Desiree. She couldn't understand fully what was going on, nor what her eyes were witnessing, but it looked as if it felt good by the way Carmella was moaning, sounding as if she were crying almost.

"Desi, yes," Carmella moaned. "You're takin' me all the way there. Momma, si! Si!"

"Dios, sabes muy bien, mi amor." (God, you taste so good, my love.) Desiree moaned. *"Déjame Vete a la mierda."* (Let me fuck you.)

Desiree was sitting up looking as if she were putting a belt on to Pepper when Carmella turned and saw her staring. She said nothing as Desiree lay on top her, only returning to making those funny sounds again. Pepper stared for what seemed like an eternity as she watched Carmella kiss and grab on her friend. Soon they both were yelling each other's names. Carmella knew Pepper was watching, but she'd wanted to learn —so she said—and if Carmella was going to teach her, she was going to give Pepper her lifestyle up-close and unfiltered. A fast and furious pounding took Carmella over the edge and she came down from her sex high a few minutes later, when she looked back towards the door, Pepper was still peeking.

"Close my door, Peppi," Carmella said aloud as she sat up in the bed.

"Oh my God! She saw that?" Desiree asked, covering her lower face.

Carmella lit up a blunt and took a few tokes. "If she wants to learn about this life I will give her all she wants to know, Desi." she said as smoke left her lungs.

"She's so young."

"That's where it starts. I don't want to hear shit about what I do with Peppi, okay?"

"No need to yell. I just don't like being an exhibitionist." Desiree said as she spread cover over her and Carmella's legs.

"A good one you are, though, ma-mi. You make me scream, woman!" Carmella said through laughter as she pulled Desiree down on top of her. "I'm going to be here for a while until I reopen Club Glitz. It'll do Peppi some good to stay out of Saint Louis for a while, too."

"How soon before you open the night club?"

"Five, maybe six months. And once I reopen the club, I'll just have this one thing in Saint Charles that needs tending to. Happy Holidays, baby. I'm back, Desi. I'm back." Carmella ended just before she kissed Desiree passionately.

CHAPTER SEVEN
BACK ON THE HOMEFRONT

Early March of 2002 found most of the Holland-Dawkins family out early in the morning working the ranch. The big three were out rustling the cattle, Kimi and Koko were slopping the hogs and feeding the chickens and Mary and Dimples were loading produce into Mary's pick-up truck to take to her produce stand.

Walee, Spoonie and Tyke, meanwhile, were out wandering around. Walee, dressed in jean shorts and a wife beater and tennis shoes with no socks, and Spoonie and Tyke, who were wearing their softball uniforms as the two had a game later in the day, traversed the land on this bright and sunny morning and made their way over to the forest to the east of Ponderosa to pick up Walee's pet turtle, Slo Moses. Walee had been taking care of the turtle since last year, keeping it in a small fenced-in area beside a swampy area on the land and feeding it regularly. The turtle was about the size of a tennis ball when Walee first found the amphibian, now nearly a year later, it was as round as a dinner plate and had a beautiful blue, yellow, orange and light green shell.

Walee scooped up his turtle and he and his sisters walked over to the pig sty to meddle thirteen year-olds Kimi and Koko, which was their normal routine.

"Hey! Hurry up and slop them hogs before we lay y'all off

today!" Walee yelled, mocking his sisters from the opposite side of the fence.

"Yeah, slop them hogs!" Spoonie and Tyke repeated simultaneously as they laughed.

"You lay us off then! Do us that favor, boss man!" Koko yelled as she and Kimi continued pouring feed onto the ground.

"Stop fraternizing and get back to work! Aww forget about it! When you finish for the day—you finish for good! I'm firing both of y'all lazy asses today!"

Tyke then chimed in, attempting to repeat Walee's statement. "Yeah, we firing, we firing both of y'all lazy—"

"You better not copy off him, Tyke!" Kimi yelled.

"I'm a slap ya' face ya' keep playin' with me, Walee!" Koko followed as she ran towards the gate.

Walee, Spoonie and Tyke ran off with Koko hot on their tails.

Koko chased her younger siblings through the dirt-covered maze inside the poultry yard and was near to catching Spoonie when the three emerged out into the open field and scattered in three different directions.

"You better not let me catch either one of y'all behinds back over here none today! Especially you, Walee! And y'all other two need to quit repeating after his filthy behind mouth!" Koko screamed angrily as she stopped running, realizing she wasn't going to catch neither of the three as they ran across the open field.

Walee, with turtle in hand, and Spoonie and Tyke following his every move, soon found themselves on the upper southern portion of the ranch. They crossed the fence that separated the cattle and horses from the upper portion of the land that the family used for farming and recreation and began mingling with calves that were being led to the stream on the east side of the ranch to be watered.

Walee had a small tree branch in his hand and he began to

lash one of the small calves strolling by as he held onto his turtle.

Tiva rode her horse towards Walee when she spotted him and her youngest sisters milling about in the calves's pathway leading towards the stream. A few bloodhounds ran by barking loudly and the calves began trotting lightly.

"Walee! Take your li'l sisters and cross back over the fence and get from 'round them calves, man!" Tiva yelled from atop her horse.

"No, ma'am! I'm—stayin'—right—here!" Walee snapped as he continually lashed the small animal before breaking out into the Carlton dance from The Fresh Prince of Bel Air.

"Look at 'em, Kimi." Koko said as she eyed Walee way off in the distance.

"Umm hmm," Kimi replied while sanitizing her hands. "He gone dance his self right into a trampling he keep goin'."

Tiva could see the calf growing agitated while Walee was dancing. "Spoonie? You and Tyke get on the other side the fence," she said as she climbed down from her horse to usher Walee to safety.

The twins walked back to the fence steadily yelling for Walee to follow them, but he ignored them both and made whipping sounds as he continued to hit the calf and breaking out into dance on occasion.

"Spoonie, watch this here!" Walee yelled aloud as he pelted the calf hard on the back to try and get it to run. Instead of running, however the calf back-kicked Walee and knocked him down and sent Slo Moses flying into the air at the same time before it took off running.

Walee gasped for air as he held his stomach and was slowly catching his wind back when Tiva, Spoonie and Tyke ran over to help him. He caught his breath just as Spoonie and Tyke began pulling him by the arms towards the fence.

"Where Slo Moses," Walee cried aloud as he being dragged by his sisters. "Grab Slo Moses! Tyke! Eh! We got a man down over here! Man down I say!"

Tiva knew Walee wasn't actually hurt the moment she laid eyes on him and she couldn't help but to chuckle at the stunt her younger brother was pulling. Earlier in the week, a rancher had fallen off a horse and as he was being drug towards the fence, Flacco was yelling repeatedly "man down". Walee was merely repeating what he'd seen and it was funny to Tiva, who witnessed the entire episode. Spoonie and Tyke, however, were certain Walee was hurt for real.

"Ohh, man that hurt! Cow kick me! Somebody grab Slo Moses! We got a man down over here! Man down!" Walee continued yelling as he was cleared of the now fast-trotting calves.

All of Walee's siblings and a few ranch hands checked on him out of concern, but they all quickly understood that the only thing that was hurt on Walee was his pride so they went back to their routines. Slo Moses wasn't so lucky, however; he was trampled amidst the confusion. His shell was crushed by the calf and he died on sight. Walee took the lose of his favorite pet really hard.

A few hours later, the family was having lunch on the patio before they left for Spoonie and Tyke's soft ball game. Spoonie and Tyke's team was in a playoff game on this day and it was a big day for the twins. Walee sat with Spoonie, Tyke and Mary and ate, but he was still saddened by the loss of Slo Moses, his beloved pet.

Kimi, Koko and the big three were at a nearby table enjoying their meal and conversing about much of nothing when Walee began to sniffle. "How can y'all act as if nothin' happened out there?" he asked his five older siblings sorrowfully as Spoonie and Tyke rubbed his back softly, trying to console him.

Naomi was at a nearby table with Doss, Dimples, Siloam and Dimples' son, Tacoma. They knew what happened as well; but everybody felt as if Walee had gotten what he asked for out in the field for agitating Kimi, Koko and the calves.

"Kimi, pass me the napkins please." Walee requested sadly.

Kimi passed Walee the napkins and he tore off a few sheets and blew his nose, producing a loud trumpet sound which caused the family to sniggle. Walee could carry on with an act and milk it dry whenever he wanted to, but he was actually hurt this day and the family seemed not to care about how he felt about losing his pet.

"Slo Moses didn't hurt *anybody* or *anything*—and that heifer killed him for nothing! She knew my turtle couldn't move that fast," Walee said as he wiped his watery eyes.

"Poor thang. Bet he never saw it coming," Koko said as she and Kimi sniggled.

"Make fun of me if you want to! But I'm tellin' y'all, that heifer killed Slo Moses on purpose!" Walee screamed as he slammed the table with his fists.

"Hey! You better get your emotions in check over there before I come over there and step on your skinny behind on purpose!" Naomi chuckled as sniggles were heard.

"Momma, he really hurt this time!" Spoonie said as she and Tyke wiped Walee's tears with the napkins.

"He shouldna been out there clownin' around! He lucky it was Slo Motives and not him." Naomi replied.

"His name was Moses not motives," Walee corrected. "Slo Moses was his name, momma!"

"Whatever his name was you put him in that position, son. Take it as a lesson learned and stop meddling people. You done went so far as to upset the animals and now your li'l buddy is vamoose. Lesson learned I say again."

"That don't ease the pain, man." Walee said as he covered his eyes and cried lowly.

"Tyke pass me the napkins, please." Kimi said softly. When Kimi sniffled slightly, Tyke was touched.

"Aww, Kimi? You 'bouta cry for Slo Moses too?" Tyke asked lovingly as she reached for the napkins.

"Girl, please! Don't nobody care 'bout that damn turtle I'm tryna get a biscuit, shucks!" Kimi snapped as sniggles began to emerge from the group again.

Tyke threw the napkins at Kimi and she quickly caught them. "Umm, hmm," she said nonchalantly while grabbing a biscuit. "After all he done did tellin' y'all about Mister Spots y'all still support his little act. Y'all gone learn to stop being his cheerleader. After that? He'll grow up—I hope."

"But he hurt for real this time, Kimi and you and everybody else actin' like he playin'!" Tyke snapped.

"We know he ain't playin'! We just sayin' we don't care about that li'l ugly turtle! He gone be all right!" Koko remarked as she stood up and did the Carlton dance. "One time for Slo Moses," she ended before she sat down and high-fived Kimi.

Mary recognized her nephew's sense of loss; but it was just a turtle by all measures. How exciting could that pet be was her reasoning. "Walee, it's a bunch of turtles out by the canal. Just find yourself another one, baby, and put it back out by the swamp."

"Find another one she says," Walee cried. "I'll never find another Slo Moses! He understood me!"

"This is where I get off," Mary said as she returned to her meal.

"Lord, the turtle understood him," T-top said lowly as she looked to the sky briefly. "Ain't nothing to understand about you but the fact that you're a silly young man. Now suck it up and get ya' self another turtle, boy!"

"Thissa cold-bloodied family, man'," Walee ended sadly as he finally began eating his lunch.

After finishing lunch and showering for a fresh change of clothes, the family headed out to Kaw Lake Park to watch Spoonie and Tyke's game. Upon leaving the ranch, a right turn led out onto a road bordered by prairie land and brush on either side that went for about two miles. A right turn would lead down to busy U.S. Highway 60, which lead into the city. Passing Mary's produce stand on the right while headed east, one would cross over Kaw Lake Bridge where Kaw Lake Park, which sat right beside the bridge and lake shore, would come into view.

Kaw Lake Park was the happening place in Ponca City along with the town's only bowling alley and Sonic burger chain, all of which sat on the far west side of town near a Walmart Center along with the town's compact strip mall. Ponca City didn't have much by way of entertainment or shopping because it was such a small town, but whenever the Holland-Dawkins family, who were well-known around these parts, were on the scene, things were pretty interesting to say the least.

Kaw Lake Park might as well been named the Holland-Dawkins Playground because that is what it was to a degree. Doss had paid to renovate the park last year when Spoonie and Tyke joined the league. Some parents buy a playland and place it in the backyard for their kids. Doss had taken things to a whole other level by rebuilding an entire park to his youngest daughters' liking.

A new concession stand was put in along with new bleachers, three boat launches and a fishing pier. The softball field had new turf put down and there was an electronic scoreboard in the outfield. Doss had shelled out $60,000 for the renovations and had received a key to the city for his efforts and was deemed Park Commissioner, a job he'd transferred to Naomi, who now managed the park's payroll and hired people and also had another avenue to wash the family's money clean.

The family, packed into three Suburbans, exited the vehicles sixteen strong and making plenty noise. Naomi was the loudest this day, yelling aloud that the stars had arrived to claim the championship as the family approached the bleachers.

All of the family members were exited for Spoonie and Tyke, who were elated to have led their team to the playoffs. The scores of people who were on hand were greeting the family, and there was even a band on hand to celebrate this day, a band that had caught Siloam's attention by the song they were playing and singing.

"...*The judge said guilty on a make believe trial...slap the sheriff on the back with a smile and said supper's waitin' at home and I gotta get to it...That's the night that the lights went* out in Georgia...that's the night that they hung an innocent man...well, don't trust your soul to no backwoods southern lawyer...'cause the judge in the town's got bloodstains on his hands..."

Twenty-nine year-old Siloam Bovina, a huge fan of music who'd had her share of the rock and roll experience by running with a small band a couple of years ago, was taken aback by the powerful voice that was shielded by scores of onlookers. She made her way through the jubilant crowd and eyed a brown-haired light-skinned little girl of Native American descent playing the drums beside the bleachers with three other youths and singing Reba McEntire's version of the song *The Night the Lights Went Out in Georgia.*

Siloam was floored. She had to find out who the little girl was, but for now, she just stood and listened in admiration as the little girl playing the drums continued singing the inauspicious song.

"...*They hung my brother before I could say...the tracks he saw while on his way to Andy's house and back that night were mine...and his cheatin' wife...had never left town...and that's one body that'll never be never be found ya' see little sister don't miss when she aims her gun...That's the night that lights went out in Georgia...*"

"Damn, I ain't know that li'l girl could sing like that," Dawk said as he walked up and stood beside Siloam and bobbed his head to the music.

"You know her, Dawk?"

"Yeah. She stay 'round my girl Oneika house on the west side. Her name Jane Dow and that's her band. The Jane Dow Band."

"How old is she?"

"She like, all four of 'em like thirteen or so I believe."

"Do they have a manager?"

"Nahh. They not that serious about it I don't think. They just play together from time to time as far as I know."

"They cared enough to give themselves a name, though. *Hmm*," Siloam said to herself as she and Dawk continued watching the performance with the rest of the appreciative crowd. Siloam had not a clue at the time, but once she got to talking to little Jane Dow, she would soon embark on an adventure that would eventually turn into her life's greatest work.

****

About an hour later the game was underway. Naomi had just yelled that the umpire needed a new pair of eyeglasses when he called a strike on Spoonie in the second inning that to her was an obvious ball.

Tyke came up to bat in the fourth inning and when she hit a double the entire family cheered aloud. The next two girls struck out and Spoonie was now at bat. Spoonie wanted to bring her sister home and she did so when she hit a triple to allow Tyke to cross home plate and their team took a one point lead before the last batter hit a fly ball that was caught in left field for the final out of the inning.

Out in front of the bleachers, Walee was ecstatic for his two sisters' performance this afternoon. He climbed the chain link fence and began booing one of the opposing team's players as she came up to bat. "You suck! You suck!" he yelled aloud.

Walee's taunt didn't sound right to one of the on-lookers. Telling a ten year-old little girl she sucked was a little over the top to him and he expressed his disgust to Walee. "Sit down and shut up talkin' like that!" he screamed aloud.

Naomi heard the man, and when she turned and looked, she saw that it was her nameless neighbor whose fish the family had eaten a while back. "*Not this old ass man again,*" she said to herself. "Hey! Leave him be! He ain't bothering nobody! If ya' get your mind out the gutter you can understand the jostling! Everybody here does it!" she yelled to the old man.

"This ain't the Chicago Cubs! They might wear the Cubs' uniforms, but it's just a kids' game for Christ's sake! He needs to sit down before somebody puts him in his place!"

Naomi stood up and removed her ten gallon hat and faced the man, who was sitting a few rows up. "Don't talk about somebody you don't know! Leave Christ outta this! And if anybody—and I mean *anybody*—say another word to me or my son today it's gone be trouble in paradise!"

"I come to watch a game! Not to hear a bunch of sexist taunts."

"I'll give you a sexist taunt you old bald-headed pus—" Naomi caught herself, refusing to call the man a bald-headed pussy-faced bastard and stooping down to a low level in public. That was reserved for the times she encountered the old man on the ranch and the two of them were left alone to argue and cuss one another out in peace. She turned and calmly sat down and counted backwards from ten to one in order to calm her nerves. "*Oooh he steams me,*" she said to herself.

"Ha! She told you she did, already old man!" Walee snapped before he turned back to the game and climbed the fence once more. "You suck! You suck!" he resumed yelling.

****

"These here items are a size bigger than the outfits we brought here the last time, so if you can still fit the other clothes, then these will be too big for now," Kimi said to a group of four girls as she and Koko began pulling outfits from two large cardboard boxes.

Kimi and Koko, at the young age of thirteen, were five foot six one hundred and thirty-five pound big-bosom teens. Their thick, wavy brown hair was to their shoulders, and their brown eyes sparkled. They were miniature replicas of Naomi, except for the long, brown hair. The twins had on a short, but loose fitting pair of tan camouflage shorts and matching tops with dark tan cowgirl hats and dark tan sandals with straps around their ankles.

"How much you paid for those sandals, Koko?" a young teen asked.

"These was like twenty dollars from that li'l store beside Walmart? And the outfit hit for like fifteen dollars. We needed something to wear right quick so we ran and snatched these up." Koko answered modestly as she held up a pair of olive Dolce and Gabbana Capri pants with a matching top.

"These clothes y'all giving away cost more than what y'all wearing now," another girl said.

"And your point is?" Kimi asked as she held up the clothes.

"I'm just, I'm just saying, we appreciate what you and Koko be doing. These clothes are really nice."

"It's nothing. And didn't I tell you they was gone be sweating them mauve sandals I gave you?"

"You did, Kimi. And they were," the young teen answered in a sassy tone as she high-fived Kimi.

"See? Y'all follow our lead and people will never make fun off y'all at that school," Koko added as she pulled out a pair Gucci jeans and smoothed the fabric out with her hands.

Naomi's middle daughters were very generous with their friends. Whenever they grew out of their clothes, instead of throwing them away or bringing them to a thrift store, they would meet their friends at the park and let the girls pick whatever they wanted. The clothes they gave away kept their friends, who didn't have much by way of money, looking good in school and whenever they were out and about. There was nothing behind the twins' generosity, other than the fact that they wanted to give back for being in such a fortunate position in life. They were the trendsetters around town. If a female wanted to know what was hot in fashion, she knew to call Kimi or Koko.

"Who can fit these jeans? They're a size six I believe," Kimi said as she held the jeans up, she and Koko going about handing out clothes to their friends.

****

"So you gone ride out with me after the game, Oneika? You and Jordan?" Dawk asked casually as he leaned up against the concession stand counter.

Seventeen year-old Oneika Brackens was a Creek Indian like

the Holland-Dawkins family; but whereas the Holland-Dawkins family was mainly a mixture of Negro and Creek Indian, Oneika's family had a Caucasian and Creek Indian heritage. She stood five foot seven and sported her one-hundred and forty pounds of flesh and bones with pride right along with her firm 34C breasts and high-yellow skin. Oneika's shiny brown hair flowed down to the nape of her neck and her big, round and brown sleepy eyes would light up any room. She always had a smile on her high-cheek-boned face and she had a very easygoing disposition, which made it easy for her fall for Dawk's smooth charisma. He'd met her at Kaw Lake Park during one of Spoonie and Tyke's games the previous summer and the two now referred to one another as being special friends.

Jordan Whispers was Dawk's other special friend. She was a seventeen year-old slender white girl from the west side of town who knew everyone and was into just about everything. She stood five foot eight and weighed one hundred and twenty-five pounds. She was a slender brunette with incredible blue eyes and curvy hips and had the most beautiful pair of long, curvacious legs in the Midwest.

Dawk had met Jordan at the town bowling alley a few months after he met Oneika. She was real open with Dawk, who'd learned she was bisexual early on. Oneika had shared a fantasy of hers with Dawk: she wanted to know what it felt like to go down on another female. Dawk realized right away that he had a couple of adventurous young women on his hands and he was willing to see just how far he could take it. If he ran things right, he knew he would have Jordan and Oneika on his team in no time.

Dawk had driven Oneika and Jordan to Tulsa a few weeks after meeting Jordan. The town was only about and hour and a half away from Ponca City, but Oneika and Jordan had never been to the area. The two were leery of one another at first, but Dawk kept things calm by asking the girls about their lives and goals. He kept them talking, and soon had the two laughing and talking to one another by the time he made it to Tulsa.

Dawk had visited the city of Tulsa a few times and knew his

way around very well. He took Oneika and Jordan shopping, buying both of them new outfits and shoes. He then guided them over to Victoria Secrets. While Jordan and Oneika were picking out negligees, Dawk pulled the two over to the side and asked them if they would like to spend the night with him at motel room he'd rented in downtown Tulsa.

The girls were cool with the suggestion and went about picking out their lingerie. Dawk was smooth with the way he handled things. Dealing with two females simultaneously was no easy task, and Dawk wanted the experience more then anything. He conversed with the young women about things happening in town and around the world as he rode through the city. It was no big rush to the motel. Dawk felt he'd already sealed the deal, but he wanted to show the girls something different; he wanted to allow them to have a time they would remember and appreciate always so they wouldn't mind doing it again if he asked.

Dawk took Oneika and Jordan to a steakhouse in town and the three had a wonderful experience. The females had never been treated so kindly by anyone. Dawk had taken them shopping, out to dinner and they'd cruised around town listening to music.

When Dawk suggested that the three head over to the motel, Oneika and Jordan were more than willing to follow his lead. It wasn't too long after showering and having a few shots of gin, that all three found themselves piled up in the bed. Oneika fulfilled her fantasy, going down on Jordan, who readily returned the favor by suggesting the two get into a sixty-nine position.

Dawk had Oneika and Jordan going down on him simultaneously soon after. They licked his rigid manhood slowly, engulfing the length until they gagged while stroking his thick tool. Oneika sat atop Dawk's face reverse cowgirl style as Jordan impaled herself on his shaft facing Oneika. The girls took turns on Dawk, who didn't mind getting used under the circumstances. He had the girls bend over the edge of the and entered Oneika slowly, allowing her to adjust to his girth before driving home hard and fast. Dawk was trying his best not to come because he knew Jordan's tight snatch was dripping wet and ready to be penetrated once more. Dawk knew he had Oneika on his team, but he was really aiming to wrap Jordan up on that night. When Oneika shuddered and fell forward onto the mattress, Dawk replaced his old condom and entered Jordan, who was waiting eagerly with her ass arched into to the air.

Jordan sighed when Dawk slipped from her inner folds a couple of minutes later; but to her delight, he turned her around and picked her up and leaned her against the closet doors and impaled her onto his throbbing erection. The two stared into one another's eyes as their bodies meshed together in pure ecstasy. Jordan was overcome with emotion at that moment. She sighed in agonizing pleasure as she closed her eyes and kissed Dawk with aggression. The two were panting heavily now, Dawk gently nibbling Jordan's earlobes and shoulder blades as she held onto his neck tightly. As her orgasm approached, Jordan threw her head back and screamed Dawk's name to the top of her lungs as her entire body trembled in sheer delight. Dawk soon began thrusting up into Jordan at a fast and furious pace, the closet doors were repeatedly being pushed in and out, making a loud clapping sound that was in complete harmony with the sounds of the top of Dawk's thighs slapping the bottom of Jordan's quivering thighs and ass cheeks.

The pleasure being produced at the junction of satisfaction had both lovers clawing and kissing one another harshly; their mouths were producing animalistic sounds and they were making faces that neither would ever produce on their own in public. Jordan screamed aloud and let go of Dawk's neck and threw her hands back against the rickety closet doors that were being nearly knocked off their hinges and surrendered completely. Her legs were now gaped open and Dawk was holding her up underneath her shoulder blades as he stroked her with reckless abandonment. Through cries and moans of ecstasy, Jordan's entire body stiffened as she squirted, having had the most intense orgasm of her life. Dawk began pistoning in and out at a frantic pace until he grunted and grabbed Jordan's waist and pulled her forward, planting her firmly on the base of his stiff phallus as he shot gobs of seminal fluid into the condom.

Ever since that unforgettable night in Tulsa last summer, Oneika and Jordan had been in Dawk's midst quite often. The two girls simply adored Dawk. He was a charismatic, six-foot four tan-skinned ponytail-wearing, muscular young man that was fun to be around. He kept the two with pocket money at all times and serviced the girls thoroughly in the bedroom. They'd do anything he asked, if only to be in his presence.

"What we gone do tonight if we ride out?" Oneika asked Dawk with a sly smile.

"You know. That thing you and Jordan be doing."

"The sixty-nine?"

"Sixty-nine, sixty-eight, you pick the number. Just let me get in where I fit in."

Oneika laughed and said, "Jordan you hear this nasty man talking?"

"He says he wants to get in where he fits in? What can he fit in?" Jordan giggled.

"That's why I love you, girl. So we on? We can chill over to the Holiday Inn with a bottle of gin, ya' feel?"

"Last time we drunk gin I woke up all sticky. Whatever, man. I'm down," Oneika replied through laughter.

Dawk laughed to himself. He had some real freaks on his hand and was looking forward to what the night had in store. Oneika and Jordan were down for whatever and he knew it all-too-well. *"Gone be another fun night,"* Dawk told himself.

****

Sixteen year-olds Bay and T-top, meanwhile, were sitting in one of the family's Suburbans out in the parking lot where Bay had just revealed to T-top a secret.

"Girl? That's what got you worried?" Tiva asked.

"Yeah, Tiva—because I don't know how people gone feel about it if I were to tell it."

"But I don't think nobody will really care, Bena. Where y'all met again?"

"At Ponca City High that day we went and took our exit exams last year, but we hooked up when we went back to get the results."

"That's right. I remember that day because me and Dawk dropped y'all off at Pizza Hut when we left the school. I never had a clue y'all was on a date that day, though. I knew you and AquaNina had become friends, but I thought you was just fuckin' around when you told them boys in Vegas you was into girls. It's cool with me, though. You my sister and love you no matter what."

"And I love you back. Kimi 'nem look up to us, though, and I just believe they might feel different about me. And what about momma and daddy?"

"Nahh, Bay. We family no matter what. I don't think nobody will ridicule you. And momma and daddy are pretty understanding parents. At least you willing to tell them and not let them find out on their own. Now that would be awkward. Weird even."

"It would be weird. I have to figure out how to tell momma this here, but I'm gone hold off for as long as possible."

"Whenever you do? Let me know. If you want me to come and back you up on it I will."

"I love you, Tiva. I'm glad to have you for a twin, thanks."

Coming out to her twin was a load off Bena shoulders. She had to tell someone and she and Tiva were very close. Having her twin not shun or become repulsed by her alternative lifestyle had made Bena feel much more secure and she now had the courage to tell her parents the truth about her friend AquaNina—that they were not just friends—they were a couple. She thanked Tiva once more and the twins hugged one another tightly before getting out of the suburban and running back into the park to watch the remainder of the game.

****

It was now the bottom of the ninth inning and the bases were loaded. Tyke was the final batter, and all she had to do was bring one person home to tie, or hit a double to bring two runners in for the win. Spoonie was on second base cheering for her twin while the entire family screamed from the bleachers. The whole crowd was in an uproar as the ball left the pitcher's hand. Spoonie swung as hard as she could, but she'd missed. That was the third strike and the last out and Spoonie and Tyke's team had lost their first playoff game of the season by one point. Spoonie bowed her head at the plate and cried silently. It was the last game of the season and she was saddened that she had cost her team the game. Now they would have to wait until August, which seemed like an eternity, before the second season started.

Doss walked up and hugged Spoonie at home plate as team mates came and patted her on the back, telling her she did good throughout the game. "You hear your friends, Shima? You did good the whole game, baby girl." Doss said lovingly as he knelt down and grabbed his daughter's hands.

"I know daddy, but the hit that really mattered was the one I didn't hit. Now I have to wait five months to play again. I may never get to hit a walk off homerun again and that's one of the most awesome plays a player can execute in this game. I'm just not good in the clutch!" Spoonie said sadly as she stepped into her father's arms and hid her face in shame.

Tyke made her way through the players on the field and tried to cheer up Spoonie, but Spoonie really wanted to hit that ball. The rest of the family soon made their way to the field to console Spoonie as well; as they did so, Walee had an idea. "Hey y'all? We should set the play back up and let Spoonie hit the ball to win the game!" he suggested.

"Oooh! I'm pitching!" Kimi yelled.

"And I'm catching!" Koko followed.

"Whoa, whoa, whoa, big and bigger! Slow y'all roll!" Walee stated.

"Like Slo Moses did this mornin'?" Kimi quickly snapped as she laughed.

Walee shoved Kimi and took off running across the field, but Kimi ran him down in seconds and placed him a head lock. "I keep tellin' you big girls can run, boy! Say I'm pitcher!" she demanded as she tightened her grip. "Say it!"

"Alright, you can pitch!" Walee stated in a muffled voice from the pit of Kimi's left arm.

The family told Spoonie their intentions and she grew happy. When the park emptied, Naomi and her seven other kids along with Dimples took the field and Spoonie stepped up to the plate. Kimi was pitcher and Koko was the catcher. The two of them were athletic, but only when they had to be; and on this day, Kimi was only trying to allow Spoonie to hit her ball and bring two players home so the family can move on to something else. She threw the ball and Spoonie swung and missed. She missed the next one as well. Koko then got up from behind home plate and went and talked to Kimi. "Hey, you heard anything about Bay 'nem going to Pizza Hut?" she asked as the two stood at the pitcher's mound.

The family stood by believing Kimi and Koko were actually trying to help Spoonie out; they were, but their main goal for helping Spoonie was to benefit themselves. "I believe so, why?" Kimi responded to her sister's question with her hands on her hips and breathing heavily.

"Because, Kimi, Spoonie in a slump and we can be out here all day. Lob one up to her so we can go eat."

"Alright then. Hey, they got a meat lover's special right?" Kimi asked.

"I think so, but they got them li'l garlic sticks with the dipping sauce, cheese sticks, girl that's the bomb right there and we can—"

"Hey! I thought y'all was talking about helping Spoonie!" Naomi yelled.

Kimi and Koko were so caught up in their conversation about eating at Pizza Hut they never saw nor heard their mother walk up on them. "Throw the ball right so she can hit it!" Naomi snapped as she turned and walked back out into the field.

"We going to pizza hut?" Kimi asked lowly.

Naomi paused, turned, and eyed her daughter with stern eyes. "Never mind, momma," Kimi stated and quickly turned away from her mother and got ready to pitch.

It took Spoonie almost an hour to hit a homerun ball, and the ten year-old was overjoyed as she ran and grabbed Doss's hand and guided him to the base and the two crossed together. The family was happy Spoonie got to hit her ball, they only wished it didn't take so long because the sun was beating down on everybody like a flame thrower.

"Hey Spoonie," Walee began to speak as the family walked off the field, "and don't take this wrong way, 'cause I love ya' like no other. They all thinking it, but ain't nobody in the family gonna say it—come August, when ya' games start up? If ya' lose again, we not doing that no more. Sometimes you have to learn that you win some and lose some."

"I already know that, Walee. But just having the family on the field playing with me and Tyke was the best game ever! Thank you everybody! Dad, you can still run pretty fast too!" Spoonie ended as the family loaded themselves into the three vehicles and finally made it to Pizza Hut, much to Kimi and Koko's utter delight.

CHAPTER EIGHT
ONE TO THE DOME

It was a month after Spoonie and Tyke's playoff game down in Ponca City—April of 2002. JunJie's Gulfstream had just landed at Midway Airport in Chicago a few minutes ago. He'd flown into town on a prerequisite with his son, Phillip Tran, and his godson Grover Kobayashi and the three were now riding with Finland Xavier in a stretched BMW limousine.

"What brings you into town on such short notice, Mister Maruyama?" Finland asked as the chauffeur wheeled the vehicle through the city streets.

"You were in my home for Thanksgiving when I had a couple of visitors. I told you the formalities of that meeting later on that night and gave you a heads up." JunJie replied as he sat back and crossed his legs, brushing lint from his silk socks.

"The Onishi brothers. I take it they didn't heed the warning you told me about?" Finland said with a curious look on his face.

"Which is why we have come. I want them taken care of because they have played with my time and my money—both of which are valuable to me and neither can I ill-afford to lose or go without." JunJie remarked as Phillip opened a briefcase and put stacks of hundred dollar bills on display in the backseat.

Finland picked up a stack of the crisp green backs and took a sniff. "Smells like murder," he said.

JunJie smiled right along with Phillip and Grover and said, "A lot is at stake, my friend. But this job will not be easy. Expedience is a must also."

"You're paying upfront this time. This is new and must be very important."

"Yes. I am paying up upfront and this job should be made a priority for you and your people. My son Phillip, Grover and I will all be away the duration of this job. I don't want to be nowhere around when it all goes down for legal reasons. All the information, the addresses, photos and the brothers' daily itinerary is inside this briefcase. Have your people complete this job as soon as possible."

"Why the rush if I may ask?"

"I've recently gotten information that the Onishi brothers are scheduled to leave in approximately four weeks for Japan to complete their deal with their investors overseas."

"They're just making the deal after all this time?"

"Funny how business works isn't it? I was all set to get things going last November, but it seems as if it has taken the Tokyo investors a little longer than expected to raise the fifteen million dollars Hayate and Isao needed to get their project underway. That mishap has worked in our favor, Finland. We have much to gain should this hit be a success. I'll fill you in on the major details over dinner." JunJie said as he handed Finland the briefcase.

"Okay," Finland replied. "I'll get in contact with my people the moment we're done with the final details." he ended.

****

"There they go walking with them guns again. I bet they slick asses go outta town soon," Martha said to herself as she sat on the balcony outside the Great Room watching Bay and Tiva

head towards the shooting range behind the stockyards with their father.

It was a week after JunJie's meeting with Finland back in Chicago, and all was quiet on the ranch. A little too quiet if you were to ask Martha Holland. A few days earlier, DeeDee and Mendoza had flown into Oklahoma City and were picked up by Doss and the big three; and in Martha's eyes, that particular visit didn't look like a social call. The men were locked away in Doss's private room a great portion of their visit and after visiting an army surplus store back in town, DeeDee and Mendoza flew back to Chicago with Dawk the following day. Something was going down without question in Martha's eyes given the men's maneuvers, but the reason behind the moves was a question she hadn't the answers to. She sat sipping a glass of white wine this late evening, wondering what Doss and her two oldest nieces were discussing as they walked east across the land, away from the setting sun.

"This here is a big pay day for the family, children," Doss remarked as he led Bay and T-top through the stockyards. "This is one of those million dollar hits I told you about a while back. Five hundred grand for each mark," he said as he showed his children pictures of two Japanese men.

"Who are they?" Bay asked.

"Their names are Hayate and Isao Onishi. Our man JunJie told Finland that these guys must be removed within three week's time—but it won't be easy from what you all's grandfather and Mendoza discussed with me during their short visit."

"Why?" Tiva asked.

"For starters no hit is ever easy. With that aside, we're facing three problems. One, these guys live separate. Two, they have to be hit on the same night and three—the weather will be a factor. That's why I want you two to practice shooting in the dark with these night vision scopes we bought from the army surplus store the other day. This will be a tough one, but I know we can do it and the money is well worth the effort."

Bay and T-top looked the photos over the duration of their walk and entered the woods and set up their rifles to begin target practice. Doss knew exactly what was on the line with this particular hit. From all information given, the Onishi brothers were major heroin dealers, but their power lay across the Pacific Ocean in Tokyo. Doss knew leaving one or both brothers alive in a failed hit would have repercussions for JunJie in Seattle because the Onishi brothers would be sure to use their resources back home in Japan and retaliate on American soil. A possible war with the Yakuza, the Japanese version of the Mafia, was at stake should this job fail and Doss understood that fact to the fullest; but the killer-for-hire had full confidence in Bena and Tiva, two of the best snipers he'd ever seen because he'd trained them specifically for these types of hits.

The whole two hours Bay and T-top practiced, they remained about a hundred yards apart. Their shots were dead on under the moonlight, but getting accustomed to the night vision scopes was a little difficult because everything was a light shade of green. The deadly duo would practice for another week straight under the darkness of night. On their last night of practice, it had rained heavily and a light fog set in, perfect conditions, Doss believed, as he led his daughters back to Ponderosa to have dinner with the family once they were done practicing.

The following day, Doss, Bay and Tiva were preparing to leave the ranch and drive to Cicero, Illinois. Martha was out on the road with Twiggy, a calculated move by Naomi, who felt her sister was getting a little too concerned over her husband's activities. Everything was now set. All Doss and the big three had to do was fulfill the contract.

****

Arriving in Cicero after a twelve hour drive and a full night's rest, Doss took Bay and Tiva over to *Eastside Bar* where their grandfather was waiting with Mendoza, Lucky and Dawk. The last time Bay and Tiva were in this building was in June of 1991 when they were only five years-old. They were just two innocent toddlers preparing to leave Illinois for Oklahoma back then. Now, just short of eleven years later, the twins were back in Cicero to meet up with long-time mobsters who'd preceded them in order to take on an assignment that would net the Chicago Gang a million dollars by eliminating the lives of two men in Seattle, Washington.

The history, the lineage, better yet the bloodline of Twenty Third Street Mafia lived on through this next generation of gangsters deriving from within the Holland-Dawkins family, who were fast becoming the strongest crew out of the Chicago Gang to date, and whose services were often called on for the fulfillment of the gang's most difficult jobs.

"Well, look what my eyes are witnessing," Mendoza said as he stood up and greeted Doss and the twins just as they entered the nearly empty bar. Patrons rarely visited *Eastside Bar* for drinks and mingling in the 21st century because it was viewed as being outdated; but the men who made power moves on the streets and controlled much of the drug traffic throughout the Midwest could be found here always—and that was the only thing that now mattered when it came to *Eastside Bar*.

"If Zell were alive he would surely be beside himself over this scene right here," Mendoza said as he walked up and hugged Bena and Tiva. "You two have got to be the most gorgeous women around," he added, forcing Bena and Tiva to blush and thank him in unison.

"Now you is gone stop flirting with my family if you don't want Francine to find out about this here," DeeDee said through laughter as he joined in and hugged his granddaughters.

"You're just mad because I'm their favorite," Mendoza joked. "You might be their family by blood, but these are my daughters at heart and in spirit."

"You girls remember this place?" Doss asked.

Bena and Tiva scanned the empty room and looked at one another and shrugged their shoulders. "Should we?" Bay asked.

"You two were knee high to my ankles last time you were in

this place," Lucky said as he pulled out two chairs. "Dawk knows the story. We've shared it with him the time he's been here. Come, ladies, it's time yous two learn what this thing of ours is really all about," he added as a bowl of pretzels and two bottles of red wine was placed onto the table.

A lesson in history, Mafia history, was about to be given to Bena and Tiva Holland; and from this day forth, the twins, along with Dawk Holland, would always be acknowledged as members of the Chicago Gang. The next to lead the organization once the old-timers turned in their guns were all present, save for Eddie Cottonwood, who was still holding things down in Saint Louis under the tutelage of Coban Benito and Humphrey Gaggi.

Bay and Tiva sat down side by side and listened intently as mafia history was revealed. Twenty Third Street Mafia's inception and its wars were revealed in full detail, uncut and raw in the most explicit form imaginable and the twins were taking it all in. The whole time the men talked, Bena and Tiva never interrupted. They waited until the proper time to ask questions and never came unnerved over the things revealed over a period of several hours. It was fair to say that by the time Bena and T-top were preparing to leave for Seattle two days later, they were wiser to the business.

****

After a 1,700 mile trek across Interstate-90 and laying eyes on some of the most beautiful scenery the country had to offer, Doss, Lucky, Bena and Tiva made it into Seattle after a thirty-six hour drive. Airport security had been tightened since the events that had unfolded with the hijacked planes on the east coast so plane rides to a hit, no matter how far away a job was, was definitely out of the question. Doss never used planes for jobs anyhow, but Seattle was in the most northern and western part of the country and it had taken an eternity to reach the city. Throughout the trek west, the group of four felt as if they were getting further and further away from actual civilization because cities, and then towns, became more and more scarce.

During one stretch across the state of Montana, there wasn't a town around for miles and miles. Nothing but lush, green fields, mountainous terrain, snow-capped peaks and crystal blue lakes. Beautiful scenery, but the occupants inside the black suburban and shiny new Cadillac Avalanche trailing weren't out to sightsee. Their deadly mission lay in a city on the Pacific Ocean and they were making a beeline for the left coast with two Dragunov rifles and two fully loaded .45 automatics.

When the crew reached Seattle, Bena and Tiva came to see why their father had them training in the elements back in Ponca City. The Emerald City was overcast and rain fell lightly. Traffic was streaming out of downtown during the evening rush. Seattle seemed no different from any other city save for its depressing grey skies and rainfall. A paper picked up at a fuel stop showed the forecast for the next three days—cloudy, a high of 59 degrees, and an eighty percent chance of rain each day. Bena and Tiva knew this job wasn't going to be as easy as the Vegas hit, but they were up to the challenge.

After checking into an inconspicuous motel on the outskirts of the city, the crew separated and began to spy their marks with the addresses provided by JunJie. There were too many witnesses at the brothers' downtown office to pull the job the crew noted, so a strike on home territory was warranted. The following day, Lucky and Tiva drove thirty miles south towards Kent where Hayate Onishi resided. The mark's luxurious three story brick home was centered in a cul de sac and tucked into a wooded hillside facing a business area, but that was all Lucky and Tiva could discern on this night because the fog was simply too thick, and it was a steady, light drizzle. They would have to sit and wait to see if the fog would clear out; and if it did, their mark still had to show.

Doss and Bay, meanwhile, had traveled about fifteen miles east of Seattle and had entered a ritzy Bellevue neighborhood littered with million dollar homes. Father and daughter cruised pass Isao's home, which sat atop a hill covered with shrubbery. A shot from ground level was out of the question because Isao's limousine would be completely blocked by the shrubs and trees that sat perched in front his home once he arrived.

Doss continued riding through the neighborhood trying to

find an angle, but the neighborhood had too many trees and hills to provide an adequate vantage point. He left the neighborhood formulating another attack method when Bay spotted a mini power station sitting on the edge of a steep-sloping tree-lined rocky hillside about ¾ of a mile away from her mark's sprawling two story mansion. There was a tall, grey steel electrical tower anchored into the cliffside where she could set up, and the countless pine, juniper, and spruce trees and shrubbery could provide the necessary cover.

"Dad, can you find the entrance to that power plant over there?" Bay asked as she pointed to the hillside on her right.

Doss rode through the area outside the neighborhood and came up on a small access road leading to the mini power station. He turned onto the pathway and extinguished his headlights and cruised to the end of the road where he and Bay got out under the falling rain and scanned the area.

Doss walked to the edge of the cliff and looked to his left and there lay Isao's mansion, the driveway to the man's home clearly visible. "We've found our spot. You gone have to climb down a bit to see the front door, though. Good job," he told Bena.

Bay, dressed in an all-black army uniform and black leather boots, draped her rifle over her shoulder while her father anchored a rope to the back of the Suburban and she slowly climbed down the rain-slickened, forested cliffside and carefully stepped onto the concrete platform holding up the steel electrical tower where she set up her rifle and lay in wait. The rain was coming down a little heavier as she lay atop the concrete slab adjusting her scope to allow for windage and gravity while Doss stood atop the cliff watching over things.

JunJie's file indicated that the brothers usually arrived home a few minutes apart, with Hayate arriving home before Isao somewhere around eight 'o' clock. After forty minutes of waiting, a sleek white limousine turned into the cobblestone driveway just before eight 'o' clock and the chauffeur got out and opened the rear door. Bay now had her mark in her line of fire so Doss chirped Lucky on his Nextel. "How you looking?"

"We can't see a thing down here. It's too foggy—even with the scope she can't see a thing."

"Did he make it home?"

"He's been home. Somebody came out on the balcony, but we not sure if it was him because we can't make out shit through this fog down here. Tonight's no good. We got no shot down here."

"Call it off," Doss said before he leaned over and whistled for Bay, who climbed back up the hillside and the two left the area. Finland said the job would be difficult and all four gangsters now understood fully what they were up against. The weather was an uncooperative factor in the scheme of things, and the forecast over the next few days didn't look any more promising.

Lucky ran his hands through his hair in frustration as he sat on the bed inside the motel room beside Tiva, who was breaking down her rifle. "If we let these guys get away, we run the risk of losing out on a million dollars, family. Not to mention the fact that this shit won't sit good with the Asians," Lucky said as he lit a cigarette and popped open a can of beer.

"We just have to time it right." Doss said while rubbing his chin in deep thought.

"We can time it all we want," Lucky remarked. "We're not the problem. This crappy ass weather is working against us and time is steadily tickin'."

"And the bad thing is the forecast isn't better tomorrow," Bay remarked as she paced the floor in frustration.

"Or the next day, or the next day, or the next day," Lucky said. "We have a problem here. Maybe we should try another way. Just bum-rush them mutherfuckas and get it over with."

"This is the only way, Lucky," Doss stated. "We can't catch these guys any other place because they're too many witnesses around. The bum-rush wouldn't work. But the plan we have in place will work if only the weather cooperates. The Onishi brothers seem to do everything JunJie says as far as arriving home at the said time. Let's just gather our heads, take a deep breath, and get back at it tomorrow."

****

For four nights in a row, the crew was hindered by Seattle's unrelenting and adverse weather conditions. Whenever Tiva was able to hit her mark, Bay would be hindered by rain and fog and vice versa. On the fifth day of their trip to Seattle, the crew had gotten word from Finland via JunJie that the Onishi brothers were headed back to Japan for a month-long business meeting in three days and the job would be obsolete should they board their flight. The crew tried for another two days to hit the Onishi brothers, but the weather was relentless. Fog and rain reigned supreme on both nights. On the eight day, the last day that would allow the crew the opportunity to fulfill the contract, the gang all headed out with the understanding that if they didn't hit the Onishi brothers on this night, the job would be considered a failure—not a good look for the professional crew of killers who prided themselves on never missing a mark.

JunJie, who was tucked away in Key West, Florida with his son and godson, was getting worried himself; if the Onishi brothers made their flight the following morning, he ran the risk of being unable to take over their businesses because he knew they were going to sign contracts with their Japanese counterparts back home and other investors would be in position to gain the reaps of their spoils should they die after signing those contracts. The tension was ratcheting up in Seattle and the Chicago Gang had to either deliver, or abort one million dollars in cash and suffer a setback in their cocaine deliveries because JunJie needed the ships the Onishi brothers owned to transport more product. A lot was riding on this last night of the attempted hit.

Arriving back in Kent on their final night before the brothers' scheduled flight, T-top sat in the backseat of Lucky's 2002 Cadillac Avalanche waiting patiently. Despite the pressure, she was calm and certain she could hit her mark. Things were good from her vantage point. There was a light drizzle, but no fog. All Hayate had to do was step outside; and from what Tiva had seen the past several days, someone, assumingly Hayate, emerged onto the patio every night shortly after his limousine pulled into the driveway. For the first time in over a week, the sky was clear enough for Tiva to recognize her mark. The weather thirty miles north, however, was not cooperating was the understanding via Doss's updates. Still, the crew was going ahead with the job in spite of the high risk.

Lucky and T-top were parked in an office park's parking lot. The business was a printing company that remained open twenty-four hours a day. Lucky's Avalanche was parked amongst many other vehicles, parallel to Hayate's home, which sat about a half mile away at the end of a cul-de sac. Medium-height buildings, which consisted of Starbuck's Coffee, Kwik Prints, and various clothing stores and condominiums, lined the street leading to the cul-de sac and the wooded hillside that held the man's luxurious home. The two continued talking for a while longer until they spotted Hayate's black Mercedes limousine turning into the cul de sac.

"Okay," T-top said as she placed the night vision scope onto her rifle. "If this guy does what he usually does when he gets home, he'll be dead in ten minutes. What time is it, unk?"

"Seven thirty," Lucky replied.

"Kinda early, but we close enough." T-top responded as she readied her rifle.

Bay, meanwhile, had used a rope anchored into the soil to descend the rain-slickened slope and was now perched on the concrete slab of the electrical tower looking down on her mark's home through her night vision scope. It was seven forty-five when headlights down below appeared and turned slowly into the driveway.

Doss was standing at the foot of the cliff looking down on Bay when headlights turned onto the access road. Bay saw the lights and she scurried up from the ledge and peeked between her father's feet only to see a patrol car's flashing lights. She ducked back down and turned to her mark, whose limousine was nearing the house. Isao's front door could be seen from this vantage point as well; Bay would just have to hunch over and kneel on one knee atop a rugged rock that set on a ledge.

"Continue on," Doss said as he threw his Nextel and binoculars down and turned around and faced the officer, who was exiting his car with his gun on his hand.

Bay was attempting to grab the Nextel, but it was just out of reach. She would have to climb back onto the top of the ledge to retrieve it and that move would alert the officer. She slipped back down the ledge out of the officer's sight, turned back to her mark and saw his scant image moving slowly up the sidewalk leading to his home and aimed her rifle once more.

"What are you doing around here?" the officer asked Doss.

"Just taking a leak, officer," Doss replied as he pretended to zip his silk suit pants.

The officer looked over to the black Suburban, which was parked several yards away from the man, and asked him, "You come way down here on this dark road to take a piss?"

"I didn't want to offend anyone." Doss replied as he stood with his hands at shoulder length.

"Well, you're offending me. Get over here and place your hands on the hood for me would you please, sir?" the officer asked as he shined a flashlight into the interior of the Suburban and saw that it was unoccupied.

Thirty miles down the road in Kent, T-top had just witnessed her mark walk out onto his balcony talking on a cell phone. "That's our guy and I got a clear shot," she said.

Lucky chirped Doss back in Bellevue at that moment and asked, "How you looking?"

The officer heard the chirp and the voice and began searching Doss's raincoat.

"You there?" Lucky asked.

At that moment, the officer looked over to the ledge, pressed his hand to Doss's back as his free hand began moving towards the radio planted on his left shoulder.

Bay, at the same time, had lost sight of her mark. He was walking beside his chauffeur, who was unwittingly shielding him from her line of fire with his body and an umbrella as the two made their way towards the home's entrance, Isao holding a briefcase while talking on a cell phone.

"It's a go on our end!" Lucky snapped.

Bay heard Lucky's remark, and despite the officer's presence, she went on with the job.

The officer heard the chirp and the voice as well, and Doss quickly sized him up. He was taller than he, but was of slender build, a young buck, maybe a rookie; whatever the case, Doss felt he could take the man down if he acted swiftly. The officer was reaching for his radio once again, and Doss, with the understanding that if this constable made that call, he and Bay would be in hot water, lurched out and grabbed the officer's Glock .9, catching the man by surprise. The two wrestled beside the car where Doss was able to slam the officer's hand against the side of the windshield, knocking his weapon out of his hand and sending it down into the mud as an intense struggle ensued.

Bay knew her father was battling the officer and she now had a life-altering conundrum on her hands—help her father—or take the five hundred thousand dollar shot. Trusting in her father's abilities to hold his own, Bay opted for the latter.

Lucky, meanwhile, wasn't getting a response on the Nextel. He thought about aborting the mission, but he and Doss had never discussed not having contact; on top of that, this was the only time Tiva had been able to lay eyes on Hayate with a clear shot. Lucky also knew the Onishi brothers were leaving for Japan the following morning, so to take down one would be better than none in his mind. The long-time gangster was now about to take the gamble of his life. Hitting one of the brothers could possibly expose the fact the businessmen had a price on their heads, but a move had to be made quickly. "Fuck it! The Asians will weather this storm and we'll back 'em," Lucky said lowly. "T-top? Take him down."

T-top had been having Hayate in her line of fire for the last minute from the back seat of the Avalanche as he talked on his phone and moved about on his balcony. Upon Lucky's order, on bended knee of the floorboard, T-top squeezed the trigger on her Dragunov and Hayate's blood splattered his patio window. He dropped his cell phone and stepped forward clutching his chest and another low-muzzled sound was heard by Lucky, who'd witnessed Hayate's head split open like a squashed tomato before his body dropped from sight.

T-top pulled her weapon back into the Avalanche as Lucky slowly drove away. She watched as a woman, Hayate's wife, ran out onto the balcony screaming just as she and Lucky cleared their line of sight. As he drove back to Seattle, Lucky again called Doss to see how he was making out. "Eh? You twos okay up there? We done down here."

Bay heard Lucky's voice again and now knew for certain that she had to take the shot. She watched from the ledge as Isao paused briefly and stared at his cell phone. Bay had the man in her cross-hairs briefly, but just before she squeezed the trigger, Isao dropped his phone all of a sudden and began running to his home and she lost him.

"Fuck!" Bay exclaimed lowly as she moved her rifle to and fro, trying desperately to find her mark in her scope once more, all the while hearing the battle her father was engaged in atop the hill. Unable to find the man with her scope, Bay moved her rifle ahead of Isao towards the front door in anticipation of his movements. When he crossed her line of sight in the scope once more, she followed him patiently. The chauffeur was in and out of Bay's line of fire, but for a few brief seconds, just before he entered his home, the back of Isao's head came into view and Bay fired one shot. The 7.62 millimeter bullet sliced through the back of her mark's skull and exited his face just below his left eye. Isao was dead before he fell into his threshold.

Bay quickly pulled herself up on to the rain-slickened ledge via the anchored rope and crawled on the ground under the pelting rain until she got up and ran over to her father, who was battling the officer something fierce beside his patrol car. The officer was laying on his back reaching for his gun repeatedly while yelling aloud for help as Doss pounded his face. Able to take the blows, the officer stopped struggling briefly and was able to reach his taser while sustaining punches and he hit Doss in his side with a power jolt. His limp body dropped down on top of the officer, who shoved him aside and scrambled to his knees and reached for his radio. "Dispatch! Dispatch! We have, we have an officer—"

The officer was silenced by a bullet that ripped off the right side of his forehead. Bay had run around and aimed her weapon and landed a fatal shot, looking the officer directly in the eyes before she killed the man. She then shot out the headlights and flashers on the patrol car and aided her father to his feet and the pair climbed into the Suburban with Bay behind the wheel.

Bay was about to pull off until Doss told her about the anchored rope, his binoculars and the Nextel he'd dropped and for her to also rip out the video inside the patrol car. While Bay gathered those items, Doss opened the glove box on the patrol car, popped the trunk and staggered to the rear of the vehicle and grabbed a two gallon plastic jug that was filled with gasoline. He and Bay scooped the officer's body up and shoved him inside of the patrol car and doused the vehicle's interior and the officer's body with the gasoline and set both ablaze to remove any remaining evidence, leaving behind one honest, hard-working dead policeman. The officer had caught many a teenager smoking and drinking in that locale and he was only making his rounds. He thought he'd encompassed the same scenario as he had many times before, only this time, he'd crossed paths with bona fide killers and it cost him his life.

Lucky was headed east out of Seattle when Doss called and explained what happened in coded talk and told him to travel on. The crew would not meet up again until they returned to Chicago. The job was viewed as a success; but the crew had unknowingly dodged a bullet. It was through sheer fate that the hit hadn't been uncovered, because unbeknownst to all involved, the Onishi brothers were wanted by another gang that'd been hot on their tail for some time.

****

The following morning, the crime scene atop the cliff near Isao's home was flooded with at least two dozen officers and crime scene technicians. The death of the Onishi brothers had sent shockwaves throughout the law enforcement community, namely the Federal Bureau of Investigation, who were onto the brothers for distributing heroin on the east coast.

The burnt out hull of the patrol car containing the officer's corpse, which was burned beyond recognition, was covered with a blue tarp as rainfall pelted the investigating officers' uniforms. Amidst the organized chaos, a black Suburban pulled up to the crime scene and a female federal investigator emerged from the passenger side. This red-haired forty-four year-old woman had been on the tail of the Onishi brothers for nearly a year, ever since she'd busted one of the brothers' buyers in Philadelphia and had gotten the dealer to give up his connect for a lesser sentence. When she'd gotten word Hayate Onishi had been killed on the same night as his brother, and an officer had been killed in close proximity to Isao, she knew nothing short of a professional hit had taken place.

The agent crossed under the yellow tape outlining the crime scene and walked amongst the officers, trying to decipher what they knew by asking numerous questions, but none of the investigators were able to offer much by way of evidence or suspects in the hits because the rain and fire had washed away all evidence, except for a few spent shells. After peeking underneath the tarp at the officer's charred remains, the woman couldn't help but to exclaim to her assistant, "What kind of an animal would do such a thing, Laddy?"

"One who's a professional?" Laddy Norcross, a thirty-two year-old blonde-haired young man of Swedish descent replied.

"The question was a rhetorical one, Laddy. You have a lot more to learn about the way I do business, guy, if you ever want to become my lead detective."

"I've only been under your wing for a few months so I'm still trying to gauge the process. But I'm most certain I'll be learning from the very best before my wings are set free. That was the right answer, though, don't you agree? I mean, had it not been rhetorical."

"Maybe. Leaning more towards yes." the woman said as she

walked towards the edge of the slope.

"Thanks. Not bad for a newbie, huh? Hey? Anybody ever tell you that you look almost exactly like Scully from the X-Files? Only thinner?"

"Yeah. The guy before you asked me that and I sent his ass back to Quantico for desk duty. Still think I look that fat bitch from the X-files?"

"What fat bitch from the X-Files? You are truly unique in beauty and brains."

"I like having my ego stroked, amongst other things, but I don't like to be patronized," the woman sighed. "You're right, though," she then said as she stood at the foot of the ledge, looking down at Isao's home where more investigators were milling about. "The shot came from this vantage point is all these people know, but hell, my Labrador retriever could've figured that one out and she's blind in one eye. I gotta give it to whoever did this—it was a helluva shot—one to the dome—from nearly a mile away. Not many in our field could land that shot given the angle and weather. Impressive. This was a professional job, by all accounts. And whoever did this needs to be removed from society because he or she, or they, are heartless people without a conscious," the woman said as she eyed the carnage.

A federal agent assigned to the Seattle office approached the woman and she extended her hand to the man."My name is Lisa Vanguard, federal agent and prosecutor. I want the names of all these guys' associates. Can we also get the cell phone records that the Onishi—"

"Your job here is done, Misses Vanguard," the slightly balding, but physically fit mid-forties Caucasian said in an aggravated tone.

Lisa eyed her fellow agent with disdain given his tone of voice and disposition. "It's Miss Vanguard. And my job is just beginning, sir. The people I was investigating have been killed and I'm now obligated to find their murderers in order to move my case forward."

"You were only sent here to investigate the Onishi brothers, who as you already know, are on their way to that metal meat slab down at the medical examiner's office."

"I had a strong case brewing! And I was only weeks away from indicting those guys until this," Lisa said as she spread her hands towards the crime scene off in the distance. "Whoever did this it is my responsibility to bring them to justice!"

"You were funded monies to investigate the Onishi brothers only. They're dead now so the plug has been pulled on your investigation. I got word this morning from the Justice Department that you and your staff are on a flight back to D.C. tomorrow. Your job is done here in the state of Washington. This investigation now belongs to the Seattle field office."

Lisa was devastated. At her core she believed had she gotten to the Onishi brothers she would have been the agent who would have taken down an entire drug network that was based in the city of Seattle. It had taken her nearly a year to sniff out the top tier players in her investigation and now it was being snatched from her hands in one swift motion. "Fine," Lisa said as she threw her hands up. "I know more about this case than all of you guys put together and I'm the one who's shut out? You people have no clue what you're dealing with. This isn't your everyday homicide."

"We know exactly what we're dealing with," the man said matter-of-factly. "We're dealing with the death of a well-respected rookie patrolman by the name of Rodney Simmons who was killed in cold blood and two drug dealers who got what was coming to them because of the business they were involved in by all accounts."

"Their profession doesn't make their deaths any less important. If you knew the game, you'd see clearly that the Onishi brothers were terminated on purpose. Maybe by a rival gang here that's trying to take over their heroin operation. Have you any references to other criminal gangs here?"

"There're several Asian gangs we're looking at, but no one's talking, of course."

"Really? What are the Asians going to say if you ask them about these homicides? 'Oh yeah, that Onishi hit? That was on us and we're all now ready for a life sentence'?" Lisa said sarcastically.

"Your attitude is the very reason I'm glad you're leaving my state and this here time zone."

Lisa rolled her eyes. "What's your name?" she asked.

"I'm agent Daniel Jarkowski,"

"Okay, agent, jerkoffski. Do you have—"

"That's Jarkowski."

"Jerkoffski, Jarkowski, same difference. Do you have a suspect?"

"No one as of yet." Jarkowski replied as he shook his head while looking down at Lisa.

"Why you looking at me like that?" Lisa questioned. "You still pissed about me mispronouncing your name? Come on, we bigger than that aren't we, guy?"

"You come here and try and uproot the Asian community by insinuating that there is an organization here that is involved in crime and I don't like it."

"I'm not implying anything. I am *convinced* that there is an Asian gang established here opposite the Onishi brothers who can kill people via the long shot. That thought ever crossed your mind? Or you can't think that far out of the box?"

Jarkowski smirked at Lisa and cleared his throat. "When we find that officer's murderer we will find the Onishi brothers' murderers and kill two birds with one stone. And this hit could've been orchestrated by the Yakuza just so you know."

"If only the Japanese Mafia did hits abroad. Sir, and no disrespect, but nobody this far up in the business walks around wearing an 'I'm a Killer' sign. And looks don't mean a damn thing to me when it comes to homicide. From infant to elderly, everybody's a suspect in my eyes."

"Is she always this difficult?" Jarkowski asked Laddy.

"I just met her a few weeks back."

"That's not what I asked you."

"He likes his job. So therefore he will not answer that question," Lisa remarked with a smile.

"We're done here," Jarkowski said in frustration. "Be sure to catch your flight in the morning—and don't go snooping around the time you have left here. The Seattle office will take over this, this unfortunate tragedy and do what needs to be done. You'll need to leave all your files at the Seattle office and make sure you're debriefed before day's end," he ended before he walked away, leaving Lisa and Laddy standing in the light drizzle.

Lisa knew what was on the line, but she would have to follow protocol. The people in charge back in D.C. were pulling her off the case despite the fact that was she was right on the heels of the Onishi brothers. She understood the fact that because her targets had been removed from the investigation via death, her job had become obsolete.

It was a crappy deal, but Lisa knew she'd lost all authority over her investigation. She would leave Seattle the following day after following protocol, but she was determined to return to the west coast to finish what she'd started as she just knew there was much more to the story involving the deaths of the Onishi brothers.

For now however, Lisa knew that whoever the killers were, they would remain free because the Seattle office in her assessment, were an inept bunch of witless agents who could care less about upholding the law and closing out the big investigations.

CHAPTER NINE
SMUGGLER'S BLUES

"Okay, that's the last one. Let's load up and be gone," Lucky told Junior and Eddie, the three having just repackaged twenty-seven kilograms of cocaine inside JunJie's warehouse in Bedford Park on 71st Street in Chicago for transport to Saint Charles. It was now September of 2002, five months after the hit on the Onishi brothers. It was a Saturday and the warehouse was closed, but the crew had free access the building anytime they wanted.

By the fall 2002, no clues as to the killers of Hayate and Isao Onishi had been uncovered as of yet. All authorities knew was that it was an orchestrated hit perpetrated by professionals given the nature of the shots and the discovery of the officer's burned corpse and scorched patrol car. Investigators never knew of the real turmoil between JunJie Maruyama and the Onishi brothers, and the man was conveniently out of town in Key West, Florida when the killings took place so he'd never become a suspect. His cunning maneuverability, and the fact that he had Agent Jarkowski on his payroll, kept him from being charged and the connection between he and the Chicago Gang was never made.

JunJie was quickly put in position to take over a major portion of Seattle's ports and within a couple of months, cocaine shipments had increased. All was going well for the

Chicago Gang by the start of fall; cocaine was moving as fast as it could be transported and everybody was making good money and staying under the radar. Business was merely continuing on as usual for all involved.

"Man, we gettin' a late start. It's two in the afternoon already. You notified Benito and Gaggi, Lucky?" Eddie asked.

"Yeah. Everybody's waiting us so let's load and get on the road." Lucky responded while pulling the door up on a truck that was backed into the dock.

"You heard from mom and granddad at the hospital?" Junior asked as he hopped onto a forklift.

"Your grandmother is undergoing tests and she's fine, son. That's what pops said. He'll update us later."

"You comfortable with mom joining us on this, dad?"

"It's a simple run, son. We've been doing this all summer."

"I know all that. But, it's mom. She gonna be okay?"

"Son," Lucky responded as he eyed Junior, "your mother insisted she join us because she's ready to get away for a while. This thing with Francine has her as nervous as all out doors, not this delivery. Besides, she won't be nowhere near the stuff. Don't worry about it."

Lucky, Junior and Eddie were going to travel down to Saint Charles and make a drop off on this cool autumn Saturday in late September of 2002. Once Junior loaded a couple of pallets of fruit intertwined with cocaine, he and Lucky headed to his Avalanche and joined Mildred, while Eddie got behind the wheel of the refrigerated six-wheeled truck.

The plan was to drive down to Saint Charles and make the switch, cocaine for cash. From there, Lucky and Mildred would head to Oklahoma with the profits so Naomi could wash the money clean through the family's businesses while Gaggi and Benito distributed the product to a few soldiers from Fox Park who helped Eddie and Junior move the weight. The crew pulled out of the warehouse and were on their way once the gate was locked.

THE HOLLAND FAMILY SAGA

****

"On that train of graphite and glitter...On the sea by rail... Ninety minutes from New York to Paris...Where by seventy-six we'll be a okay...What a beautiful world this would be... What a glorious time to be free..." Pop and Jazz singer Donald Fagan's song, *I.G.Y.* (What a Beautiful Word), blared loudly inside Lucky's Avalanche as he headed south on Interstate-55 towards St. Louis, Missouri, about thirty minutes into the trip and having just made a fuel stop with Eddie.

As he rode with his parents, Junior repeatedly shook his head at the song being played. "Every time, man," he sighed. *"Every—freakin'—time* I get in a vehicle with you it's like going back in a time machine!"

"You just don't know good music, son." Mildred remarked making Lucky smile; proud that his wife was taking up for him.

"You sidin' with dad? You sidin' with *dad*? You didn't say that back at the gas station when you were complaining about the fact that he needs to step out his time machine and play more up to date music."

Lucky dropped his smile and looked over at Mildred; the woman was trying to keep her composure, but she knew all-too-well she had made that statement. Mildred was a fun-loving and easily entertained woman, and hearing her son repeat her words caused her to chuckle.

Lucky could look at his wife's face and tell right away that she had made the statement. "You think that's funny, Mildred," he asked. "Step outta my time machine, eh? You callin' me an old timer? You callin' me an old timer you, you—"

Before Lucky could get Mildred's favorite saying from out his mouth, Mildred was already beginning to erupt into laughter, her body was heaving as she tried not to laugh, but Mildred couldn't help herself as she just knew it was coming.

"Ohhh!" Lucky yelled aloud over the music.

"Ahhhhh!" Mildred screamed in loud laughter as she slapped her legs and rocked back and forth in her leather seat. "Don't say it no more! I'm gonna piss my pants!" Mildred said as tears ran down her face from the laughter.

Junior was in the back seat laughing at his mother. Mildred had an infectious laugh, and her laughter soon had Junior and Lucky laughing uncontrollably and Lucky wasn't going to stop no time soon. Since Mildred and Junior laughed at his choice of music, Lucky decided he would get back at one of them at least, that one being Mildred. "You gonna piss your pants? You betta not piss your pants in my fuckin' Cadillac you, you —"

"Lucky, stop! Don't say it! Don't you say it!"

"Ohhh!" Lucky yelled aloud.

"Ahhh! You mutherfucka!" Mildred screamed through laughter as she grabbed the dash board with both her hands, her eyes wide and filled with tears as she looked straight ahead.

Lucky and Junior saw the expression on Mildred's face and they couldn't help but to laugh. For whatever reason, Mildred had caught the giggles at this moment. What Lucky was saying wasn't really that funny, but Mildred thought the entire scenario was more than hilarious. Soon, Lucky and Junior were laughing along right along with Mildred; and every time Lucky yelled "ohhh", Mildred would scream out in laughter.

"Hey, son, ya' see there? I'm milking your mother like them heifers down on Naomi's farm!" Lucky said through laughter.

"Ohh boy! Foot in ya' mouth dad!" Junior stated under his breath as he watched his mother's face grow serious.

"You callin' me fat, Lucky?" Mildred asked angrily, changing her entire demeanor.

"No! You took that statement the wrong way, alright? I was stating how when you calm down, I make you laugh again and you almost piss your pants each time. I was milking your laughter is what I was doing."

"Bullshit! You sittin' over there *tryin'* to make me piss my pants!"

"Ehhh, hold the fuck up! You was laughing the whole time!"

"Yeah, but I kept asking you to stop!"

"You didn't stop until you heard the word heifer, and no, you nowhere nears fat. You look the same as the day I met you at the ball park in April of seventy-one."

"You still remember?" Mildred asked with a sweet smile.

"Of course I do. I remember what you had on too."

"What did I have on, Faustino?" Mildred asked as she reached out and stroked her husband's muscular biceps.

"You had on red shorts, black tennis shoes with a red and white stripped blouse. I remember because you looked like a fuckin' Cardinals fan."

"I told you I was Cubs fan that day, but secretly, I was going for the Cardinals." Mildred chuckled.

"I knew it! That's why—all these years and you only watched the Cubs when they play the Cards! Hey, son? We got a traitor amongst us! Your mother's a Card's fan! Maybe they playing today, how about we drop you off at the stadium when we get to Saint Louis? How about we do that? You can watch them instead of going to Spoonie and Tyke's game you, you —"

"Don't you start that again!" Mildred screamed as she eased away from Lucky.

"Fuckin Cards fan, ohhh! Unfuckin' believable!"

"Ahhhhh! I told you not to say it! I'm gonna piss my pants! Pull over now! Now before I wet myself, Lucky!"

Mildred had to force Lucky over at that point. He quickly pulled over, and called and had Eddie slow down. Mildred hid from sight, squatted and urinated, and before long they were back on the highway. Once everyone was situated and the group was back behind Eddie, Lucky grabbed his phone and called Doss, who was on the ranch lying low with his family, and told him they were on the highway.

****

Doss and the big three hadn't done much since the Seattle

job. They only practiced shooting on a daily basis and spent time with the family. Killing an officer was serious business, and the Chicago Gang had requested that Doss and the big three lay low. Doss was to make $400,000 dollars off the hit, but when DeeDee and Mendoza heard all the details, they kicked in another $150,000 dollars.

Doss and his family walked away with over half the payoff. Another two hundred thousand dollars was given to Lucky. Once DeeDee and Mendoza got their twenty percent cut each of the remaining profit, the one hundred and fifty thousand remaining dollars, was tucked away in a rainy day fund for the gang to use for lawyers and bail money. That was the usual order of things on big hits within the family, with Doss getting a forty percent markup off the top for his services. A few hours after he'd talked to Lucky, Doss got a call from Mendoza, who seemed a little unnerved in his tone of speech.

"Everything okay?" Doss asked as he sat in his private room.

"It's Francine," Mendoza said sadly. "Francine has breast cancer and she may need a double mastectomy in order to save her life."

"The tests didn't go well, I see. I'm sorry to hear that, man. You called Lucky and told him?"

"I don't want to put that on his mind while he's working. Him or Junior. I'm, I'm gonna step aside for a while until we get through this. Have Lucky call me as soon as he arrives on the ranch, he'll have to take the reins for now."

"You got it. Your family will be in me and Naomi's prayers, my friend."

"Thanks, Doss. That means a lot. DeeDee's here with me. He says he's not gonna fly down for Spoonie and Tyke's softball game and says you will understand."

"Of course I understand, Mendoza. And Francine's a strong woman. She'll fight this battle and win it without fail."

"Yeah," Mendoza said in an unsure tone before he hung up the phone and went and sat beside DeeDee in the waiting room in total shock.

"You got in touch with Lucky?" DeeDee asked.

"No. I talked to Doss down in Oklahoma. I'm gonna wait to tell Lucky. He's doing that thing, you know, so I don't want to upset him and my grandson."

"That's understandable. Francine's a fighter. She'll pull through."

"How right you are. You wasn't, you wasn't around this day back in sixty-eight when these broads got racist with Naomi." Mendoza said, reminiscing about happier times to lighten the mood in the waiting room.

"Francine told me about that day." DeeDee said as he smiled and reached over and poured him and Mendoza a cup of coffee.

"Hey, thanks. Just what I need to work out the kinks. Yeah, Naomi, she, she couldn't have been no more than twelve or thirteen at the time, and Francine had to be in her late thirties then, il mio amico. Man we kicked some tail that day. I remember walking across the street watching Francine and Naomi thump this broad while she was on the ground," Mendoza broke into laughter at that moment. "And I went over there and called them women some of the worse names imaginable let me tell ya'," he added.

"Serena even got in on the action Francine told me." DeeDee chimed in.

"Serena most certainly did. Hey, she surprised everybody with that move. Ohhh, that was a scrappy one there when it really got down to it, Doss."

"Umm, hmm. She and Kevin were good people, too. Good parents to Naomi."

"They were a calming force in Naomi's life. And good friends to Francine. I know Francine wishes they were around today. The Langleys, the Langleys had a way of making everything seem okay, you know? No matter what the circumstances were at the time. I could use their uplifting spirits now because I really don't wanna lose Francine. She's my best friend you know?"

DeeDee sat upright with his coffee and asked, "And what am I?"

"Chopped liver is what you are," Mendoza replied as he and DeeDee shared a quick laugh. Mendoza then sighed and looked down into his cup of coffee. "It's something we all have to face, Doss."

"What? Death?"

"Yeah. I wonder how it'll all end for me. There really isn't much time left. I have many more days behind me than in front that's for sure," seventy-one year-old Mendoza remarked somberly.

"Don't think about it, man. Not now anyway," seventy-one year-old DeeDee replied as he patted Mendoza's shoulder.

"I can't help but think about it. I went to the doctor myself last week and you know what he told me?"

"Was it good or bad?"

"Indifferent is what it was."

"Okay. What'd he say?"

"He said, and he was smiling, too, when he told me, 'You're in good health, Mister Cernigliaro. Just make sure you eat plenty fruit because an apple a day keeps the doctor away'."

"Is that right? What's so bad about that?" DeeDee asked as he stirred his coffee.

"Nothing. But I'm not finished with the story. I just look at the guy with a blank stare. I been knowing him for years, so I'm able to express myself candidly you know? I look at 'em and I say, I says, 'Doc, it's no secret between you and I what I do for a livin''."

"What he say back?"

"Nothing at all. He just smiles at me and I says back to him, 'Now, you like to say an apple a day keeps the doctor away. Well, I say, you can eat all the fuckin' apples you want, but if you go down in my line of work it ain't gonna be because you forgot to eat your fuckin' fruit'."

"You told your doctor that?"

"Sure as hell did."

"What he say back?"

"He told me I should find another line of work and sit my old ass down and eat some fuckin' apples." Mendoza replied as he and DeeDee laughed lowly. "How ya' like them apples?" Mendoza added. The two lifelong friends would share more laughter to keep the mood upbeat, but deep down inside, Mendoza had never been so scared in all his life. If he were to lose Francine, for Mendoza, it would mean the loss of the most valuable thing in his life without compare.

****

A few miles to the northwest of Saint Louis lay the city of Saint Charles. A medium-sized city, population 60,000, and the home base for Chicago Gang affiliates, 63 year-olds Coban Benito and Humphrey Gaggi. The lifelong mobsters had a smooth set up in a neighborhood right behind Lindenwood University on the corners of Elm Street and Lindenwood Avenue. This was a densely populated neighborhood filled with homes and small businesses that were all anchored by a bar and grill that had been owned by the Egan's Rats since the 1920s.

The people here basically kept themselves and minded their own business; and although many knew the dealings that went down on the corners of Elm Street and Lindenwood Avenue, the place had been a part of the neighborhood for decades and Benito and Gaggi were two of the most well-respected men on the block. They were known to aid businesses by giving loans and sometimes never asking to have the loans repaid. That in itself kept the men with a certain amount of respectability.

This part of Saint Charles, although dense, was a quiet area occupied by young and established married couples while the rest of the homes were being rented out to students who were sharing the rent in order to attend the nearby college. There were numerous small businesses in the tranquil community as well. On Elm Street, where most of the activity took place, there was a large three story cleaners on the corner across the street from *Connections*. A deli, bookstore, and an urban clothing store was on the block as well, all catering to the nearby college campus' students and the neighborhood in general.

Elm Street was a calm place by all outward appearances, but in all actuality, it was the headquarters of one of the biggest cocaine operations in the Midwest. Down from *Connections*, on the opposite end of the block on the same side as the bar, lay twenty-seven year-old Eddie Cottonwood's two story white wooden Victorian-style home. Eddie had been tight with Doss ever since he'd helped him, Lucky and Junior pull off a job inside Cabrini Green projects back in 1992. He moved down from Chicago to the Saint Charles area with his two younger brothers and daughter when he got in good with Benito and Gaggi and started making large amounts of money. He was now Benito and Gaggi's muscle. Eddie's younger brothers, seventeen year-old Jason David A.K.A. Jay-D, and fifteen year-old Donnell, A.K.A. Dooney, were under his wing and steadily learning the business.

Jay-D was sitting on the front porch of the home with his niece, ten year-old Nancy, braiding her hair while his brother Dooney washed the Cottonwood family's dark blue 2001 Lincoln Navigator. The family was relaxing for the minute, but soon, Jay-D and Dooney would have to stand guard for a delivery that was scheduled to arrive from Chicago.

"Jay-D, why you braid it this way?" Nancy asked as she squinted her eyes. Her uncle had a way of braiding her hair so tight she could barely blink.

"I'm hurtin' your skull again?" Jay-D asked his skinny, dark chocolate-skinned knot-kneed little niece.

"Yes, sir. But I can take it. I just know you braiding it to the side again and it makes the other side of my face hurt the first day. Feel like all my skin be pulled to one side."

"You don't like the lady down the street to do it and you asked me to do it."

"Because I know you gone take me somewhere for sitting through this agony," Nancy replied.

Jay-D laughed lowly and said, "I have business down the street to take care of when your daddy get in, so whatever you have in mind we'll do it tomorrow, okay?"

"Aww, man! I coulda waited 'til tomorrow?"

"That's what ya' get for tryna be slick," Jay-D smirked just as a Spanish girl ran onto the block chasing a puppy on a leash.

"Heyyy! That's a pretty puppy," Nancy said. "I played with it the other day."

"You know that chick?"

"Not her name. I didn't ask. But she lets me pet her dog whenever I do see her."

Jay-D whistled to Dooney and nodded towards the jogger and the two watched as she ran up the block where she stopped halfway, tied her dog and walked up the stairs of the neighborhood deli and took a seat on the patio.

"You ever seen her before, Dooney?" Jay-D asked from the porch.

"Nahh. But I think she go to Lindenwood because she had one of they gym uniforms on."

"That don't mean shit, Dooney. You know what's up today," Jay-D replied just as he finished Nancy's hair. "Niece, go on in and pop some popcorn and turn on the TV. They got some new movies on the DVD player in the den."

When Nancy entered the home, Jay-D and Dooney stood on the corner and watched the woman from a distance. She'd ordered a sno-ball and hopped up just as soon as the six-wheeled truck rounded the bend onto Elm Street. Jay-D and Dooney grabbed two Tech-9 semi-automatics from the rear of the jeep and began walking slowly towards *Connections* as the truck backed into the alleyway behind the building. The two eyed the female, who casually jogged past them with her puppy while sipping her sno-ball, before heading down to the bar

The small six-wheeled truck turning onto the block was what the woman was looking for on this day, just like every other day she'd been on the block for the past few weeks unnoticed by those whom it truly mattered to; when she passed Eddie's home, she rounded the corner, picked up her puppy and ran through the woods onto Lindenwood College campus' parking lot and hopped into a white Ford Focus.

"What did you see today," her male counterpart asked.

"A small truck backing in. The same one as last time, and those two boys that was in that house on the corner by that jeep was walking back down there," the girl said as she changed clothes.

The man grabbed his cell phone and text the words, *It's going down*, and slowly pulled out of the parking lot.

****

Eddie and Junior, meanwhile, were already unloading the cocaine when Jay-D and Dooney walked up.

"Hey, look who decided to join the party," Junior said as he stood on the concrete dock with the last sealed box of cocaine.

"I told y'all to be down here when we got here," Eddie scoffed as he hopped down from the docks. "Anything outta the ordinary?"

"Some lady jogging. Dooney think she go to the college down the street. I don't know about that one."

Eddie looked at his younger brothers curiously as the two walked towards the end of the alleyway back out onto Elm Street. "What went down?" he asked as he began looking around cautiously.

Inside *Connections*, meanwhile, Lucky, Benito and Gaggi were at the bar counter having just finished counting $486,000, all banded into thousand dollar stacks and placed inside of three leather satchels. The crew wasn't on the clock for no more than fifteen minutes and were preparing to leave when Mildred ran into the bar. "I gotta tinkle before we hit the road, love," she told Lucky.

"Be quick about it," Lucky snapped.

"Care for a drink while you wait," Benito asked from behind

the bar.

"No. I'm drivin'. And you twos really need to cut that shit out. This is when the real work begins and you two are reaching for the bottle. One of yous grab a bag and help me stash these in the jeep." Lucky said as he grabbed the two remaining bags.

Back outside the bar, Jay-D had just run down what he thought about the woman jogger to Eddie and Junior when two black Crown Victorias with dark tinted windows swung the curb off Lindenwood Avenue with blue flashers circulating in their windshields. Junior and the Cottonwood family knew the sight all-too-well—the feds were coming down on this day.

"Rollers! Rollers! Get the fuck outta there! It's a raid!" Junior, Eddie, Jay-D and Dooney yelled aloud and at random before they took off running in all directions.

Lucky was near the front door and could see the cars stopping and officers jumping out wearing all black, including black ski-masks and gloves, and toting assault rifles. He turned around with the two satchels of money he was holding onto and yelled, "Mutherfuckas! Mildred! Get the fuck outta here! Run, Mildred!"

Benito and Gaggi ran out the side door. They were nearing their BMW when two agents grabbed them and shoved them back inside without uttering a word.

Lucky, meanwhile, had busted in on Mildred, who was washing her hands. "It's a raid! The feds are out there!" he said out of breath.

Mildred was beyond scared and began palpating. "A raid!" she whispered. "Oh my God!"

"You gone need him now more than ever," Lucky said as he ushered his wife out the bathroom towards the same side door Benito and Gaggi had attempted to run out of; when Lucky and Mildred emerged, they were both greeted by one lone agent who was welding a gold-plated handgun. "Inside," the female commanded through her ski-mask as she shoved the two back into the building and locked the door.

Lucky, Benito, Coban, Gaggi and Mildred were all placed onto their knees in the center of the wooden floor inside the dimly-lit, cavernous bar while four agents stood over them. The the other four agents had went about confiscating the drugs and money in an organized and timely fashion, careful not to make any unnecessary noise.

Mildred was crying her heart out, "I'm going to jail, Lucky," she cried aloud.

"You're not going to fuckin' jail, okay? You only came in to use the bathroom and you knew nothing about this," Lucky said under his breath as he held his hands behind his head. "That's your story. Get used to it because you're gonna have to tell it over and over again."

"*Esto es todo!*" (This is everything!) the female with the gold-plated handgun remarked as she walked from behind the bar holding a duffel bag.

"You checked the safe, Carmella?" one of the females asked, causing all eight of the agents to freeze in their tracks.

"*Perra dices mi nombre?*" (Bitch you say my name?)

"What the fuck kind of raid is this?" Gaggi asked as he turned to face the four agents standing behind him. "Are you sons-of-bitches real cops even?"

The question Gaggi asked had set off a fuse. The man standing behind him pulled the trigger on his silencer-tipped AR-15 and shot him in the back of the skull and he fell forward onto his face with blood pouring from his mouth. Benito clutched his heart and called out to God just before he was shot two times in the back of the skull.

"We got ya' in this place. You girls can finish the job. We gone be outside," the man who'd shot Benito and Gaggi said as he and his three henchmen walked towards the door.

"Si! We got these two," Carmella remarked.

Q-man and his crew had watched the Chicago Gang for nearly five months, had learned their routine and set up the sting. They now stood outside eyeing spectators off in the distance counting down the seconds anxiously. Carmella and her crew had to move quick lest they be discovered.

Back inside the bar, Mildred was going ballistic. She crawled away from Benito's shivering body and huddled under a bar stool just as Lucky jumped up and lunged at the agent approaching him with her gold-plated handgun. She fired a muzzled shot that hit Lucky in the arm, but he still managed to grab hold of the woman. The two fought toe-to-toe for a few seconds. Lucky hit the woman in the head with a forceful left jab, knocking her over the table and chairs behind her. The woman quickly jumped as Lucky shoved the table aside.

Lucky was going for his gun until Toodie ran up and fired a shot from her silencer-tipped AR-15 that hit him in his back. He was propelled forward by the gun blast, falling onto the woman he was fighting as he stumbled to the floor. As he fell, Lucky pulled the woman's ski-mask off and could see for the first time that she was a Colombian. "It's a hit! It's a hit!" he yelled out to no one in particular as he coughed up blood.

"You're right, pa-pi," Carmella said as she pressed her boot to Lucky's chest, pinning him to the floor. "It is a hit!" she hissed as she aimed her weapon and shot Lucky in the face as he lay on his back. She then walked over to Mildred, who was reciting the Lord's Prayer with her eyes closed. "Your god will not save you today, old lady," she said before she placed her gun to the top of Mildred's skull and pulled the trigger.

Carmella, Toodie, Phoebe and one of their young soldiers from Fox Park then fled the scene with the three satchels of money and three duffel bags containing an unknown amount of cocaine. They met up with Q-man outside the bar and the crew hopped into their cars and backed away from *Connections* and peeled off down Lindenwood Avenue, leaving behind a scene of unbridled carnage that would become known as The Massacre on Elm Street.

THE HOLLAND FAMILY SAGA

CHAPTER TEN
A COLD PIECE OF WORK

"I'm rollin' with thugs and felons ughhh, cuz that's his own killaz...we gon' teach you ole punk ass niggas to respect us authority figures...throw one of a kind boy when we be pourin' up in the club...you going down boy too bad fuck ya' sorry for ya'...that's when that spot get shook, but I ain't the one to come look...'cause all I can tell the police is..."

"I am not a crook!" Carmella, Toodie and Phoebe said in unison as they all threw up peace signs and laughed aloud after quoting part of the rapper Mystikal's verse.

Li'l Jon and The Eastside Boys song *I Don't Give a Fuck* was pumping hard inside the interior of the black Crown Victoria as Carmella wheeled the ride eastbound on Interstate-70 headed towards East Saint Louis. She lay back into the soft leather while still dressed as an F.B.I. agent, complete with lettered jacket and fake badge, her left hand now draped across the steering wheel and her right hand rubbing her chin softly as she drove in deep thought. The Saint Charles hit was by far one of the coldest tactics she'd used to date and she'd succeeded in removing some major players from the game, just as she'd promised over a year ago. She then thought about letting what happened back at *Connections* slide, but she just couldn't, nor was she willing to take the chance.

Toodie and Phoebe were bobbing their heads to the music

and absorbing the lyrics while counting the stacks of money. Carmella bumped Toodie and nodded to the backseat briefly.

"Si, boss," Toodie said.

Toodie then grabbed her phone and texted Phoebe. When she read the message, Phoebe said aloud, "Figured that a while ago."

"Me too," Toodie responded as she continued on with the counting of the stolen loot.

The young female in the backseat grabbed her phone and began texting. Carmella quickly took notice and she jumped to attention. "Who you talking to?" she asked as she looked in the rearview mirror while turning the volume down.

"She texting her momma," Phoebe remarked.

"I'm talkin' to her li'l young ass!" Carmella snapped.

"I thought we was going back to Fox Park. I have to do something for my momma," the young girl stated in a meek tone.

"Your momma gone have to wait on that shit because we on our way over to the spot on the other side that water. Let me see that phone," Carmella demanded as she placed her hand over the front seat and wiggled her fingers. Carmella called Q-man and told him to meet her over by the abandoned warehouse in East Saint Louis. "You know where it's at right?"

There was a brief pause and Carmella responded by saying, "I know we said over there, but something came up. Just push out now and we gone meet up about the same time. I'm rolling that way now. Get the keys to one of the rides from that li'l girl in the house and you drive it on the other side for me. Not the yellow one, though. I got you covered when we hook up."

When Carmella hung up the phone, the young girl asked to use it to call her mother. "I told you, you will do that shit later. Just ride." Carmella snapped as she dialed another number. "Peppi? You okay?"

Carmella chatted with Pepper for a few minutes, telling her

she'd be home shortly and hung the phone up once more, denying the young girl in the backseat the use of her own phone again. She then called Desiree back over in Denver and talked briefly as she cruised over the Mississippi River Bridge and entered East Saint Louis.

At that moment, Toodie and Phoebe began sliding clips into their .9mm Berettas and the entire mood inside the car had gone from calm to fright. Toodie and Phoebe knew what was about to go down, and the young girl seemed to pick up on the play as well.

"I'm sorry I said your name," the sixteen year-old told Carmella.

Carmella shook her head and sucked her teeth. "All the fuck you had to do was watch and report back to Q-man, bitch," she sighed as she shook her head in disbelief. "Your ass didn't listen, and now you fuckin' sorry?" she asked calmly.

"I forgot! I just slipped up for a minute! But we was gonna kill them anyway!"

"Fuck that! I gave you one order! One test! For you to not to say my name and you failed it! Had shit gone wrong my name woulda been out there," Carmella argued as she exited onto Saint Clair Avenue and rode in between the interstate pylons towards the abandoned warehouses.

"Carmella, no!" the young girl whined as Phoebe cocked her gun and placed it to her side. "Phoebe! Please! I ain't gone say nothin'! I won't tell nobody what we did I promise!"

Neither Phoebe nor Toodie uttered a word as Carmella wheeled the vehicle to the back of the empty warehouses and slammed on the brakes and threw the car in park where she, Toodie and Phoebe jumped out with their handguns cocked and surrounded the ride. The sun had just slipped beneath the Saint Louis skyline on the opposite side of the river and a dark blue hue encompassed the area as the cool wind begin whipping about.

The young girl began screaming in the backseat, her voice echoing throughout the hallowed warehouses, landing on nothing but the bare brick walls and the area's non-human inhabitants. Carmella turned up the music to drown out the girls' screams just as Toodie snatched her from the rear seat of the car and drove her into the concrete dock head first. The young teen fell onto her stomach and Phoebe kicked her over onto her back and began stomping her face repeatedly with her boots.

Carmella then picked the young girl up and threw her onto the docks and climbed up onto the concrete and dragged the semi-conscious teen, who was weakly crying out for her mother, inside the warehouse where the three beat the youngster mercilessly. If anybody were watching from a distance, it would look as if three federal agents were abusing their arrestee; but no witnesses were on hand for this all-out assault on one lone teen that'd gotten in over her head.

The girl was slammed against the brick walls and steel beams inside the small room where the beating had escalated into a violent frenzy. She was cut all over her body with razors, one of her ears was nearly sliced off and she had hair ripped from her skull. She was left a bloody, heaping mass of flesh by the time Carmella and her girls grew tired of whipping her ass. A single shot to the face from Phoebe's .9mm ended her life and her body was covered with old cardboard boxes and insulation and left where it lay, dead, bloody and stiff.

Carmella, Toodie and Phoebe were emerging from the building when Q-man and his crew pulled up. The men exited a money green 1973 Buick Skylark on 26 inch chrome rims and Toodie's white Navigator with guns in hand and waited while the girls jumped down from the docks. Carmella went to her car and grabbed a duffel bag and a suitcase and set it atop the trunk of the Crown Victoria and waved the boys over.

"We came out with four hundred and eighty-six thousand dollars and twenty-seven kilograms." Carmella told the Somalis. "The money all in thousand dollar stacks so it's a even split—two hundred and forty-three stacks apiece and thirteen kilograms even. You and your people can have the extra brick for delivering our ride."

"It was four of y'all at first. Where your other girl at? The one that I was dealin' with?" Q-man asked as his boys took down their cut.

"She had to go home. Just like I do." Carmella said as she walked around the driver's side of the Crown Victoria.

"You a cold pieca work, yeah?" Q-man said, looking at the bloodstain on the concrete dock. "She fucked up at the end and you kill the bitch? You had it in mind to kill those people anyway," he reasoned.

"That's how I do my business. I have no time to be fuckin' around with these li'l girls out here in this game. Them li'l young bitches need ta' recognize what they gettin' involved in when it comes to me and mines. Everybody wanna be a fuckin' gangster but they have no clue how to be real with it."

"Hmm. You just gone leave her here?"

"Fuck you worryin' bout that bitch for? Everybody paid now so let's go get it!"

"Fuck it, man. We headed back to the Ap tonight. Me my fam be in touch next month," Q-man said as he shook his head and walked off.

The Crown Victoria was taken several miles north of East Saint Louis and set ablaze. Carmella and her girls then headed back towards Fox Park in Toodie's ride, minus one soldier, and thousands of dollars richer.

"Awww," Phoebe suddenly sighed from the backseat.

"What happened?" Carmella asked.

"I was reading our homegirl's last text."

"What it say?" Toodie asked.

"I love you mommy," Phoebe sang before she laughed.

"See there? She was just a fuckin' baby," Carmella said through laughter as she wheeled the vehicle onto the Mississippi River Bridge. "She wouldn't have lasted long in this business so I did her a little young ass a favor," she ended as Toodie took the cell phone and tossed it over the side of the bridge into the murky waters below.

After dropping her girls off at the trap house in Fox Park located on Ann Avenue, Carmella jumped into her yellow Spider and headed over to her home in Crestwood, an upscale neighborhood on the outskirts of Saint Louis. Crestwood might as well have been on an island in the Pacific as it was a slice of paradise. The area was quiet and draped with oak trees, sculpted parks and golf courses amidst the mini mansions that dotted the area. The home was a two story light grey and white five bedroom brick home with specks of black running throughout. The roof was made of white clay and the lawn was trimmed and edged to perfection with a large moss-covered oak tree on either side of the driveway. It was the smallest of the four mansions Carmella owned, but it was luxurious nonetheless.

When Carmella exited her Ferrari, eleven year-old Pepper opened the door and ran out the house to greet her. Carmella had to run into the home and deactivate her alarm before it went off, barely making it in time. "Pepper, remember not to open the door without deactivating the alarm." she said softly.

"I'm sorry. I forgot."

"People die for forgetting, you know?"

"Why? How?"

"Never mind. What did you do here today all by yourself?" Carmella asked as she traversed the stairs of her home, removing her jacket and badge.

"I read the English book you gave me and took that test you left in the dining room."

Carmella had never placed Pepper into a school because she was always on the move with the child. Not to mention the rapport that she had with the little girl may be uncovered should she enter the system. Still, Carmella made sure that Pepper was able to learn curriculum that matched her age and then some so as not to have the child grow up illiterate. When Peppi Vargas was old enough, Carmella was planning on taking her to a high school so she could take a G.E.D. exam and earn her diploma. Until then, she would keep the child's nose in text books whenever possible.

"How you think you did on your test, Peppi?" Carmella asked as she entered her twelve hundred square foot master bedroom.

"I passed."

"You're very confident."

"You said to always be sure of yourself and know what you are capable of doing. I'm sure I passed that test because I was capable to do it."

"Able to do it, Pepper. You were able to do it." Carmella said as she sat on the bench before her bed and removed her boots.

"Okay. Why're you dressed like that? Are you the police?" Pepper inquired, sitting beside Carmella.

"I was for about five minutes. Not even that long."

"I've never seen you wear your hair in a ponytail. What did you do today?"

"Started a war, Pepper. Your Auntie has started a war."

"People die in wars. Are you going to die in this war?"

"You ask a lot about death."

"I know. I saw my mother die and I can't forget it. I'm scared to die."

"No one gets out of life alive, Peppi. Death is something we all have to face. Either late in life or early in life, it will inevitably arrive at our doorstep. I was scared to die once, but when you've looked death in the face, it no longer bothers you. It's like going to sleep."

"I wanna live a long time."

"So do I, Pepper. But bosses don't always live long. Remember that if you ever become a boss, okay? We don't live long," Carmella ended somberly as she stripped out of her clothing, turned on the TV and walked towards her bathroom.

Pepper climbed onto the bed and watched the news while Carmella showered. A few minutes into the program, she saw a story that detailed a shooting that took place in a town called

Saint Charles.

"In what has to be one of the worse shootings ever in Saint Charles' history, three people were gunned down and another critically wounded inside a bar that was the reputed headquarters of a now defunct Italian Crime Family known as the Egan's Rats. The suspects in what has come to be known as The Massacre on Elm Street, were said to have been dressed up as FBI agents when the shootings occurred. Rumors ranging from a drug deal gone bad to old Mafioso rivalries or a combination of both are fueling the investigation. Witnesses report hearing no gunshots, but some grew curious when the purported officers left holding bags believed to contain drugs and money without arresting any suspects. A local deli owner discovered the bodies and authorities were soon notified. Investigators have no clues and the only living witness is listed in critical condition and has little chance of surviving. Authorities are resting their hopes on the chance that the lone witness, who's being guarded by police, is able to pull through and give an account of all the events that transpired leading up to this terrible tragedy. More details on this story as the investigation unfolds."

Carmella was drying herself off and had caught the last vestiges of the news report and she trotted out of the bathroom butt naked. "Now someone may remember she said my name. I did right killin' that whore," she said somberly as she stared at the fading images on the TV.

A surprised Pepper eased back on the bed and pulled her knees up to her chest. "You did that to those people?" she asked lowly.

"What do you think, Peppi?"

"I think so. But it's our secret." Pepper replied as her eyes welled up. "Please, don't hurt me," she whispered.

Carmella saw right away that Pepper was deathly afraid of her; but she need not be. A special place inside her heart shed light on Peppi Vargas and she couldn't hurt the little girl even if it called for it. Carmella then briefly thought about the sixteen year-old she'd killed, a girl similar to Pepper who looked up to her and only wanted to fill her shoes. She then asked herself that if it were Pepper who'd said her name inside that bar, would she do what she'd done to the young female over in East Saint Louis a couple of hours earlier to Pepper, and her only answer was that of maybe, maybe not.

"Are you mad at me?" Pepper asked, shaking Carmella from her thoughts.

Carmella walked over to one of the walls in the room that featured rows of neat wooden squares filled with neatly folded clothes with the tags still attached. "I'm not mad at you," she told Pepper as she removed a tag and slid into a pair of loose-fitting cotton shorts "It's just that sometimes this business gets too complex even for those who are on top. Understand?"

"Not really. Can you tell me why you killed those people? Did they something to you?"

"Yes they did. They got in my way, baby. They just got in my way." Carmella said as she popped a tag and pulled a t-shirt down over head. "I'm going to fix us a good meal now, Peppi. What would you like for dinner?"

"Enchiladas!" Pepper exclaimed as she stood up and began jumping up and down on the soft mattress. "Chicken enchiladas!"

"Okay," Carmella responded as Pepper jumped into her arms. Carmella caught the little girl while laughing aloud before gently placing her back onto her feet and leading her out of the room. "I haven't used my kitchen but once when we first got to this place in the summer. You just relax and let me handle everything while you finish studying."

While gathering items for the enchiladas, Carmella called Toodie. The Perez sisters had seen the same news broadcast. They knew just as well as Carmella that there was one survivor, the only problem was that neither knew who the person was; the authorities were tight-lipped about the matter, refusing to release the names of the victims, the lone survivor, and were unwilling to say whether they had a list of suspects or not.

"We must keep a low profile for a while, Toodie," Carmella said as turned on the water faucet. "I'm going out of state. You two head over to the other spot."

"We moving now," Toodie said as she eased up from the couch and called for Phoebe. The two of them readying to move the cocaine they'd stolen a couple of hours earlier over to another trap house they operated in East Saint Louis, Illinois while things died down.

Carmella, meanwhile, was planning a trip to Denver, Colorado and visit Desiree the following evening. She'd missed her friend and lover the time she'd been away. As she began seasoning the boneless chicken breasts in the sink, Carmella again thought about the hit she pulled and couldn't help but to release a sly smile. She had a good crew indeed. Whatever carnage lay behind in Saint Charles, Missouri would have to be absorbed by those who'd felt her wrath because Carmella could care less about the damage she'd done to her enemies.

CHAPTER ELEVEN
THE SEARCH FOR ANSWERS

The crime scene on Elm Street had been cleared of the carnage. Mildred, Benito and Gaggi's bodies had been taken to the medical examiner's office in Saint Charles and Lucky had been transported to Mercy Medical Center near the junction of I-270 and I-64 and was undergoing surgery for three gunshot wounds to the lower back, left arm and lower left jaw. A few officers were still on hand out in front *Connections* filing reports and talking to witnesses, all of whom gave the same story—eight or nine people dressed up as federal agents had robbed *Connections* and shot up the place. No one mentioned drugs, but Benito and Gaggi were known criminals so that specific detail went without saying as far as authorities were concerned.

When Carmella and her crew drove up, Eddie, Junior, Jay-D and Dooney had fled the scene; now they were beside themselves having realized they'd abandoned the bosses under pretense. The repercussions could be severe; abandoning the bosses warranted death for those who were supposed to stand guard. Things had to be smoothened over and explained thoroughly in order to prevent the entire crew from getting wiped out; but only twenty-six year old Eddie Cottonwood seemed to understand that fact.

"Sons of bitches wasn't even cops," twenty-four year-old Junior said in disbelief as he paced the floor of Eddie's kitchen a couple of hours after the hit. "We fell for that play and look what happened! I want every set in this bullshit ass town hit right now!"

"Yo," Eddie said as he held up his hands, "we don't even know who in the fuck these people are, Junior. Maybe we should get our soldiers around town to open their ears and close their mouths so we can find out who's behind this shit before we go out and start killing people that don't have nothing to with what went down."

"Fuck that! They kill my moms and pops while I'm there? Anybody can get it as far as I'm concerned!" Junior said as he eyed Eddie with rage in his eyes.

"That's the wrong move, man. I'm just sayin', before we start a war, let's think this out and go about it the right way."

"We already at war! And the right way is to strike back at everybody!"

"Hit everybody," Eddie as matter-of-factly as he eyed Jay-D and Dooney, who shook their heads somberly. Junior was making no sense at this moment and Eddie and his brothers knew it.

"I know you want payback and so do I," Eddie told Junior from across the table. "We all were out there on the corner when that shit went down and we all made the wrong move, man. Running off was the biggest fuck up we ever made to date. At least it's the biggest mistake me and my family ever made. We all should've stayed. But because we jump ship, my life and the lives of my brothers is on the line. We gotta face the music, brother."

"Don't give me that brother shit, Eddie! And the only music I want to hear is the sound of Chicago pianos ringing aloud on the streets of Saint Louis! You think I give a fuck about what my granddad or DeeDee says? It was my mother and father who took those bullets!"

"Benito and Gaggi went down—"

"Fuck Benito and Gaggi! I could give a fuck less about those two sons-of-bitches!"

"You not in the right frame of mind," Jay-D spoke up. "What you plan on doing ain't gone do nothing but draw heat," he said as he watched Junior repeatedly pace the wooden floors inside the kitchen.

"Jay-D right," Eddie chimed in. "Let's call the people who can make the right decisions and guide us through this episode the right way so there won't be any unnecessary bloodshed is all I'm saying."

Junior stopped passing the floor and eyed Eddie. "You saw my mom's brain's splattered on the floor of that bar," he asked lowly. "Some punk asses swoop in and take my family out in cold blood?"

"This ain't just about your family, Junior! We still have to run a business!" Eddie retorted as he pounded the table with one fist.

"This is way beyond business! This here is personal!"

"You can't go at it that way, man! Let's make some calls. Let's take it slow," Eddie reinforced.

Junior wasn't trying to hear Eddie's reasoning. He threw his hands up and stormed out of the kitchen. "Fuck it I'm gone!"

Eddie quickly gave chase. "Don't you go and do something crazy, Junior! Let me call some people and get some leadership reestablished," he said once he'd caught up to Junior in the foyer.

"I'm the fuckin' leader now! What part of that shit you don't understand, Eddie?" Junior asked as he walked backwards towards the front door with his arms spread.

"Where you going, man? Don't you go out on your own and start wildin' out down here."

Junior laughed at Eddie's remark. "How the fuck you're gonna tell me what to do," he questioned as he pulled on his suit jacket. "You do what you have to do. Call whoever you like and think is in charge."

"I just wanna talk to the people in charge, Junior. It has nothing to do with you, man."

"Sure it doesn't—for now. But when I get my way? I'm gonna hit every dealer in this town. I'm going back to the hospital and check on my pops. But if I find out on my own who did this? It ain't gonna matter what nobody says because I will kill all of them by myself if need be."

Eddie sighed a sigh of relief at that moment, happy Junior was not going to start riding around to the crew's several trap houses and start issuing ill-advised orders to soldiers to start hitting other sets; but he still had it in him to go off on his own and that would be dangerous on his part. When Junior left the block, Eddie got on the phone and called Doss.

****

Elm Street was a tranquil place early Sunday morning. Soldiers from around the Saint Louis area were on hand to protect the Chicago Gang's home turf from further retaliation. A few were hiding out in the old cleaners across from the bar and several men were parked in SUVS up and down the block.

Eddie stood outside the entrance to *Connections* in an olive silk suit and black gator shoes talking to one of the crew's most trusted soldiers in Saint Louis, seventeen year-old Malik Gomez, who ran a trap house in Fox Park.

"Anybody said anything last night about what happened around here over where you at, Malik?" Eddie asked as he tucked his hands inside his silk slacks.

Malik Gomez, a five foot nine one hundred and seventy-five pound muscular Mexican with short black hair, shook his head slowly and said, "Nothing of any value, homes. But this set over on Ann Avenue back in Fox Park? Business been picking up for them the past few months. A few buyers say they have a connect coming out of Mexico. I can't say if they were in on this thing or not because I don't know enough about them."

"You know their names?"

"Some of them. They just a bunch of crazy Mexican girls if ya' ask me. I'll check them out some more if that is what you want done." Malik replied as he scanned the block, making sure the guys he'd brought with him were in the right place.

"Look into that for me. They might be the type to do some shit like this. You know their names?" Eddie asked as he looked down at Malik.

"The only names I know off Ann Avenue is Toodie and Phoebe. They're sisters who run that block and a few other spots in Fox Park."

"Keep your ears open for me. If they was involved in this here, it'll come out soon enough."

"Si, boss. Who we waiting on again?"

The question had barely escaped Malik's lips when a black Suburban with dark tinted windows pulled up in front of *Connections*. Malik, and two other soldiers standing outside of the bar with him and Eddie watched as four people, a man dressed in a dark brown silk suit, followed by a young male and two identical twins, all emerged from the interior of the vehicle.

The young male wore a cream-colored suit and black dress shoes. The identical twins were dressed in baggy jeans and tight-fitting shirts and all three were clutching a .45 automatic handguns. The group walked slowly up the sidewalk leading to the establishment.

Doss had driven up from Oklahoma overnight when Eddie had called and he was planning to get the crew on the same page until he could talk to Mendoza and DeeDee in person back in Chicago. He greeted a few of the workers before he and the big three walked into *Connections*.

"What do we know?" Doss asked he walked over to the bar where Eddie was now standing with his younger brothers.

"All we know is that before the raid, a Spanish broad jogged onto the block with a puppy on a leash," Eddie stepped forth and replied. "She bought a sno-ball from the deli and then left. Next thing we know we gettin' hit. Whoever did it disguised themselves as federal agents and raided the joint. We believe this Spanish chick was in on it, but we don't have a clue where she's at right now."

"Where were you and your people when this went down?" Doss asked as he walked behind the counter and eyed the register and safe, which hadn't been touched.

Eddie rubbed his face in frustration and said, "We were, we were on side the building when they rode up, Doss. They had these lights flashing, badges and even had the jackets and shit that the FBI be wearing. We thought it was a legitimate bust so, so we, we umm—"

"Y'all took off running?" Doss asked calmly as he eyed Eddie seriously.

"Yeah, man. When they left without making arrests, we came back but by then someone else had found the boss."

Doss stared down at the floor in deep thought; he knew the only way the crew would ever get hit would be for someone to have talked. Eddie should have stayed regardless was his thinking. A man could still fight behind bars, and the feds for the most part could be beaten if one had the money required to obtain a top notch lawyer.

"We can't change what's happened," Doss remarked as he approached the bar from behind the counter, "but we most certainly can't let it happen again. I'm not saying be stupid and open fire on the police and go for suicide, but had it been an actual raid, we would've been in a better position to fight this thing maybe. And had we stayed we could've defended our turf, you see?"

"I know, boss. And that's what got me pissed." Eddie said as he slapped the counter and backed away in frustration.

"Junior vacated too, so the Italians can be held in contempt as well. That is where you should be given a pass, but it's no guarantee, Eddie."

"I told Junior last night before he left that I'm willing to face the music, Doss. If anybody should be held responsible, it should be me. I don't want nothing to happen to my brothers over there. They were only following my lead."

"I'll do what I can to smooth things over in Chicago. Next

time, though, should it be a next time, take the hit. It's what we pay you for and everybody involved in this business understands the risks—up to and including death or jail. Can't do much about our immortality, but we have a damn good lawyer who will defend us and plenty of money to fight the charges to go along with it, and outside of Jesus, he's the best thing going when it comes to fighting the law."

"Take the hit next time. Got it. You talked to Mendoza?" Eddie asked, a little relieved that he wasn't asked by Doss to take a ride.

"Not yet, but he knows what happened thanks to my wife. Me and my family will be on our way to Chi-town after we spend time with Lucky. Now, what I want done is for us to establish a new base of operations for the time being. You got somebody in mind we can use? Somebody reliable?"

"Yeah. My man Malik here is solid. He run the biggest trap we got over in Fox Park. Strong soldier with good street intellect that knows how to move weight fast."

"Okay," Doss said as he turned towards Malik. "Young man, you up next. You the man behind the man now. You just been bumped up to a Lieutenant."

"I won't let the family down, Doss."

"Try not to," Doss said as he turned back to Eddie. "I'm gonna have Fin set up a rental space so we can deliver for the time being. We have enough artillery to hold our own during this transition, Malik?"

"Every set got at least two Tommy Guns and three AK-47s. We good on guns, boss." Malik responded.

"Okay. Eddie? You're taking lead for now down here with Gaggi and Benito out of the equation. But you only operate on my orders."

"What about Junior? He wanna go all haywire and just start killing any and everybody."

"Junior isn't running anything. Mendoza and my father are still over this organization, so they have the final say so. I'm only telling you to do what I know they would want done for the time being. We should have about eight left, I want six of those broken down into ounces and the rest cooked up until it's offed. By then we'll have another shipment brought in and we can pick back up where we left off."

"Thanks, Doss." Eddie remarked.

"What you thanking me for?"

"Man, I swear, I thought you were going to have us killed for running off like that, brother."

Doss took a few steps towards Eddie, looked him in the eyes and said in a serious manner,"I been knowing you since before you were able to walk, Eddie, not to mention me and your father did good business together back in the day and you like a son to me. I can't say I'm not disappointed because I'd be lying to you, but this here wasn't a double-cross. We took a hit —a big hit—but business must go on. I know you won't let us down from here on out and will do all that's necessary to make it right—given your mistake."

"Whatever I gotta do, Doss. Just give us the orders."

"You have orders for now. And I'll vouch for you with Mendoza and my father. I'm going sit with Lucky for a while. We'll be in touch in a couple of days." Doss ended as he and the big three left the bar.

****

"On our own turf," Mendoza said somberly as he and Junior sat inside his home in Cicero after leaving Mount Sinai Hospital, a day after meeting with Doss. "We find that Spanish girl Eddie mentioned to Doss we can crack this thing wide open and track down those responsible."

"This hit could've come from anywhere. Someone has to be talking for this to happen, granddad." Junior said as walked over to his grandfather's wine rack.

"I don't think so, son. This was a hit. And the people we have in charge have had solid reputations for years and were groomed for this business."

"But they're not Italian." Junior said as he began pacing the living room floor.

Mendoza eyed Junior with disdain as he sat up in his lounge chair. "Are you implying that one of our own set this up? If so, who? And why?"

"I don't know the why, but Eddie could be the who."

"Are you serious? Eddie was around before you were even brought into this thing of ours, Junior."

"Loyalty sometimes comes with a price! It can be bought!"

"Eddie took a loss with the rest of us! And you yourself left the area! I can make the same accusation towards you!" Mendoza said as he stood up on his feet.

"You'd believe an outsider before you believe your own kind?"

Mendoza eyed Junior with a quiet anger. He was shocked that his own grandson would dare to insult the race of people who'd been most loyal to La Cosa Nostra for the last forty years or so. "Have you lost your mind, boy? Would you even say what you're saying to me if DeeDee, Doss or Eddie were even present? You call our most loyal allies outsiders?"

"What difference does it make? You would take their side anyway!"

"There are no sides with this thing of ours! Never had there been a *side*! It is only us! *Us*!" Mendoza yelled.

"Us is right. If the blacks were of any importance, Zell would have made them."

"You really have gone off the deep end, boy." Mendoza remarked as he looked at his grandson with a disheartened look. "All these years I never knew you to have a racist bone your body. Your grandmother, mother, father and I aren't and wasn't like that ever. Where is this attitude coming from?"

Junior stood up and paced the floor with his glass of wine. "Eddie tried to usurp my authority," he said. "I ordered for him to hit every set in Saint Louis but he wouldn't listen."

"He was right not to do so."

"Are you serious," Junior asked. "With Benito and Gaggi dead and my pops in critical condition, I'm next in line to run the business."

"Your mother is dead, and your father is this close to death," Mendoza said as he held two fingers close together. "And your grandmother is preparing to have a double mastectomy. And all you worry about is who will lead the business? Where's your heart? Or better yet your head and the brain inside it?"

"My heart is set on revenge! What happened was slip in judge—"

"I'm not done talkin' you son-of-a-bitch!" Mendoza yelled. "You shock me with your racist attitude and the lack of remorse for what your family is going through! We have people that can run the business! Your main focus should be on that of burying your dead mother, your wounded father and your ailing grandmother! The streets will take care of themselves!"

"Not without a leader, granddad. So tell me," Junior said as he picked up a bottle of wine and gulped from the bottle. "Tell me who's in charge?"

"Doss will lead the family through this episode and you will stay here with me and deal with what's going on in our immediate family is what you'll do!"

"Like the hell I will," Junior said as he headed for the front door.

"Lei rià il Suo asino qui! Io che gli parlo non sono fatto!" (You get your ass back here! I'm not done talking to you!) Mendoza yelled.

Junior paused, closed the door and turned to his grandfather and Mendoza could clearly see streams of tears pouring down his face. Junior was hurt to his heart over what had happened. "I'm sorry, granddad. I shoulda fuckin' stayed," he cried as he took to one knee and pounded the floor with his left fist. "I ran like a coward and it cost my mother her life! My pops ain't doing too well either! I'm going outta my fuckin' mind!"

Mendoza walked over and knelt down before his grandson

and placed a hand on his shoulder. "Look at me, son," he said lovingly. "You have nothing to be ashamed of. The fear and anger I can understand—but rebelling against the family would only contribute to the problem. Here, at least for now, here is where you belong. I do what I do to protect you because I know you will only run out there and get yourself killed. Cooler heads are on this job. When the time's right, you'll get back out there, but for now, I need you here with me."

"I understand, granddad," Junior said as he stood up and ran his hands through his hair. "I haven't cried like this in years."

"Not since you were a young lad that fell off the swing in your mother's backyard," Mendoza replied, believing Junior was getting back into the right frame of mind.

"I'm, I'm really gonna miss my mom's laugh. It was infectious, you know?"

"That it was. I ever told you the story of how your parents met?"

"At the ball game back in nineteen seventy-one, right?"

"Yeah. The ball game—but let me tell it again—with a little more flair."

"I'd love to hear it. Hey, you wanna fix a meal? Let's fix my pop's favorite meal."

"We have to get some ground beef. And a couple of steaks."

"Okay. I'll pay."

"You're paying? Well, let me throw my wallet down just to make sure ya' cheapskate."

Junior laughed and said, "You're right, man."

"About you being a cheapskate? Hell I saw that before you were able to walk."

"Not that, granddad. About me belonging here in Chicago. We have a good crew. I owe those guys an apology. Even if they didn't hear what I said, I owe it to them to stand up and apologize." Junior said as he coughed lowly and eyed the floor.

"That's what men of honor do, son. And honor runs in all of

the Chicago Gang's blood." Mendoza replied as he turned towards the door.

"*Not always,*" Junior said to himself as he followed his grandfather out the front door.

****

"Doctor Obadiah Wickenstaff you're needed at the emergency entrance. Doctor Obadiah Wickenstaff you're needed at the emergency entrance."

"*What a weird name. I wonder what nationality someone with the name of Obadiah Wickenstaff would be,*" Naomi thought to herself as she walked across the pristine waxed floors of Mercy Medical Center. She strolled past smiling nurses, her pointed stiletto heels leaving subtle imprints in the vinyl tile as she approached the main desk and asked could she see a man by the name of Faustino Cernigliaro Senior.

"Yes, ma'am. He's responsive at this moment, but he can't speak."

"I talked to his doctor yesterday and he said his chances aren't good. How is he responsive if he's so gravely injured?"

"He can open his eyes and blink. That's how authorities were able to communicate with him, ma'am."

"Can you share what they've…never mind…I know it's an on-going investigation and I'm out of line."

"He must mean something to you. I can see the hurt on your face," the nurse remarked.

"Lady," Naomi said as she smiled proudly, "that man was my best friend next to my husband. As a matter of fact, he introduced me to my husband. And from that came eight children and a lifetime of memories."

The nurse smiled back at Naomi. "I'm sorry this happened, miss?"

"I'm Naomi Holland-Dawkins."

"Naomi? Your friend, Faustino? He's a strong man, but the wound to his lower jaw is a critical one."

"Will he recover?"

The nurse shuffled papers around her desk. She sniffled with tears forming in her eyes and said, "The doctors are never around for these things. They leave it up to us to tell loved ones. Like we're the bad guys in all this and it brings us joy to share what we know."

Naomi stepped back at that moment and placed a hand over her mouth to hold back her cries. She knew where Lucky had been shot, and she herself didn't think his survival was favorable. The nurse only confirmed her beliefs, but she had to know what she would face when she entered her friend's room. "What's the prognosis?" Naomi asked lowly.

The nurse looked Naomi in the eyes and held back tears. "We do what can here to save lives," she said lowly. "Sometimes, though, the trauma is beyond our abilities and we're only able to make the patient as comfortable as our God-given talents would allow until the inevitable. Mister Cernigliaro is paralyzed from the chest down. The bullet that went through his lower jaw severed a vertebra in his neck, Naomi. He can't breathe on his own and he can't feed himself. Control over his bodily functions is nonexistent and the, the agonizing thing for your friend is that he knows all of this. He's been put into a living hell."

All the hope and happiness she had been carrying with her left Naomi after the nurse had spoken. She was hoping to at least see her friend smile this day, but Lucky didn't have a damn thing to smile about. Knowing Lucky, however, Naomi knew her friend wished he'd died rather than have to live life as a quadriplegic. She thanked the nurse and rode the elevator up to Lucky's room where she encountered DeeDee in the waiting room.

"Doctors tube fed him about thirty minutes ago. He's awake, just staring at the TV." DeeDee said with concern as he hugged Naomi. "How's the family handling things on the ranch?"

"DeeDee, they were so worried about you. The kids kept asking about you. The family is mostly preparing for Mildred's funeral. I talked to Doss earlier. He's back in Chicago with Fin.

He says the Asians know we took a hit, but it's business as usual on our end."

"Doss is in charge of the whole thing now given the situation with Mendoza's family, so he and my grandkids may be busy for the time being."

"I understand. Lucky ever say who did this?"

"I asked, but he can't talk. It seems as if he wants to say something, but I can't put my finger on what it is he's trying to say. I can't communicate with him."

Naomi knew Lucky had information that would be valuable to the family, only he couldn't relay the message. She came up with a plan of her own as she entered her friend's room and eyed him for the first time in a few months, and four days after the events had unfolded in Saint Charles. It took everything within Naomi not to gasp over what her eyes were witnessing. Lucky was in an unrecognizable state with his shaven head and wires that were holding his jaw together. His hands lay limp on his sides, his once muscular legs appearing frail and immobilized. Heart monitors increased somewhat and the respirator moved slightly faster the closer Naomi got to her friend.

Naomi picked up a sponge and a plastic bowl and went into the bathroom and filled it with warm water and grabbed a bar of Ivory soap and a hand towel. She returned, pulled a chair up to Lucky's bedside, dipped the soap into the water and rubbed it gently into the towel. After wringing the towel out, she lowered Lucky's pristine, white bed sheet, bringing his naked body into view. The respirator increased as she did so, but Naomi only smiled and said, "I've been knowing you since you were shooting dog water. There's no need to be shy now, Mister Cernigliaro."

Rapidly blinking eyes had caught Naomi's attention. "You like what I said? I was only trying to lighten the mood. I'm sorry it took four days for me to come, but I knew you'd hold on for me. I had to calm the family and get things in order on the ranch, but I'm here now, il mio amico."

Lucky blinked his eyes again and Naomi caught on. "Okay,"

she said as she ran the soapy towel over Lucky's chest and stomach. "Now we can talk. Blink once for yes and twice for no. Can you do that?"

Lucky blinked once and Naomi smiled. "Resilient man you are," she said as she dipped the towel back into the warm water. "Is this bath bothering you?"

Lucky blinked twice that time. "I know you have a witty remark, something along the lines that if only Doss could see his wife scrubbing my naked ass on this day, it would've all been worth it."

Lucky blinked once and Naomi laughed aloud. "I'm sure he wouldn't mind, Lucky. Do you know the full story? Junior talked to you about Mildred?"

Lucky blinked once and the respirator increased in speed once more.

"We're all upset over this thing, Lucky, but you know something. Now, DeeDee has tried, but you and I are talking, now. Do you know who did this to you?"

Lucky blinked once and Naomi continued washing his body. She was getting somewhere with her friend, but garnering information pertaining to the hit wasn't her sole purpose for visiting Lucky. Naomi genuinely cared about her lifelong friend and was hoping he'd pulled through; she was doing her best to give him the strength to continue fighting for his life.

"I guess I made fifty dollars off doing your homework when we were children," Naomi chuckled. "Good money for the times. But the main thing I'll never forget is the day you brought Doss over to Kevin and Serena's home. The baseball game we went to that day? Child, I can't even tell you who was playing nor did I care. I was so into Doss nothing else mattered."

Tears streamed down Lucky's face hearing Naomi talk about that that day. The baseball game where he'd met Mildred was amongst the last of the conversations he'd had with his wife before calamity struck. God he loved that woman; of all people, Mildred Cernigliaro did not deserve to die. What kind of people were his family dealing with was a thought that was running through Lucky's mind constantly. In spite of his own troubled state, the man was more worried about the survival of those he loved rather than his own plight. He just couldn't relay all the things he felt and believed, however, given his incapacitation.

Naomi dabbed the sweat around Lucky's temples and then wiped his tear-stained cheeks. "I'm takin' you way back now aren't I?"

Lucky blinked once.

"You want me to stop?"

Lucky blinked twice that time.

"Okay, il mio amico. Now, Finland? You were a real piece of work during that time let me tell ya'," Naomi said through laughter. "I thought I'd never get you to see things my way, and Finland is now one of the most important people in the family. All because you chose to be his friend. You are a damn good man, Lucky."

Naomi washed Lucky's private area without giving it a second thought; there were no boundaries to her caring for her friend because she understood Lucky's state to the fullest. Reluctance would only signify a boundary in her eyes and she wanted Lucky to know that what she did was genuine. Tears ran down Lucky's cheeks once more as Naomi wiped his legs. Here was this black woman, a woman not his wife, who he'd learned had died, who cared enough to sit and talk to him and make things as normal as they could be.

Naomi and DeeDee were the only ones who'd made Lucky comfortable. He understood why his father hadn't visited given his mother's plight, and that went without saying, but Junior, Lucky's own son, had disappointed him; but it was a fact he could not relay, nor did he care to share, even if he could. He lay wondering what would become of his son because suddenly, Lucky no longer saw himself in his own offspring the way he saw Doss's demeanor inside of Dawk. The family would be in good hands if the Holland-Dawkins family took the reins was his thinking as Naomi wrapped up such a soothing bath, because something about Junior, if Lucky had to tell it, didn't sit right with him, only he couldn't convey the message.

After placing lotion onto Lucky's body, and dabbing him with cologne, Naomi pulled her chair up near her friend's face, leaned in and said, "We have an issue, Lucky. Can you tell us who did this?"

Lucky blinked once.

"Do you have a name?"

Lucky blinked once again and Naomi grabbed her purse and pulled out a legal pad. "I'm going to recite the ABCs. When I get to the letter of the person responsible, blink once for me, okay?"

Lucky again blinked once and Naomi began to slowly recite the ABCs as she stared him in the eyes. When she reached the letter C, Lucky blinked once.

"C," Naomi said as she wrote the letter down and started over. The moment she said the letter A, Lucky was blinking again.

"A," Naomi said and started once more.

Naomi could see in Lucky's eyes that he was eager to tell her what he knew. She believed he wanted to say the name of the person behind the hit, in which he did, but Lucky had much more to say; only he couldn't communicate his thoughts given his adverse condition. When Naomi reached the letter R, Lucky blinked again.

"R," Naomi said as she wrote the letter down. "Carmine? Carmicheal?" she then asked.

Lucky blinked twice.

"Okay, umm, was it a male?"

Lucky blinked twice.

"Hmm," Naomi said. "A female did this. Was she black?"

Lucky again blinked twice.

"White?"

Two more blinks.

"Italian? Russian? Hispanic? Colombian? Asian?" Naomi was calling out various races and Lucky's eyes were going berserk. She slowed her pace and began backing up. When she said Colombian, Lucky blinked once.

"Okay. A Colombian female. This wasn't a bunch of stick-up-kids, now was it? You don't have to answer that." Naomi remarked.

Lucky stilled blinked twice and Naomi started over again. "I have the letters C, A, and R. Let's continue." she said. When Naomi got the letter M, Lucky blinked once. Not knowing where to go with the last letter she'd obtained, Naomi started over from the letter A, once more, and when she got to the letter E, Lucky blinked again.

"C-A-R-M-E," Naomi said aloud. Filling in the rest of the letters, Naomi said the first name that had come to mind that matched the flow of the letters. "Could it be the name Carmella?" she asked.

The respirator went ballistic and Lucky's head began jerking violently at that moment. Nurses soon rushed in. "What happened," the nurse asked as she ran over to Lucky's bedside. "We need all non-essential personnel out of this room stat! Set me up a sedative and alert Mister Cernigliaro's doctor!" she yelled as Naomi was escorted out of the room.

CHAPTER TWELVE
TAKING THE SHOW ON HE ROAD

The Royal Flush had been the most happening place in downtown Denver since its opening a few months back in April of 2002. By the end of September of 2002 it had become the go-to place after the Denver Broncos home games on Sundays. Many people knew about the new club—including Carmella Lapiente`. She and Pepper had been in town for just over a week with Desiree, having left the day after the Saint Charles hit. Carmella spent her first day with Desiree shopping around town while being given details on the up and coming competition.

The name Asa Spade was ringing out in the streets of Denver according to Desiree, but his face was unknown. The two soon began moving about town and had scoped out a trap house over in Shorter Arms where Asa Spade was known to appear, and had followed an Asian lady to a condo which they'd assumed was a stash house. Carmella had learned the names and faces of certain crew members in Asa's crew, but the man himself hadn't been fingered as of yet.

Carmella and Desiree followed the Asian woman to a club called *The Royal Flush* and it was there that they'd surmised that the face of the man named Asa Spade could be revealed. The two weren't sure who ran the joint, however, so Carmella decided to send a lurker inside so as to put a face to the name of Asa Spade.

Asa and his team had cornered the market in Colorado in under a year's time and were now worth several millions dollars. They'd opened *The Royal Flush* and had acquired a mansion in Boulder, about an hour's drive northwest of Denver and a condo in downtown Denver that was used to store money and guns that were run through the trap house in Shorter Arms and a few other hot spots around the city; but it was the condo and the Asian woman Carmella had latched onto that'd led her and Desiree to *The Royal Flush*.

Carmella had no trap houses in Denver. She sold her weight out of hotels in the city to customers in and around town and also out of state. She had connections to cocaine dealers in Boise, Idaho, Cheyenne, Wyoming, and as far away as Reno, Nevada and Sturgis, South Dakota. Motorcycle gangs, Indian tribes, conservative right wing militias and left-leaning tree-huggers were her clientele. Carmella didn't discriminate when she was moving weight. Whoever had the buy money and their background checked out got served. Carmella would sell cocaine to the Pope and the Dali Llama himself, if he came correct.

This one woman was responsible for a vast majority of the psycho-stimulant drugs that had plagued the western states a couple of years ago and she was aiming to gain control of that market once more by eliminating the competition—her usual method of operation. Carmella couldn't get to the man named Asa Spade as of yet, but eventually, he would have to step aside and let her do her thing or else he'd get the same treatment the Italians received. In the meantime, Carmella was planning on sending her adversaries a warning—in her own special way.

****

"Niggas on the block say them rollers been ridin' through hot the past hour," Dougie told Percy as the two sat a table inside their main dope house inside Shorter Arms with Ponita Felton and Francesca Aranello, two of Asa Spade's old prostitutes who'd now gotten involved in the dope game with their former pimp. The two females counted money and prepared it for

Xiang Nyguen, where it would be taken to the crew's condo in downtown Denver until it was ready to be picked up by JunJie's son Phillip Tran at Loveland Airport in Fort Collins, Colorado, about a hundred miles north of Denver.

With most of the cocaine already in the hands of the crew's dealers, or on its way to its final destination in other cities and states, Ponita and Francesca were ready to let their hair down so-to-speak on this night. They'd been grinding right alongside the cousins and were ready to kick back until the next shipment, which was about a week away. Xiang wasn't on hand to make the pick up this night because the crew was closing down for the week.

"Them laws just had a shift change about a hour ago. You know how they like to shake shit up before they go park somewhere." Percy said as he and the crew separated $175,000 dollars in mixed bills. "Everybody been paid already this week so what we have here all goes back over to the condo when we done counting."

"Broncos won today, y'all. You know what that mean," Ponita remarked as she banded stacks of hundred dollar bills together.

"It's a big deal tonight is what it means," Francesca said as she rolled a blunt. "The Royal Flush gone be packed tonight and I'm going man hunting once we drop this loot off."

"You know it," Ponita chuckled. "Dougie being stingy with the dick already, so—"

"You know you lying," Dougie said, cutting Ponita short. "Fran can do whatever she want—but your sexy ass is staying home with daddy tonight."

Dougie and Ponita had been messing around for about a year now, but things really kicked off for the two during the Thanksgiving holiday the year before. Ponita was a beautiful twenty-five year-old woman with an Argentinian background. She spoke fluent Spanish and could be a loyal woman despite her past.

Percy thought Dougie was crazy for getting serious with an

ex-hooker, and Dougie sort of agreed in the beginning. The more he analyzed the situation, however, the more Dougie began to see the good inside Ponita. She was by far the most down female he'd met; she handled guns okay, could be trusted to watch his back and above all else, Ponita Felton was just a woman who loved; and despite her flawed past, she had good intentions when it came to Dougie and the rest of the crew.

Francesca Aranello could best be described as a sophisticated woman with a freaky twist. She had a certain class about herself and demanded respect from others. She rarely spoke on her past, but it wasn't out of shame or regret, it just wasn't anybody's business. Sex at age ten willingly left little to the imagination for Francesca; she'd seen and done just about everything. One thing she particularly loved doing was dressing up in costume and role playing with her sex partners.

Francesca knew how to have a good time when not hustling. She liked using a bong to smoke weed and loved walking around naked in front of people as she was a high exhibitionist. Francesca was cool with everybody in the crew, but when it came to the workers, it was another story. She would come down hard on the crew's dealers when they came up short and had gotten into several fist fights with some the boys. Percy and Dougie both knew the only reason Francesca behaved the way she did at certain times was because she'd been getting pimped herself most of her life. Now that she had a little power, karma was in full effect on some days. With that aside, Francesca was good for the crew—a truly rough and rugged woman by all outward appearances, but she could be a little weird at times—tonight was one of those nights.

"Eh," Francesca said as the crew sat around a coffee table in the living room of the small two bedroom apartment running bills through a money counter, "guess what the hell I saw last week that got me on the radio for a couple of minutes?"

"Not that crazy ass story again," Ponita laughed.

"Yes! That crazy ass story again," Francesca replied. "People see Elvis in Hawaii, the Virgin Mary on toast and UFOs in the sky so why I can't see what I saw in the woods?"

"What you saw in the woods, girl?" Percy asked.

"We was out back of the mansion gettin' fucked up last Wednesday," Ponita said through laughter as she stood up. Francesca tried to hit her friend playfully, but Ponita stepped aside and said, "Percy? All of a sudden ya' li'l fuck buddy over there stood up and leaned forward and said, 'looka that Bigfoot over there'!'"

"You saw a Bigfoot, Francesca?" Percy asked as he Dougie laughed aloud.

"It's called a Sasquatch, Percy. And yes, I did see one walking in the woods to the right of the house."

"She done smoked some good shit let me tell ya'," Ponita quipped. "We was listening to this show called Coast to Coast with Art Bell while we was outside that night and they was talking about vampires and shit like that and her ass went ta' trippin'. She laid up there and called that man show and had him believing her bullshit."

"You told somebody that shit?" Percy asked through laughter.

"Not just somebody, big dog. This bubble eye bitch called a national radio show—high as the fuck—but the man on the radio sound like he was smoking right along with us and both of 'em went ta' trippin' that night." Ponita said through laughter.

"Where that shit at y'all was smokin'? They got more left?" Percy asked as he scanned the coffee table. "I'm gone sit out there and get high and see if I see me a Bigfoot."

"See, y'all makin' fun of a bitch," Francesca remarked as she sat back and stared at her friends while rolling the blunt. "Sasquatch real, trust me. Most people that see that creature is white. I'm a black woman sayin' it so it's something to it."

"What being black gotta do with seeing Bigfoot, Francesca?" Ponita asked as she stuffed a stack of bills into the money counter.

"Black people don't see what I saw and tell other people about it, Ponita. It's like I'm validating what's true."

"Listen to you," Dougie laughed. "You ain't validating a damn thang. Your ass Italian anyway."

"My daddy black, so I'm black. And this black woman says Bigfoot is real!"

"White, black or other—people who claim to see a Bigfoot is coo-coo for cocoa puffs," Dougie replied as he brushed Francesca off.

"For real though," Francesca remarked as she leaned forward in her seat, stating her case. "This one here was tall and had black hair and was running through the woods. I'm tellin' y'all the truth."

"You ain't see a Bigfoot, your ass saw Shaq runnin' behind our house," Dougie laughed.

"Ha! Now that's a Bigfoot mutherfucka right there! You should go down there and see if you see some footprints then." Ponita said through laughter. "Shaq black ass runnin' behind our house," she laughed lowly as she banded another stack of hundred dollar bills.

"You comin' with me, Ponita?" Francesca asked.

"Fuck no! You and ya' Bigfoot can kiss my ass on that!"

"See? You know it's real."

"It ain't real. I'm just not crazy enough to wander around in no woods looking for something that don't exist."

"They elusive like that." Francesca said matter-of-factly.

"Bitch," Ponita snapped. "They have satellites that can read a license tag from four hundred miles up in space and you mean to tell me they can't find a wild monkey in the woods? Get the fuck outta here with that!"

"What about flying saucers, Francesca? You think they real too?" Dougie asked.

Francesca placed a hand on her knee and stared at Dougie. "Are you serious, man," she asked in wonderment. "Ain't none of that stuff real. Little green men don't come here. Why they wanna come to this fucked up planet?"

"To see what the deal is. They might be happy to know it's other life in the universe." Percy chimed in.

Ponita curled her lips to the side. "You gone get high with her ass and go out there and look for a Bigfoot, huh, Percy?"

"We find one we be famous, Percy! Ain't that right?" Francesca said as she extended her hand for a high-five. Percy left his girl hanging, though; he picked up the blunt instead and asked her for a lighter.

"Fuck you, traitor," Francesca quipped as she kicked the legs on Percy's chair.

"You can play around in them woods if you want to. You ain't see nothing but a black bear standing on its hind legs." Percy said.

"Can't share nothing with y'all," Francesca remarked. "Pass that weed."

"Hell no. Next thing you gone tell us is they got a alien in the bathroom," Percy remarked through laughter.

The crew chided Francesca for a while and talked about their plans for the night once their profits were banded and separated. Dougie was going to head over to *The Royal Flush* to check in with Asa Spade while Percy, Ponita and Francesca rode back to the condo with the money.

****

Glitz was another happening spot in Denver. Located on the northeast side of the city, the upscale two story 35,000 square foot entertainment complex catered mainly to the Hispanic population in Denver. Desiree Abbadando had designed the place, opting for a tropical theme. The large shark tank situated before a second floor balcony was the main attraction, along with the many birds of paradise that sat perched in palm trees planted inside the club. *Glitz* had a large V.I.P. clientele. Many of its parishioners were well-to-do people, and the lines waiting to get in usually spanned the length of the block nearly every night from both directions.

On any given Sunday night in Denver, *Glitz* would be packed to capacity around this midnight hour; instead, Desiree worked alone inside the club that had been closed for a special occasion. Desiree was on the second floor of the club on the balcony overlooking the large shark tank spreading out plastic and setting up tables and chairs in eager anticipation of the party that was to come. She was making sure that everything Carmella had requested be done accordingly before she set out to fulfill the rest of her lover's plan.

****

Carmella, meanwhile, was over to her mansion in Cherry Creek kicking back with eleven year-old Peppi Vargas. She was stretched out on the floor of her spacious bedroom lying on a Persian rug in a black slip, her auburn hair styled to perfection in braids and curls and her body draped in all the accessories from lip gloss to platinum jewelry.

Carmella lay in a relaxed state on her carpeted floor, being propped up by several lush pillows and rolling a blunt as Pepper knelt before her putting lotion on her legs. When done, Pepper stood up and grabbed a lighter and lit Carmella's blunt. Carmella had Pepper doing a little bit of everything for her on this cool September night in Denver. She had the little girl massaging her neck and shoulders, painting her toenails and fingernails and was also teaching her how to load a .9mm semi-automatic. It was as if Carmella had her own little Mini-me sometimes and she would milk it dry whenever she felt like doing so.

"You're going to be alone for a while tonight, Pepper because I'll be attending a party." Carmella said as she blew smoke out of her lungs.

"Okay. You're coming back, though, right?" Pepper asked as she rubbed lotion onto Carmella's legs.

Carmella laughed lightly as she took another toke. Pepper always asked her that same question whenever she told her she would be away and it made the young woman feel wanted each time. To know someone would miss her if she were to leave carried a lot of weight with Carmella, and it was one of the reasons Pepper was being treated so well, at least from Carmella's point of view.

"Yes, Peppi, baby," Carmella said as she smiled at Peppi. "I promise I'll be back. Maybe not before the sun comes up, but I'll be back. Put some of that lotion on my heels. A woman should never leave home with ashy heels."

"Must be a big party." Pepper said as she cupped Carmella's heel.

"People will be talking about this one for some time let me tell, ya', my love," Carmella said just as her phone rung. "Hola?"

"Everything is set here," Desiree said. "I'm on my way over to The Royal Flush after I shower and change."

"Do not get a V.I.P. table, Desiree. I know how your ass love to floss. You need to remain as low key as possible. Stay near the bar and I'll meet you there later," Carmella replied before hanging up the phone. "Okay, Pepper. Dinner time. Steak burritos okay?"

"Perfect," Pepper replied as she picked up the .9mm from her side.

"You remember how to rack it?"

"I pull this top part back," Pepper said as she struggled to cock the empty pistol. "I pull this top part back and make sure the red button is not showing and I'm ready to shoot."

"The red button must be showing in order for you to shoot a round, Pepper. Remember, red for fire."

"Right. I get confused sometimes."

"You're still learning. Come on, let's go and make dinner before I leave," Carmella said as she got up and stretched and checked her appearance in the full length mirror. "Not bad. Not fuckin' bad at all."

****

"Soul controller...rap Ayatollah...kids hate when they get older I put cracks by the stroller...I'm a registered voter... mutherfuck a quota...give me some baking soda and quarter... bet it jump straight up out the water..."

Asa and Xiang stood side by side in the office overlooking the huge dance floor inside *The Royal Flush* as they bobbed their heads to P. Diddy and The Family's song *Let's Get It*. *The Royal Flush* was laid out like a palace; black marble columns running throughout set off a Roman theme while two large bars on opposite ends of the club served the finest of liquor. A huge sunken, black marble dance floor surrounded by theatrical-style stairs created a pit inside the club. A walkway above the dance floor spanned the width of the club and led up to the second floor where the V.I.P. Rooms were located.

Desiree walked into the club dressed exquisitely and showed a guard her V.I.P. pass, which cost $2,500. She was escorted across the private walkway that sat fifteen feet above the dance floor. It was a place to make it rain money, but Desiree hadn't the money to drop green backs on the crowd. She reached the bar at the end of the walkway and was offered her choice of champagne before being led up another flight of pristine marble stairs where she was greeted by a woman she knew to be named Xiang.

"I've never seen your face before. This has to be your first time here," Xiang remarked over the music. "Let me give you a quick tour so you can become familiar with our accommodations."

"Is there a kitchen is all I want to know? Because lady, I'm starving!" Desiree said over the loud music.

Xiang laughed and said, "A kitchen we do have up here! We have a gourmet chef and staff that cooks to order. Let me take you to your booth and get you a menu."

"Can you smoke in here? And I'm not talking about cigarettes or cigars." Desiree didn't know it, but the moment she'd set foot inside of *The Royal Flush*, she had erred tremendously.

Xiang looked at the woman in a perplexed manner for a brief second. No one had even dared asked that question before. What kind of an establishment did this woman think was being run here was Xiang's thinking. She was undoubtedly new, but her question had opened Xiang's eyes to possible ulterior motives.

"If you do smoke, you will have to close the partition. You have your champagne. I will be back shortly with your menu," Xiang replied. "But before you do anything, give me one minute."

"I'm gone like this place," Desiree said as she entered the private room and situated herself inside her booth with her champagne.

Xiang followed the woman into the booth, watching her every move until she was seated. "Anything else you need right now?" she asked through a polite smile.

"I already want the New York strip steak and grilled shrimp platter. Baked potato on the side with a salad with ranch dressing and garlic bread."

"A woman who knows what she wants," Xiang remarked. "I'll send a waitress over to take your order."

Xiang left the lavish room and tugged on Dougie's t-shirt, signaling him to follow her and the two walked over to the office where they saw Asa Spade on the phone. They waited patiently until he hung up.

"There's a woman in room eleven asking about smoking weed." Xiang stated matter-of-factly as she ran her hands through her long, black hair, awaiting Asa's reply.

Asa raised his eyebrows. "Asking to smoke weed? What she think we running a hooka hut?"

"I don't know what she is thinking," Xiang said as she frowned and looked back towards the hall where the woman's booth sat. "She paid cash for a VIP booth and I have never seen her in here before. She also knew the menu before I even presented it to her. She just seems suspicious to me. I mean, who in the fuck asks could they smoke blunts in a place like this? You either know or you don't know. And if you don't know you don't ask."

"Room eleven, huh? Dee let's go scope this broad out." Asa said as he grabbed a .45 automatic from his top desk drawer and tucked it inside the waistband behind his dark grey silk suit jacket.

Asa and Dougie went and stood outside the room looking over the balcony, all-the-while stealing peeks on the woman. She seemed to be scoping the club out from her booth. She was subtle with it, but Asa Spade wasn't a fool by a long shot. He'd been around for a while and was now running a legit business. The last thing he wanted was to be set up by the authorities or somebody off the streets trying to earn a quick dollar through an armed robbery attempt. After three songs, Asa Spade walked into Desiree's room to put her up on his game.

"I hear you want to smoke herb in my building," Asa said as he walked through the sliding door.

"I only asked. The hostess said I could so long as I close the partition." Desiree remarked as she smiled at Asa.

"She spoke out of term on that. See? I don't know you from Eve. You walk in here dropping thousands like it ain't nothing and now you wanna smoke weed in my spot? I run a tight ship over here and as far as I'm concerned, you can be part of a stick-up crew or the feds."

"Feds? Would I smoke cannabis if I were a federal agent?"

"Yeah, you would. And I've known agents to do much worse. I'm gone ask you to pay and leave. You not welcomed here. Whatever you selling, I ain't buying."

"I need to make a phone call," Desiree said, hoping to be able to call Carmella and have her arrive sooner than later.

"Let me explain what the deal is, bitch. You're not wanted up in here, ya' got me? Now, as the saying goes, we can do this the easy way, or the hard way." Asa Spade remarked coldly. "And as far as you makin' a call? That shit ain't gone happen until you pay your tab and hit the parking lot," he added as Dougie walked up behind him and pulled out a chrome .9mm once he'd closed the partition.

"I paid twenty-five hundred dollars to come up here, mister."

"Don't mister me, bitch," Asa Spade said as he and Dougie flanked the mysterious woman inside the booth. "I don't give a fuck if you paid twenty-five thousand dollars to walk into my shit. You looking 'round like you scoping me out and I don't like it. I'm not hard up for cash so you can take your money and spend that shit somewhere else. But you gone pay me before you leave this room."

Desiree now understood that she'd walked into a snake pit. The people she were sent to eye were sharper than she'd given them credit. They'd latched onto her scheme before she knew what happened and she feared the potential outcome. Carmella had given her specifics, but she'd failed to follow orders wanting to floor show. She had no more cash on her as she'd spent her grip getting into V.I.P. under the belief that she could get an up-close view of the people who were running Shorter Arms to better aide Carmella. She'd succeeded, but the men sitting on either side of her seemed as if they would do more than just escort out of the club if she refused to pay.

"I have a credit card." Desiree said hesitantly.

"Cash, credit or blood is what we deal with. You got credit? Let me see it," Asa remarked.

Desiree handed Asa Spade a gold Master Card and he left the table, leaving Dougie behind, who held his gun to her side as Asa closed the partition.

****

"If I hear one more thing about a fuckin' Bigfoot I'm gone drive this jeep into a brick wall inside this garage," Percy snapped as he wheeled his 2002 Navigator through the underground garage of the condominium complex where the crew's stash house lay. He backed into a parking spot on the second level and exited the vehicle with Ponita and Francesca, each toting duffel bags of cash as they made their way towards the elevators. The three were still mocking Francesca about her Bigfoot sighting when three men in ski-masks dressed in all black emerged from behind two parked cars with guns drawn.

Percy, Francesca and Ponita had no time to react and now found themselves staring down the barrels of semi-automatic machine guns in the still of the night. Two of the men snatched the two duffel bags Ponita and Francesca held onto just as a black cargo van pulled up with the side door open. The three were shoved into the van's cargo bay at gunpoint and the gunmen hopped in and sped off.

CHAPTER THIRTEEN
THE CARD PARTY

Carmella had just turned onto 25th Avenue in her Hummer headed towards *The Royal Flush* when her phone rang. "Hola?" she answered.

"No need to go inside the club," Desiree said in frustration.

"What? Why not?"

"A fight broke out and everybody scattered. It was a big mess. Where you at?"

"I'm riding up to the club now," Carmella said as she cruised pass *The Royal Flush*. "People still waiting to get in. How was it a fight happened?"

"They must've cleared it up or something."

"You sure them people didn't learn your ass was—hold on I got another call. Hola?"

"Somebody gone come in let us in?" the male voice asked happily.

"Hold on," Carmella said as she clicked over. "Bitch," she said, "where you at now?"

"I'm north of Mile High Stadium."

"Make your way over to the other spot. And if I find out you lying to me about what happened inside that club tonight I'm gone fuck you up!"

"I would never lie to you, you know that. Come on now, this me!"

"Okay, 'this me'! Start that way and I be there!"

Carmella drove until she was able to make a U-turn where she cruised past *The Royal Flush* again. She saw a group of people wearing Broncos jerseys, young folk around her age who seemed to be having a good time. She pulled up alongside the group and let the passenger side window down and leaned over. "Excuse me," she called out. "I was about to go into the club, but somebody said they had a fight. Were they fighting in there? Because if so I don't want any trouble."

"Fighting? The only thing you had to fight in there was your way to the bars!" a female, who was undoubtedly drunk, said through laughter. "You have nothing to worry about at The Royal Flush! The owners don't play that shit!"

"Figured that!" Carmella said as she drove off.

Carmella drove in silence. She now believed Desiree had lied to her, but she was unsure as to why. Maybe she grew nervous and left before she arrived, or maybe there was much more to the story. Not one to leave a door open, Carmella would be certain to get to the bottom of the matter before she overreacted with her lover. She then grew happy when she realized that the biggest portion of her plan had succeeded. "Going to a card party," she said as she bounced in her seat and continued on her journey over to *Glitz*.

****

Barely two hours ago, everything in Percy, Francesca and Ponita's lives was heavenly bliss. The three were cracking jokes the entire ride over to their condo and were planning on kicking back with the crew for a few days at the mansion in Boulder and fuck around with Bigfoot while getting high. Now, the three found themselves butt-naked and bound to chairs while staring at a large fish tank as four unknown men and a woman milled about smoking weed and drinking liquor.

Desiree had never seen the Somalis until she arrived at *Glitz*.

Carmella had described the men to her, but her descriptions didn't do the guys justice. Desiree was expecting to see a group of slovenly dressed, unattractive men when she pulled up to Glitz in order to let the men in with their captors.

To the contrary, the Somalis were perfect specimens of men with their muscular physiques and thick heads of curly black hair. Black baggy jeans and long sleeve white t-shirts and white tennis was the Somalis attire. The guy who went by the name of Q-man was female eye candy for Desiree. Muscular with smooth, tan skin and long braids, he stood out from his counterparts, who all sported curly Afros. Q-man stood over six feet tall with a set of pearl white teeth and a neatly trimmed mustache. He was a man Desiree would readily do without apprehension. *"Maybe,"* Desiree said to herself before she escorted the Somalis to the back entrance of the club in order to secure their captives.

"What happened at the club?" Q-man asked as he passed Desiree a blunt, barely ten minutes after the crew had entered the club and secured their captives.

"A fight broke out so I had to leave."

"So your girl didn't meet you there and scope the place out like y'all had planned?"

"I had to leave before all that happened."

Q-man eyed Desiree with a look of uncertainty. He was guessing she'd gotten thrown out for whatever reason, but it wasn't because of a fight. That was a lame excuse in his mind. "I know your girl ain't gone like that shit. She a stickler for detail, you know? I hope y'all work that shit out."

"We'll do fine," Desiree sassed. "A good round of pussy-eating will resolve this issue."

"No wonder I can't get in that ass, fellas," Q-man said as his boys laughed lightly.

The cage being raised on the first floor alerted everybody; Q-man and one of his boys descended the stairs with guns in hand and greeted Carmella while she was lowering the steel barricade once more.

"We got it all set up," Q-man stated.

"Good. At least there's someone in this town I can count on."

"We gone stick around for a while, but after that we jettin' back to the Ap."

"Did they have any money on them, Q-man?"

"About one seventy-five large."

"Our deal for this kidnapping was one hundred grand. Keep all of it," Carmella said as she jogged up the stairs. "You boys are well worth the price."

"Nuff said," Q-man replied as he followed Carmella up the stairs.

Carmella was furious with Desiree for lying to her; but when she laid eyes on her lover upon reaching the balcony, her heart softened. What she'd planned on doing had melted away given her lover's pleading look of apology. Desiree was sorry, Carmella knew; she'd made a mistake, nothing more in her eyes and she didn't warrant such a cruel fate. She'd done her best, and despite her failure and knowing lie, Carmella found it within herself to forgive, because she cared about Desiree just enough to do so. She decided to not address what Desiree had done in front of the Somalis, the subject would lay dormant until the two were alone under the covers.

Carmella then turned to the captives sitting off in the distance. "What fun me and my Somali friends are going to have with you guys tonight," Carmella said as she walked over and stood before her three captives. "But before we all get acquainted, I would like to have me a drink. I will be back shortly," Carmella said through a smile as she backed away from the three.

To say that Ponita, Percy and Francesca were terrified would be an understatement. Never before had either individual encountered such callous attitudes. The plastic spread out on the floor was unnerving, and the two menacing sharks inside the tank were seemingly growing impatient by the minute. They kept circling the tank and surfacing near the humans before dipping back below the surface of the hazy, light green water.

Music was turned on and bottles of liquor was brought out from the office to the rear of the balcony and Carmella and her gang sat at a large table overlooking the tank and the entire club and drank and smoked and got caught up on operations in various cities throughout the Midwest, ignoring their guest, but knowing exactly what they were going to do the whole time.

An hour or so later, Carmella jumped up all of a sudden. "How rude we've been, people! We have guests over here and haven't offered them a thing!" she said, barely keeping her composure. "At a party, people love to play cards. You three wanna play cards?" Carmella asked with a wide smile on her face.

Percy, Francesca and Ponita refused to respond, they couldn't even if they wanted to given the duct tape around their mouths. The whole time they were trying to free themselves of plastic ties that bound their hands to the chairs they were sitting in, but neither was successful.

"You can't answer with that shit around your lips," Carmella said. "How rude of me. I will answer for you then! I want to play a game of cards with you guys, okay? Okay!" she snapped as she pranced over to the bar and grabbed a set of cards. Carmella skipped back over to her guests and slid a small table before the three individuals. She then grabbed a chair and sat before the trio. "When I was a little girl, my Ma-Ma knew this lady who was a gypsy. She could tell people's future by looking at these cards. Cards like these," Carmella said as she held a deck of tarot cards up for display.

Percy, Francesca and Ponita only stared in silence; neither had a clue what was going on inside of this woman's head nor that of the horror to come. They watched as the woman went through the deck of cards, selected the three specific cards she wanted, and placed one face down before each of them and stood up. It was obvious to everybody, including Carmella's hostages, that their fates had been sealed long before the card game had ever begun.

Carmella was enjoying being master of ceremony over this

maniacal macabre meeting of opponents, even if she and her bunch were the only ones who understood the reasoning behind the action. As far as Percy, Francesca and Ponita knew, they could've merely been picked at random to be robbed and just happen to encounter some sick individuals. But no matter which way the chips fell, and who thought what, the fact was that Carmella had three of her opponents dead right and it wasn't a damn thing they could do to stop what was about to happen. Anything her heart desired was possible on this night. She went back over to her table and lit up a blunt and poured herself another drink while the rest of her crew lingered around conversing as they smoked and drank, occasionally tuning in to watch Carmella do her thing.

"Now guys," Carmella said upon her return to her makeshift fortune teller's table, "I will flip one card at a time and then tell you what your future has in store. Is that okay? Okay!" she snapped happily, as if her captives were really going to answer as enthusiastically as she was making this twisted game of torture out to be while being happy participants.

Carmella reached out and flipped over Ponita's card which showed a skeleton dressed in a black knight's suit sitting atop a white horse. "This is the death card," Carmella remarked in mocked somber, her head shaking from side to side in a slow fashion. "You will die a slow death tonight and will never be seen again," she told Ponita, who seemed to gag as tears began streaming down her face. "Don't cry ma-mi! It is what the cards say must happen to you." Carmella said as she leaned forward and gently stroked Ponita's face.

Ponita jerked her head away and Carmella stood up and smiled down on her. "Where are you going? Huh? No-fuckin'-where! You're going to sit your ass right there in that seat and take what's coming to you! Okay? Okay!" she ended happily as she sat back down in her seat.

Carmella then turned to Percy, and after taking another toke of her blunt, and a slow sip of her tequila, she flipped over the card and showed him the image, which was a crucified man hanging upside down on a cross. "This is the hanged man card, amigo," Carmella said. She then pointed to Ponita and said,

"You will watch her die a slow death, and then I will make you tell me what I want to know. How quickly you give me what I want to know will determine how quickly you die, because the card says you shall remain in suspended animation for a short time and then you must die. Okay? Okay!"

The look on Percy's face, which was sheer terror, was priceless to Carmella. The fear she was instilling in her captives was a high she couldn't get enough of; it was nearly orgasmic. Leaving her second captive to marinate and reflect upon on his own impending martyrdom, Carmella slid her chair a few paces to the left, sat before Francesca, placed her hands on the table in a prim and proper manner and merely smiled in silence for a couple of minutes.

"What a beautiful specimen of woman you are," Carmella finally complimented. "If you were any other woman? I would take you and make you mines for the night. I would have so much fun with you, brown sugar," she said as she picked up the card and showed it to Francesca, who only tilted her head up slightly to see the image of the planet Earth encased in a wreath. "This here is the world card," Carmella said. "You will have the weight of the world on your shoulders shortly and you will be the last to die. But lucky for you your death will come quickly. I will have no use for you other than for you to die. I hate to do it to you because I really would rather fuck your brains out, but this is for business not for pleasure. Okay? Okay!"

Francesca was still struggling to free herself. She knew not what state of mind Percy and Ponita were in, but if she could find a way to break free, she was going to cause mayhem and force the people around her to kill her quickly. Sitting by idly while awaiting death was a fate she cared not to endure. The plastic ties were doing their job, though, and escape seemed nearly impossible for all three captives. Francesca mumbled something inaudible to Carmella, who merely laughed as she stood up and said, "Don't worry, Foxy Brown. Soon, you'll be yelling nonstop."

****

Asa Spade, Xiang and Dougie had just returned to their

condo and where expecting to see Percy, Francesca and Ponita lounging around. Instead, they were met with dead silence. Everything seemed in order inside the pristine pad, but something wasn't sitting right with the three. No words were spoken as texts and calls began going out to the three missing members. Asa and company tried for nearly an hour to get in touch with their cohorts, but the numerous texts and calls had gone unanswered.

"One of the boys down at the trap said Percy 'nem left like two hours ago with the re-up," Dougie said in a worried tone. Dougie and Percy had done their own fair share of dirt from kidnapping to murder and he knew foul play when he saw it. Something was wrong with this night most certain, only neither he, nor Asa Spade and Xiang knew what was going down exactly.

"Let's back track," Asa Spade said before grabbing the keys and heading for the door with Xiang and Dougie following his lead.

Asa and his crew rode over to *The Royal Flush* and saw an empty parking lot. They then headed back over to the trap in Shorter Arms and woke three soldiers who were laid up in the house. The men had no clue as to the whereabouts of Percy, Francesca and Ponita. Two hours later, Asa Spade was cruising through the parking lot of the condo when he stumbled upon Percy's 2002 Navigator that was properly parked in one of the slots. A quick search around the surrounding area uncovered Ponita's cell phone on the ground with the missed calls and texts that Francesca had made and sent earlier.

"That woman at the club," Xiang remarked, "she may have something to do with this."

"It's a good chance," Asa said. "She used a credit card to pay the bill. Let's go back to the club and go through the receipts and get her name and see if we can track her down."

****

The sharks inside the tank inside of *Glitz* were in a frenzied state as flesh splashed down into the water. If ever there were a real life horror flick, then the events inside this club would definitely qualify. True to her word, Carmella had delivered a slow death to Ponita Felton. Francesca and Percy were forced to sit and watch as their friend was crucified to a plywood board with small steel spikes and her body dismembered while she was still alive.

Ponita's arms were cut off with a chainsaw. The sounds she made, coupled with the blade slicing through her bones were nothing short of heartbreaking. She'd begged to be killed, but had remained alive for nearly a half hour until her legs were severed and she bled out completely. Her murderers were now throwing pieces of her flesh into the tank and the two bull sharks were swallowing the body parts whole and circling for more.

While her comrades entertained themselves by feeding human flesh to the aquatic carnivores, Carmella picked up a machete and she and Desiree approached Percy. Blood splatter was on Carmella's chin, but she refused to wipe it off, merely letting it trickle down her neck as she, too, was in frenzy—a murderous frenzy fueled by a sincere determination to eradicate those who unknowingly stood in her way.

Desiree removed the small table before Francesca and Percy, and Percy's chair, with him in sitting it, was picked up by two of Q-man's henchmen and placed atop the plywood that still had remnants of Ponita's blood and flesh splattered about. Carmella stepped forward and stood before Percy soon after.

"You," Carmella hissed as she pointed her machete at Percy, "when I remove the tape from your lips I want you to tell me the name of your boss and where he lives. And then I kill you quickly to put you out of your misery."

Percy said nothing as he sat bound and naked. Slowly, Carmella pulled the tape away. "You might as well kill me now bitch because I ain't tellin' you shit!" Percy yelled.

"Did you hear that bitch gurgling and begging to die when that chainsaw cut into her ass?" Carmella asked through laughter. "You are hard, okay? You're hard. But don't make this more difficult than what it has to be."

"Fuck you!" Percy yelled.

"Fuck you!" Carmella yelled as she knelt down and hacked off half of Percy's left foot. "Now he wants to cry," she said over Percy's immediate screams of agony as she stood up once more and spread her arms. Carmella showed no mercy when she raised her arm and slammed the machete into Percy's clavicle, slicing through it completely and leaving his left arm dangling. "You're now half the man you once were, mutherfucka!" she yelled. "Your boss! Who's your boss? Who do work for?"

Percy began coughing uncontrollably and vomiting onto himself, still he wouldn't give up names. Carmella raised the machete again and slammed down into Percy's knee, slicing off a portion of his knee cap. His cries brought tears to Francesca's eyes. She wished he would just say the name and end it all for everybody, but she had to admire his resilience. It was a resilience that was forcing her to fight for her own life. She sat wrestling with her plastic ties, determined to break free as she watched her friend's eyes roll to the back of his head.

"Hey," Carmella yelled as she slapped Percy's face with the bloody machete. "Amigo, you woke?" she asked.

"I think he died," Desiree said while checking for a pulse.

"The tourniquets," Q-man said.

"Say again?" Carmella asked, nearly out of breath, as she looked back at Q-man.

"You wanted to kill that man so bad your ass forgot the tourniquets."

"Shit. You're right." Carmella laughed as she took her machete and sliced Percy's throat, making sure he was dead. She then turned to Francesca and said, "That leaves you, bitch. I want the name of your boss and where he lives!"

"As much as we would like to stick around for the show, we need to get back to our room so we can get ready to leave out later on," Q-man said as he stood up and stretched.

"You're not going to watch me murder this bitch?" Carmella asked.

"If you've seen one murder you've seen them all," Q-man

remarked as he and his boys headed for the stairs with the money stolen from their enemies.

"Okay then. Call me when you get back to the Ap," Carmella said as she and Desiree followed Q-man and his crew downstairs, unintentionally leaving Francesca alone as all were high out of their minds and had become lackadaisical with the securing of their last surviving captor.

When the group disappeared from sight, Francesca saw her opportunity. She'd broken free shortly before Carmella had sliced Percy's neck and was only awaiting the right time to make her move. She eased up from her chair and crept over to Percy and saw that he was dead. The gate being raised on the first floor let her know her captors were all the way to the front of the club. The only way out was through the small office behind the plywood and plastic laying on the floor so she tiptoed over to the door and eased it open.

Once inside, Francesca saw a single door that led to a fire escape. It was the same door she and her friends had been ushered through shortly after their capture. She ran over to the door only to discover that was padlocked from the inside. The cage being lowered alerted Francesca to the fact that Carmella and her crew were returning to finish her off. She grew frantic as she paced the office, opening drawers and flipping over sofa cushions in hopes of finding a gun, but she came up empty-handed. The voices from her captors were growing closer and Francesca knew she had to act fast. Out of desperation, she grabbed a chair and threw it towards the small window beside the office door and it shattered, giving her a way out onto the fire escape.

Carmella and Desiree heard the noise and they rushed up the stairs to find an empty chair, Percy's dead body and an open office door with a shattered window. "Fuck!" Carmella yelled as she ran into the office where she saw Francesca climbing out of the window.

Carmella made a mad dash for Francesca, but she'd fallen out the window and dropped about four feet onto the metal walkway of the fire escape. Francesca wasted no time in getting up and running down the stairs butt-naked as gunshots from Carmella's .45 automatic rang out into the night.

Bullets ricocheted off of metal and concrete as Francesca reached the bottom of the stairs, dipped behind several dumpsters and disappeared into the night, forcing Carmella and Desiree back inside to clean up their crime scene as both were certain that their escapee would notify authorities.

CHAPTER FOURTEEN
PIECES OF A PUZZLE

"You said one of them was named Desiree?" Asa Spade asked Francesca as she lay in her hospital bed about four hours after her ordeal. Francesca was treated for cuts to her stomach, inside left thigh, and the bottom of her feet; very minor wounds given her potential outcome. Police had taken a report, but Francesca's fabricated inability to identify her supposed attackers left the authorities with nothing to go on. It was little they could do, save for hope for a potential lead that would never arrive.

"Desiree the only name I remember. Something else was said about some Somalis. I don't think they're from 'round here because one of the guys said something about going back to the Ap. I don't know no neighborhood called the Ap here in Denver." Francesca replied.

"What's the Ap?" Dougie asked.

"I don't know what the Ap is, man," Francesca sighed. "They had us right. I should be fuckin' dead. But they was so high they forgot about me when they went to let some of them out."

"There was a lady we think was scoping the club last night," Asa said. "She used a credit card to pay her tab and we found out her name was Desiree Abbadando. I don't think it was coincidence. We got hit by this woman and her click. We find her, we find out who did this and why. In the meantime, I'm gone pay JunJie his cut outta pocket and business will go on."

Just then Dougie's phone rang. He answered and chatted briefly before hanging up and said, "Ace? They found my cousin in the park in Shorter Arms."

Asa looked over to Dougie, who was at a loss for words. Francesca had given the crew the lowdown, but now Dougie was feeling the full impact. Percy was like his brother; the two had been in the crib together, slept and pissed in the same bed when they were kids and had each other backs on the streets of L.A. and Vegas and rose to the top of the game, going from slanging crack to moving bricks and making more money than they'd ever imagined. Denver, however, would be where Percy Hunt's journey through the game would come to an utter halt. The rise to the top came with a price—a heavy price. And for Douglas 'Dougie' Hunt, the cost of success came with the loss of his blood.

Asa could feel Dougie's pain. He knew all-too-well what his boy was feeling because he'd loss a nephew who'd been like a son to him two years ago. He knew where Dougie's heart was also—it was set on revenge no doubt. "We gone get through this shit, Dee. Let's go get Percy ready to be sent home. Then we gone track down this Desiree. We got an address off the credit card she used." Asa ended.

****

Carmella, meanwhile, was over to her mansion in Cherry Creek eating breakfast with Desiree and Pepper as she thought about the events that had transpired hours before. Neither she nor Desiree had slept a wink and both were drunk and high as all out doors; but despite being in an inebriated state, Carmella's mind was in overdrive this early Sunday morning. The woman she knew as Ponita Felton had vanished, having been fed to the sharks entirely, the other person who she knew as Percy Hunt, his body had been wrapped in plastic and dumped in the park inside Shorter Arms. It was Carmella's way of showing respect to the woman named Francesca Aranello for not bringing the police into the situation when she had the chance to do so. Still, the finding of Percy's body had drawn heat to Asa Spade's main hustle spot. He would have to move to another locale for the time being was Carmella's best guess; but she knew she had to be on high alert because Francesca was sure to give the location of the club where the drama went down. She had Q-man and his crew stay in Denver instead of heading back to Minneapolis-Saint Paul in order to help her move weight and provide extra muscle for whatever battle may unfold. She would be heavily guarded when out on the streets.

Carmella sat staring at Desiree with disdain. She was beyond words as she watched the woman talk happily with Pepper as if what she'd told her last night in bed was no big deal. Desiree was so high, she'd told Carmella exactly what she'd done when she walked into *The Royal Flush* and Carmella was incensed.

"You think you in good with me after what you did last night, Desi?" Carmella asked, having grown tired of watching what she perceived was a nonchalant attitude being put on display by her lover.

"What? I did all that you asked last night. You're not satisfied, Carmella?"

"I'm not talkin' about what we did here! This is about the V-I-P shit you pulled! That is the problem this morning!"

"I didn't get a V-I-P!"

"That's not what you said! The drugs! You were so high you laughed yourself into a confession you fuckin' dummy! You told me you went into the V-I-P section last night in the bed! And whether you did or didn't there was no fight last night at The Royal Flush so that means you lied to me!"

Desiree was at a loss for words. She stood up and walked over to Carmella. "I'm, I'm sorry I did that."

Carmella didn't say it, but she was admiring Desiree in her short negligee with her smooth thighs covering the sweet pleasure palace she loved to suck and lick on until her heart was content. She couldn't let on that she was turned on by the sight, though, because the move she was about to make was far from that of a sexual advance.

Pepper was staring at Desiree herself. Again she'd watched Carmella and Desiree go at on top of the sheets and she had gotten a thrill herself. The things the two women did to one another looked as if it felt good and she now took the time to eye Desiree up-close in near nudity.

"Pepper, go to your room," Carmella snapped, noticing the little girl's hard stares.

"But, I'm not done with my sausages and—"

"I said go to your fuckin' room, li'l girl! This is grown women's business!" Carmella yelled, forcing Pepper to hop up from her seat and dash out the dining room. "Your li'l hot ass!" she added as she watched Pepper trot down the hall and out of sight. "You gone get what you lookin' for around here you keep playin'! 'Cause I'm the right one to put it in your young ass life!"

"Carmella, baby. I'm sorry. I'm so fuckin' sorry." Desiree said as she stood before Carmella with her eyes welling up.

Carmella eyed Desiree coldly as she eased her chair back from the table. "Everybody is always sorry in this business! I'm sorry this, I'm fuckin' sorry that! I get tired of hearing that shit, Desi! Why can't people just do as I ask? I know what the fuck I'm doing here!"

"I won't let you down again, baby. I promise."

Carmella hopped up from her seat in her night gown and walked into the living room with Desiree on her heels. She went straight for her gold-plated .50 caliber lying on the coffee table, turned around and aimed the gun at Desiree's stomach. "I told you if you lie to me I was gone fuck you up," she hissed.

The look on Desiree's face was one of shock and fear. Carmella had never gone this far with her. Sure, she'd curse her out like the whore she was, slap her around like she owned her, which she did, but she'd never pulled a gun. "You're, you're going to kill me for making a wrong move, Carmella? I thought you loved me!" Desiree pleaded.

"Get on your knees and crawl over here," Carmella demanded.

"Baby, please. This isn't—"

"I said get on your fuckin' knees and crawl over here!" Carmella yelled as she racked her pistol and pointed to her fur-tipped stilettos.

Desiree began crying heavily as she sunk to her knees while shaking her head from side to side. "There's no need to do this," she lamented as she crawled across the floor in her negligee, staring Carmella directly in the eyes.

"This is how I will make things right," Carmella said as she held the gun at her side, watching her mate creep across the floor slowly, like that of a dog in search of its master.

"Please, no!" Desiree pleaded as she reached out and clutched Carmella's legs and cried heavily.

Carmella stared down at the top of Desiree's skull, slowly bringing the pistol up to the top of her head. "I love you Desi," she said as she squeezed the trigger.

Desiree nearly jumped up out of her skin when she heard the gun click. She cried heavily upon realizing it was nothing more than a game of manipulation, a warning of sorts from Carmella to let her know just how far she was willing to go to protect her business. "If you ever lie to me again, the next time the gun will be off safety," Carmella said before she stepped back and walked away from Desiree. "I don't want to see your ass until we leave tonight for the club. Dismiss yourself from my presence," she commanded.

"Si, Carmella. Thank you," Desiree remarked as she got up off her knees and ran into one of the spare bedrooms, where she would remain the rest of the day.

****

While events were unfolding in Denver, Colorado, six hundred miles away in Ponca City, Oklahoma, on the same day, there was much happening down on the ranch. Walee had just run into Ponderosa shortly before eight A.M. and crept into one of the bathrooms on the first floor where he stripped off his clothes and showered. Wrapping himself up in a towel and placing his jeans, underwear, shirt and socks into a trash bag, Walee ran out of the home's side door on the east side and stashed the bag in one of the family's dumpsters before climbing the stairs to his bedroom to put on a fresh set of clothes.

A couple of hours later, the family took to the land and it was alive with activity as usual on this early Sunday morning. Naomi had been riding a tractor around the front portion of the land in between the home and the barn picking up refuse. She rode over to the dumpsters to discard the trash and when she opened one of the lids she was hit with one of the most foul stenches ever. She backed away and grabbed a stick and began poking at the trash and pulled out a small pair of jeans, jeans she knew belonged to Walee. *"What has he gotten himself into now,"* Naomi questioned in silence.

Naomi first thought Walee had fallen off into a pile of cow dung, but on closer inspection she could see that the source of the odor was deriving from within the denim jeans. She threw the jeans back inside the dumpster and returned to Ponderosa in search of Walee. She walked into the kitchen where she saw Doss placing dishes into the dish washer and asked, "Baby, have, have you seen Walee?"

"Not yet," Doss replied as he kissed his wife's lips. "But it won't be long before we hear him," he joked.

Naomi only sighed as she rubbed Doss's broad shoulders and walked away. When he questioned his wife her over her seemingly troubled soul, she made light of the situation, stating that it wasn't a big deal and she was just wondering where he was because she hadn't seen him in a while. Naomi then went into the theater room where she saw Spoonie and Tyke watching ESPN. "Have either of you two seen your little big brother?" she asked.

"We went into his room and he said he wasn't feeling well and for us not to tell anyone," Tyke responded.

Naomi chuckled as she walked out of the room and climbed the grand staircase and walked into Walee's room where she saw her son tucked under his covers. On any given day, Walee would be leading the way through the stockyards with Spoonie and Tyke following, on his way to meddle Kimi and Koko out by the chicken coops. Naomi thought it to be strange that her son would still be in bed this late in the morning when the entire family was up and about. She walked over and sat beside Walee, pulled his covers down and saw that he was crying.

"I didn't mean to do it, momma," Walee said lowly.

"Accidents happen, son. But throwing your clothes away? What happened?"

"I got scared."

"Scared? Scared for what, baby? What happened, Walee?"

"I was by the canal looking for another turtle," Walee began. "I wasn't making noise or nothing. Just walking down the middle of the canal when that man back there ran down the hill and pushed me down."

Naomi tucked her chin. "He pushed you down?"

"Yeah. I got up ran, but, but—"

"But what?" Naomi asked, her heart pounding as she scooped Walee into his arms. "What happened?"

"He threw me down and pointed a shotgun at my chest and said he was gone kill me for makin' fun of him at the park," Walee said as he heaved. "He scared me! And I, I wet my—"

"You don't have to say it, son. Don't say it," Naomi whispered through tears as she held her son close to her heart and ran her hands through his thick hair.

"Momma, don't say nothing! Don't tell my daddy and Dawk what I did. Promise you won't tell."

"Okay, son. Okay. But, can, can I go and talk to our neighbor on your behalf and get him to apologize to you?"

"No. Let's just let it alone."

Naomi didn't respond. She understood her son's fear, but to just 'let it alone' was not in her make-up. She wasn't built to just let things slide. And she felt her nameless neighbor had no right to confront her son and literally scare the shit out of him. He would have to answer for that one.

"It'll be our secret, okay? But I will talk to him. I have to, son." Naomi said in a near whisper.

"Okay. Thank you, momma."

"And Walee? As long as you live don't you ever be ashamed of what happened today, okay? Grown men have done worse under fewer circumstances so don't you be ashamed. You have people that love you and will protect you."

"I'm gone protect myself, too."

"That's what you do, Walee. Fear is a powerful thing, but fighting for your life is to be honored. When you get older you'll remember this ordeal and handle the situation accordingly. But don't worry about it for now—momma has this one covered for you."

"What are you going to do?"

"I'm just gonna talk to our neighbor friend woman to man. We adults have a way of getting, getting our point across to even the most stupid of people we encounter. And that man is stupid and should not be feared."

"Okay. I'm sorry I let you down, momma."

"You didn't let me down, son. You were only caught off guard. It's okay, baby. Now, there's pancakes downstairs, and Spoonie and Tyke are near about ready to go and harass Kimi and Koko, but they can't do it without you, son."

"I'm not in the mood. Can we just go and help Kimi and Koko today?"

"Well," Naomi said as she smiled proudly. "Someone's ready for a job already."

"I can do it. I wanna do it."

"Okay. We'll, umm, we'll get you started tomorrow and I'll join you and your sisters so you can learn how things go."

"I can't wait," Walee said with a smile.

The incident with the family's nameless neighbor had seemed to bring about a certain maturity within Walee in Naomi's eyes and she liked it a lot. Kimi and Koko were to the point that they were constantly asking their mother for more responsibility, and with Walee coming on board now, Spoonie and Tyke were sure to follow, and that meant that Kimi and Koko could move up in the family's business. Naomi knew exactly the job she would begin training her middle daughters for, but that was a way's off. Her immediate goal, however, was that of rendering an apology from her neighbor on behalf of her youngest son.

After pulling out a new outfit for Walee, Naomi got up and left his room, intent on confronting her neighbor. She was halfway down the grand staircase when she met Doss, who was ascending the stairs with a somber look on his face. "What now?" she asked through a sigh.

"Lucky." Doss said sadly.

"What about him? He's making progress," Naomi asked happily.

"Baby? My father called. Lucky had a stroke this morning. Doctors said it was a blood clot in his brain. My father said they tried, they really tried, but they couldn't save him. Lucky died at six twenty this morning during surgery."

Naomi sat down on the stairs and cried her heart out. This was a crushing blow—and an unexpected one to say the least. She'd visited Lucky the week before for a second time, had spent several days with her friend and he seemed to be doing fine, even regaining movement in his fingertips.

"We buried Mildred a little over a week ago," Naomi said through tears. "Now we have to give Lucky a home going? Junior's a mess and Francine is sick. Mendoza? How's he dealing with things?"

"As best a man could given the circumstances. Me and the big three will be away for a while after Lucky's funeral to handle things in Saint Louis. We have to maintain business and get back at those responsible for disrupting the order of things and killing our friends."

"I understand, Doss. But be careful. We're dealing with an animal—this Carmella woman is an animal."

"We'll get her soon enough. Soon enough, baby. Umm, I'm gone make some calls and get things set up with Eddie and the boys over in Saint Louis. We'll notify the family during lunch."

CHAPTER FIFTEEN
GOING OUT IN STYLE

"And now...the end is near...and so I face...the final curtain...my friend...I'll say it clear...I'll state my case...of which I'm certain...I've lived...a life that's full...I've traveled each and every highway...and more...much more than this...I did it...my way..."

Lucky's funeral was one of the biggest Cicero had seen since the celebration of Zell's death back in 1992. A long line of cars, those of mourners, followed the lavish light grey hearse that held Lucky's body as it cruised down Twenty Third Street one last time. A loud speaker was atop the car, intertwined with the countless bouquets of flowers planted on the roof of the hearse, and Frank Sinatra's song *My Way* blared loudly as scores of mourners stood by on both sides of the pavement paying their respects by singing along with the lyrics and tossing more flowers into the street.

Mendoza trailed his son's hearse, his eyes wet with tears as he eyed all the people who loved and respected his son. He pulled Francine, who demanded to be a part of the ceremony despite her illness, close to his heart as the song played on.

"I've planned...each chartered course...each careful step... upon the byway...but more...much more than this...I did it...

my way..."

As the song approached its crescendo, Mendoza and Francine both broke down in tears. Losing their son was such an unexpected tragedy, but given the nature of the business, it was an unsaid possibility that had become a sudden reality that they were forced to deal with head on. Mendoza couldn't help but to reflect on the words Zell Verniche` had spoken to him in August of 1992 as the hearse came to a halt in front of *Eastside Bar.*

"Fuck you asshole. And I mean that not in a disrespectful manner, but in a comical one because you're grateful for me allowing you to do something that I feel may very well destroy not only your crew, who I love so much, but your whole fuckin' family. I'm, I'm not going to be around to see that happen if it ever happens."

"Never have words been so truer," Mendoza said aloud.

"What was that, dear?" Francine asked as she dabbed tears.

"Nothing, honey. Just reflectin' upon words from a wise old man who lived years ago," Mendoza said as the chauffeur opened the door, allowing him and Francine to step out under the bright morning sun where they were greeted by numerous mourners, all offering their condolences.

The Holland-Dawkins family trailed Mendoza's limousine in three separate limos of their own. All were wrought with sadness over Lucky's departure. He'd been an uncle to the kids, a big brother to Mary, Martha, Twiggy, Regina and Siloam, and a loyal ally to Doss. Blank, tear-stained faces sat in a daze behind tinted windows as the caravan slowed to a halt.

Martha sat eyeing Naomi, who wore a pair of dark sunshades that did little to hide the pain coursing through her heart. Martha knew Lucky was a gangster, but she never fully understood what power the man held on the streets. This was her first time visiting Cicero, but it didn't take long for her to figure out the weight forty-eight year-old Faustino 'Lucky' Cernigliaro Senior carried on the streets of the underworld at the time of his death. Lucky's funeral was like no other in

Martha's eyes. It was like a huge parade, or the arrival of a beloved political figure or famous athlete who'd returned to his or her respective neighborhood to be revered by those who'd admired them for their accomplishments.

Forty-three year-old Martha Holland had seen many a man, and woman for that matter, get laid to rest in Jackson, Mississippi, but no funeral she'd ever witnessed had been respected in the manner in which Lucky was being sent home on this day. He was going out in style in her eyes. For all those who'd died in Ghost Town, none were celebrated in this manner—a street laden with flowers, scores of people lining the sidewalks, music, t-shirts with Lucky's image on the front worn by quite a few and a procession of cars that spanned two long city blocks. Martha saw the big picture, and in her mind, Naomi, Doss, Dawk, Bay and T-top were all caught up in something that was far bigger than she could have ever imagined. She knew not what to say, and could only eye Naomi with a look on her face that said, *"I understand your pain, sister."*

"It is what it is," was the look on Naomi's face as she stared at Martha through her dark tinted sunshades for a few seconds; she then let her head drift towards the window to stare at the mourners, the sisters' silent remarks towards one another never being acknowledged, but understood nonetheless.

Naomi was grief-stricken. Lucky was her best friend; her first friend outside of Kevin and Serena. The first kid who'd been kind to her and never made fun of her race. Lucky in fact, upheld Naomi's heritage and celebrated in her triumphs. He was a wonderful friend in her eyes. He'd introduced her to Doss, was godfather to all eight of her and Doss's kids, whom he cherished, and he'd basically set Naomi on her journey to prosperity when he spoke on her behalf to Zell when she'd wanted to exact revenge upon those who'd nearly eradicated her family's once-humble existence down in Sylacauga, Alabama. It was fair to say that if it weren't for Lucky, the woman Naomi Holland-Dawkins was today, and the Holland-Dawkins family itself, would not even exist. Naomi sat reminiscing about the good times as Dawk walked up to the car and opened the door.

The whole ride to *Eastside Bar*, Mary was wondering the reasons behind Lucky and Mildred's deaths. Naomi had given few details, only saying he and Mildred was shot inside a bar down in Saint Louis. It came out the night before that both had been caught up in a robbery. Mary, like Martha, understood that Lucky was a gangster, but even she was beginning to wonder just how much of a role Naomi and Doss played in the overall scheme of things as she exited the limousine.

****

Mourners filed into the bar to view Lucky's body after the family paid their respects. His coffin was placed at the end of the bar in the center of the room. His body, which was decked out in a tailor-made light grey silk suit, black shirt, and light grey tie, black gators and a black velvet fedora, lay in peace as if he were asleep, his hands lay gently on his lower chest, both pinky fingers clad with diamond rings. No expense was spared on forty-eight Faustino 'Lucky' Cernigliaro Senior, a well-respected mobster who'd met the same fate that he'd dished out to so many others before he himself crossed over into the afterlife.

A couple of hours later, *Eastside Bar* was filled with people who'd come to pay their respects. Dinner was being served and stories about Lucky's life were being shared when forty-seven year-old Finland Xavier entered the establishment decked out in a black silk suit and his bald head polished enough to cast a reflection. He walked through the barriers and stood before Lucky's coffin and wiped tears that had begun to form away from his eyes.

Like Naomi, Fin was heartbroken over the loss of his friend. To him, Lucky was a stand-up guy, a great business man, and a fiercely loyal friend. He would miss having dinner over to his friend's home with his wife, who'd also died in that tragic episode. "Cicero will never be the same without you, il mio amico," Finland said as he patted Lucky's hands and went to the back of the bar where he met up with the rest of the family.

Fin sat with Mendoza, DeeDee and Doss and entertained a plate of creamy lasagna and a T-bone steak while updating the men on the operation. He'd just flown back into town from

Seattle after meeting with JunJie to discuss the family's shipping arrangements.

"Our associate in Seattle is getting nervous over this impending war and wants a reassurance that we can still conduct business throughout this process. He's sending a shipment of guns with the next delivery to help us out," Finland remarked as he stirred his lasagna.

"We have the new drop zone you established a while back," Mendoza remarked. "Our buyers are still willing to deal with us, but not in Saint Charles and that is how we would rather things go for the time being. And we most certainly could use some extra firepower."

"We have a rental home set up in Granite City for the time being. Low key and quiet," Doss said.

"Good," Finland remarked. "We'll give it two weeks, see how it goes and I'll report back to our man. The thing that bothers me is the fact that our affiliates in Colorado are also facing adversity. They had to bury one of their own and the other? The other was fed to sharks inside a night club."

"Fed to sharks?" Mendoza asked. "Who in the hell does that?"

"Someone with a serious agenda if you ask me," Finland answered. "We've been in business for ten years now, gentlemen. And given the nature of this occupation, this is about the average time for a war to kick off in any organization."

"Our affiliates," Doss asked, "are they able to handle their end of this thing? Because I have no doubt in my mind that me and my family will come out on the winning end of our battle."

"They're capable, but they don't have much by way of muscle."

"We have plenty muscle despite our losses," DeeDee said as he leaned forward and rested his arms on the table. "I see an opportunity to reap more profits for our unit. Tell our friends in Colorado should they need our services we're available—for a price, of course."

"Duly noted," Finland ended.

"I got Junior on the job with those women who our guy in Fox Park believes killed that Spanish girl Eddie told us about early on," Doss said. "It's gone take some time because they're heavily guarded is the word. It may be next year before we get 'em, but we're all on alert and on the offense looking to strike at the opportune time. Business as usual for us. Tell your man in Seattle that we still have a green light."

"Will do. You know you guys may be battling for some time, right? Years maybe before it's all said and done."

"It is the nature of the business, fellas. War is necessary." Mendoza said. "Takes heart to be in this business. And those behind us have plenty of it. I don't doubt them. Doss? This war will be yours to finish, but me and your father are never far away should you need counsel."

"I won't hesitate to take advantage of the guidance, family," Doss said as he stood up and poured glasses of wine for everyone seated at the table. "This here endeavor will make men and women out of boys and girls. May we succeed by any means necessary. Salute."

"Salute," everybody replied as they all raised their glasses and toasted rims."

****

Junior, meanwhile, was outside the bar hanging with the crew from Saint Louis. Eddie Cottonwood, his younger brothers Jay-D and Dooney, and the crew's up and coming newly-appointed Lieutenant from Fox Park, Malik Gomez, had traveled from Saint Louis with Doss and the big three to provide protection during Lucky's funeral.

It was understood by all involved that the family was in the beginning stages of a war that was being instigated by a Mexican gang of drug dealers from Fox Park—Malik's neighborhood—and Junior, who was scheduled to return to Saint Louis shortly after his father's funeral, had an assignment for Malik, who'd given the family some valuable information.

A week earlier, Malik had showed Jay-D an article that

detailed a missing young female from the Fox Park neighborhood. Malik always read the paper and watched the news while over to his trap house and he believed that the missing girl had something to do with what down in Saint Charles because she was known to hang with two sisters off Ann Avenue. The girl's mother mentioned in the article that her missing daughter's last text was that of, *"I love you, mommy."*

When Jay-D saw the picture Malik had showed him in the papers, he immediately recognized the young female as that of the woman who'd jogged onto Elm Street with the puppy on the leash the day of the robbery and relayed the information to Doss. Doss, in turn, took that news and informed Junior that the names Toodie and Phoebe Perez were connected to the hit.

The Chicago Gang now had The Perez sisters on their radar, but they weren't easy targets, nor were they the only ones in on the hit, the family knew. To add to the difficulty, Malik Gomez operated in the same neighborhood as Toodie and Phoebe, so his life would be in jeopardy if ever the click from Ann Avenue learned he was working for the crew in Saint Charles.

Tactic would have to be used in order to take down Toodie and Phoebe without bringing repercussions on Malik, who was willing to bear the brunt of the storm whenever the Chicago retaliated against two of those they now knew, were responsible for the hit on Benito, Gaggi and Lucky.

CHAPTER SIXTEEN
RANDOM ACTS

Eighteen year-old Dawk was the middle of a game of dominoes at the last booth inside *Connections* with Jay-D and Dooney on a cool and rainy night shortly before nine 'o' clock. It was now mid-October of 2002, two weeks after Lucky's funeral and another search for Toodie and Phoebe was about to get underway on this night. A fresh shipment of cocaine was being moved and all the crew's soldiers in the Saint Louis vicinity were armed with M-14 submachine guns supplied by JunJie. The streets weren't talking much, but they need not be; the Chicago Gang knew who they were gunning for—the Perez sisters—the only problem was the fact that Toodie and Phoebe were nowhere to be found. It was as if they'd vanished into thin air.

Dawk made a fifteen count play and was soon greeted by Tiva. "You going do that thing with Malik tonight?" she asked her brother as she took a seat.

"Yeah. We just gone spin a couple of corners in Fox Park and head over to the safe house in Granite City."

"You gone be okay?"

"Yeah I got it." Dawk answered.

"You going solo tonight, homeboy," Jay-D said as he laid a domino down. "What's up with that, player?"

"Got a li'l something I wanna try out on dude. Malik stay over in Fox Park, you know?"

Seventeen year-old Jay-D ran his hands through his braids and under his chin and said, "Man, I put you up on Malik at Lucky funeral. He solid."

"I know that's your boy and all, but we gotta be sure we can trust this cat, understand?" Dawk asked as he leaned in and stared Jay-D in the eyes coldly.

"I feel ya'. Do what you gotta do then, big dog."

Fifteen year-old Dooney sat across from T-top mixing the dominoes for a new game, all the while smiling at the sexy seventeen year-old. Whereas Jay-D was a slender dark-skinned young man with a thin beard and braids, his brother Dooney was a light-skinned bald-faced chubby lad with a smooth, baby face. He looked every bit like his oldest brother, Eddie Cottonwood when he was younger, only lighter.

"Say, T-top," Dooney said, putting on his killer smile, "want you come and sit next to me and let me tell ya' something good."

"I can hear you from here, Dooney." Tiva sighed.

"Nahh. They got too many ears hustlin'. This here private."

"Boy, ain't nothing you gotta say to me private."

"You gone come around one day. I'm good for you, already."

"You get on my nerves, already."

"Already," Jay-D said as he sipped on a Heineken. "Yo, Dawk. You sure you don't need nobody to go with you on this one?"

"Nahh," Dawk replied as he hopped up from the table. "I be back in a couple of hours."

At age eighteen, Dawk Holland stood 6'4" and weighed a solid two hundred pounds. Years of working the ranch had given him a near perfect physique and he was in the best shape ever. It was obvious he had Native American blood flowing through his veins from his tan complexion, somewhat flat face and long, black hair, which he often wore in single ponytail, but other facial features, namely the dark eyes and full lips, put his African American side on full display. Dawk's physique and rugged appearance left nothing to the imagination, one could merely look into his dark eyes and knew he was a man about business and could handle his own. He eased through the lounge area of *Connections*, his muscular frame towering over most of the people inside the bar as he made his way to the front door and stepped outside where he met up with Junior.

"Eh, I thought you was never gonna come outta there. All set?" Junior asked as he stood out in the rain with an umbrella alongside two soldiers.

"Yeah. I'm gone take the Escalade. You put that tool up in there?" Dawk asked as he zipped his black leather jacket, placed a pair of sunshades over his eyes and pulled down on his black skull cap

"Yeah. Got it all set," Junior said as he stepped back under the canopy, trying to keep his silk suit dry as the rain had picked up. "How the fuck can you see wearing those shades at night?"

"When you get on my level you'll understand one day, youngin'." Dawk joked.

"Youngin'? While you were out chasing chickens I was puttin' in work."

"I don't doubt it."

"Hey, you shouldn't. Where you gettin' off on interstate forty-four? I killed two guys right there you know? On the opposite side at the red light."

"Your daddy told me about that. That was about ten years ago, right?"

"Nearly to the day. A few months over, but yeah. Two Crips that had it comin'. That neighborhood been poppin' for years. I wasn't surprised when Malik said the people behind that shit came outta there, but I wasn't expecting it. Them mutherfuckas probably was babies when I was out there puttin' in work."

"As days go by," Dawk said as he pulled out his cell phone

and called Malik. "I used to chase chickens. Look at me now," he ended as he dapped Junior and walked off. "Yo, I'm on my way. Meet me at Mickey D's in twenty minutes," Dawk told Malik before he started the SUV and pulled off.

"Two hours!" Junior yelled as Dawk bent the curb, blowing the horn as he cruised pass *Connections* and left the neighborhood.

****

"Tienes el producto listo para el swap, perra?" (You got the product ready for the swap, bitch?) Toodie asked Phoebe as the two pulled into the parking lot of the McDonald's on Jefferson Avenue, just outside of Fox Park.

"I got your bitch, hoe." Phoebe snapped as Toodie pulled the Hummer up to the drive thru speakers and ordered three double quarter pounder meals and a ten piece nugget combo.

"Y'all pull around," the cashier remarked.

Toodie and Phoebe had been on the move ever since the hit in Saint Charles, moving back and forth from their main trap house on Ann Avenue back to their other trap house in East Saint Louis. The Perez sisters knew their previous actions in Saint Charles warranted retaliation and they were always on alert. Laying their heads in the same place for an extended period of time would be a dumb move on their part so they were always on the go, just like tonight; but they were steadily making money despite their peripatetic lifestyle.

Toodie pulled up to the drive thru window, music blasting, she and Phoebe toking blunts and talking plenty trash as they waited for their order.

"Mueva el lento asnos!" (Move your slow asses!) Toodie yelled from behind the wheel.

"Cierra tu boca, Toodie!" (Shut your mouth, Toodie!) one of the servers replied through laughter.

Everybody in Fox Park knew and loved Toodie and Phoebe. The two were very popular females in the neighborhood and received much love. Whenever they came through the drive thru at the McDonald's on Jefferson Avenue it was always an event because the crew inside the business all resided in Fox Park. Cars would wait longer than usual because Toodie and Phoebe would always hold up the line with their antics.

The manager inside the place sold ounces of cocaine on the side and whenever she needed to score, she would have Toodie and Phoebe ride up to her store and place a special order. Upon receiving their food, whoever was driving would tell the cashier she was shorted on her order and the bag would be handed back to the manager with the cocaine inside. The order would then be handed back to the driver with the buy money tucked inside by the manager. Sometimes the manager took longer than normal because she had to be careful not to be seen. On this night, however, things went smoothly. Toodie grabbed the bag with the buy money and pulled out of the drive thru and made a left turn onto Jefferson Avenue, headed out of Fox Park towards Interstate-44.

A few minutes later, Malik and Dawk had both pulled into the McDonald's at the same time. Malik dapped his soldier and jumped out his Cadillac STS and ran and hopped into Dawk's Escalade, both gangsters unknowingly having just missed Toodie and Phoebe, who'd vacated the drive thru only minutes earlier and were now headed over to East Saint Louis for a week or so.

"What's up, homes?" Malik asked as he hopped in and pulled the hood down on his sweatshirt. "Fucked up night tonight, man. I don't think nobody gone be out tonight. So unless we plan on doing a kick door, we wasting time."

"You never know what you gone see in this here game," Dawk said as he wheeled out of the parking lot and made a right turn onto Jefferson Avenue, headed into Fox Park.

Dawk and Malik circled the neighborhood several times. Cruising down Ann Avenue once, and passing by Fox Park itself, which was located on Saint Louis Street. Just as Malik had said earlier, the entire neighborhood was dead.

"Maybe tomorrow or the next day we can catch 'em slipping, Dawk." Malik remarked.

"You right," Dawk replied as he pulled into a convenience

store's parking lot where he removed a .38 revolver from his jacket and sat it in the console. He then asked Malik if he wanted a drink. Malik declined, but when Dawk entered the store, he watched Malik's moves. The young man sat still, only looking around on occasion to guard his back.

"We need to ride over to Granite City and pick up some loot right quick," Dawk told Malik once he returned to the vehicle with a bag of potato chips. He grabbed his .38 and tucked it back into his jacket and began pulling out if the parking lot.

"Granite City," Malik asked causally. "If we gone ride way out there, I want me a beer, homes." he said as he opened the passenger side door.

"I got you," Dawk replied as he pulled his .38 out again and sat it on the dash.

Malik eyed the chrome handgun gun as it lay on the dash and chuckled slightly. This was the fifth or sixth time Dawk had sat his gun down in front of him; to Malik, it seemed as if Dawk was trying to get him to pick his gun up the whole time they were riding together. Malik had an idea what was going down so he picked the gun up, willingly going along with the play he believed was unfolding. When Dawk climbed back into the Escalade, Malik pulled the gun on him and cocked it.

"This is what you was wondering, right?" Malik asked calmly. "Would I do this shit here or not, right?"

"You got the ups on me, dude," Dawk said as he eyed the barrel of the gun. "Pull the trigger if you want to."

Malik aimed the gun at the floor board and pulled the trigger, but the gun didn't fire, just like he knew he wouldn't. "The one you got behind your back is the one I need to be worrying about, right, Dawk?" he asked.

"How you know?" Dawk asked as he pulled a .9mm from his backside and laid it down on the dash.

"My daddy taught me the loyalty test a long time ago, homes." Malik said as he sunk back into his seat.

"So, you didn't have it your mind to kill me tonight?"

"Or any other night, homes. I'm down with you and your people, already. Who taught you that trick, though?"

"My father had a suspicion that this man that worked for him was trying to rob him," Dawk began as he pulled out of the parking lot. "So he had the guy stay behind and help count money, making sure there was only one gun inside the building that was within reach. My daddy said he laid a three fifty-seven down on the black jack table and got up to get a drink."

"What happened, homes?" Malik asked as Dawk guided the SUV onto Interstate-44 headed east.

"My father told me when came back in the room his soldier was holding the gun and putting all the money in a paper bag. The then man started for the door, calling my daddy names and telling him how stupid he was for trusting him and he was a dead man. When he went to pull the trigger, though, the gun didn't fire because my father had filed down the firing pin. He pulled his gun and killed the guy on the spot and dumped his body in a landfill."

"That's fucked up, homes."

"It was. This business, this family? It goes back generations. There was never a double cross in the ranks in its history. I'm just tryna make sure you down with us no matter what."

"I understand. That was, that was slick. But you coulda just asked me, Dawk. I been dealing with Jay-D for a while now. He didn't vouch for me?"

"Jay-D was in your corner one hundred. This was all my idea. I just had to make certain."

"I feel you. What now, though?"

"You in," Dawk remarked. "As of now, the family still on the clock with the Perez sisters. That's job one for us. You from Mexico?" Dawk asked Malik as he rode down Interstate-44 towards downtown Saint Louis.

"No, man. I was born here in America in Yuma, Arizona. My parents, my parents now live in Santa Fe, New Mexico where they own a small supermarket. They have a li'l money," Malik said. "But I'm my father's son. He was a hustler—a loyal hustler—and so am I."

"How you learn about the loyalty test?"

"My father was a mule from Tabasco, Mexico," Malik replied. "He smuggled pounds of marijuana in a back pack across the desert and over the border down by Nogales, Arizona before he became a major distributor. When his best friend failed the loyalty test my father killed the man. After that, he retired. He always said that the drug business sometimes turns best friends into enemies and he didn't want to have to kill any more of his friends."

"Crazy world, ain't it?"

"Who you tellin'? Yo, where we going now?"

"Over to the safe house in Granite City to pick up some money. From there we head back over to Elm Street for a li'l welcoming party set up for you."

"That's what's up, homes." Malik remarked, calmly, knowing he'd just been officially accepted by the crew.

****

Desiree had just closed *Club Glitz* and was on her way over to Cherry Creek to spend the night with Carmella. A couple of Q-man's soldiers had escorted her to her car where they immediately parted ways at Desiree's behest. There hadn't been any confrontations as of late and Desiree was certain she would make it home safely on her own.

Snow flurries were raining down on Denver, Colorado on this cold October night in 2002 as Desiree drove through the vacant city streets in her white '02 Range Rover. The car that had begun following her halfway to her destination was of no bother, just people headed to the same neighborhood was her reasoning. When she pulled up to Carmella's mansion, however, Desiree spotted four people dressed in all black hopping out of the car that was following her and they were running her way. She ran towards the front door, soon finding herself having to dodge bullets. The home's brick columns in front of the doorway shielded her, allowing her to open the front door and scurry inside as bullets slammed into the walls of the entrance.

"Ex un exito! Carmella, han venido a por nosotros!" (It's a hit! Carmella, they've come for us!)

Desiree had slammed the door shut, but it was immediately kicked open, but by that time, she had a .9mm millimeter in her hand and had opened fire. The masked gunman was struck in the leg and fell down in the foyer, allowing her to run deeper into the home.

Carmella, meanwhile, was in her bedroom helping Pepper with her studies as she lounged around in a red silk night gown when she heard the commotion. "Pepper," she said frantically as she pulled the little girl down to the floor and shoved her under the bed, "hide and stay there until I return!"

Carmella then jumped up from the floor and grabbed her gold-plated .50 caliber, wrapped a PPD-40 submachine gun that was laying on her nightstand around her shoulder and ran out her bedroom towards her living room in her bare feet towards the erupting gunfire. She neared the end of the hall and saw someone dressed in all black wearing a ski mask peeking down the opposite hall and let loose with her .50 caliber. Whoever the person was, his body seemed to explode when Carmella pumped five rounds of white hot lead into his body. Blood splattered the wall as his body dropped from sight. Carmella then dropped her .50 caliber and racked her PPD-40 at that moment and crept towards her living room.

"Desiree! Ve a la biblioteca al Kalashnikov!" (Desiree! Go to the library and grab the Kalashnikov!) Carmella yelled as she stepped into view and let loose with her German-made PPD-40 submachine gun that held a seventy-one round clip.

Carmella's elegant domicile, set against the back drop of the Rocky Mountains, had been transformed into a war zone in a mere matter of seconds. Bullets shattered fine China, ripped through the best of Italian leather and shattered crystal vases, but the woman had a fight in her that was resilient to the death. She would rather die in her home than surrender to a bunch of inferiors who knew not the caliber of woman they were up against. Bullets spat from her PPD-40 shattered the windows on the front of her home, detaching pictures from her walls and shredding wood and marble like lettuce as her attackers took cover, unable to withstand the fierce ordinance raining down on them.

"Todos podemos morir hoy! Traelo, mutherfuckas!" (We can all die today! Bring it, mutherfuckas!) Carmella yelled as she emptied her gun and ducked behind a marble column in her living room.

Carmella's attackers took the opportunity to strike back when the gunfire seized from the home's interior. They entered the home again and emerged from the foyer firing M-14s at random, tearing up the home's insides as they stepped into the living room.

At that moment, Desiree emerged from the opposite side of the living room with a fully automatic Kalashnikov holding a seventy-five round clip. The Russian version of the AK-47 sent the three remaining gunmen running for the front door, sending one to the floor in the process as Carmella reemerged with a fully loaded PPD-40 and opened fire.

When the gunmen fled, Carmella waited a few seconds before she ran to her front door and saw her potential killers speeding up the block out of her neighborhood. Desiree emerged from the opposite side of the room and the two eyed one another, both out of breath with wide eyes, rapidly palpating hearts and sweat trickling down their temples.

Carmella looked around at the damage done to her home, lucky to have survived the first attempt on her life in over three years. She went over to one of the dead men and pulled off his ski mask and recognized the man as one of the men she'd seen in Shorter Arms.

"Asa Pala ha dejado su tarjeta de visita, Desiree. Es ahora, mi amor." (Asa Spade has left his calling card, Desiree. It's on now, my love.) Carmella said somberly as she headed back to her bedroom to check on Pepper with her head bowed in disbelief.

****

Naomi was out on the back portion of her land feeding turkeys in order to fatten them up for Thanksgiving, which was about a week away. It was now late November of 2002, a month after Asa Spade's failed attempt on Carmella. Earlier in the day, Naomi and Doss had discussed the war the family was engaged in where he told her he was disappointed that his crew hadn't tracked down Toodie and Phoebe as of yet. Cold weather had also set in, so the crew was at a stale mate until further notice. Naomi also knew of the problems in Colorado, but at the time, no one affiliated with the Chicago Gang or Asa Spade's crew knew that they were actually battling the same organization.

To add to the mounting frustration, no one knew of Q-man and his crew from Minneapolis-Saint Paul. Things weren't going well for Asa Spade and the Holland family at this point as far as the war was concerned, but the cocaine side of things was going along smoothly. Money was coming in and being washed clean on a monthly basis and Naomi had in mind to buy more trucks in the spring to further expand business.

The Holland Ranch's land was capped with a layer of snow about six inches thick on this cold and cloudy November morning. Naomi walked amongst the turkeys spreading corn onto the ground and smiling as she watched the birds peck at their breakfast. "Eat up boys," she said as she continued spreading the feed around. "I got my eyes on two of you delicious looking rascals and a nice deep fryer to sit you in to make you all nice, warm and cozy, yes I do."

It was early Sunday morning, an off day for the ranch hands, but Siloam, Dimples and Twiggy were out on the land spreading hay for the cattle and Flacco was on hand clearing the truck's path so a couple of truck drivers could leave out later on in the day with loads of hogs. Not much activity was going on around this time of year because of the weather and the upcoming holidays.

DeeDee was in town, having visited Francine before he left Chicago. She'd had her double mastectomy two weeks earlier and was recovering nicely and was planning on spending the Thanksgiving holiday with Mendoza, Junior and Fin back in

Cicero. A semi-hiatus was underway for most, and Naomi was really looking forward to spending the day in the warmth of Ponderosa watching NFL with the family while preparing a pot of seafood gumbo and stuffed bell peppers.

"Be nice if I could have some fish to fry, too," Naomi thought aloud as she looked over to her nameless neighbor's land and reflected on the days when her kids were bringing home buckets of catfish. She stood and stared at her neighbor's land for a minute and then thought—she hadn't seen the grumpy old man in a few days. On any given day he'd be out riding across his land in his old, beat up orange Ford F-150 pulling up tree stumps to cut firewood.

The land the man owned on the other side of the canal was laden with decades old hickory trees. His man-made pond had frozen over with a layer of thin ice and the trees had lost their luster. The man's house was also deteriorating at a rapid pace. There was so much potential in the land opposite the canal in Naomi's eyes. The family could double their acreage and build more homes, sell timber and expand in agriculture. Naomi felt the land was going to waste. She looked over to her right towards a bend in the land where the man's home sat before a thick grove of hickory trees and saw his pick-up truck parked out front covered in a thick layer of snow.

To Naomi, it appeared as if the old man's truck hadn't moved in days. She and her neighbor had a few words more than three times when she'd confronted the man over his actions concerning Walee and the man denied that he'd ever pull a gun on her son. Naomi believed Walee all the way, however, and since he'd never given her an apology, she took each and every opportunity to let the man know just how much she despised him by hurling every conceivable gross insult she could think of whenever the two were alone. Naomi was hoping to get a chance to curse the old man out again his morning, but the more she stared over at his home and his truck out front, the more she became engulfed with an ominous feeling.

Naomi left the turkey pen and dusted her leather gloves. She locked the gate and looked towards the north portion of her land and saw no one in sight. The twenty-four degree weather had forced Dimples, Siloam and Twiggy back inside Ponderosa the moment they were done spreading hay. Naomi also saw Flacco's black Nissan Titan riding off the land. Now alone, she removed her .44 magnum from her waist and tucked it inside her tan wool trench coat pocket and began a leisurely walk over towards the man's home, looking back on occasion to make sure she was the only soul out on the land this early Sunday morning.

Naomi's knee length, tan leather boots sloshed across the snow-covered land. She descended the hill down into the canal and stepped onto the ice, which gave way and turned into a muddy slush. Undeterred, Naomi crossed the shallow channel, climbed the hill opposite her land and made her way over to her neighbor's home. She stood outside the man's two story cabin-style log home admiring what was obviously a lovely home once upon a time. She then turned around and looked at the man's vast span of land and saw potential in the unkempt property. The old man hadn't done much the time he'd been around because the area was in decline. The space around the man's home was unkempt as well. A rusted fifty-five gallon drum that had been gutted out to make a grill sat beside the wooden porch, dead weeds were growing up through the wooden stairs and the home's wooden rails were failing. Some of the logs on the home appeared to be rotting, and when she stepped back and looked up, Naomi could see that the home's roof was in need of repair. Birds were nesting in the attic for the upcoming winter and the bricks on the chimney looked as if they were about to crumble.

"Hello?" Naomi called out as she walked up the ice covered stairs, purposely tapping the wooden rails to make noise as she did so. When she tapped the right wooden railing lining the front porch a third time, it fell off into the snow, followed by several wooden rafters on the home's covered patio. "Anybody home?" Naomi called out as she approached the front door cautiously, never getting a reply.

Naomi walked over to one of the windows and peeked in, but she couldn't see a thing because the screens were caked with grit. She walked back over to the front door and twisted the knob and saw that the door was unlocked. She removed her gun and gently nudged the door open and remained on the porch. This man was a strange man, and for all Naomi knew, he could've been trying to lure her in in order to shoot her. She called out again. "I say, is anybody home? Your door is unlocked, mister!"

Still getting no response, Naomi slowly entered the man's home with her cocked pistol and stood in the living room with a disgruntled look planted on her face. The place was atrocious. Old, dusty furniture covered with stained sheets, unlit lanterns on top of tables, and every piece of junk known to mankind was stacked up in piles against the walls from hubcaps, to old water hoses, broken TVs and radios that looked decades old. The old man was a pack rat that threw nothing away was Naomi's best guess as she walked to her left and entered the kitchen.

Naomi was taken aback as she slowly rounded the kitchen table that was filled with old dirty dishes, some with mildewing food sitting in them. There on the floor, lying on his back, was her nameless neighbor. The grey-bearded, bald-headed, skinny old man eyed Naomi and licked his severely blistered and chapped lips and looked towards the sink. Naomi followed the man's eyes and looked towards sink and pointed at the faucet with her glove-clad hands.

"Thirsty?" Naomi asked as she eyed her neighbor coldly.

The old man was so weak he couldn't speak. He uttered an incoherent phrase and extended his hand briefly, but it seemed as if it pained him to do so. He groaned and let his hand drop to his side and heaved a dry cough. Naomi quickly surmised what'd happened to her nameless neighbor. She hadn't seen him for three days in a row, and that was the key clue. To her, it seemed as if the old man had stumbled in his kitchen and injured himself a few days earlier and was unable to move or call out for help.

Three days was about the length of time a human being could go without water, Naomi knew; and her neighbor was desperate for a drink. Not one to be disrespectful, Naomi reached over and grabbed a dirty glass off the table and filled it with tap water and knelt down before the old man. "I think we got off on the wrong foot, il mio amico," she said calmly as she held the glass of water just out of reach of her neighbor friend. "I mean, the name calling and angry rants? We carried on like a bunch of angry teenagers you and I. And you did accuse me and my family of stealing your fish once upon time," she added as she smiled brightly. "My youngest son? I believe him. I believe you pulled a shotgun on him a while back. He crapped his pants you know? Just like you as a matter of fact. Tell you what, I'm gonna let by gones be by gones, okay? You and I have much bigger issues to deal with, right? Right," Naomi said as she stood up and poured the water down the drain before setting the glass back in its proper place on the table. "You take care yourself, now. And have a happy Thanksgiving," she ended as she walked out of the kitchen and left the man's home exactly as she'd found it.

The old man's body was found in January of 2003 by a city worker who'd been sent out to inspect the man's home for an appraisal. The cold weather had held back his decaying corpse's stench and if it weren't for the home appraiser, there was no telling how long the man would've lay dead on his kitchen floor because Naomi was the only person who'd known of his inevitable death, and she wasn't going to say a thing.

As for the rest of the family, no one was really moved by the man's death. He'd been a thorn in just about everybody's side for years and it couldn't have happened to a better person was the reasoning for many on the Holland Ranch.

The old man's death had opened his land up for possible sale within a couple of months. And by the start of spring of 2003, Naomi was attempting to buy the land from the Kay County Board of Commission at $2,500 dollars per acre, far less than what her land was now valued at. Another 213 acres of land was up for grabs and Naomi would use all her lawyer credentials to make sure that the old man's property came under the family's control. It would be a long and laborious fight, because the commissioners were resolved to holding on to the land for an extended period of time to increase its value, but Naomi would be there every step of the way, waiting and watching.

****

The start of spring of 2003 had also thawed out old bones of contention in Denver and Saint Louis. Asa Spade had licked his wounds on the failed hit against Desiree and Carmella, a hit in which Dougie had taken a bullet to the leg and was forced to flee the scene with Francesca, the two of them leaving behind two dead soldiers from their main trap house in Shorter Arms, and having regrouped during the cold months.

The Chicago Gang, meanwhile, had intensified their search for Toodie and Phoebe. And as the weather began to heat up, so did the streets in both cities. Shootouts erupted on occasion between drug dealers who were siding with Carmella in Denver, and those who were riding with Toodie and Phoebe back in Saint Louis. The tension in both these cities was so thick one could barely breathe. Every day was lived as it was the last and nothing was being taken for granted.

Doss and his crew were intent on retaliating, however; it had been too long since the hit on Benito, Gaggi and Lucky and someone had to answer. The war between these two factions was now about to reach its first apex as the summer of 2003 got underway; and whoever made the wrong move first would surely pay a heavy price because these gangsters were all gunning for one another without fail and were on a straight up collision course.

CHAPTER SEVENTEEN
CAUGHT SLIPPING

Sitting just south of Interstate-44 and Russell Boulevard, which ran east to west, and east of Jefferson Avenue, a street that ran north and south, lay Ann Avenue—the main trap house for the Perez sisters in Saint Louis. Tucked in between California Avenue to the east and Ohio Avenue to the west, this short city block was a fortress all unto itself. Cars coming in from either direction looking to do harm would have a hard way out because Toodie and Phoebe had gunners on each corner.

The two story red bricked row houses, which resembled many a brownstone in New York City, sat a ways back from the street and sidewalk and weren't easy to access on this particular block. Creeping in between the homes was nearly impossible because they were bunched together in units of three or more. Toodie and Phoebe's trap sat in the middle of the block in a five block unit, dead center. Numerous Mexican female soldiers were always out on the block and here, the Perez sisters felt safe. This was their stronghold when it got down to it.

Well aware of the attempted hit on Carmella and Desiree in October of the previous year, the Perez sisters were on guard for possible hits as they conducted their business throughout the months. Things were going good for the crew in Fox Park.

Q-man and his crew had gotten a firm hold on a neighborhood in Cincinnati, Ohio known as Over the Rhine, and they'd also expanded into the cities of Kansas City, and Indianapolis, Indiana.

Carmella had increased her shipments of kilograms coming in from Valle Hermoso, Mexico on through Brownsville, Texas from forty-eight a month to seventy-two per month and the monies being made hadn't been this respectable in years. Ounces on up was the only product was being moved and even then, Carmella could barely keep pace. During this summer July month of 2003, she was down in Mexico looking to further increase her shipments in order to maintain her grip on the markets she served.

Twenty-two year-old Toodie and twenty year-old Phoebe's pristine Cadillac Fleetwood sat out in front their trap with music blaring as the two shared a blunt while watching the block. Every so often a car would pull up and a worker would escort one lone buyer inside. The trap wasn't more than a furnished two story drug lab. Tables were all around the living room with one long suede sofa and a single table set up with cocaine was in the kitchen. Four female soldiers welding AK-47s to secure high dollar deals milled about on the first floor and three queen sized beds and TVs were on the second floor. When a two door Cutlass pulled up to the set, Toodie whistled and one of the young Mexican females, a fourteen year-old girl named Simone Cortez, jumped up from the stoop and ran to the edge of the sidewalk.

Fourteen year-old Simone Cortez was as cool as fan and razor blade sharp. She'd grown up in Fox Park and had been in the neighborhood all her life. Toodie and Phoebe had been knowing her since '99, and had been having her eye on her for a while. When Carmella went down in Memphis, Toodie and Phoebe put her on when she was only ten years-old. She had seen a lot in her young years and was more than hip to how things flowed in Fox Park. It was fair to say that Simone Cortez was the crew's next up and coming soldier at the tender age of fourteen.

"*Medio ladrillo.*" (Half a brick.) Phoebe told Simone.

Simone, a heavy set tan-skinned female with a bald-faded haircut, nodded towards a dread-locked black male and followed him back into the house. The man walked in and saw two females standing on either side of him in the home's pristine living room and he paused momentarily.

"Come on, man," Simone snapped. "Stick and move," she said as she walked around a small wooden table.

The man pulled out a knot of money and Simone went to work. "*Pepper, quiere un medio.*" (Pepper, he want a half.) she said as she walked towards one of the tables in the living room and began separating the money in order to place it inside the money counter.

Twelve year-old Peppi Vargas was now getting her feet wet in her benefactor's occupation. Before Carmella left for Mexico, she stopped over in Saint Louis and dropped Pepper off and told Toodie and Phoebe it was time for her to get her feet wet in the game and for them to look after her throughout the process.

The first time Simone laid eyes on Pepper, it was an instant bond. She was the little sister Simone never had. The two spent a lot of time together and Pepper was learning a lot from Simone, but the twelve year-old still had a dislike for Toodie and Phoebe because she knew they could care less about her life. Phoebe was trying, but she went with the flow of things, doing little to suppress Toodie's verbal abuse. Simone didn't care all that much for Toodie and Phoebe herself because she knew they were shady, but Simone knew how to run game and go with the flow; and for that, she was always in good standing with the Perez sisters.

Pepper was sitting at the table in the kitchen by her lonesome, a .380 caliber pistol tucked in her backside with rows of ounces, quarter kilograms, half kilograms and entire bricks staring her directly in the face.

"*Medio ladrillo, Pepper!*" (Half a brick, Pepper.) Simone snapped from the living room.

Pepper was still green. Street math was a little confusing for the twelve year-old at times. Simone had broken the cocaine down from smallest to largest, but Pepper would still get confused. She picked up a neatly-packaged quarter kilogram and walked out of the kitchen timidly and handed Simone the package. Right away Simone saw the mistake, but instead of yelling at her the way Toodie always did, she walked young Pepper back into the kitchen and broke the math down for her again from smallest to the largest.

"*Ahora lo tengo.*" (I got it now.) Pepper said lowly. "*Lo siento.*" (I'm sorry.)

"It's all good. You still learning. Stick with me you be all right." Simone remarked as she left the kitchen, served the young man and sent him on his way.

When the guy left with his product, Phoebe turned to Toodie and said, "Let's go up to the Mickey D's on Jefferson Ave and get the hook up on some lunch."

"That McDonald's is gonna be the death of your ass," Toodie snapped towards Phoebe before she took a toke off the blunt she was smoking.

"We all gotta die from something someday. Come on! A bitch hungry!" Phoebe chuckled as she tugged on Toodie's shirt.

"This bitch here," Toodie sighed. "What time is it?"

"Three 'o' clock. Way pass lunch."

"I guess, girl. Simone? Hold it down! We going get lunch for everybody." Toodie said aloud.

"I want a Big Mac meal!" Pepper yelled as she ran to the front door.

"Get your young ass back inside!" Toodie snapped. "Ain't nobody ask you shit!"

"Damn, Toodie! She been in there all day! Let her breathe," Phoebe snapped as she watched Pepper walk back into the home dejectedly.

"Fuck her!"

"Yo, Phoebe," Simone called out as she stepped out onto the

stoop. "Two Big Mac meals for me and Pep!"

"I gotcha, homegirl!"

"You too nice to them li'l hoes, yeah?" Toodie said as she hopped behind the wheel of the Hummer.

"Somebody around here has to be," Phoebe ended as her sister pulled off from the curb.

****

"Bring out the big guns when you go out there tonight," twenty-five year old Junior told Dawk, Jay-D and Malik as the three of them left Jay-D's home and walked down the block towards *Connections*.

"Who ridin'?" Malik asked.

"Me, you, and Bay," Dawk answered.

It was business as usual for the crew over in Saint Charles in July of 2003. Junior, Dawk and Malik had just returned from the crew's trap house over in Granite City where Doss was repackaging product with Eddie, and the three of them were going have a late lunch inside their headquarters with Dooney, Bay and T-top as four 'o' clock approached. *Connections* still operated as a bar and grill in the neighborhood and did good business. It was mainly busy at lunch hour and around seven at night. The down time around this time of day afforded the crew time to spend together and discuss business.

The group entered the bar, which had all but a few customers, and walked towards the last booth. The short order cook emerged from the kitchen and asked did they want a bite to eat.

"Eh, take a break," Junior told the middle-aged man. "I'm gonna fix my crew whatever they want today."

The cook left and Junior got up and walked into the kitchen where Tiva was in front the grill deep-frying an order of lemon pepper chicken wings and french fries for a waiting customer. *Connections* was one of the coolest places in the neighborhood. It wasn't nothing for one of the crew to fry up a burger and fries, a grilled steak, pork chops or whatever the menu held for a customer. Ever since the infamous hit nearly a year ago, many people came to the bar, if only to say they'd hung out and had a meal or drink, or both, in what was known as a gangster's domain. *Connections* was revered in the area, and so were the new faces who now ran the establishment.

"You need a hand, baby?" Junior asked.

"I got it," Tiva replied calmly, all the while eyeing Junior and smiling sexily.

Tiva and Bay had turned eighteen a couple of weeks back in early July and it didn't take long for Tiva and Junior to become involved. Tiva had only one lover before Junior back in Ponca City, but Junior was her heart. And he'd done the right thing by asking Doss and Naomi during the twins' birthday party if they'd mind him dating Tiva. Both parents were surprised, but they respected Junior's approach, especially since he'd come clean on some ill-will he'd been harboring for some time.

Last year, shortly after his father's funeral, Junior had invited his grandfather, Doss, Naomi, DeeDee and Eddie Cottonwood to his parents' home in Cicero for an elegant dinner where he apologized to everybody for being disrespectful of the family. Naomi, Doss, DeeDee and Eddie would've never known of Junior's brief battle with envy had he not told them, but they all respected him even more so for doing so; and Mendoza's presence only aided in Junior's successful attempt to smooth things over.

Doss and Naomi knew what Tiva was involved in and if it weren't Junior, Tiva would've had to find someone not involved in the business to become intimate with; with that aside, Doss gave his approval based on Junior's loyalty to the family and Junior and Tiva were now in the early stages of a budding romance.

To Tiva, Junior was a sexy man. She remembered him being a little on the chubby side when he was younger, but at the age of twenty-five, Junior looked exactly like his father. Lucky was a muscular bow-legged man with rugged features and a square jawline. Junior was built the same way, save for his red hair and his mother's blue eyes. The first time the two made love, which was a week ago, Tiva had shed tears the experience was so good. Junior complimented her body perfectly when he lay on top of her and when he took from behind he engulfed her completely, able to stand up in it while pulling her short black hair and kissing her like a man possessed. Sitting atop her man was the best for Tiva. Junior had a chest full of silky red hair and she loved to run her hands through it while he gripped her ass cheeks and drove up in her, the two staring one another in the eyes in the most intense way imaginable. Theirs was a special kind of love that both wanted to last a lifetime.

"You need anything you just let me know," Junior said as he slid pass Tiva, purposely brushing up against her rear end as he went over to the stainless still island counter and began setting up the meat slicer in order to cut fresh sirloin steak for the crew.

"What I need from you can't be given to me up in here that's for sure," Tiva said as she shook the basket inside the deep fryer.

"No it can't. Give me a rain check."

"You don't even have to ask, baby." Tiva answered.

Back outside in the bar, sixteen year-old Dooney sat shuffling a deck of cards preparing to deal out a hand of spades for his self, Dawk, Bay and Malik while Jay-D kept score. "Bay," Dooney said through his trademark smile and baby face.

Bay leaned back and sighed as she looked off into the openness of the bar. Dooney was a relentless flirt, a sex hound so to speak. He'd loss his virginity when he was eleven years old and couldn't get enough of sex. If a hole was available, nine times out of ten Dooney was going in hard. He'd tried to get next to Tiva, but when he learned she was interested in Junior he backed off.

The twins were all out sexy and it was a given. They stood five foot nine and weighed a solid one hundred and forty-five pounds. Smooth tan skin and short black hair with slender eyes and luscious lips accentuated near-perfect physiques and the outfits they wore only added to their exquisite beauty. The entire crew knew Dooney had no shot, no shot at either twin; and Dooney himself knew he had not a chance, he just loved flirting with the twins as he'd never been around such adoring, mirror imaged women in his life. He took every opportunity to engage them in conversation, albeit aggravating, but everybody knew Dooney meant no harm and actually had a better chance of winning the mega ball or getting struck by lightning rather than getting either twin to drop their panties for him.

"You hear me talking, Bay," Dooney said as he began dealing out the cards. "You and me is partners in this game, baby, so you should hear me out."

"What? What you gotta say, Dooney?" Bay asked as she picked up her cards.

"Let's go to the movies tomorrow. My treat."

"I'm not going on a date with you, man. Didn't I tell you I gotta girlfriend?"

"I know," Dooney snapped. "That's what I'm saying. Me, you and your girlfriend can go out to the movies, dinner and take it from there."

"We ain't takin' it nowhere and you know it. Ship ain't leaving the dock. How many books you got, boy?"

"Three," Dooney said as he smiled at Bay. "I have ménage a trois."

"You a relentless soul, yeah?" Dawk said as he chuckled over Dooney's remark. Dawk was stacking his cards but couldn't help notice how Malik kept staring at the floor outside the booth. "What you keep looking at on the floor, Malik," he asked.

Jay-D shook his head at that moment and said, "This fool think he know how to do floors. Talkin' bout he wanna lay down some new wood in the bar."

"I can, homes." Malik replied causally. "Look at this wood. The polish isn't working anymore and it's rotting. I can take that wood up and put down some fresh cherry wood that'll set this place off."

"You do that kind of work?" Dawk asked.

"Yeah, man. I mean, I only work on my parents' home in Maplewood, but, someday? Someday I'm gonna have my own renovation company. This here game ain't a career, no?"

"I like that," Dawk said. "What's your plan?"

"I have two guys under me in Fox Park that love to do renovation too. They help me out around the house sometimes. Together? Together we gone buy all the tools we need? A couple of vans, do some advertising and build up our clientele. Just like I do now with the game."

"I respect that," Dawk said. "We gone make that happen for you, homeboy."

"That's hard work," Dooney said. "Me and Jay ain't working hard now and don't plan on workin' hard later."

"For once he said something that makes sense," Jay-D nodded in agreement.

"What's y'all plan?" Bay asked.

"Shiiit," Jay-D said as he leaned forward and sipped his Heineken. "Me and hot nuts here gone get in the music biz. Find us a hot rapper tryna make it in the game and invest in his ass and ride 'em straight to the top. We gone be next No Limit or G-Unit."

"Roc-a-fella and Cash Money got both of them beat, homes. Why not be the best of the best?" Malik asked.

"You just worry about what color uniform and name tag your ass gone be wearing while you work on these here floors," Jay-D joked. "And while you doing floors? We gone be in New York poppin' bottles with a buncha freaks."

"A bunch of freaks?" Malik said in a matter of fact tone as he straightened his cards. "You gone have millions of dollars and you gone have 'a buncha freaks' at your table? That's the best you can do, homes? Why not Angela Bassett, Nia Campbell or Sanaa Lathan instead of a buncha freaks?"

"A buncha freaks was like, like metaphoric for bad bitches," Dooney said.

"Y'all gone have some bad bitches at your table, already. Fuck around and catch that gangsta," Bay stated. "How many books you got again, Dooney?"

"Trois."

"You got three, I got six, that's ten. Put the wheels on it." Bay said quickly.

"Boston," Jay-D sang as he wrote down the score.

"Whoa, whoa, whoa!" Dooney snapped. "Where you learned your math, Bena? Three plus six is nine all day where I'm from!"

"We got ten, trust me. Sit down and play. Go 'head Dawk."

"I don't know where to start," Dawk said. "I ain't even bothering to straighten these out."

"Say, Dawk? You saw that new diamond Rolex?" Malik asked.

Bay and Dooney leaned back in their seats. "Dock 'em three books, Jay-D," Bay said.

"Dock us three for what?" Dawk asked.

"Y'all talkin' cross the table, man. You know what y'all doing." Dooney said.

"I just asked a question, Bay," Malik responded.

"Okay. Go 'head. See where cheatin' get y'all," Bay said.

"Nahh, I'm gone have check that new rollie out though," Dawk said as he threw out the Ace of diamonds. Bay merely shook her head as she threw out a three of spades and cut his suit.

"Already!" Dooney said as he threw out a four of diamonds.

Bay and Dooney won eleven books and set Dawk and Malik on the first hand, thereby ending the game before it even started. "Bay did that!" Dooney said as he stood and reached out to hug Bena.

"Get the fuck outta here! I ain't huggin' your nasty ass!" Bay snapped as she hopped up from the table to check on the food.

THE HOLLAND FAMILY SAGA

****

Several hours later, after enjoying a sirloin steak dinner, the crew had closed *Connections* and were now preparing for a ride through Fox Park. The kitchen's island counter, which was once filled with an assortment of vegetables, seasonings, meats and cooking utensils, now held an arsenal of weapons ranging from semi-automatic handguns to assault rifles. The sun was beginning to dip behind the hills of Missouri and the neighborhood had grown still and quiet.

Junior, Dawk, Bay, T-top, Jay-D, Malik and Dooney were loading bullets into clips and greasing guns when Doss called and had them unlock the front doors for him and Eddie.

"Okay, family," Doss said upon entering the building as he removed his suit jacket. "We got the product out on the streets, brought in some more profits and we are dead tired. What's going on with that other thing?"

"Going through the plan now. Gone ride down Jefferson Avenue and bend a few corners in Fox Park. Toodie and Phoebe been on the move, but word is they been posted up on Ann Avenue." Bay answered.

"I hate that spot and love it at the same time," Eddie remarked.

"I understand," Doss replied as he took a seat at the bar and was handed a cold beer by Dooney. "Love it because it's a perfect fortress, and hate it for the same reasons. Don't ride down Ann Avenue tonight. They guard that place like the white house and I got a bed feeling about that there."

"Stick and move if you can and stay on main Ave," Junior chimed in. "We know some of their soldiers, so if you see anybody you know that's affiliated with the Perez sisters you got the green light, okay?"

"Cool," Bay said as she grabbed a Chicago Piano, A.K.A. the Tommy gun, with a thirty round drum attached and headed for the front doors with Dawk and Malik following close behind, each welding powerful semi-automatic assault rifles.

****

"Yo, we got another sale from our girl up to Mickey D's," Toodie told Phoebe as she snapped her phone shut.

"Already. Let me see if these li'l girls want something while we up there," Phoebe stated.

"Fuck them, Phoebe! Let's just go drop off and come back!"

"Kathy, them girls been trappin' all day. The least we can do is feed 'em before they knock off."

"Knock off? You run this shit like General Motors or something. I be in the car," Toodie sighed.

Phoebe returned with a list of orders and she and Toodie were on their way up to McDonald's on Jefferson Avenue with Simone and Pepper in tow. Toodie had resented the two youngsters riding with her, but the immaculate 1975 black on black Cadillac Fleetwood with the big chrome wheels that kept spinning even when car wasn't moving and the suicide doors was the best ride the Perez sisters owned and it was a beauty that begged to rode in.

Toodie swerved onto Russell Avenue headed east blasting Master P's song *Players From the South*. The d-girl ride slid up the avenue in seeming slow motion with bass thumping and blunt smoke billowing out into the open air. Enthralled by the song, which seemed to be dragging, Pepper couldn't help but to ask, "Simone, why it sound like they rappin' in slow motion?"

"You ain't never heard a chopped and screwed out record before, girl?" Simone asked as she tapped Phoebe's shoulder to get her to pass the blunt.

"What's chopped and screwed?"

"It's when the Dee-Jay slow a song down like it's in slow motion or something. Tight ain't it?" Simone asked before took a long toke and passed the blunt back to Phoebe.

"Yeah," Pepper said as she bobbed her head to the music, listening hard to the gumbo thick bass and gangster-laden lyrics.

"*...eliminating niggas like Calgon...if this was a*

mutherfuckin' band I be a baritone...see the P is from that mutherfuckin' Calliope...where them niggas boot up with gold teeth don't give a fuck about a hoe...and niggas stuntin' on that water water...you know we bout bout it but don't give no fuck about seeing no mutherfuckin' tomorrow..."

Toodie turned off into McDonald's, all heads inside the car bobbing to the music and the bass shaking the windows on the building as the group approached the drive thru speakers where she turned the music down and placed a special order.

At the same time, Dawk, had just exited Interstate-44 from the west and had made a right turn onto Jefferson Avenue in a beige 2001 S-Class four door Mercedes on 20" chrome wheels. Traffic was light on Jefferson Avenue as it was getting late, but McDonald's had a line wrapped around the drive thru. When Dawk cruised by, Malik recognized the Perez sisters' Cadillac at the drive thru window. "There they go, homes!" he exclaimed from the back seat, his glove-clad hands repeatedly tapping the back window.

Dawk wheeled into a small office complex beside the restaurant, which sat a few feet lower than the McDonald's and looked over and saw the wheels spinning on the Perez sisters' ride.

"You sure that's them?" Bay asked as she grabbed a ski mask.

"They been riding that car for a minute now. If it ain't them then it's somebody out they crew. We got the green light to hit anybody out they crew and it don't get no better than this! Let's move," Malik stated lowly as he grabbed a ski mask and slid it over his face.

****

"You gone give me my order, already!" Phoebe yelled aloud to the cashier. "And don't short a bitch on the ketchup and shit! We strugglin' back here and can't afford groceries!"

The crew inside McDonald's was joking around with the Perez sisters until the manager made the switch and received her product. Toodie had just pulled off and Phoebe was checking the bags when she noticed four orders of fries were missing.

"Stop the mutherfuckin' press, Toodie, these hoes done shorted a bitch on the fries!" Phoebe snapped.

"What? Girl, forget that shit!"

"Nahh! The fries is the most important part of the fuckin' meal!"

Toodie pulled forward and placed the car in park and stared at Phoebe.

"What?" Phoebe asked.

"I know you don't think I'm going get that shit!"

"Toodie come on now! I paid for it! Just run in and get the shit while I roll this other blunt."

Toodie hopped out the car and slammed the door. Pepper soon followed saying she had to use the bathroom. The two went inside the building where Toodie approached the counter and Pepper headed to the toilet.

Simone was in the backseat bobbing her head to the music playing low on the speakers. Pepper had just emerged from the restaurant and was walking back to the car when she saw three people dressed in all black creeping out from behind a row of bushes and a few parked cars on the opposite side of the parking lot. She was wondering what they were up to, but said nothing as she continued walking towards the car.

At the same time, Phoebe was rolling a blunt when she spotted three people dressed in all black, one of them running up on the Cadillac with a chrome Tommy gun on full display. Her eyes grew wide as she dropped the weed.

"Ohhh, fuck!" Phoebe yelled as her adrenaline began to flow. *"Peppi, llamada Toodie! Llamada Toodie!"* (Peppi call Toodie! Call Toodie!) she frantically screamed as she tried to reach up under the driver's seat.

Simone looked up and nearly pissed her pants when she saw the cannon the gunman was welding. She opened the back door and rolled out onto the ground in between the car and the curb leading to the sidewalk just as gunfire erupted.

The windshield and front passenger side window on the Cadillac shattered and bullets lodged into Phoebe's right side, forcing her against the driver side door. She was reaching under the front seat for her sister's mini Uzi when the gunman ran up and sprayed the interior of the Cadillac, shredding her body and splattering her intestines and brains throughout the pristine car's interior.

Bullets from the assailant's gun sounded like a bunch of empty fifty-five gallon barrels crashing down onto concrete at random and the sparks from the gun's barrel and chamber was radiating in the darkness, coming off like a strobe light from a disco tech as the ski-masked assassin lit up the interior of the Cadillac. A couple of cars sped out of the driveway and several people had left their cars behind, jumping out and running away from the violence in sheer terror.

Phoebe lay on her back, looking her dispatcher square in the eyes as bullets pumped into her body in rapid succession until everything in her world faded to black. Just as fast as twenty year-old Phoebe Perez had lived, so had her life come to an abrupt end. She died on the front seat of her sister's car in a hail of semi-automatic gunfire.

Pepper, meanwhile, was frozen stiff. She stood by and watched as Phoebe's killer ran past her, looking her directly in the eyes before turning away and running off into the darkness with the other two gunmen.

Toodie ran out of the building and knocked Pepper down in her attempt to reach her sister. When she reached the car, however, Toodie knew right away that it was no saving Phoebe. She lay on her back looking up at the car's roof, her eyes half-closed and her mouth slightly open. Brain matter was seeping from the back of her open skull and spilling out onto the white leather seats right along with her intestines, which were spilling out from her midsection. Toodie walked away from the car and went and sat on the curb and hid her face as she began to scream aloud in agony, knowing she'd just been dealt a serious blow at the hands of her enemies.

THE HOLLAND FAMILY SAGA

CHAPTER EIGHTEEN
COUNTRY BUMPKIN BRUISING

"How was the trip to Chicago," eighteen year-old AquaNina asked Bay as the two dressed inside their master bedroom after showering together.

It was two weeks after the hit on Phoebe Perez. Early August of 2003. Fox Park had suffered the loss of one it's most revered hustlers the night Phoebe was killed and the neighborhood was still in mourning. Teddy bears and flowers were placed under the McDonald's drive thru window and many who rode through would often bless themselves in remembrance of their downed comrade.

Carmella had flown back into town for her girl's funeral and had sent her off right. She and her girls partied for two days straight in honor of Phoebe and had even tried to retaliate a week after, but riding through Saint Charles was a suicide mission. The place was heavily guarded at all times, so striking back on the Chicago Gang's home turf was out of the question for the time being. Carmella would have to let things die down before she could devise another plan to counteract what'd been done on her main hustle spot down in Saint Louis.

Bay dried her legs and fell back onto the bed and pulled AquaNina close. The two had been lovers for nearly a year now, but Bay had come out to the family on her eighteenth birthday, the same day Junior asked permission to date Tiva.

Most in the family weren't surprised over Bay. AquaNina had been her only friend for a while. The two did everything together, from going to the movies, dinner, shopping and hanging around Ponderosa and showing up at Spoonie and Tyke's ball games and the town's bowling alley together. They were an obvious couple, but their lifestyle was accepted by the family.

Bay and AquaNina's alternative lifestyle was disapproved by some youngsters around town, however, and they would sometimes encounter ridicule when out in public. It took a lot within Bay to not bring out her true self to her peers in Ponca City because she knew the people who harassed her and her baby really didn't know the things she was capable of doing; and it was for that reason, that a lot of the mockery she and AquaNina endured was being handled with tact and grace on Bena's part so far.

"It went well," Bay said as she kissed AquaNina's forehead. "Lotta logistics to learn."

"I missed you the whole time you were gone. You barely called."

"I know. I'm sorry for that, but moving around like we do don't allow for much free time, you know? By day's end I be dog tired. But I always text you good night."

"You do. And I appreciate that, baby." AquaNina replied as she nuzzled her nose against Bay's neck and inhaled her scent as she began singing softly in her ear. "*I know you got a little strength left...I know you got a lotta strength left...*" AquaNina cooed.

"I so love it when you sing that song," Bay said as she kissed AquaNina's forehead tenderly.

Eighteen year-old AquaNina Mishaan was nothing short of exquisite. She was a five foot eight one hundred and thirty-five pound full-bloodied Navajo Indian with thick brown hair and clear brown eyes. She was a slightly slender young woman, a little shorter than Bay and ten pounds lighter. A lot of boys around town were envious of Bay because they couldn't figure out how one of the baddest women in Ponca City had ended up in her arms.

AquaNina was nothing short of Bena's heart. She would do anything for her love, up to and including providing a condo on the town's north side so the two of them could be alone like they were on this day. AquaNina still lived with her mother and father, as did Bay, but the two really were making plans to be together for life. For now, though, both were happy with the arrangements. They could get together over to the condo, make love freely, have dinner together and play board games. Their time alone was cherished and neither wanted what they had to end.

Bay lay back with AquaNina in her arms, the smooth sounds of Maxwell's song *This Woman's Work* playing low on the stereo, one of her favorite songs that she loved to hear AquaNina sing to her, as she reflected on the events that had transpired up until this point in her life.

Four—that was how many people eighteen year-old Bena Holland had killed to date—and she knew their names and could vividly recall each encounter. A dude who'd called himself Whip down in Vegas in August of 2001, a man named Isao Onishi and an officer by the name of Rodney Simmons in Seattle, Washington in April of 2002, and her latest victim as of August 2003, a woman named Phoebe Perez just two weeks ago over in Saint Louis.

Bay understood that she was a killer not only by occupation, but by nature, and truth be told, she loved the job and the life that went along with it. Killing people gave her power over others; she held the key to their future and she wasn't the type to set them free. The little girl who'd she'd eyed as she fled the murder scene shortly after killing Phoebe was a mere afterthought. Had her gun not jammed, whoever the little girl was, she would've gotten it too, just for being affiliated with the Perez sisters. Whoever was in the backseat of that Cadillac that night had escaped death for the same reason as the little girl Bay had eyed, but the main target had been eradicated and Bay knew full well that the hit she'd pulled was more than enough for the Chicago Gang because she'd taken a major player away from the family's enemies.

Phoebe Perez was a special life taken for Bay. She knew she'd gotten one of the people responsible for Lucky's downfall and hoped she'd done one of her mentors proud from his grave while bringing about some comfort to the surviving members of the Cernigliaro family.

The look on Phoebe's face as she moved about in desperation inside of that black Cadillac would forever be etched into Bena's psyche. Bay saw fear, a pleading for mercy and a sense of helplessness in Phoebe's eyes just before she squeezed the trigger and ended her life. The way her body twisted and turned on the front seat of the car and the horrifying screams would never be forgotten, nor would they be shared amongst those outside of the business. The life Bay led outside of Ponca City would be her big secret, a secret that only few in the family knew, and that was the way Bena Holland and all involved in what was going down outside of the ranch intended on keeping things as it was a rule that needed no repeating. If Bay had to tell it, AquaNina would never come to know the dark things she had done and was prepared to do should she be called upon.

After dressing, Bay and AquaNina headed over to Pizza Hut where AquaNina once worked in order to pick up several pizzas for the family back on the ranch. The two were enthralled in their own conversation, discussing how to further decorate their two story three bedroom condo and AqauNina possibly opening an antique shop in downtown Ponca City, when five young males entered the parlor.

Bay was facing the door and she caught sight of the boys, two blacks and three whites, as they entered. Bay knew the boys; she'd had words with them earlier in the summer at the movie theater when they hurled insults at her and AquaNina. Funny thing was, two of the white boys had tried to get with her and AquaNina, even offering money to sit and watch the two have sex in a hotel room on the west side of town. Bay despised the young men, and she knew they were going to start trouble the moment one of the boys tapped another's shoulder and pointed in her and AquaNina's direction.

AquaNina, meanwhile, as she sat with her back to the

entrance, was overjoyed as she expressed her desire to purchase a handcrafted wooden head and footboard for the queen-sized bed that was going to go inside one of the condo's spare bedrooms, totally unaware of the situation.

When Bay nodded her head towards the front door, AquaNina turned around and eyed the boys.

"Oh no," AquaNina sighed. "Bay, what are we gonna do now?" she complained.

"Let them be. Our pizzas almost ready so just chill."

To 'chill' was Bay's plan, but the five boys had other intentions. They boldly walked over to Bay and AquaNina's table and pulled up chairs. "We need a ride back over to Kaw Lake Park and you two gonna take us," one of the boys said, despite the fact the five of them had rolled up in an old, dark green pick-up truck.

Bay leaned back in her chair and looked off into the openness of the pizza parlor and laughed to herself. She would never underestimate anyone, but these guys were a true bunch of wannabe hard asses. The thing around Ponca City for those who had nothing else better to do with their life was to name themselves, go out in their little group, and pick on other people just for kicks. "What kind of pizza y'all ordered? Can we have a slice?" one of the boys asked.

"We ordered two meat lovers, a vegetarian and two pep—" AquaNina stopped talking when she saw Bay eyeing her with a blank stare.

"It's obvious who the man is in this here deal," another one of the boys said as he and his friends laughed lightly. "You be using a strap on when you fuck this one?"

"Why? You want me to use it on your punk ass, boy?" Bay retorted.

Amidst 'oohs' and 'ahhs' the young male knocked the salt, red pepper and Parmesan cheese shakers off the table and leaned back and smiled.

"Aww, man! Look what you did! Why you do that?" Bay mocked through laughter just as her and AquaNina's order was brought to the front. The two hopped up amid taunts, being called everything from clit lickers to freaks of nature as they left Pizza Hut.

Bay may have been laughing and brushing the boys off, but on the inside she was furious. Time and time again she'd taken taunts and had let it slide, but when she saw AquaNina in tears and heard her ask 'why people treat others that way', she now felt the desire to get some payback.

******

"If you don't move that funky plate of couscous from outta my face it's gone be trouble on the home front," fifteen year-old Koko told Spoonie as she sat out on the patio with Kimi and Tyke, the four sisters entertaining themselves by picking out clothes to order from a Neiman Marcus catalog.

"It's better than that meat lover pizza Bay bringin' here," eleven year-old Spoonie snapped as she poked out her tongue.

Koko picked up a bottle of hot sauce and said, "Stick it out again!"

Tyke poked her tongue out that moment and laughed.

"See," Kimi chimed in as she grabbed her cell phone. "Me and Koko asked Bay to get y'all a vegetarian pizza, but since y'all wanna be smart we gone cancel that. Bay pick up!"

"Wait!" Spoonie and Tyke said in unison.

"Ha! Apologize to the both of us." Koko said.

"I Apologize." Spoonie said.

"No, ma'am. We need y'all to say we apologize Misses Koko Dawkins and we apologize Misses Kimi Dawkins." Koko remarked.

"We just gone eat the couscous before we go through all that there," Tyke ended.

******

"It's so good...loving somebody...and somebody loves you back...and that's a fact...it's so good...needing somebody and somebody needs you back...say you got seventy thirty...you got

sixty forty...talkin' 'bout a fifty fifty love...yeah..."

Doss's private room was the place to be at this time for the men in the family. He and his father along with Mendoza, Dawk and Walee were hanging out in the room listening to music while playing chess and eating. Everybody with the exception of Walee was vibing to Teddy Pendergrass's song *When Somebody Loves You Back.*

Dawk could appreciate the music, and Teddy had taken Doss, back to the days when Naomi worked at the law firm in the Sears Tower in the early eighties. His music was hot during their time before the kids came along and good memories were being brought back.

DeeDee was reminiscing about Sharona Benson, his love who'd left him in his old age and Mendoza was enjoying the song while slicing into to a hearty T-bone steak and challenging Walee on the chess board.

"Ohhh. This is good stuff right here, let me tell you guys," Mendoza said as he chewed on a succulent piece of fat he'd cut from the meat.

"If you lived here my wife would make no money. You'd eat every last bull on the ranch." Doss remarked as he uncorked a bottle of red wine.

"All eight hundred of 'em I would." Mendoza replied through laughter as he slid his queen across the board.

"That's some of the wackest music I done heard in my life!" Walee snapped as he slid a rook into position. "Check, Mister Cernigliaro."

Mendoza sat his plate down and leaned forward and eyed the board. "How did I get myself into this situation?"

"Listening to that dumb music got you in trouble, man," Walee laughed as he stood up and cracked his knuckles.

"Grandson, someday you'll understand these songs we've been listening to all day," DeeDee chuckled. "When you're alone with your woman about to get it on? You would want some Teddy and not that b-bop you be listening to all the time."

"What would I do alone with a woman?" Walee asked sarcastically.

"If you have to ask, then you're not ready, son." Mendoza remarked as he moved his king out of harm's way.

"What's the big deal about females? Have any of you ever even seen a woman naked? Stuff hangin' off they chest and long nails that dig into your skin. And if they ain't clean they smell like rotten fish."

The men laughed aloud at that moment. "Where'd you learn all that?" DeeDee asked.

"Cable TV has it all. Real Sex on HBO tells me all I need to know. Sex is yucky."

"Sex is yucky?" Dawk repeated. "If I remember correctly, you used to take my Penthouse magazines and stay in one of the bathrooms for like an hour."

"I was doing research," Walee snapped. "You ain't have to say nothing about my research, Dawk."

"Yeah, research. It gets better when you study the real thing you know, il mio amico?" Mendoza said as he leaned back into the sofa cushions.

"I'm a be by myself. Women cost. And I ain't coming off none of the loot the family owns!"

"Oh you right about that," Doss chimed in as he poured up glasses of wine. "You most definitely gone pay for your own woman. Now, your grandfather can help you out with that because he done paid for nearly every woman in his life."

"And they were worth every dollar," DeeDee said proudly.

"That's why you be having a knot of money when you going see Oneika and Jordan, Dawk?" Walee asked.

"Stay out my business, boy. What's it to you?"

"It ain't nothin' to me. I'm just tryna learn how not to go broke that's all." Walee said as the men laughed aloud.

"It's gone be fun watching you come of age, son." DeeDee ended through laughter.

THE HOLLAND FAMILY SAGA

****

Meanwhile, upstairs inside the master suite, Francine was showing Naomi, Martha and Twiggy her implants. She'd had her double mastectomy in November of last year and had completed her plastic surgery several months earlier and was doing well, having beaten her bout with breast cancer.

"One hundred and seventy-three thousand dollars out of pocket for the entire process ladies," Francine said as she stood naked from the waist up in front of a large mirror.

At age seventy-three, Francine still had a nice physique. A few wrinkles around the eyes and the corners of her mouth with slightly greying hair, but she was in good shape for a woman her age and looked years younger. She wasn't afraid to share what she'd been through, either, and forty-seven year-old Naomi, and forty-three year-olds Martha and Twiggy were all concerned about breast cancer given their ages.

Francine discussed her fears, treatment and the feelings she'd encountered once she'd made the decision to have her breasts removed and gave valuable insight to the women. "My best advice is to you ladies is to have your mammograms done annually or bi-annually. Naomi, I don't know if you know if cancer runs in your family or not for certain, but it is a contributing factor. Along with diet and exercise of course."

"Serena discussed those things with me, but I never paid it any mind, really. Now that it has hit close to home I'll heed the warning."

"As you should. You all should. I went to the doctor often, but he didn't catch the cancer until the latter stages. I was angry over the mastectomy because I didn't feel like a woman afterwards. But these are better than the real ones. Look how they sit up," Francine said happily. "Mendoza can't keep his hands off them. He touches the fake ones more than the real ones, that's for sure."

"Okay, I'm done." Twiggy snapped as she walked away from the mirror.

"Did I upset you, Irene?" Francine asked as she turned

towards Twiggy. "Here, let me cover up and stop discussing my bedroom."

"No you didn't upset me, Francine. I'm just going…well, shit I can just ask you. I been a part of the itty-bitty-titty committee all my life. Can your doctor just throw a couple of thirty-four Cs up in here on GP?" Twiggy asked while pointing to her small breasts.

"Why not just go all out and get the forty-four double D max package like I got?" Naomi said as the woman burst into laughter.

"And tip your light ass over every time you lean forward," Martha ended through laughter.

****

Back down in Doss's private room, Walee was the only one still not understanding the music and the conversation over women. He was ready to hear some more Slick Rick and Ice Cube, something he could relate to at his young age, even if the raps were from the nineties. Tired of hearing the adults and his older brother tell him he just didn't know women and good music, Walee got up to leave the room.

"The game isn't finished, you know?" Mendoza called out.

"I had you beat, man," Walee said as he left the room. He was headed to the patio when he met Bay and AquaNina coming through the front door with stacks of pizza in their hands.

"'Bout time, man! Where y'all been?" Walee asked as he rubbed his hands together.

"Never mind. Where Dawk and T-top?" Bay asked as she marched pass the grand staircase.

"Dawk in daddy private room listenin' to garbage with grandpa 'nem. Tiva takin' a nap in her room. Why?"

"Never mind," Bay said as she hurried off into the kitchen and sat the pizzas on the counter. She then climbed the back stairs and walked into T-top's room and shook her from her slumber.

When Bay told Tiva what was up, she jumped from her bed, threw on an old pair of Jordan's and placed a baseball cap onto her head and the two headed back downstairs where they met Kimi, Koko, Spoonie and Tyke in the downstairs kitchen.

Tiva had already called Dawk on his cell phone and he met his sisters as they were headed towards the front door. "Y'all ready?" he asked.

"Where y'all goin'?" Kimi as she followed her siblings towards the front door.

"Bay, no!" AquaNina cried, realizing what was about to go down.

"'Nina they done tried us for the last time! You take it if you want, but I'm not puttin' up with it!"

"Oooh!" Koko snapped. "Them five boys got at y'all again?"

"Damn straight! They at Pizza Hut right now and we goin' back over there and whip that ass!" Bay assured.

Kimi and Koko knew a couple of the boys that hung out in the group personally and had a vendetta out on them. The boys had asked the twins to have sex one day while they were at Spoonie and Tyke's ball game a few months back and both were insulted and appalled. The boys, after being read their rights by Kimi and Koko, spread a rumor around the park and on the west side of town that the two gave it up easy. Ever since then Kimi and Koko had been looking for some get back. The day had finally arrived and they were overjoyed.

"Let me get my purse," Kimi quipped happily as she trotted up the stairs.

"Whoever ain't in the car when I pull off gettin' left so hurry up," Bay said as she ran towards the front door.

"They goin' fight! Tyke, come on!" Spoonie said through a wide smile as she grabbed a slice of vegetarian pizza and ran and caught up with her oldest sisters and brother.

While the adults were talking the day away, another portion of the Holland-Dawkins clan was preparing to ride into town and cause some major conflict. The kids were emerging from the house at random, each eager to claim a seat inside Bay's ride in order to partake in the upcoming festivities. And everybody had his or her own reason for riding—Bay, who'd had it up to her neck with the harassment, Tiva, who would ride side by side with her twin to the depths of hell and back. Dawk, for added muscle and to make sure his sisters handled their business, Kimi and Koko, mad at two of the boys for asking them for their precious kitty cats and spreading a rumor, and then there was Spoonie and Tyke, who were going along just for the sheer thrill of it all.

Walee wanted to go, but he was in the kitchen trying to keep AquaNina from going hysterical. She was crying and worried Bay was going to get hurt or worse and he was doing his best to calm his sister's girlfriend down and prevent her from walking down the hall that led to his father's private room.

"Listen to me!" Walee yelled as he slapped his hands together and stomped his feet. "You can't go around here crying and carrying on because you gone get Bay and everybody else in trouble. Shut up about it!"

"You shut up, Walee! Bena gone go and get herself and everybody else in trouble! Mister Dawkins!" AquaNina yelled as she ran out of the kitchen.

Walee ran up on AquaNina and turned her around. "If you tell my daddy about this? I'm gone tell Bay I saw you with another girl while she was up in Chicago!"

AquaNina paused at that moment. "That's a lie and you know it," she cried as her lips trembled. "I would never do that to Bena."

"Bay don't know that. She told me to keep an eye on you and she's gonna believe everything I say."

"Why would you do that to me?"

"Why would you do what you're about to do to Bay?"

"Because I care about her, Walee!"

"If you cared you'd let this go down, already." Walee snapped, silencing AquaNina for the moment.

THE HOLLAND FAMILY SAGA

Back outside in front of Ponderosa, Bay had just popped the trunk on her ride. "I got two bumper jacks and one of Spoonie and Tyke's aluminum baseball bats back here," she said as she rummaged through the rear of the vehicle.

"I want the bat!" Kimi and Koko said in unison.

"Nahhh, I got the bat," Dawk said. "Tiva take this tire rod. Here go the other one, Bay. Let's ride."

Walee ran to front door and saw Bay peeling out with his siblings in Bay's ride and he threw his hands up. He'd missed his opportunity, so he went back into the home and searched for AquaNina.

Bay had gotten her grandfather's DeeDee car for her eighteenth birthday and had just gotten it out of a detail shop in Oklahoma City a day after she'd arrived back on the ranch. The 1972 four door Lincoln Continental was repainted lightgrey like DeeDee had when he drove it, and Bay had gotten a Crutchfield sound system and four 7" TV monitors with two in the headrest and two in the visor.

The interior was white plush leather and Bay had placed 26" chrome Assassinator rims on the car. She had also placed suicide doors on the car. When all four doors were open the car looked as if it had wings, but what everybody loved most about Bay's car was the rims. The rims on the old Lincoln made the long, sleek, dark-tinted gangster whip look as if it was being pulled on a conveyor belt when it rode down the highway because the rims never moved.

Bay's car skated smoothly across the fresh asphalt leading off the property, Tiva in the front seat next to her and Dawk on the passenger side. Kimi, Koko, Spoonie and Tyke were bunched up in the back seat as the clan sped off the land where Bay made a right turn onto the road leading back into to town.

"For all the lies they told I'm gone be sure to get me some licks in today!" Koko yelled from the back seat as Bay sped back to town.

"I never liked them punks anyway," Dawk said as he flipped though Bena's CD collection in search of some music.

"They been messing with Bay and 'Nina for a while now. They got it comin'," Tyke snapped.

"What y'all small behinds gonna do?" Kimi asked.

"If Tiva give us the bat we'll show you." Spoonie answered.

"Y'all just stay out the way, Spoonie and Tyke. We got this here," Tiva snapped as Bay made a right turn onto Highway 60 and headed west towards town.

When the bass from Project Pat's song *Gorilla Pimp* came across the speakers, the entire clan went into a frenzy.

"I'm gone split a bitch head to the white meat!" Tiva yelled over the music.

Mary was at her produce stand with Dimples. Her business was filled with customers when she saw and heard Bay's car barreling down the highway with Dawk hanging out the passenger side window holding onto a baseball bat and Kimi leaning out the back passenger side window yelling aloud. The engine on the car was revved up high with its dual exhaust pipes wide open and it was cutting into the wind like a hot knife through butter.

"Marrryyyyyy!" Kimi sang aloud. "Be right back for some Granny Smith apples, Auntie!"

"Here the part! Here the good part come!" Koko yelled as the group prepared themselves for the upcoming chorus they were waiting to sing all but two words…

"…*I'm gorilla on a hoe…*"

"Dig that," all seven siblings yelled aloud as the car cruised down the highway.

"*I'm a pimp nigga you ain't know…*"

"Dig that," they all screamed in unison.

"*I'm a mack man onna stroll…*"

"Dig that!"

"*I'm out here out tryna break a hoe…*"

"Dig that," the siblings all yelled as Bay's car bounced onto

Kaw Lake Bridge with the music steadily thumping.

Siloam was out on the park with Jane Dow, the band she was now managing and she, too, had seen and heard Bay's car glide by at a high rate of speed headed into town with loud music playing. *"What are they up to,"* Siloam wondered as she grabbed her cell phone.

Bay's cell phone soon began vibrating. She looked and saw Mary's number and sent it to voice mail. Dawk did the same thing to Siloam as the clan approached the intersections of Highway 60 and Highway 77, a major intersection therein town.

Bay was in the right lane preparing to make a right turn when she spotted the boys' dark green pickup truck making a left turn off of Highway 77 onto Highway 60 headed east towards Kaw Lake Park.

"They tryna get away!" Bay yelled as she hit the gas.

"Whoa!" Dawk yelled as he sat up in his seat.

"This here ain't legal. We ain't legal right now. Watch out for the police. Where the, where the police?" Tiva asked cautiously as she held onto the dash, watching for oncoming traffic.

"They gettin' away!" Kimi yelled.

"I see 'em! They going towards Kaw Lake!" Tyke yelled.

"Back it up! Back it up," Dawk said calmly as he eyed the traffic. "She just learnin' how to drive, y'all!" he yelled aloud to onlookers. "Be cool, we workin' it out!"

Bay had ignored all the traffic signals, and from the right lane, she'd made a wide U-Turn, crossing three lanes of traffic on her left side in an attempt to turn the car around in order to head east. Cars that were approaching from the north and south, cars whose drivers actually had the right of way, had to slam on their brakes to avoid a wreck as they blew their horns frantically. People headed east watched as the long Lincoln held up traffic in all directions, Bay trying to right the car to give chase.

Dawk was hanging out the window, bat still in his hands, eyeing the oncoming traffic as if they had a problem with what his sister was doing as they blew their horns impatiently. "We be done here in a minute! Chill the hell out!" he yelled aloud as Bay went from reverse to forward repeatedly, jerking the car violently while trying to straighten out the elongated vehicle. Even with all the room allotted, Bay still had to back the long Lincoln up several times before she was able to peel out after her intended victims.

By now the five boys knew what they were up against. One of the three boys sitting in the back of the pickup began yelling aloud, "Here they come! It's all of 'em!"

The driver of the pickup sped up as he headed towards Kaw Lake Bridge, but by now Bay was hot on his tail. Scared of retribution, the driver pulled into Mary's produce stand to alert Mary of her family's intent, but that did little to stop what was about to go down.

Bay wheeled in right behind the boys and all seven siblings hopped out the car and ran towards the boys, who were running towards Mary. "Miss Mary we was just playin'!"

"Playin' what? What's going on here?" Mary questioned as she stepped from behind one of her wooden bins.

None of the boys answered when they saw Dawk, Tiva and Bay running their way, Bay and T-top gripping tire rods. Customers began scattering through the parking lot headed for their cars as the five boys broke out running in different directions.

Dawk jumped on the back of the oldest boy, a nineteen year-old black guy named Tonto Jamison, who'd been Tiva's first boyfriend, and took him down. He punched Tonto in the back of the head and stood up and began stomping his back. "My sister something to play with, boy?" he yelled aloud as he continued stomping Tonto's back.

Bay and Tiva had cornered another one of the boys in the gravel parking lot near the open road and both were going in something fierce. Bay had the seventeen year-old in the headlock, preventing him from moving as Tiva pounded his body with her fists. "You—don't—fuck—with the—Holland family—like that bitch!" T-top said as she punched the boy in his rib cage repeatedly.

Kimi and Koko, meanwhile, were getting the best of one of the other boys. Together, Naomi's middle daughters couldn't be beat. They were more than enough with their heavy hands. They were slapping the fifteen year-old around like he was their own child. "You wanna tell people you slept with me, boy?" Kimi asked. "Say you lyin'!" she added as she grabbed the boy's braids and yanked him forward while Koko beat his back.

"Say it!" Koko yelled as her heavy hands landed on the boys back, producing hollowed sounds that knocked wind from the teenager. "Say you was lyin'!"

They youngster was trying to speak, but Kimi began kneeing him in the stomach, sending him down to the gravel. He was calling out for help as best he could as customers soon began gaining control of the melee along with Mary.

"Why you runnin'? Get back here!" Tyke yelled as she and Spoonie chased another fifteen year-old boy through the shaded aisles of their aunt's produce stand, Tyke gripping her aluminum baseball bat.

The frightened youngster was knocking over racks of produce as he made a hasty retreat. He really had nothing to fear because Spoonie and Tyke were paper thin, but he knew they played softball and could swing a bat so he wasn't willing to challenge the youngest of the group. Tired and out of breath, the youngster fell up against a bin off bananas and fell onto the concrete under the wooden canopy. Spoonie and Tyke went stood over the boy and eyed one another as he lay on his back screaming out for help.

"What now?" Tyke asked.

"We should hit 'em one time with the bat." Spoonie said.

"Okay," Tyke responded as she raised the bat into the air.

Just then, Dimples ran up and grabbed Tyke's arm. "You tryna kill somebody, Sinopa? What the hell done got into y'all today?" she yelled.

By then, the entire family back over to Ponderosa had made it over to Mary's produce stand as AquaNina had ignored Walee and reported the matter to Doss. A couple of state troopers and eight Kay County Deputies were on hand to sort out the incident. Fights were common in the city, and the parties involved always knew one another, such as was the case on this hit summer day in August of 2003.

The authorities all knew and respected the Holland-Dawkins family, and upon hearing the entire story, no citations were issued, namely because Bay had filed a sexual harassment complaint against Tonto, the oldest of the five boys. She'd used the law to her advantage, advice given to her by her mother that had earned her a reprieve on this day.

Doss would later counsel his oldest three and remind them of the business they were involved in and incidents like this one was not to be tolerated and had to be avoided at all cost. The big three had to understand that the people in Ponca City weren't of their caliber and they shouldn't stoop down to their level. It was an experience that was to never be repeated again was the understanding, but the adults understood the kids' frustration and willingness to go to bat for Bay so-to-speak. No punishments were issued, but the remainder of the weekend, Dawk, Bay and T-top had to undergo counsel from their father, grandfather and Mendoza and they would all take heed.

With that aside, the siblings had all earned their respect; and after what was deemed the Produce Stand Powwow—it was understood by all around town that if you messed with one Holland-Dawkins sibling—you messed with them all. And if people around town didn't understand that fact, they'd best be prepared to face the repercussions of their actions.

CHAPTER NINETEEN
JUST ANOTHER EXECUTION

It was now September of 2003, a month after the melee in Ponca City. Things had returned to normal for the Holland-Dawkins family, but six hundred miles to the west, trouble was brewing.

Smoldering ash billowing up from the right side of *The Royal Flush* in downtown Denver left little to Asa Spade's imagination as to what'd happened to his night club. It took three firefighter units to extinguish the flames, but not before half the club was destroyed. Preliminary investigations were pointing to arson, and all roads, for Asa, were leading back to Desiree Abbadando. She'd been off the scene for a while, avoiding *Glitz*, but she'd struck with a vengeance that left Asa without a base of operations.

On top of that, traffic in Shorter Arms was at a snail's pace because of the numerous shootouts and buyers were beginning to pull away from Asa Spade and his crew. This faction of the organization was up to its neck on the losing end of a battle that was taking a toll on profits and the problem had to be rectified before Asa Spade found himself shutdown completely. Without much by way of muscle, Asa decided it was time to put his pride aside and make a phone call.

****

Carmella sat inside her home in Cherry Creek with Desiree and Q-man, the three of them laughing over the fact that they'd burned Asa's club the night before. Carmella knew exactly what she was doing in Colorado. Her home may have been hit once, but she knew Asa Spade and his crew were under the impression that it was Desiree who was running things in the city and that's the way she wanted things to go so she could remain behind the scenes, doing just as her mother had suggested. She may have been on the losing end of the battle in Saint Louis by early September of 2003, but she was kicking ass in Denver, Colorado and forcing the competition off the scene. Satisfied that she couldn't be touched, Carmella began planning a birthday party next month for Desiree that was to be held inside of *Glitz*.

"Everybody will be at your party, Desiree. My girl Toodie from Saint Louis will join us too. Q-man? You and your boys coming back for the celebration?" Carmella asked before she downed a shot of Jose Cuervo.

"We be in. Won't you set us up with some hot Mexican pussy when we come down?"

"We can swing that, pa-pi," Desiree said as she got up and sat in Carmella's lap. "But the birthday girl and her host is most certainly off limits."

Q-man just stared at the two women as he rolled a blunt. They were all out sexy, but the way they swung kept them just out of reach. "Give me a show," he said, deciding to try his luck.

Carmella laughed and leaned forward and tongued Desiree hard. "How much are you willing to pay, Q-man?" she then asked as she backed away laughing.

"Shiit, we got all this champagne and weed sponsored by my ass and we just kicking back celebrating another victory. Come on, show a man some action," Q-man said as he leaned back, took a toke and gripped the crotch on his baggy jeans.

Carmella was an exhibitionist at heart. She loved people watching her have sex. "I do something, just a little something for you Q-man, because I like your style," she said as she patted Desiree's ass to get her to ease up from her lap. Carmella then stood and pulled up her white all-in-one dress, revealing her bald-shaven vagina as she wore no panties, and spread her pussy lips. "Lick my clit, Desi," she said sexily as Q-man stood and blew her a shotgun.

While going down on Carmella, Desiree tugged on the zipper of Q-man's jeans. "I wanna taste this, Carmella. Can I taste this?" Desiree pleaded.

"She's feeling frisky, Bahdoon," Carmella said through a smile. "You're in luck, amigo. Let's all undress and go to the Jacuzzi then if we're going to do this thing."

"That's that shit I'm talking about," Q-man said as he grabbed the weed, a couple of bottles of champagne and followed Carmella and Desiree towards the Jacuzzi in the master bedroom, where the three would spend a great portion of the day smoking, drinking and sexing.

****

Eighteen year-old Bena Holland was out on the southern portion of the Holland Ranch with a Nikon D70 camera with a telephoto zoom in lens. She was taking pictures of the land her mother was attempting to purchase as Walee, Spoonie and Tyke milled around in the canal down below.

It was now late September of 2003, a couple of weeks after Asa Spade's club had been set ablaze. A week earlier, Finland Xavier had traveled to Seattle and met up with Asa Spade and JunJie and had been handed down another contract on a woman by the name of Desiree Abbadando. Asa Spade had tried to kill the woman himself shortly after his club was burned, but he couldn't get close to Desiree, who was now being guarded by several men who were only known as the Somalis.

Asa Spade was the type of man who went after the head of the snake, and as far as he knew, Desiree was at the helm of the crew he was fighting against. Asa never understood the fact that it was someone behind Desiree who was actually pulling the strings, however, but the job was now in the hands of the Chicago Gang, a crew of professional killers who were unknowingly on the verge of exposing Carmella and bringing the on-going war to end once and for all.

Bay continued snapping away with her camera until she ran out of film and returned to Ponderosa. She entered a dark room she had set up where the film was slowly developed and the pictures were hung out to dry. The photos were okay, but there was room for improvement in areas of focus was Bay's assessment.

Tiva Holland, meanwhile, was out behind the stockyards practicing shooting targets as Kimi and Koko milled around, occasionally firing off a twelve gauge shot gun. T-top was to take the shot on Desiree during the hit, a shot in which she couldn't miss because Desiree would surely go into hiding once more. Five-hundred thousand dollars was on the line for the crew so accuracy was of the utmost importance.

Bay and Tiva practiced the remainder of the month, Bay learning to use the camera, and T-top honing her shooting skills, and by the second week of October, they were satisfied that they were ready for their next job. They left a week before Halloween under the guise of heading to Chicago to help their father with his warehouse business, but they'd actually met up with Dawk and Junior in Denver to complete their job.

The first few nights were unsuccessful. Desiree wasn't on the scene outside of *Glitz* and going into the club for further surveillance was too risky. The crew regrouped and emerged on the fourth night and snow began falling, a heavy snow that was to be expected, but unwelcomed nonetheless. When Desiree finally appeared, she was surrounded by the Somalis and two unknown women as she approached the front entrance to the club.

"Okay, ladies," Junior said lowly as he started the F-150 the crew was riding in, "our mark is on the premises, so go do your thing. We got you covered down here on the ground."

Bay and Tiva exited the vehicle that was parked in an alleyway across the street and down the block from the corner from the club and climbed a snow-covered ladder that led to the roof of a small dentistry that gave them a perfect vantage point to see their mark. Dressed in all black leather, including black trench coats and leather boots, the twins crept across the snow-covered roof and headed for the building's ledge where Tiva set up her bi-pod and the two lay in wait.

Back inside *Glitz*, Desiree was having the time of her life. She'd been treated like a queen by Carmella, the two drinking the best of champagne and partying with the crowd in celebration of Desiree's twenty-eighth birthday. The two had worked themselves up into a sexual frenzy atop their balcony overlooking the shark tank and the club, and soon had to escort partygoers from the loft in order to be alone.

"Come on, people," Carmella yelled over the music as she walked towards the double doors. "You can finish partying downstairs!"

"I know what's about to happen. Can me and my boys stay and watch?" Q-man asked, reminiscing about the time he'd spent with the two woman the previous month.

"Q-man, you leave with everybody else. Take your boys with you," Carmella said through laughter. "This is our time."

"You said you was gone hook a brother with some of that Spanish cat, though."

"All them senoritas down there? You better put your game face on and go fuck somebody!" Carmella snapped as she escorted Q-man and his crew towards the doors leading to the balcony.

Once Carmella locked the door leading to the balcony, she and Desiree moved towards the office, gripping and kissing one another hungrily as they entered the room. Desiree leaned up against the large desk, stripped and walked seductively towards Carmella, who was sitting on the soft leather couch inside the cozy domain. Desiree then began purring and meowing like a hungry cat as she sunk to her knees in the middle of the floor. She looked sexy to Carmella, her dark eyes boring into her skull, her taut ass swaying side to side and her pert breasts with hardened nipples sitting up close to her body as she crawled over to her lover.

Carmella held her legs wide and tilted her ass up. "Kiss me all over my little kitten. God, I love this little game we play," she moaned just before Desiree extended her tongue and dove straight into Carmella's vagina and began sucking hard.

Carmella placed her arms inside her thighs, holding them up in the air as she bounced up and down. Desiree tongue-fucked Carmella's vagina relentlessly, moaning in delight, happy to be servicing her lover. Carmella soon began rolling Desiree's head and she quickly got the message and rolled her entire face over Carmella's vagina causing Carmella to begin thrusting her hips up and down.

"You want me to fuck your face, Desi? There, I'm fucking your face! How's it feel, baby?"

Desiree called out to Carmella, moaning her name before rising up from between her thighs and the two women locked lips, Carmella tasting her own juices on Desiree's tongue. Desiree then stood up and Carmella turned her around and smacked her ass hard and bent her at the waist, positioning her over the couch. She licked Desiree from behind for several minutes and backed away from her and stood up.

"*Tengo una buen cumpleaños sorpresa para ti, nena.*" (I have a nice birthday surprise for you, baby.) Carmella said as she reached under the couch and pulled out a strap-on dildo. She ordered Desiree to remain with her ass in the air and hands planted to the sofa as she garnished the sex toy.

Carmella stepped forth and rubbed Desiree's back gently as she slid the huge dildo into her moistened vagina and began to slowly piston in and out. She leaned back and looked down and could see Desiree's tight pink vaginal lips being pulled back and pushed in by her dildo as she stroked her and the sight was driving her wild. Before long, Carmella was fucking Desiree like a woman possessed as she smacked her ass cheeks. She stroked her for all she was worth while working up a sweat, fucking Desiree as if the strap-on she wore was a real penis.

"*Por favor, cariño, me llevas que no.*" (Please baby, you wearing me out I can't.) Desiree moaned deeply, her mouth hanging open and her hair now in disarray as Carmella took her from behind.

"I'm right there. I am going to fuck you until I come," Carmella grunted through closed eyes as she pummeled Desiree. "Come with me, Desi," she moaned as her face contorted. "I'm fucking coming. I'm coming!"

Desiree moaned and began throwing her hips back at Carmella. *"Cógeme fuerte! Es difícil!"* (Fuck me hard! Fuck it!) Desiree yelled like a woman possessed.

Carmella threw her head back, arched her back, and let go of a loud guttural groan as her entire body began convulsing. Both women collapsed beside one another in complete satisfaction.

Desiree turned over, pulled Carmella on top of her and the two kissed passionately. "I can't move no further, Carmella. You make me feel so good, ma-mi!" Desiree said with a chuckle.

"I think I love you, my little kitten." Carmella remarked through panting breath as she smiled.

"Where'd you get that dildo?"

"Bought it earlier today."

"I was surprised—but I liked it. Will you fuck me again later, please?"

"You don't have to ask, Desiree," Carmella said lovingly. "Letss shower and mingle some more downstairs." she ended.

****

"What's the deal over in the Lou?" Q-man asked Toodie as two sat at the bar drinking Coronas and chasing it with Patron on the first floor of *Glitz*.

"We chilling. Since Phoebe died ain't been much."

"I know you ain't gone let them folks over in Saint Charles get away with killing your sister."

"It ain't like we ain't be trying, Q-man. Since that lick we pulled over there them mutherfuckas been hard to get next to."

"You know what you gotta do, right?"

"What I gotta do?"

"You need to see if you can get somebody to flip. Find a weak mutherfucka out they crew and get 'em to give you something you can use."

"They ain't going for that play. That crew is jam tight."

"What I do know about that click is the fact that they have a structure. They put people in position of power."

"That's why I say ain't nobody over there going for that shit."

"See? That's where you wrong," Q-man said as he lit up a Black & Mild cigar over 50 Cent's song *In Da Club*. "When a crew have bosses? It's always somebody jealous looking to move somebody out of position. Just something to think about. So, you gone let a real nigga get that pussy tonight or what?"

"We have bosses in our crew, too, Q-man," Toodie said over the music as she poured herself another shot of tequila. "I appreciate your insight and all, but as far as pussy is concerned? The bosses in this crew don't rock like that."

"Some of y'all do." Q-man said as he reached over and poured himself a shot of Patron.

Toodie downed her shot glass of tequila and laughed lowly. "They made you sip champagne outta both of they ass cracks in that Jacuzzi. Sat they pussy on your face and came in your mouth back to back so don't think you that mutherfucka that's gettin' pussy on the slick and gone run through the whole crew. This may be a man's game, but the women is running everything," she said as she took the Black & Mild cigar from Q-man's lips and took a puff. "Hmm," she said as she looked at the tip of the cigar and frowned, "this taste like asshole."

"How the fuck you know how it taste then?" Q-man asked as Toodie got up from her bar stool.

"Dueces!" Toodie ended as she disappeared into the crowd.

"Carmella ain't have to tell a man business like that, my dudes." Q-man told his cohorts, who were laughing over

Toodie's last remark. "Well, at least I fucked the bitches," he spat in defense of himself.

****

Fireworks were bursting into the cold air as *Club Glitz* began emptying out at 2:30 in the morning. Junior and Dawk sat watching the festivities from the F-150 as clubbers exited the building and stood out in the street and on the curb looking up into the air. The Hispanics knew how to throw a party in their eyes. The club had stayed pack even though it was a crisp twenty-three degrees out.

"This guy Asa Spade says there may be more people involved in this thing you know?" Junior told Dawk.

"I know. It has to be more people than just the ones we know of. This crew here nearly shut that man entire operation down from what I hear." Dawk replied as he watched the crowd spill out into the area in front of the club.

"This shit has all the trademarks of what went down with us and that Mexican gang back in Saint Louis." Junior said.

"Hallmarks," Dawk replied..

"Say what?"

"The right word is hallmark not trademark."

"Since when you decided to get all technical and shit?" Junior chuckled as he rested his left arm on the back of the seat.

"My girl Oneika must be rubbing off on me," Dawk chuckled. "She taking classes in college back in town and ever since then she been correcting my speech."

"You like that broad?"

"She, she good for me, man. Don't dip in my biz, keep a clean apartment I got her set up in back in the Ponc and she know how to cook."

"How that sex game?"

"I ain't answering that," Dawk laughed lowly.

"Why?"

"Because you gone get to talkin' about you and T-top and don't care to hear that."

Junior laughed and shoved Dawk's shoulder. "I would never rub that in your face, man. What's up with Jordan? The other chick you was dealing with?"

"Jordan ass a straight up head case. She too easy, man. She do everything I say without question. It's like she can't think for herself and that right there turns me off."

"Hmm," Junior said through closed lips. "A compassionate pimp. There's a new one."

"I'm not a pimp, man." Dawk smirked.

"You may not see it, but you and Walee are becoming you twos' grandfather. Like it or not."

"I just have to be careful who I deal with, ya' dig? And Jordan crazy ass could get a man entire spot blowed up. I ain't going out like that. Oneika the truth, me and her might be something later on down the road if she grow a little more."

"What you gone do with her? Jordan I mean?"

"I might pass her down to Walee."

"See? You pimping."

"Nahh, I just know Jordan stupid enough to go along with it," Dawk said through light laughter. "A real woman wouldn't let me do what I do to her. And it's for that reason that I'm reluctant about Oneika. I mean, she allow me to sleep with Jordan and she know it. Hell, she join in most times. It'll work itself out in time I guess."

"All things do, il mio amico. But back to the topic, this does have the, the hallmarks of what we going through in Saint Louis with what's happened to this guy Asa Spade. He fighting Mexicans, we fighting Mexicans. I'm just saying. Could be an angle."

"You right. You right. But it's a lot of Mexican clicks out here that move weight and some of 'em want it all to themselves."

"True that. But it's a small world, il mio amico." Junior ended as fireworks began erupting overhead.

****

"Damn they is throwing down out here in Denver," Bay said as she and her twin eyed the fireworks display with admiration, Bay occasionally snapping photos of the exploding pyrotechnics.

"A nice show it is. But we gone make some fireworks of our own once this girl show her face." Tiva responded as she looked through her night vision scope and focused in on the club's main entrance.

"*New Orleans...come on and raise up....take your shirt off... twist it 'round your head spin it like a helicopter...Saint Louis...come and raise up...this one's for you...this one for who...us, us, us...*" Desiree had just been handed a fresh bottle of Cristal as Petey Pablo's song *Raise Up* blared loudly over the speakers of the emptying club as she led the way towards the front doors.

"*Feliz cumpleanos! Feliz cumpleanos!*" (Happy birthday! Happy birthday!) was yelled repeatedly as Desiree emerged from the club dressed in a red mink coat and matching mink hat and red knee-length leather boots. She led the way out onto the sidewalk, floor showing and show-boating while throwing hundred dollar bills in the air. Clubbers were all around, some yelling and scrambling for the money as Desiree danced around at the foot of the curb.

Tiva, meanwhile, now had the mark in her crosshairs. She was on bended knee with her Dragunov set up and ready to shoot while Bay snapped pictures of the people surrounding Desiree. "I'm ready to shoot. You got enough pictures? 'Cause they all gone scatter once this woman go down."

"Yeah. We good," Bay answered as she fired off rapid shots with her camera. Just then, a woman caught Bay's eye through the zoom-in lens and she'd grown wide-eyed because she recognized the woman, but before she could utter a word, Tiva had squeezed the trigger.

Desiree was just about to throw another stack of hundred dollar bills into the air when a bullet slashed through the right side of her face and exited the bottom left side of her skull. She collapsed to the ground, still clutching money and was dead before she'd even stretched out completely on the snow-covered sidewalk.

Only Carmella, who was standing right beside Desiree, knew what was going down as other clubbers began laughing, believing Desiree had slipped on the frozen sidewalk.

"*Ella golpeo! Ella ha galpeado!*" (She hit! She's been hit!) Carmella yelled hysterically over the music as she knelt down before Desiree as scooped her head up into her arms. "No, Desi! Desi?"

A crowd soon surrounded Carmella and when club patrons realized Desiree had been shot, some began running away; others went about grabbing money up off the ground, totally unconcerned about Desiree being shot.

Back atop the roof, Bay and Tiva were gathering their items.

"We got a problem here, T-top," Bay said in a hurried tone.

"What's the matter? The police down there don't even know where we at."

"That's not it," Bay responded. "I saw Toodie Perez out there. Whoever pulling the strings behind Desiree is running both the crew here in Denver and the one back in Saint Louis. Our family and Asa Spade are fighting the same click."

CHAPTER TWENTY
A MEETING OF THE MINDS

A sleek white limousine pulled up before *Eastside Bar* and JunJie Maruyama exited with Asa Spade and Dougie following close behind. The men were greeted by Junior and Finland and escorted inside the bar. It was the first week of December 2003, five weeks after the hit on Desiree Abbadando and the war between the three factions was ratcheting up again.

Carmella had killed three more of Asa's crew shortly after the hit on Desiree, nearly depleting him of soldiers, and she now had Q-man and his crew riding through Saint Charles periodically, but it was easier to bust off shots outside of Fort Knox. With so much tension in the air and danger lurking about, Cicero was the best place for the bosses to hold a power meeting.

Once inside, JunJie and his clan were escorted to the back of the bar where Doss, DeeDee and Mendoza were all waiting.

"Asa Spade," Doss said as he stood up and greeted the man, "I've heard a lot of good things about you, brother."

Doss's first impression of Asa Spade was that of a man with strong character. A hustler by nature and a man dedicated to crew and business. A stand up guy. He liked him right away.

"I heard a lot about you as well, Doss, although your name and face has been in anonymity until this day," Asa replied through a smile.

Asa Spade's first impression of Doss was one of respect. Asa had pimped women, bodied a few men in his time, but here was this killer-for-hire that actually murdered people for a living, stone-faced, yet just as calm and inviting as an undisturbed body of water. Doss was a man's man in Asa's eyes. Someone he could easily trust and the polar opposite of Finland Xavier. He liked him from the start.

"That job in Vegas changed my life. I appreciate what you and your crew did for me, Doss," Asa remarked, breaking the brief moment of silence.

"It was just a job that needed doing. Now, given this photo of Toodie taken the night Desiree was hit, we all seem to be battling the same enemy in two different cities."

"Seems like it. The only problem is we don't know who's pulling the strings." Asa replied as he ran his hand across his wavy head of hair.

"You're right, but we have some leads," Doss said as he handed Asa a stack of photographs that Bay had developed back on the ranch shortly after the hit on Desiree. "Recognize anybody else besides Desiree?"

Asa gestured his hands towards the table before him, requesting permission to sit. Doss reciprocated by stepping aside to allow Asa, JunJie and Dougie to have access to the booth.

Once the men were situated, Asa looked the pictures over and acknowledged one of the people, a man only known as the Somali.

Dougie grabbed the photos and eyed them and recognized one person right away. "This woman here was in the house the night we went after Desiree," he said as he pointed to Carmella's picture.

"Gentlemen," JunJie said cordially, "since the hit on Desiree Abbadando, the bloodshed has escalated in Denver and I've have to decrease shipments to that city. This war is now interfering with our business in a most unfortunate way."

"That we agree on, and things have gotten a lot more violent in Saint Louis ever since we loss three of our people in that fake drug bust last year." Doss remarked.

"Do you know who it is that you're looking for, Doss?" JunJie asked.

"Yeah, we do. Not too long before Lucky passed away, he said a woman by the name of Carmella was in on that job. We don't know her last name, but we do know she's a Colombian."

"A Colombian named Carmella?" JunJie asked as he raised his eyebrows.

"Yeah. You know this person?" DeeDee asked.

"I've heard the name before," JunJie replied, a little intrigued. "My guy south of the border mentioned to me once upon a time that he was angry at a Colombian named Carmella Lapiente` for killing nine people he did business with."

"We may be staring at Carmella," Asa Spade remarked, as he tapped the photograph.

"Quite possibly, Asa," JunJie replied. "We may very well be on to something here, but let us not jump the gun. Let me see those photographs if you don't mind, Mister Doss."

JunJie had remained out-of-the-loop the duration of the war, but now that his money was being interfered with, he felt a need to get involved directly and become more hands on with the matter in order to help rectify and bring about an end to the bloodshed. In his mind, the Chicago Gang was strong enough to hold their own; Asa Spade's crew, however, had been weakened by the war and was on the verge of total collapse.

"What I am going to do is take these photographs and have my friend down south look over them. I'm suspecting that this woman here," JunJie said as he pointed to an image of Carmella, "I'm suspecting that this woman may be a woman by the name of Carmella Lapiente`. If it is so, then we have a bigger problem than we've suspected."

"How so?" Doss asked.

"If this woman is able to eradicate nine respected drug dealers in Mexico, stand up to our associate south of the border and wage a war in two cities here in America, then she has plenty power."

Mendoza couldn't help but to smile. "Mister Maruyama? You tellin' me we got the name and the face of the person responsible for killing my son and his wife and our guy down south knows this person?"

"I can't confirm, Mister Cernigliaro, but let me look into this for you all and I'll get back in touch upon my return. I'll have to make a trip abroad and get in touch with my associate and see if he can finger the woman in the photo as being that of Carmella. In the meantime, I think it's best we all take a short hiatus until we can put all the pieces together. Everybody has money put back to weather the storm until next year I assume?"

"We're comfortable," Mendoza replied. "You just make sure you notify us once you hear anything be it good or bad."

"I'm a man of word, Mister Cernigliaro. And we haven't been doing business all these years for me not to come through."

"I meant no offense. But this war has taken a toll on both crews and it must end."

"Trust me, Mister Cernigliaro, we'll get to the bottom of this. I'll get you your information concerning Carmella Lapiente`. You and your family work on finding those Somalis."

The Chicago Gang and Asa Spade's crew were slowly putting the pieces together. Still, they weren't sure exactly who they were fighting against. After a leisurely dinner where further business was discussed, JunJie made his way back to his private jet in preparation for a trip abroad to meet one of the most powerful men involved in the American drug trade.

CHAPTER TWENTY-ONE
THE BOSS OF BOSSES

It took several weeks of careful maneuvering and diligent flight planning in order for JunJie to take a flight out of the country, but by early January of 2004, he was able to garner the necessary documents and forge flight plans in order to make the trip. After refueling in San Diego, the pilots crossed over into Mexican air space and made their way down to South America where they landed on a small air strip just outside of the city of Porlamar on Margarita Island.

Porlamar is a small island located on the eastern side of the country of Venezuela and is surrounded by the Caribbean Sea. The town was once a small fishing village until it gave way to tourism in the early nineties. The now-popular tourist destination is filled with beautiful, white sand beaches and clear, turquoise water. Boutiques and restaurants span palm tree-lined streets of the small city, giving the island of Margarita one of the most extravagant night lives Venezuela has to offer. Wealthy actors, big time music and movie producers had often traveled to Porlamar to enjoy the city's night life, a world of its own whose concept was borrowed back in America to build up South Beach.

JunJie exited his private Gulfstream jet on a desolate runway on the island's north side and was greeted by one lone figure wearing dark shades, dressed in a black silk tank top, flip flops and khaki cargo shorts who'd exited a white on white four door 2003 Bentley Arnage. "JunJie, Grover and Phillip Tran. It's good to see old friends again," the man said aloud with a wide smile on his face.

"Gacha, how's business?" JunJie asked as he extended his hand.

"That is something I should be asking of you, Mister Maruyama," Gacha replied with a firm handshake. "But me and my family are living like kings and queens down here if you must know. The Venezuelan President is very friendly, because we support his presidency of course."

"You're the FBI's biggest celebrity and the U.S. Marshall's favorite fugitive. You could never return to America." JunJie chuckled.

"May the sweat from my cojones drip onto their faces, no? Here they can't touch me. And even if I could return the city on the hill, why would I ever want to return to such a place? Look around you, Mister Maruyama. I live in paradise. You should've come down for New Year's. I threw a party for the entire island. Oh and, please, excuse my attire, I went for a dip in the Caribbean before you arrived."

"This sure beats the snow back in Seattle that's for certain," Phillip remarked.

"It does doesn't it? You can't beat the weather or the women in this town. Long before there was South Beach in Miami, there was Porlamar. Take me at my word." Gacha replied through light laughter. "Come now. Let us return to my villa where we talk in private, my friends."

Rafael Gacha, a muscular, well-tanned and fit man with numerous tattoos on his neck and arms with a thick head of curly black hair, was the American network's supplier. He was a thirty-six year old Colombian from Bogota that'd fled the South American state with a duffel bag full of hundred dollar bills just before Pablo Escobar was killed in December of 1993. The then twenty-six year-old Enforcer for the now-defunct Medellin Cartel began purchasing cocaine for as little as three-thousand a kilogram and started shipping the product back to the United States where he sold them for twenty-five thousand dollars each. He'd muscled his way to the top by eliminating rival traffickers and paying off politicians and police and soon opened his own cocaine processing plant back on the Venezuelan main land just outside of the city of San Joaquin.

Whereas JunJie was a distributor, Rafael Gacha was one of the top cocaine suppliers in the business and was responsible for a high percentage of uncut powder that entered the United States. On top of that, his organization was backed by the Venezuelan government. Rafael Gacha, a multi-millionaire up in the low-nine figure range, was practically untouchable in South America and proudly wore the crown of Boss of Bosses. Everything involving the movement of weight for JunJie Maruyama and all involved started and stopped with Rafael Gacha—he was the man behind the men back in America.

JunJie, Grover and Phillip rode to Rafael's home that sat atop a cliff overlooking the Caribbean Sea with a couple of cars trailing the group; men packing Uzis for everyone's protection. Rafael had many enemies, the Sinaloa Cartel was after him for disrupting routes into America via Tijuana and the Gulf Cartel had him marked for death because he'd disrupted their shipping lane through Eagle Pass, Texas. Here on the island of Margarita, however, he was impossible to assassinate. In spite of his assured safety, Gacha was not one to take chances, armed body guards were a must wherever he traveled on the island.

After a short ride into the mountains, the group reached Rafael's six thousand square foot villa, which sat on over one thousand acres of land. The home was surrounded by palm trees and lush foliage and even had a waterfall in its garden area. Horses ran about freely on the low land and farm hands picked oranges from the grove in the valley below. Rafael led the way onto his patio overlooking the Caribbean Sea and extended his hand, allowing his guests to have a seat. A four-man wait staff emerged from the home and one of the men stepped forth. "What would you and your guests like to drink, Senor Gacha?"

"Bring us all glasses of orange sangria. Make sure the oranges are fresh. Use the ones picked earlier this morning along with the chilled vodka." Rafael answered as he watched his servants reenter the home. "Now," he said as he turned back to JunJie and crossed his legs and diddled a few petals on the gladiolas rooted in one of his many gardens, "what is it that I've done to deserve such a meeting?"

"I need info on the Lapiente` Family. You've told me about the problem you've had with them in Valle Hermoso a while back and I'm now under the impression that we now have a problem with them in America."

Gacha's eyes lit up immediately as he righted himself in his chair. "Lapiente`," he said lowly as he removed his sunshades and stared at JunJie. "How can you be certain it is them you're fighting against?"

"Take a look at these photographs," JunJie remarked as he placed the pictures in Rafael's lap. "Anyone there look familiar?"

JunJie leaned back and crossed his legs and watched as Rafael flipped through the photos. He knew where the photo that may be that of Carmella Lapiente` lay and he stood up and tucked his hands into his slacks the moment Rafael paused. "So it is her," he said matter-of-factly.

"As sure as the day is long." Gacha replied as he stood up and ran his hands through his hair in frustration. "This woman has been a thorn in my side for some time now."

"I say the same. She's nearly wiped out one of my partners in the city of Denver and has the other caught up in an on-going battle in the city of Saint Louis."

"No one in your organization can kill this woman on American soil?" Gacha asked, a little perplexed over the situation.

"She's like a ghost that's rarely seen. We hit her on her home turf in Denver once, but we didn't have enough firepower. Now she has a gang of Somalis on board for muscle. I have a friend who says the best way to deal with a viper is to cut off its head."

"Ahh," Rafael sighed. "But you've been grabbing the snake by its tail, my friend. It is a dangerous thing because a snake grabbed by the tail is surely going to strike."

"I can't disagree with that assessment. But I'm now left wondering what is it that we can do to close this woman's organization down because she's knee deep in everybody's ass in America."

The servants returned with the men's drinks and Rafael and JunJie took a seat once more upon their departure. "The best place to hit Carmella would be on her home turf, my friend. Valle Hermoso. I've been trying, but I can't reach her from here. I can't penetrate her organization. They would see me from miles away because they know how badly I want them."

"Valle Hermoso? That's risky don't you think? Striking on her home turf? If you can't get to her, what makes you so certain that me and my organization will get her?"

Rafael looked at JunJie and smiled through closed lips in an overly assured manner. Without a doubt he was a master manipulator on a scale far larger than JunJie and those whom JunJie did business with back in America could ever hope to be. He knew everything that went on in South America and Mexico and had angles upon angles that he could use to steer his entire network whichever way he wanted and needed it to go in order to keep things running smoothly.

For several years, ever since Carmella had killed nine buyers of his, he'd had it in for the woman. The only problem was the fact that he couldn't leave Venezuela unless the F.B.I. and/or the U.S. Marshalls or D.E.A. arrested him. He was limited in what he could do outside of the country he lived in, but he was well-informed. He knew as Carmella grew stronger over time, she would cause problems in America. Some would have to die before the ramifications would begin to impact JunJie, he knew, but Gacha was willing to sacrifice a few, to save many. It was only a matter of time before word got back to him and JunJie had just delivered that message.

"I have a lot of fate in you, Mister Maruyama," Gacha said

after a few brief seconds. "And I'll back you by using every contact I have to aide you along the way, my friend. If we plan this thing right," Gacha said as he lit a cigar, "if we lay a plan out right and bring about something unexpected we can get her —on her home turf. I want her dead more than anything and will do all I can to make sure that comes about."

"You seem to have a sincere hatred for the Lapiente` family. May I ask the history?"

"This guy Damenga Lapiente` was Carmella's brother. The Lapiente` family was once the people on the front lines for my organization in America—but Damenga was a hot head. When Carmella came out of her coma after she was shot, Damenga told me that this guy down in New Orleans killed three members out of his crew and shot Carmella in a home invasion in Memphis, Tennessee. I almost approved of the retaliatory hit."

"But you called it off. Why?"

"Damenga told me this guy raided his home in Memphis before he ever met the guy. I called the hit off because that dealer was offing at least a hundred kilo a month. It was just the nature of the business we are in, and I don't think that guy would have pulled that hit if he knew Carmella was Damenga's sister—but this loyalty thing blinded Damenga and his brother Alphonso. They broke off from me and cut off the shipping lane through Valle Hermoso. We were at war over the route going through Valle Hermoso when Damenga` and Alphonso was killed in New Orleans." Gacha said as he took another sip of his sangria. "For all I care, that guy in New Orleans did me a favor by killing those two brothers. If he were around I'd shake his hand and congratulate him on a job well done."

"Seems as if the Lapiente` family has burned a lot of bridges."

"That is an understatement. It took me many months, and a lot of money and lives to establish a new route, and for that, I have a bounty on my head from the Sinaloa Cartel and the Gulf Cartel. I had to step on other people's toes to keep my ship afloat."

"Carmella got in your way and forced you into a corner." JunJie remarked as he sipped his sangria.

"Yes she did, but if we remove her, I just may be able to bring about a truce."

"Because you'll have your old route back into America that's closer to your markets in the southeast. Clever, Mister Rafael."

"Thank you, my friend. We have a common interest here. The ultimate goal for me is to gain access to Valle Hermoso, and it would be of great benefit to you and your partners back in America," Gacha responded. "Let me use the resources we have here to try and track Carmella down. This move will take some time, but once we know all we need to know, we'll be able to take the Lapiente` family down once and for all, or at the very least, deal them a major blow. Don't worry, Mister Maruyama, we'll get her soon enough. Here's to the death of those who oppose us and all that we stand for," Gacha ended as he stood and raised his glass and the group all touched the rims and shared another drink.

To use his own men would force Rafael to kill his most trusted soldiers once the job was done to prevent the finger from being pointed back towards his self. It wasn't something he wanted to do because he would only open himself up to the Sinaloas and Gulf Cartels, organizations he could deal with so long as he had his trusted soldiers by his side. The Americans, however, the Americans, with a little backing, could do the job and settle a score for him at the same time. He would sincerely help them eradicate Carmella, but in his own manipulative way. Thereby keeping his hands clean and remaining in good standing with the Venezuelan government, who were turning a blind eye and a deaf ear towards his activities, so long as he kept the American authorities out of their affairs.

With the information received, the green light was now switched on for Rafael to move the pieces into place to take down and old enemy who had a debt to pay with blood, and set the ship right once more with an organization he'd been holding in high esteem for some time now.

CHAPTER TWENTY-TWO
LOSSES AND GAINS

"Uno de ellos murió el año pasado, pero estaba equivocado. Debería haber sido Toodie en vez de Phoebe," (One of them died last year, but it was the wrong one. It shoulda been Toodie instead of Phoebe,) were the first words she'd said the moment she was left alone.

Thirteen year-old Peppi Vargas had never visited her mother's grave the three years she'd been in America, but this hot summer day in August of 2004 was a special day for her because she was finally able to have a moment of peace in her heart, to shed the tears that had been held deep inside her soul since the moment her mother had passed away.

It was a hurting thing for Pepper to endure, witnessing her mother's death, and her life had been forever changed by that tragedy. She stood over her mother's grave holding a bouquet of red carnations as tears dropped down into the dirt beneath her feet. She could still remember the days her mother would take her dancing in the town square while Mexican salsa musicians played harmoniously with their trumpets, maracas and guitars. Picking tomatoes was another outing mother and daughter enjoyed, ironically from many of the groves owned by Carmella's family. Those were the fun times. Times filled with laughter and so much to learn and enjoy about life. Happy days.

She had such a beautiful smile, Pepper's mother; it was a broad beam, separated by pearl white teeth and high cheek bones with a long mane of jet black hair that flowed towards the center of her back. Pepper looked every bit like her mother, save for her thin knot knees and short, curly, coal black hair. Everything else, from her beautiful tan-skinned face, the cheek bones and the lips that curved downward to produce one of the most gorgeous smiles one could witness, was Peppi's mother through and through.

With a dead father and an uncle who could care less about her because he was too busy robbing banks in Monterrey, Peppi had no one else to turn to in life except for the people she believed had killed her mother. The thirteen year-old knew not the reasons behind her mother's killing, maybe she got in the way was her thinking, but in the way of what was the question Pepper always ended up asking herself. She sat the bouquet of flowers atop her mother's grave and knelt down in the dry dirt and said a prayer for her mother. She then opened her eyes and said, "You were the only thing that ever really mattered to me, momma. Carmella looks after me, but she's been troubled lately. People die all around me, but I'm learning how to live—me and Simone."

Carmella, meanwhile, was sitting behind the wheel of her H-1 Hummer while DeAngelo and a dozen or more soldiers lingered around outside the graveyard guarding her and Peppi. She was in town to secure another delivery for her crew back in Saint Louis and to visit her mother as it had been a few months, early spring, since she'd last visited Valle Hermoso. Staring at all of the tombstones inside the cemetery had forced twenty-three year-old Carmella to reflect on Desiree Abbadando. The night she'd lost her lover was something that was rehashed over and over again inside of Carmella's mind like old episodes of some tragic drama series that'd gone away years before. Sometimes she would just cry. Today was one of those days.

The way Desiree died, so abruptly, and being hit from a distance, was one thing Carmella never saw coming. She'd had Q-man and his crew to protect the woman; Desiree never went anywhere without bodyguards after the attempted hit inside

Carmella's home; but one shot, a shot clear out of the darkness of night that came from only God knows where had shattered her life. Who was behind the hit was another mystery in itself. Asa Spade didn't have the muscle to pull a job of that caliber, Carmella knew; but on the other hand, maybe she'd underestimated the man. She'd retaliated by killing three men in Shorter Arms, but shortly after that, Asa Spade had reopened *The Royal Flush* and was back pushing kilograms. It seemed, to Carmella, that the harder she fought, the problems she had before only multiplied in intensity, but quitting wasn't in her nature. She would battle until her last breath, until the last bullet left the chamber, all the way down to her last heartbeat.

Carmella waited patiently for Peppi even though she'd been ready to leave minutes after her caravan had arrived at the neighborhood's graveyard. She felt the least she could do, however, was not rush the child being that she was responsible for her mother being dead. Carmella reflected on the night the Perez sisters went on their rampage and wondered how life would have been for Peppi had her mother not been the one standing out in the front yard of that kids' party to stop a speeding bullet. Maybe Peppi wouldn't be selling kilograms to men and women twice her age and carrying a pistol now-a-days. The guy she'd ordered Peppi to shoot inside of Fox Park on a cold February night wouldn't be in a wheelchair—maybe. Can't cry over spilt milk, though; Peppi Vargas was now involved in the life completely. With one shooting victim under her belt and numerous drug sells, she'd come a long way in Carmella's eyes, but she still had much to learn if ever she were to move up. *"I hope I'm around to see her become a woman,"* Carmella said to herself as she watched Pepper walk back to the jeep.

"You all set, Peppi?" Carmella asked as the young teen hopped back into the backseat.

"Yes, ma'am. Where're we going now?"

"To see my ma-ma. She cook for us today."

Pepper said nothing as she bit her bottom lip and stared at her mother's grave as Carmella and her crew slowly pulled away from the cemetery.

THE HOLLAND FAMILY SAGA

****

Back on the ranch, while Carmella was down in Mexico, the Holland-Dawkins family was going about their usual routine. Things had changed a little over the months; thirteen year-old Walee, and twelve year-olds Spoonie and Tyke were now in charge of feeding the chickens and slopping the hogs and sixteen year-olds Kimi and Koko were now working side by side with their mother in her office on the first floor of Ponderosa.

Naomi had been schooling her daughters on how to close out bills of ladings on loads delivered from the trucking firm the family owned and they were coming along superbly; but there were ulterior motives for mother training her middle daughters, and on this hot summer's day in August of 2004, she was aiming to bring them up to par on how things actually ran when closing out bills at the end of each month.

Naomi led the way down the long hall, pass the theater room and her private room towards the west side of Ponderosa and entered her office that had a panoramic view of the middle field where Mary grew her crops. She was toting a duffel bag and dressed as if she were entering a conference room to deliver a presentation before a group of CEOs. Kimi and Koko followed, dressed neatly in tight-fitting silk pant suits and stilettos as they trailed their mother into the office.

"Okay," ladies, "Naomi said as she closed and locked the double doors. "Today we are going to do things a little different."

"In what way, momma?" Koko asked as she and Kimi walked over to their large double desk and powered up their laptops.

"Deposits are made every month. You've traveled with me to Oklahoma City to make bank deposits so you understand how that goes. Today I'm going to show you what goes on before the deposit."

"Okay," the twins replied in unison.

Naomi walked over to her daughters' desk, stood before them

and opened the duffel bag and began pulling out stacks of money. Kimi and Koko eyed one another and then stared at the money their mother was putting on display. Money was nothing new to Naomi's children, they'd all seen large amounts of cash around the house in their father's private room, the kitchen, and even Mary had large amounts of money on the table at the guest house from time to time. This stack of money was in uncharted waters for the twins, however; their mother was pulling out hundred dollar stacks, stacks of fifties and bundles of twenties.

"This is what one hundred and twenty-five thousand dollars looks like up close, ladies," Naomi said. "Now, we can't deposit the money all at once for tax reasons," she added. "Uncle Sam doesn't play when it comes to paying taxes, but there are laws that we can and will use to work around the laws our beloved Uncle Sam has in place."

"What kind of laws?" Kimi asked.

"The same laws the politicians use to keep from paying taxes themselves." Naomi replied as she reached into one of the bill of lading bins and pulled out the monthly earnings on one of the family's trucks. "Truck number one forty-two grossed fourteen thousand dollars, and this was a slow month for that driver. What you have to do is upgrade the gross on this truck by increasing the number of livestock on each load this particular driver ran by a sum of one. One extra bull every other load. The driver ran twenty loads of cattle at two thousand per head. Eight bulls were on board, but we bumping it up to nine. Got me?"

"I guess," Kimi replied cautiously. "So with one extra bull every other load, that'll be an additional twenty thousand dollars on the gross, right?"

"Very good. Now, that rule will apply to the six remaining trucks that have run this month. Half the loads ran on each truck should have one additional head of cattle added to the load, until the one hundred and twenty-five thousand dollars is covered. Whatever is left over, I'll take care of it myself."

"Are we allowed to do this?" Koko asked in an unsure

manner.

"Don't seem like it." Kimi whispered.

"Let me tell you two a story," Naomi said as she rested one side of her body atop her daughters' desk. "A long time ago, men came to this country and claimed to have 'discovered' the Promised Land. But there were others here before them. Some were our ancestors. Creeks, the Cherokees you see over in town, Sioux, and Lakota Indians and many, many more tribes."

"What does that have to do with us adding heads of cattle to the trucks?" Koko asked curiously.

"Laws were soon put into place that prevented the original inhabitants of this country from operating in their natural state. Laws that usurped our ancestors' culture. Laws that they couldn't understand, nor did they care to adhere to. And for that, they lost everything."

"We know the history, momma," Kimi remarked. "We just wanna know if this is legal or not."

"In the eyes of many it isn't legal. But we're making so much money I can barely deposit it fast enough. We take hit after hit on profits and have a heavy tax burden at the end of the year. Last year we paid out over a quarter of a million dollars in taxes. All we're doing is easing the tax burden by using the same laws that have been in place since this country's founding. Nothing more. And no one is going to get into trouble over this. Okay?"

"If you say so," Kimi replied.

"Look ladies," Naomi said as she eyed her daughters with a serious, yet comforting look, "this is all a part of the business we run. Companies all across this country do the same thing with billions more dollars and you never hear about those people getting into trouble do you?"

"What about Enron?" Koko asked.

"Different animal. Moving money is one thing, which is what we're doing, stealing money is an entirely different entity, which is the case with Enron, and that we will have no part in. We can't steal from ourselves now can we?"

Kimi and Koko looked at one another and shrugged their shoulders. "Explain this one more time so we can make sure we properly understand exactly what it is that we're supposed to do, momma." Kimi said.

Naomi explained the procedures once more and left her daughters to work alone in silence. When she left the room, Koko looked over to Kimi and asked, "You know what we're doing here, Kimi?"

"Yeah, I know. Do you?"

"Yeah," Koko answered lowly as she grabbed a stack of bill of ladings.

"We're laundering money," the twins replied in unison as they carefully went about their tasks.

****

Later that same day, Dawk, Junior and Jay-D had just returned from Minneapolis. They'd learned through Asa Spade that the Somalis used the term 'the Ap' the night they'd kidnapped three of Asa's crew and had surmised that the term was used in reference to Minneapolis-Saint Paul, which had a huge Somali presence.

The crew had made several trips to 'Little Somalia' in Minnesota's Cedar-Riverside neighborhood, but the people there didn't take kindly to outsiders. Asking about another Somali was out of the question as the crew knew word would get back to the person they were looking for. The man's face in the picture hadn't been seen neither of the few times the Chicago Gang had ridden up and down Lake Street in the heart of the neighborhood, and entering Riverside Towers, a large housing complex dominated by Somalis, was a sure death sentence. If the crew had a name instead of a face, the job would be far easier, but they would have deal with the hand they were being dealt and stay on their toes because they knew the Somalis knew who they were and where they were located down in Saint Charles.

"How'd it go this time?" Eddie asked as Junior, Dawk and Jay-D took seats at the bar.

"We can't penetrate that place," Junior remarked as Dooney slid a glass of scotch across the bar. "Thanks, Dooney. Boys? I thought we Italians stuck together. But that place there? If you wasn't born there, or come from overseas you ain't welcome."

"What about the Latinos up there?" Eddie questioned.

"There's nobody we trust," Dawk chimed in. "If we could just connect a name to this face we'll be in business," he added as he threw the picture with Q-man's image onto the counter.

"We should bring Malik with us next time and see if he can get in with somebody, you know? Maybe expand a little bit," Jay-D chimed in.

"That's not a bad idea," Eddie replied. "How the market look up there?"

"Them Somalis is rolling in the dough," Jay-D answered. "Whips everywhere, niggas posted up on corners and shit. They got some clicks up there and the Somalis running camp, but we might be able to finagle our way in with the Latinos and loop back around and find this dude," he ended as he nodded towards the picture.

"Stay on it, fam," Eddie said. "It won't be too long before we get that thing done with Carmella, too."

"No shit? What's the word on that deal?" Junior asked as he sipped his drink.

"I met Doss over in Granite City yesterday when he was dropping off and picking up, before he left, he said our main man JunJie puttin' something together to get us close to her so we can take her down. Should be in a few months, but in the meantime, we keep moving weight, stay on guard and continue looking for those Somalis. Things been quiet in Fox Park and in Denver, but that don't mean this war is over." Eddie concluded.

CHAPTER TWENTY-THREE
THE UNEXPECTED

"You think I should buy it, baby?" nineteen year-old Tiva asked Junior as the two walked around the Mercedes Benz showroom in downtown Oklahoma City in the middle part of September, just a few weeks after Junior's return from Minneapolis.

Tiva wanted something speedy to get her and Junior down to Brownsville, Texas by the end of the week so the two could set up in a hotel and wait on a special delivery coming in from south of the border with Jay-D and Doss. She had her eyes set on a convertible, black 2005 two-seater Mercedes SLK350 priced at $60,000 dollars.

Junior ran his hand across the emblem on the car's trunk, admiring its sleek, compact design and chuckled slightly.

"What you smiling over?" Tiva asked.

"My father used to love telling stories. The day y'all left for Seattle back in two thousand two he told me how you got your nickname for like the dozenth time."

"How I got my name?"

"You don't know why everybody calls you T-top?" Junior asked in surprise.

"Nahh. I thought it was because of my pointed chin and

round forehead."

"No," Junior laughed. "This guy, Zell, Zell Verniche` gave you that name because you used to laugh so freakin' loud whenever your daddy was pulling up to the bar in Cicero in that red T-top Camaro he keeps covered up behind the barn back on the ranch."

"Yeah? He keep sayin' he gone fix up that old Camaro, but he be so busy he ain't never got the time to do it. And he won't give it to me like my grandfather gave Bay his car so she could pimp it out like she did."

"You always laughed whenever Doss rode around with that T-top open and it was Zell who gave you that nickname and it stuck."

"Well, Zell must've known what he was talking about because I'm definitely feeling this ride right here. And I got the money to buy this thang myself."

"Shit, I got the whole thing covered if this is what you want, babe. Give your family a good Christmas with that loot you planned on spending on this nice car here."

"Really? You gone buy this Benz for me today?" Tiva asked with a smile.

"I know that doesn't impress you because you most definitely can hold your own in this life. That's what I love about you, woman."

"But?"

"But as your man I feel obligated to do this. I'm not gone stand here and watch you spend your money when I can do that and more."

"More meaning?"

"Move to Chicago with me, Tiva." Junior said seriously as he stepped closer and stared Tiva in the eyes.

Tiva knew what Junior was going to say, but she'd hoped he wouldn't. For a while now he'd been trying to get her to move in with him in the home he'd inherited from his parents, but Tiva wasn't ready to take such a major step just yet. Her love for Junior was sincere, and she knew he loved her just as much, but leaving Bay behind was something Tiva couldn't imagine. True enough, Bay had a life of her own with AquaNina, but at the end of the day, she always returned home.

Tiva and Bay were just too close at this point in time in their lives to be without one another and Tiva had no intentions on breaking the bond she shared with her sister just yet.

"Never mind," Junior said, reading the look on Tiva's face while shaking his head slowly, fully aware of her reluctance to move to Chicago. "I never worry about you going behind my back with another man, but I never thought I'd be in competition with your sister."

"You make it sound creepy, Junior," Tiva said in a somewhat disheartened manner. "You know how I feel about you, but Bay my heart."

"And what am I?"

"The love of my life, my future. Just give me more time."

"Ohh, I suppose," Junior quipped as he hugged Tiva and kissed her lips tenderly. "My offer still stands, though concerning this car. And from here we can head down to Brownsville a day earlier, find us a five star hotel if that wretched place has one, order in, and I'll still, even after you've turned me down again, I'll still cater to your every need."

"I appreciate you understanding this thing between me and Bena, Junior. I don't know what it is, but I'm connected to my sister more than anybody could even begin to understand."

"That's a special thing, baby. I won't come between that—unless this thing turns into one of those weird identical twin situations where one twin starts to take over the other twin's life. I'd hate to have to kidnap you and take you to an island somewhere and hold you hostage."

"If it gets to that point I'd welcome it. I want a life with you, Faustino, and someday, we'll make that dream a reality. Now, can we talk to a salesperson?" Tiva asked through a sexy smile.

The following morning, Junior and Tiva arrived in

Brownsville, Texas on a hot and sunny, cloudless day where they obtained three rooms inside the Courtyard by Marriot near Brownsville International Airport.

Once inside their suite, the two showered and ordered breakfast. Tiva sat on the toilet inside the bathroom as she placed lotion onto her legs and arms. After several minutes, she looked over and saw a positive sign on the pregnancy test she'd obtained from a store in the lobby. She grew happy over the fact, easing out of the bathroom and sliding along the wall while eyeing Junior as he watched TV, biting her bottom lip and barely able to contain her joy.

Junior was lying back on the bed naked, his muscular bowed legs and hairy chest being admired by his woman as she eased up from the wall and walked over towards him with a wide smile on her face.

"What?" Junior asked as he lay with his hands behind his head.

"You ready for breakfast, baby." Tiva asked as she crawled up Junior's body like a black panther on the prowl where she kissed her man's forehead softly before lying beside him and hugging him tightly.

"Yeah. I'm ready to eat," Junior said as he rose up and hovered over Tiva's sweet-smelling, naked body.

If Junior had to tell it, he was laying eyes upon one of the most beautiful women ever created. From hair tip to toe, she was near perfect. Deep, dark eyes that radiated love, soft, tan skin and pert breasts with caramel nipples that stood at attention, aching to be tweaked and licked. Well-toned legs that led to a bald-shaven vagina with pink labia that glistened with sweet secretions, secretions he loved to savor.

Tiva shuddered and her heart pounded with joy and anticipation. She knew what was in her immediate future as she slid up to the leather headboard and let her legs fall open while running her hands through the hair on Junior's broad and muscular red-haired chest. Her eyes were transfixed on her lover as she imagined what their unborn child, or children, would look like once they entered the world.

"I love you," Tiva said as Junior planted kisses on her neck and trailed down to her breasts and took a nipple into his mouth, forcing her to moan softly in appreciation. Junior went from left breast to right breast, sucking gently while inhaling Tiva's vanilla scent. He licked his way down to her belly and tickled her navel with the tip of his tongue.

Tiva squirmed and exhaled as Junior began moving slowly towards her center. This was one of the things she loved about her man—he knew how to eat. The moment Junior's sensual lips touched her lips, Tiva palmed his head and thrust forward, lifting her lower body off the mattress as she entered into a slow, circular gyration. Her motions, coupled with her hands gripping the back of his head spurred Junior on further. He loved his woman's responsiveness, almost as much as he savored her taste.

The feel of Junior's tongue against her clitoris and his strong hands kneading her ass cheeks, him pulling her closer to his face, was more than Tiva could take. She couldn't help but to cry out in delight as she wrapped her legs around Junior's head and let go with a loud scream as she shuddered. She could feel Junior sucking the juices from her insides as she came, her body trembling uncontrollably and her nipples erect and her hair splayed across her face.

Junior pulled back from Tiva and eased up her body and kissed her deeply as he drove deep inside. She turned her head to the side and nuzzled her cheek up against his as she grabbed her ankles, raising her legs high and wide, allowing her man full access to her hungry sex.

"Feed me," Tiva moaned aloud, her body jerking in near slow motion as Junior stroked her hard and steady.

"So fucking good, baby. So damn, good," Junior groaned as he raised himself up by planting his hands on either side of Tiva and began stroking her deep and fast, driving hard into her snug center. The two were soon moaning aloud as the mattress began shaking violently.

"Feed me, Faustino!" Tiva begged.

"Oooh, baby!"

Junior eased up and pulled Tiva up from the bed and turned her around, slapping her ass cheeks repeatedly as she planted her face down into the mattress and gripped the sheets tightly in anticipation of another treat Junior often gave her whenever the two were intimate. The wind was nearly knocked out of Tiva when Junior slid into her from behind, his feet planted on either side of her body as he crouched behind her and drove home long and deep.

"Pull my hair," Tiva requested. "Pull it hard and feed me!"

"You ready, baby? I'm ready!"

"Give it to me!"

"I'm fuckin' there! I'm there!" Junior moaned aloud as he thrust in and out of Tiva at a blinding pace. He exploded deep inside of Tiva and collapsed down onto her body, the two breathing hard and laughing lowly, their bodies slick with a light coating of perspiration as they brought their session home by kissing one another deeply.

This was the first time Tiva had asked Junior to 'feed' her and he never questioned her words. Assuming she only wanted him to come inside her as he'd done many times before. Tiva, however, was in a constant orgasmic state knowing she was due to have Junior's baby and she wanted his seed deep within her on this day in order to further 'feed' the seed that was developing within her body.

"I'm full," Tiva chuckled.

"You done?"

"Are you?"

"Let me grab a bite of this food and I'll be right back."

"We'll be waiting," Tiva said as she turned over and rubbed her belly while smiling.

"Are you serious?" Junior asked. "You mean?"

"Yes. I'm carrying your baby, daddy." Tiva said with a wide smile as Junior walked over and swooped her up into his arms and twirled her around several times.

"I'm gonna be a father!" Junior exclaimed joyfully.

****

Doss and Jay-D were awaiting Junior and Tiva's arrival to their suite the following morning. They'd driven into town the night before and were up bright and early having breakfast when a tap came across the door. Jay-D got up holding a Mac-10 semi-automatic as his dark-skinned, tall and lanky frame eased over to the door where he looked through the peep hole before he let Junior and Tiva in.

"It's about time you two made it here. I'm not gonna ask what the delay was. Our guys should be here within the hour." Doss said as he poured a glass of orange juice.

"We was looking over some names, daddy."

"What kind of names?"

Tiva pulled a chair up beside her father, sat next to him, grabbed his hand and looked him in the eyes with a serious gaze. She and Junior had talked the day before, discussing whether or not they should tell Doss right away or wait until they were done in Brownsville.

Junior opted for the former, but Tiva chose the latter. She knew her father, and how he would respond, and she only wanted to give him as much time as possible to make whatever adjustments that he would need to make because she knew after the trip to Brownsville, she would be going offline for the next year or so until she had the baby and recovered. Still gazing into her father's eyes, Tiva hadn't spoken a word, when Doss asked, "How far along are you?"

"How you know, daddy?"

"Besides the look of joy on your face and Junior over their sweating because he thinks I'm gonna go ballistic?"

Tiva laughed. "How do you feel really?"

"Of course you'll be done once we leave this town until you have my grandchild, but I'm one way or the other about it. You do know that a child will complicate your life and cut into your career, right? Was this planned?"

"No, it wasn't planned—but I feel good about this, daddy. And we'll have plenty of help around the ranch."

"Are you two going to marry?"

"We've talked about it, but I wanna wait."

"You having this baby at a young age isn't a problem with me because the child will be well taken care of, but if you're not going to marry? Then I definitely have a problem with that."

"See, Tiva?" Junior said as he walked over to the table were Doss sat. "There's nothing wrong with us marrying, baby. I'm willing to do it."

"Y'all gone be a li'l family and shit," Jay-D chided as he ate a bowl of cereal. "That's what's up, though. Let me be in the wedding."

"If we have a wedding, Jay-D. If we have a wedding," Tiva remarked. "I really just wanna go to the justice of the peace and get it over with. Bay be into that all fairy tale princess stuff not me."

"What woman don't want a big ass wedding?" Jay-D asked.

"This here woman. We was already talking about this. Junior, baby, what you want a big wedding or a small one?" Tiva inquired.

"A big wedding would be nice."

"That's a first," Jay-D stated, still clowning Junior. "A man wanting a big wedding. Usually the man wanna get the papers signed and go on the honeymoon. But you already had your honeymoon so I can understand why it ain't no big deal on the wedding."

"Screw you, man. I just want this here to be special. Tiva deserves it and I know how she feels about certain things."

"What things?" Tiva asked.

"You know what things. If we marry, you'll want to stay where you are."

Tiva then thought about the conversation she'd had with

Junior in Oklahoma City two days before about moving to Chicago and knew what he was getting at. "Oh that," she said. "I really would like to stay behind. What we can do, though, is have like a big reception. One big reception for everybody to attend. But I only want to go down to the justice of the peace with your grandparents and my parents as witnesses and get married in Illinois. I really don't want a big affair."

"I can go along with a huge formal reception. We can rent a big hall and invite everybody." Junior replied.

"I like the sound of that. Dad, what you think?"

"I'm in agreement. I'm just thinking how the women in the family will feel. This is a sudden and unexpected change of events after all."

"It is. But they'll be happy to help with the planning of the reception. Baby," Tiva said as she went and stood before Junior and grabbed his hands, "I believe we'll make it work."

"Me too, Tiva. We both new at this thing, but I'd rather do this with no one else in the world but you. I love you."

"Nigga, please," Jay-D snapped as he backed away from the table "If that ain't the corniest shit ever! Won't you get down on one knee and shit and ask her right, Casanova?"

"I will. But that's private. Eh, Jason, I'm gone have me a wife pretty soon. What you got?"

"A bunch of hoes is what I got. I ain't wifing nobody—but if I ever would? It'll definitely be somebody like your future bride, homeboy. Congratulations, Tiva. Tame his ass, tame his ass!"

Doss chuckled and said, "Tiva, the family will support you and Junior one hundred percent. Congratulations, Faustino. You done weaseled your way into my family," he added just as his cell phone vibrated. Doss talked for a couple of minutes and snapped his phone shut. "Alright lady and gentlemen. Our contacts south of the border is on their way up," he said as he wiped his mouth with a cloth napkin.

A few minutes later, two men were entering Doss's suite, each of the professionally dressed, tanned, toned and black curly haired men were holding two large suitcases. After a brief greeting, the men, who were two of Rafael's soldiers, laid the suitcases on the bed and unzipped the tops to reveal the contents.

"These are the badges," one of the men said calmly. "The jackets are authentic and these are the decals you'll need to apply to your vehicles."

"What about the border?" Doss asked as he scanned the items.

One of the men picked up two silk bags and pulled out a stack of money. "On the day of, make sure you approach the outer most lane on the U.S. side. We have a guy planted there always. Give him this bag of dough and you're done with the first move. When you get to the Mexican side, you must take the inside lane on the far left. Our guy will wave you through once you give him the second bag of money. Use the decals, do the job and you will be forwarded the payment."

"How will we know when to move?" Doss asked while picking up a couple of D.E.A. badges.

"Next month you will move," the other man replied as he reached down into one of the suitcases and handed Doss a cell phone. "You'll need to be back here in Brownsville at the start of next month. The day of your arrival, you're to turn on this phone. You will sit just outside of the outbound border entrance and wait for a message with two words—green light. It may or may not come on the first day or the second day or the third day, but it will come within a week's time. Message back red light once the job is done, discard the phone and return home, using the far outer lanes on both sides on the inbound side."

"Sounds like a piece of cake, except for the waiting part." Doss replied as he eyed the cell phone. "But everything looks good on paper. We'll do our part—I'm counting on your man to uphold his end of the bargain. I don't wanna stick my neck out on this and have this thing backfire."

"Our boss's word is as good as the ten commandments. This move will make a lot of you Americans richer than what you already are and we have a heavy vested interest in this deal as well."

"How heavy?" Doss asked.

"Three million dollars heavy enough? Your associate in the north west guarantees the money once the job is done and our boss will be ready to move more merchandise—if you can handle the job."

"We can handle the job," Doss replied in a confident tone. "But let's not count our chickens before they hatch. One step at a time on this, and my word is also written in stone."

One of the men reached out and shook Doss's hand and wished him good luck. "We will have our end covered. That is a promise. Now, we have another engagement in Mexico City we must look into today to aide in this job. The plan is all set, all you have to do is act. My boss never fails—and we've heard the same about you, Mister Dawkins. We'll be in touch, amigo."

The men left the room and several hours later, Doss and Jay-D traveled back to Saint Louis with the suitcases and Junior and Tiva headed back to Ponca City to break the news of her pregnancy and marriage to the rest of the family.

THE HOLLAND FAMILY SAGA

CHAPTER TWENTY-FOUR
ONCE AND FOR ALL

Carmella's jet had just touched down in Valle Hermoso only minutes earlier. The weather was hot south of the in the border on this fall evening in the first week of October 2004, but it didn't stop the woman from dressing in beige army fatigues, a black tight-fitting t-shirt and black leather knee length boots. Sunshades covered her eyes and her auburn hair was tied into a neat ponytail. $67,000 dollar platinum dog tags with her name engraved in diamonds draped her neck and a $90,000 dollar platinum and black diamond Jacob's Rolex watch adorned her wrist. She exited her plane and was greeted by eight female soldiers standing before her three black Jaguars where she hopped inside one of the cars and headed towards her family's warehouse.

"She's here now. Should be a couple of days or so," DeAngelo spoke into his cell phone as Carmella's caravan pulled into her family's tomato plant and rolled to a halt in front of the building.

"Good. You uphold your end of the bargain and we'll see you soon, my friend," the voice on the other end of the phone told DeAngelo.

"Is everybody okay?"

"Everyone is fine. You've spoken to them already just

minutes ago. Stay focused on the task at hand and all of this will be over within a week's time."

"Have your people send for me."

"Two of my guys are in Mexico City waiting for you to do as I've asked. After it goes down, you head to Mexico City and you'll come here and take them back home."

"Si," DeAngelo said and hung up the phone and hopped from the docks and greeted Carmella a she exited the car holding onto a black leather satchel. "We have one hundred and forty four on hand," DeAngelo said as he hugged Carmella. "Just as you've ordered, boss. We should be done packaging in the next couple of days or so."

"Good," Carmella responded. "That'll give me time to relax with my Ma-Ma. How's everything else down here?"

"Going along smoothly without any problems. The mayor is still in order and our friends from Sinaloa say they will send a squad up to Denver to rid us of our competition next month. They were finally able to send a team to get the job done."

"Tell them gracias."

"It has been a long time coming, boss." DeAngelo ended as he escorted Carmella into the plant where she greeted her workers and handed out $5,000 dollar stacks of money to each individual before she left and headed over to the villa to kick back with her mother for a couple of days.

****

"You're winning the war in Denver I hear, Carmella." Quintessa said as she and her daughter sat in their formal dining room eating dinner.

"Not quite, Ma-Ma," Carmella responded as she placed a helping of pasta onto her mother's plate before serving herself. "By next month, though, everything will be taken care of."

"Our friends in Sinaloa are very loyal to our cause."

"Only because we make them a lot of money, Ma-Ma."

"So do we."

"Our risk runs higher here in Valle Hermoso," Carmella said as she poured a tomato, sausage, jalapeno and garlic sauce mixture over her and her mother's pasta and said a prayer.

Quintessa picked up a napkin and spread it over her lap. "You don't like the arrangement?"

"It is working for now," Carmella answered as she uncorked a bottle of red wine. "But once they win this battle for us in Denver, we will grow in strength and numbers. I say within a year, it'll be time to renegotiate the terms of our agreement."

"Si." Quintessa said before sipping her wine. She sat the glass down and picked her fork and wiped it clean with another cloth napkin before she began eating.

Carmella looked over to her mother in surprise. "You agree, Ma-Ma? You think they will give us a better deal?"

"Why wouldn't they? We will let them take the risk in America. Desiree's death has to repaid and they are willing to do it for us. We grow like you said, and they will not be able to resist us, Carmella. Cheers," Quintessa said as she raised her glass of wine once more and toasted with her daughter.

Mother and daughter went on to share dinner before visiting Damenga and Alphonso's graves, which was their normal routine whenever Carmella was in town. They then spent the remainder of their time tending horses, working the garden and rowing a boat back and forth across the land's lakes while feeding ducks. It was a time to be cherished, but it wouldn't be long before duty called once more.

Two days later, Carmella was watching a trailer being loaded from front to back with fresh tomato sauce. Intertwined with the load was one hundred and forty-four neatly packaged kilograms of cocaine. She'd called her team in Houston and had them ready to break the load down upon its arrival and everything was on schedule and in order.

"Once we set this down in Houston, I'll be on my way back to Denver to finish this thing with Asa Spade and his crew. The same day, Q-man and his team will hit Saint Charles once more." Carmella said to DeAngelo as the two walked outside of the warehouse.

"Toodie says the place over in Saint Charles is a fortress. You may want to rethink going after the Chicago Gang on their home turf."

"We're moving ahead with our plans, DeAngelo. Our first go around with the Chicago Gang was a success. This second hit will finish them off for good. Everything will turn out fine," Carmella responded as she donned a bullet proof vest and walked around the eighteen wheeler, giving the vehicle a brief inspection. "Good, they've removed those old tires," she said. "What time will the driver be pulling out?"

"Five fifteen, this evening, just before sunset."

"Okay. I'm headed back to the airport to fly into Houston. I will call you when I arrive in Texas."

"Si, boss." DeAngelo answered as he helped Carmella into the backseat of one of her Jaguars before she was driven off the dirt covered parking lot.

When Carmella reached the airport, she saw her pilot walking around the plane doing an inspection. The old, slender, white haired Canadian was scratching his head in confusion, placing his hands on his hips and shaking his head in disbelief as he looked up at the nose of the plane. Carmella paid him no mind as she hopped out of her car and began trotting up the stairs leading into the interior of the idling small jet.

"I hope like hell you aren't in a hurry to get outta here," the pilot said dejectedly as he walked around from the front of the plane.

"Why? What is the matter?" Carmella asked, pausing halfway up the stairs.

"Somebody had the audacity to shatter the windshield."

"What? How?" Carmella asked in dismay as she scampered down the stairs.

"Shot the son-of-a-bitch one time just enough to put a quarter-sized hole in it to where it'll need replacing. And knowing this town, it ain't a fuckin' business around for miles and miles that has what I need to get this thing fixed before nightfall, not to mention the next couple of days. We can't fly for a while."

Carmella looked around at the females standing out beside the cars. This was no accident, she knew; who was behind it, however, was the sixty-four thousand dollar question. She eyed her soldiers cautiously, awaiting their reaction. If they were staging a coup, now would be the perfect time to strike. After several minutes of no action, Carmella walked over to her girls and told them the situation.

"Que vamos a hacer ahora jefe?" (What are we going to do now, boss?) one of the females asked.

Carmella nodded her head at that moment, understanding that her soldiers weren't involved with what was going down. Without bothering to answer the question posed to her, she turned back to the pilot and pulled out her gold-plated .50 caliber. "Who paid you off? Who paid?" she yelled as she racked her gun.

"What the fuck are you talking about? I been flying you around since you been out the hospital. I don't deal with anyone but you, Carmella," the French Canadian remarked as he turned to inspect the windshield. The sixty-seven year-old man was ex-military and was once a Royal Canadian Mounted Policemen and he was unfazed by criminals. He went about his business with his back turned to Carmella, but quickly took to one knee when she let one bullet fly out of her hand cannon that penetrated the back of his leg and shattered his left knee cap. "Shit! What the fuck is your problem? I don't know what's going on!" he yelled as he turned, sat down in the dirt and faced Carmella while clutching his shattered knee.

Carmella and her soldiers walked and stood over the pilot as he sat in the dirt underneath the nose of the plane. "You had one job down here when not in flight and that was to watch the jet!" Carmella yelled as her girls stood behind her.

"I, I went and had some fuckin' drinks last night! Bought a hooker and had myself a good time! The plane was safe here! How the fuck was I to know this was going to happen?"

"Batir la verdad de el." (Beat the truth out of him.) Carmella ordered her soldiers as she stepped aside and gave them room to do their job. The young females beat the pilot for nearly a half hour trying to get him to tell who was behind the sabotaging of the plane, but he never gave a name.

"Ese tipo no sabe nada, jefe." (That guy knows nothing, boss.) one of the women said. *"Hicimos todo lo que no cortamos los cojones."* (We did everything but cut off his balls.)

"Puede caminar?" (Can he walk?) Carmella asked as she lit a blunt and toke several long tokes.

"Ambas piernas y brazos están rotos. Y la bala que puso en él no está ayudando a nadie." (Both legs and arms are broken. And the bullet you put in him isn't helping none.)

"Entonces es inútil." (Then he's useless.) Carmella sighed as she eased up from the front seat of her car and walked over to the pilot, where she pulled her gun again and pointed it at the man's skull.

The pilot was now lying motionless in the dirt looking up at the sky, blood covering his face with several limbs bent in awkward directions. He said nothing as he closed his eyes. A brief pop that sounded like a sledge hammer slamming into the side of a steel dumpster was heard and it was all over for the officer gone bad. Carmella had let off one bullet that crashed into the man's face and cracked the top of his skull.

"Tenemos que salir de la ciudad ahora si vamos a estar por delante de la expedición." (We have to leave town now if we're going to stay ahead of the shipment.) Carmella said lowly as she parted her way through her girls and returned to her Jaguar.

Carmella had a lot on her mind as she was being driven back to the tomato plant. Someone was after her and she knew it. She had to speak with DeAngelo in person before she left town to inform him of the new arrangement and she also had to check on her mother before she headed back north. When she reached the factory, DeAngelo was on the dock overseeing the cargo being loaded. He eyed Carmella seriously as she approached. "Thought you were leaving, Carmella," he said in wonderment.

"Someone has tampered with the plane. I asked you was everything okay here and you said it was." Carmella replied in frustration as she stood before DeAngelo.

DeAngelo took a couple of steps back. "Everything was fine, boss. When I talked to the pilot he said he was going to go to bed inside the plane."

"He left last night and went into town drinking and whoring so I had to kill him. Send someone to cut up his body and bury it afterwards. I have to drive to Brownsville and catch a flight from there to Houston now. Move this load as soon as possible. We're falling behind," Carmella remarked angrily as she turned and walked away.

"You're leavin' now, boss?" DeAngelo asked.

"We'll fuel one last time and I'll be on my way."

"Let me know when you're on your way out. I'll have the driver of the truck trail you out."

"Si." Carmella replied as she trotted back over to her Jaguar and hopped in the back seat.

****

"Green light," Doss said as he sat in the driver's seat beside Bay with Jay-D in the backseat.

Bay pulled down her ski-mask and flipped out her DEA badge and Doss and Jay-D did the same. Junior, Dawk and a soldier out the crew followed Bay's lead in their ride, while Malik and three more soldiers from Fox Park brought up the rear. The three, black GMC Suburbans with dark tint pulled into the far right lane just as their contacts had instructed and a U.S. Border Patrol agent waved them forward just as the sun began to set.

Doss pulled forward and flashed his DEA badge and the agent eyed him for a few seconds. "Inside left lane," he said calmly as Jay-D handed him a silk bag stuffed with hundred dollar bills.

The caravan moved forward and approached the inside left lane and a Mexican border agent flagged them down. "You here for the green light?"

Doss responded by handing the man the second silk bag of money. "You're looking for three black Jaguars riding north. That is your marks. I'll delay as many people as I can. Far right lane when you return. Good luck," the Mexican border agent said as he backed away from the SUV.

Doss nodded and rode off into Mexico, headed down a lonely desert road as the sun began to dip behind the mountains in the far off distance to the west.

****

Carmella's caravan had just turned onto the highway leading up to Brownsville. Carmella's driver, who wore a dark pair of sunshades with her head covered in a black headscarf, was listening to Bob Dylan's song *Knocking on Heaven's Door* as she wheeled the car down the highway. The crew's eighteen wheeler, loaded up one hundred and forty-four kilograms of cocaine was only minutes behind, the driver's headlights able to be seen a short distance back as he tailed Carmella and her caravan, counting on them for protection all the way up to the border.

"Call the airport in Brownsville and see what flights they have going to Houston in the morning." Carmella said aloud to one of her soldiers.

"Si, boss," the young woman replied as she turned down the radio and got on her phone.

Carmella and her crew of eight were riding deep underneath the moonlit sky. Armed with AK-47s and plenty of wine to drink and weed to smoke along the way, each of Carmella's crew members' minds were drifting off into the future. It had been a while since they'd traveled with her to the border because she'd always flown out of the city, but this trip had been made dozens of times with the driver of the tractor trailer, and each time, it went like butter.

Carmella's crew was on short notice so they wouldn't be able to cross over with her on this run. The plan was to escort Carmella to the border and she would take a Jaguar and enter America on her own. The driver of the tractor trailer would pick up the car and drive it back to Valle Hermoso once he'd dropped off his trailer at the port of entry. No one riding in the caravan had a clue, however, that they were headed into the teeth of a cataclysm that would play out in the middle of the desert, miles from nowhere and under the silvery darkness of a starry, full moon-lit night.

The four-lane road traveled was a lonely one with the occasional headlights from a single car on the opposite side headed south towards Valle Hermoso and the silhouettes of lone coyotes scurrying across the highway and disappearing into the night. Music was thumping from the cars as they sped north armed to the teeth, but under a false sense of security nonetheless. Death was in the air, but as far as Carmella's crew from Mexico was concerned, it was just another routine run to the border with their boss.

"I need to see how Pepper is doing and call my Ma-Ma also." Carmella said to no one in particular as she grabbed her cell phone.

****

Pepper was sitting in the window of the second floor of the trap house on Ann Avenue watching Toodie and several females as they stood out on the sidewalk in a small circle. The weather was crisp and a little cool as the sun dipped beneath the horizon in Saint Louis. Pepper hated sleeping at the trap house. The place was neat and all, she ate good and had a little money now, but the place was boring. All she ever did was sell drugs and watch TV. If it weren't for Carmella and Simone Cortez, Pepper would've been run away. She had stacks of money, her weekly payouts for working the set, but she could never enjoy the money because Toodie wouldn't let her leave her sight.

Pepper looked over to the TV and got up and grabbed her sack of weed off the dresser and sat down on the bed and began rolling a blunt when her phone vibrated. Her eyes lit up when she saw Carmella's name flash across the screen.

"Hola!"

"Hello, Peppi what it is?" Carmella smiled as she choked off the weed she was smoking.

"When you coming back here?"

"In a couple of days. How's everything?"

"Boring. I wanna go shopping, but Toodie won't take me and she won't let me leave."

"Won't let you leave?"

"Yeah."

"If you wanna go somewhere you gonna have to get around on your own. You can catch a cab anywhere you want to go, Peppi. You have money?"

"A lot of money. I don't like sleeping here. Somebody might take my money."

"Nobody on Ann Avenue will fuck with you. Where's Simone?" Carmella asked while being driven down the dark and lonely highway.

"Downstairs watching TV."

"Get her take you to the mall tomorrow, okay? And when I get back we'll take us a trip to New York. Would you like that?"

"I would love to go to New York! Can Simone come with us?"

"If you want, baby. I miss you."

"I miss you too. I feel better now, too."

"Good. I'm going to hang up and text call my Ma-Ma, okay? We'll talk again tomorrow. Call me when you're ready to go to the mall. I'll tell you where to go and get Toodie off your ass."

"Yes, ma'am. Bye."

"Bye, baby," Carmella said just before she let out a short gasp that was heard by Pepper.

"Bye," Pepper responded somewhat apprehensively. "You

okay," she then asked.

Carmella's eyes had caught sight of something that gave her an ominous feeling just before she ended the call. She picked up her gold-plated .50 caliber and tapped her soldier sitting in the passenger seat. The female turned around and saw her boss nod her head towards three sets of headlights approaching from the opposite direction riding in close proximity.

"*Quién es?*" (Who's that?) Carmella asked anxiously as her heart rate began to accelerate.

Carmella's soldier righted herself in the seat and leaned forward and she and Carmella watched as the cars approached. "*Mirar como el de la ley. Qué están hacienda?*" (Look like the law. What are they doing?) the young woman asked in confusion as she grabbed her AK-47 and racked it.

At that moment Carmella's driver's cell phone vibrated and she answered. "Hola?"

"*Compruebe los jeeps de pasando por el otro lado.*" (Check those jeeps out passing by on the other side.) the driver in the lead car said.

Carmella's crew was waking up to the fact that danger was lurking about as the SUVs approached, but they weren't certain. Heads were turning, blunts were being discarded and semi-automatics were being locked and loaded. Law or not, Carmella's crew was preparing to battle.

"Carmella, you there?" Pepper asked.

"I'm here, Peppi. Hold on, baby."

Carmella sat her phone down and eyed the three sets of headlights headed her way from the opposite direction. The dark tinted Suburbans cruised by and Carmella swore she saw DEA emblems on each of the vehicles' driver side doors. She bowed her head briefly when she saw the SUVs' brake lights light up as all three vehicles made U-turns in the middle of the road, prompting her to pick up her phone.

"I love you, Peppi." Carmella said lowly.

"Okay," Pepper responded.

"I'm sorry about your mother, okay? Be good to your friends." Carmella said before she ended the call and racked her gun.

Pepper removed the phone from her ear and stared at it. She'd never heard Carmella speak in this manner—ever. She placed the phone back to her ear and asked, "You okay? I love you too, Carmella. I forgive you for killing my mother."

Carmella didn't hear Pepper's reply because she'd ended the call. She was too busy watching the headlights on the SUVs as they sped past her tractor trailer, making a beeline for her caravan with their blue lights flashing. Carmella then began thinking about the events that had led up to this moment and two things stuck out in her mind: her plane was sabotaged, thereby preventing her from flying out of harm's way, and DeAngelo kept asking her when was she leaving for America and he'd wanted a signal.

"Uno de mis propias. Me fuckin' DeAngelo!" (One of my own set me up. That fuckin' DeAngelo!) Carmella said in disbelief as she turned around and slumped down in her seat as her car continued traveling up the road towards the U.S. border.

The hit in Saint Charles then quickly ran through Carmella's mind and she now believed she was facing the same maneuver. *"Son American! No rendirse! Matarlos a todos!"* (They're American! No surrendering! Kill them all!) she yelled as her caravan readied themselves for a gun fight.

The female in the front passenger seat of Carmella's ride let the window down and extended the top half of her body out the side of the car and opened fire with her AK-47 on the lead car trailing Carmella's vehicle.

Malik swerved the jeep just as the passenger side window shattered and one of his men screamed aloud. When he slowed, Dawk sped past him and Jay-D rose up through the sunroof and opened fire on Carmella's car with an M-16. The left rear tire exploded and the trunk popped open on the Jaguar as the driver skidded out of control, veering over into the oncoming lane and running off the opposite side of the highway into the desert sand.

Seeing their boss's car swerve off the road and come to a halt, the two remaining cars in Carmella's caravan stopped in the middle of the highway and six females welding AK-47s hopped out of their rides and opened fire under the silvery night sky, determined to take it to whoever it was that dared to impede their venture onto American soil with a tractor trailer loaded down with kilograms of uncut Colombian white powder.

Doss and company had strategically set up their Suburbans. Two were parked across the northbound highway horizontally, giving the Chicago Gang cover from the gunfire while Malik and his three remaining soldiers, with their SUV parked on side of the road facing Carmella's remaining two cars, fired off shots from a vantage point located behind the two parked SUVs about fifty feet before them on their left side.

Carmella, meanwhile was pinned down, her car in between her attackers and the two cars that had stopped to help her wage battle. She crouched on the ground to the rear of her car as bullets lodged into the bulletproof windows and flattened the tires where she lay on the ground. She soon caught sight of one the shooters kneeling beside the hood of one of the Suburbans and let off rapid shots with her .50 caliber.

Bullets from Carmella's gun penetrated the hood on the SUV nearest her and she heard a man gasp as he fell forward, yelling he was hit. Doss pulled the man back behind the Suburban and fired on the rear of the car and Carmella scooted back behind it as one of her soldiers fell dead beside her.

Carmella crawled to the front of the car and eyed her girls across the way, who were engaged in an all-out battle, but were obviously being overcome by the gunfire themselves.

Bay, meanwhile, had scooted over to the second Suburban and came up from the rear of the vehicle with her Dragunov. Others in the Chicago Gang were spraying sporadically trying to hit anything moving; Bay however, was selecting her targets purposely. She'd taken down both drivers of the two Jaguars just ahead and was locked in on another soldier. She squeezed the trigger and the woman collapsed to the ground, leaving Carmella and five soldiers, three who were severely wounded and could no longer fight.

Carmella's driver grabbed her amid a lull in the gunfire and the two made a beeline for one of the Jaguars. They were halfway to the car when more gunfire erupted. Malik was still in on the action, and the gunfire from him and his remaining soldier had sent Carmella and her driver to the asphalt in the middle of the road.

Jay-D and another soldier were closing in on the two remaining soldiers, who'd surrendered under the belief that they were going to be arrested by the U. S. Drug Enforcement Agency given their jackets and badges. They dropped to their knees in the desert sand beside the cars with their hands in the air, believing they would be taken to into custody.

Jay-D, however, walked up on the two women and opened fire with a Tommy gun, killing both females instantly and giving no reason for their being murdered as they turned and jogged back towards the jeeps.

Doss, meanwhile, had walked up on Carmella and her last remaining soldier. Two bullets to the heart from his .45 semi-automatic ended Carmella's last surviving soldier in quick succession as he went and stood over the wounded woman.

"Who are you? Who is sending me on my way?" Carmella asked as she lay on her back looking up at the star-lit sky.

"Remember Saint Charles?" Doss asked as he pointed the gun at Carmella.

"*Chicago? No quiero escuchar mierda tienes que decir, American! Carajo! Simplemente me mata!*" (Chicago? I don't want to hear shit you gotta say, American! Fuck you! Just kill me!)

Doss only understood the last two words Carmella had spoken, 'kill me'. "Not a problem," he said as he let off three shots that slammed into Carmella's face, ending her life.

The gun battle had lasted all but a minute and a half, but it'd seemed like an eternity. As the corpses of Carmella and her crew lay sprawled out in the desert and along the highway, the Chicago Gang headed back to their two remaining rides to clear out the scene.

Carmella's tractor trailer pulled up at that moment and came to a halt. The driver saw the flashing lights and bodies laid out in the middle road that was blocked by what he believed to be DEA agents and he readily surrendered.

Dawk was nearest to the driver and he approached the old man cautiously. Ironically, it was the same old man that had given Carmella the gold-plated .50 caliber hand gun back in 2001 that she'd used to kill Lucky in Saint Charles.

Dawk, unaware of the man's history, pulled out his .45 semi-automatic and shot the driver in his forehead, dead center, from a distance of forty feet, thereby closing a chapter on a bloody feud that had lasted just over three years. He returned to the Suburbans where he saw the crew struggling to get Junior and two more wounded soldiers inside the vehicles.

"We good, dad?" Dawk asked.

"We got a major problem, son. These guys may not make it, but we can't leave 'em here. We have two options," Doss said as he doused Malik's incapacitated jeep with gasoline preparing to set it ablaze. "We can take our people to Valle Hermoso, where all hell is sure to break loose, or we can cross back into our country and figure out what to do from there."

"What you wanna do, dad?"

"Let's go home. I'll figure something out before we get there," Doss answered as he and Dawk walked back towards the two remaining SUVs, leaving behind a burning jeep and ten dead bodies on the ground.

****

Gunshots were ringing out throughout southeast Valle Hermoso. Word of Carmella's demise had spread quickly throughout the town and riots were erupting in and around the drug lord's stomping grounds. Her safe house was destroyed by bandits under the belief that money lay hidden inside the walls, but none was found. When government jeeps rode through the area, everyone that bore witness knew what was about to go down.

Quintessa Lapiente` could hear the gunfire in the distance and see the orange flames billowing up into the air. She stood on her balcony watching as soldiers near the front of her property began spraying gunfire on approaching vehicles. Two of her bodyguards ran into her room and she turned and faced them. "Who is it? Who's attacking my home?" she asked in a rage.

"The mayor has sent military men, Senorita Lapiente`. We will not hold them off for long!"

"Has he lost his mind? My daughter will crush him!"

Quintessa's bodyguards eyed one another and then turned to her. "You, you haven't heard, Senorita?"

"Heard what? What should I know?'

"Carm—your daughter is dead, Senorita Lapiente`. She was hit some miles north of here just minutes ago," the man said somberly.

Quintessa's heart sunk to the pit of her stomach at that moment. "What?" she asked in disbelief.

"We have to go, Senorita," one of the bodyguards spoke in a hurried tone as he reached for Quintessa's hands.

"No!" Quintessa yelled as she snatched away from her protectors.

The gunfire outside was growing ever intense. Lapiente` soldiers were falling all around and the Mexican military was closing in on the villa. The mayor, whose daughter had been kidnapped by the Lapiente` family three years ago, had learned that Carmella had been killed and it was music to his ears. He'd been wanting revenge ever since he was forced to submit to Carmella's will, but had always feared a reprisal. The woman's death had released him of his fears. He was now sending a paid band of Mexican military men to finish off the Lapiente` family once and for all.

"Senorita, Quintessa," one of the men said anxiously, "if we don't leave now we will all die tonight!"

"No!" Quintessa cried aloud. "My entire," the grief-stricken woman rested her hands against her balcony and looked over the land at the Mexican soldiers running towards her villa and knew the end was near. "My entire family! My family!" Quintessa cried as she looked back at her last two remaining soldiers.

"They're coming! Do you know a way out?" one of the men asked in a frantic manner.

"Si!" Quintessa said as she led the way out of the bedroom. "I know of a way!"

The gang of three ran through the home towards a set of stairs and hurried down to the first floor and emerged in the courtyard under the stars. Men were screaming aloud in Spanish far off in the distance as automatic gunfire erupted sporadically, horses and goats ran through the courtyard. An explosion near the front doors sent Quintessa and her bodyguards scattering through the villa. Quintessa ran towards a bench near a bush of roses and opened a hatch just as Mexican soldiers entered the courtyard from the opposite side.

"Run, Senorita Carmella! They're here!" one of the soldiers yelled as he opened fire with a M-16 rifle.

More screams were heard as Quintessa disappeared into the belly of the tunnel. She sighed as she knelt at the foot of the ladder, listening to the intense gun battle unfolding above ground. More explosions were heard, followed by rapid gunfire.

"Where's the woman? Quintessa? Where is she?" echoed through the courtyard.

"She lives to fight another day!" Quintessa said lowly as she began traversing the tunnel towards the opposite end.

Quintessa's mind was working overtime as she traveled the tunnel. Her best bet was to link up with her suppliers from Bogota and rebuild. Avenge her daughter's death and reinstitute a pipeline back to America. She had a bullet-proof Land Rover waiting inside the barn on the opposite end of the tunnel and the keys were inside.

The nearer Quintessa got to the end of the tunnel, the happier she grew. Her escape was certain, but she was hit with a dose of reality when the door leading up to the tunnel was pulled open. Quintessa paused and watched in horror as three grenades landed at the base of the ladder. She ran towards the opposite end of the tunnel screaming aloud and calling out to a higher source. God was nowhere to be found on this night, however; just as the three grenades exploded back to back to back, shaking the tunnel violently and releasing a torrent of smoke, the door on the opposite was opened and four Molotov cocktails slammed down into the tunnel followed by two grenades.

The explosions, coupled with the gasoline bombs sent flames shooting throughout the tunnel. The lights were shattered and the cavern was illuminated with an orange hue whose flames were rapidly turning the supposedly secret passageway into a large oven. Quintessa screamed aloud in agonizing horror under the realization that she was being cooked alive. What lay before her watery eyes was a pure vision of hell. A vision of hell she knew she could not escape. The hatches on both ends of the tunnel were open, supplying oxygen to the flames. The walls inside the tunnel were hot to the touch and Quintessa was finding it hard to breathe. She stood in the center of the tunnel screaming in terror and agony as the oxygen evaporated from the cavern and she was slowly engulfed in flames.

Mexican soldiers stood by in silence, listening to the horrific screams of Quintessa Lapiente`, who was being burned alive in what was supposed to be her escape. Flames soon shot up from both ends of the tunnel and the Mexican army celebrated by releasing multiple rounds of bullets into the air inside the courtyard. The Lapiente` family and all their strength, had been eradicated on this night. They were a family betrayed and a cartel defeated, on their own turf to add insult to injury.

The mayor had taken back what rightfully belonged to the people—the town of Valle Hermoso itself. How long he held control of the city was unknown; one thing was certain, however—the Lapiente` family would no longer pose a problem in this arid desert town just south of the U.S. border. They were now a defunct and irrelevant organization who would only be remembered in conversation and short-winded tales that would chronicle their demise.

THE HOLLAND FAMILY SAGA

CHAPTER TWENTY-FIVE
WHAT'S REALLY GOING ON

Doss and the crew had crossed back over into Brownsville and were now in the underground garage of their hotel walking around the two Suburbans tallying up the damage done on the hit. Bullet holes riddled the left side of one SUV and the passenger and rear windows had been shot out the other, but the bullets to SUVs were the least of the crew's problems. One of the soldiers from Fox Park had died before the crew had even made it back to America.

Doss thought about dumping the guy in the desert, but had Bay or Dawk been killed, he would've risked getting captured or worse in order to take his children home and give them a proper burial. The dead soldier from Fox Park deserved the same treatment was his reasoning. The guy was twenty years old and had a two year-old son and lived with his baby's mother. Her child's father deserved a proper burial in Doss's mind and she would be paid handsomely for her loss. Doss also knew he couldn't leave the guy behind because if his body was ever found, the hit would possibly be traced back to Saint Louis, but the bigger picture was the fact that Doss cared enough to bring the guy home and not dump his remains on side of the road.

Dawk and Malik had placed the man's body inside a body bag, stored his corpse in the Suburban's cargo area and Bay and a couple of soldiers was making repeated trips to an ice machine and pouring buckets of ice inside the bag to keep the guy's body from decaying. Another soldier from Fox Park caught a couple of slugs in both legs, but he was maintaining, sitting in the bullet-riddled SUV smoking a cigarette and drinking brandy to deal with the pain, handkerchiefs tied around the three slugs in his lower legs.

Junior was the biggest worry for the crew. He'd taken a slug to the left armpit and it'd exited out the top of his shoulder blade. Carmella had gotten off a lucky shot that hit an open area on the bullet proof vest Junior had worn. He was sitting quietly in the front seat of the second Suburban with his eyes closed in obvious pain.

"He's hit pretty bad," Doss remarked as he stared at Junior, who was trembling slightly.

"We can't take him to the hospital, though, so we're in between a rock and hard place." Dawk responded.

"Maybe not. I'm gone make a call. Junior, can you hold on for another four or five hours?" Doss asked as he leaned into the SUV and eyed Junior's wound.

"How the fuck, how the fuck would I know, man? It hurts every time I breathe. That bitch landed a million dollar shot." Junior gasped through clenched teeth.

"We can't go to a hospital. I'm gonna make a call, brother. Hold on for us, Junior." Doss said as he grabbed his cell phone.

****

"Won't you take me to...funky town...won't you take me to... funky town...won't you take me to...funky town...won't you take me to...funky town..."

JunJie was sitting inside a booth of *Goddesses*, a high end strip club he owned just outside of The Chinatown-International District in Seattle, Washington, watching several eighteen year-old Asian strippers dance on stage to Lipps Inc.'s song *Funky Town*. It was early in the day and the club was closed. Only JunJie, Finland, Phillip and Grover, and three Asian females were on hand on the first floor. *Goddesses* was where JunJie plotted a lot of his illegitimate schemes and conducted business of a street nature.

The crafty businessman had his hands in nearly every conceivable venture outside of the law while posing as a real estate mogul. Drug deals and the sale of guns went down inside this strip joint, but a far more lucrative business, that of adult entertainment, was also conducted inside of *Goddesses*. The second floor, which was rife with traffic on this day, was the site where numerous Asian pornographic movies were filmed and developed.

Money never stopped for JunJie Maruyama, the Sensei of Asian hustling and a gangster with street credentials that where unparalleled in Seattle's Asian community. He sat tapping his feet to the music as he watched the dancers perform with his family and Finland. The vibrating of the his cell phone caught his attention and he answered over the thumping bass of the music, the phone crammed to his left ear and his right index plugged inside the other.

"We have a situation and we need your help ass soon as possible." Doss said calmly.

JunJie knew the hit was going down on this day through Gacha. "What went wrong?" he asked.

"The job is done. One guy is on ice and the other two need medical attention immediately."

"Where are you now?"

"Just on the other side in Brownsville."

"Okay. Okay, umm. I have to make a flight plan. It'll be at least five hours before I can get down there. Can your men hold on?"

Doss looked over to Junior, who was sweating profusely and grimacing in pain while taking long, deep breaths of air. The soldier from Fox Park was moving around in his seat talking to Dawk and Malik, but he was obviously in pain as he tried to keep his mind focused off his wounds. "They have no choice as of now," Doss said. "We left a lot of damage behind just south of here and the heat may spill back over onto this side.

We can't stay here much longer. You'll have to take us to a safe place."

"I have that covered, my friend. I'll be there A-S-A-P," JunJie replied before he hung up the phone and contacted one of his pilots.

"Everything okay?" Finland asked.

"Our friend completed the job, but there were casualties."

"Damn," Finland sighed as he rubbed his forehead. "Who was it?"

"I'm not certain, but Doss is okay. It was him who called."

"You want me to join you?"

"No. Stay here and enjoy yourself, Finland. Phillip and Grover will take you to my home where you can relax and they will make sure you catch your flight tomorrow afternoon."

"If any of the family needs notifying, call me. I'll handle it. In the meantime," Finland said as he poured himself a glass of gin, "in the meantime, I'll be at my second home." he ended as he eyed the stage once more.

"Enjoy yourself," JunJie replied before he left *Goddesses*, headed to Boeing Field/King Company International Airport where his Gulfstream was located in order to make a flight down to Las Vegas.

****

The Chicago Gang, meanwhile, had moved Junior and the wounded soldier up to one of the hotel rooms they'd rented. Junior was lying across the bed in silence, having taken one of the morphine pills Doss always brought along on hits for just such an occasion. The entire left side of Junior's body was numb and he had no movement in his left extremities. He was cold all the time, so the heat was turned on inside the room and he was draped with a blanket.

The soldier from Fox Park was complaining about severe pain in his legs as he sat at a small desk and swallowed a morphine pill and downed another shot of brandy. Everybody was on pins in needles inside the hotel room, but no one showed emotion as they paced the floor in silent, deep thought, contemplating their next move should the inevitable transpire with Junior, who was the most severely wounded.

Taking bullets on the job was something that couldn't be planned on, no matter how real the possibility. It would've actually been easier to move around with dead bodies, but when it goes down the way it had gone for the Chicago Gang, time was of the essence in order to save a life. Everybody was counting on JunJie to arrive sooner than later. This was a tense time for the crew; they'd succeeded in killing Carmella and her crew down in Mexico, but they were now stuck in Brownsville, Texas in a state of suspended animation while awaiting JunJie's arrival and all they could do for the time being was toe the line in silence as the minutes ticked by at an agonizingly slow pace.

****

Back in Ponca City, Naomi was sitting in her office with Kimi and Koko, the three of them closing out bills of ladings for the week when Naomi's phone rang. She answered and heard Doss's voice on the other end. Kimi and Koko eyed their mother briefly and returned to their duties. A minute later they heard their mother gasp.

"What? Will he be okay?"

"Who?" Kimi asked worriedly. "What happened, momma?"

Kimi and Koko, ever since they realized their mother was training them to launder money for the family, began wondering exactly where all the currency was coming from. This was more than agriculture in their eyes. They'd seen the numbers, knew what cattle went for, and how much freight was leaving the ranch. They began focusing in on their father, Dawk, Bay and Tiva more and more and had a feeling that there was much more to what they were being told. When they asked their mother about the profits being made, Naomi told them that the trucks ran other freight besides livestock, but her answer didn't sit right with Kimi and Koko, the numbers didn't add up, except for on paper after they were done moving money around. Now, this strange phone call was received and

Kimi and Koko were both worried that something had happened to their father, or maybe Dawk and Bay, who'd traveled with their father to Chicago nearly two weeks earlier.

Naomi hung up the phone and looked over to Kimi and Koko. "Everyone's fine," she said. "Your father, Dawk and Bena will have to stay out a little while longer back in Chicago that's all."

That was all Kimi and Koko wanted hear. Nothing else mattered. So long as their family was safe, they would have no problems and ask no further questions. They resumed working as Naomi got up from behind her desk and quietly left the room.

Tiva, meanwhile, was in the library sitting at the large oval table reading a book containing baby names. The nineteen year-old mother-to-be was hoping to have a baby girl. She wanted to see if the family myth was true—that Holland females come forth as twins. She would be more than honored to be the first of the grandchildren to further add to the family heritage by birthing twins. She sat sipping Gatorade and listening to her MP-3 player as she scanned a host of names.

Naomi soon found Tiva in the library and entered the room slowly. "Hey, momma," Tiva said happily as she removed ear plugs. "I was looking at a bunch of names for the babies."

"Babies?"

"Yeah. I don't know yet, but you knew before Spoonie and Tyke were born you was carrying female twins. I think I am too. I looked at boys names? But they not sticking with me. When I look at the girl names, though? I just get this feeling in my stomach like that's what it is."

"Tiva, listen to me, baby," Naomi said softly as she sat down beside her daughter. "You know, sometimes, sometimes we go through life thinkin' everything will turn out just fine. We move about making plans as if tomorrow will come, right up until the moment we're blindsided with a brick."

Tiva knew what her father, brother and sister and Junior had sat out to do. She was with Bay and Dawk when they were training on the ranch with M-16 rifles, practicing herself and sitting in on every discussion right up until their departure. They were going after a fierce woman in her homeland. The job was the most difficult by far and casualties were a possibility. She leaned back in a weakened state and eyed her mother as tears welled up in her eyes. "What happened?" she asked as her body began to tremble.

"The job went well. Carmella has been taken down."

"But?"

Naomi crossed her legs and looked Tiva in the eyes and said, "Junior took a hit and it doesn't look good."

"Will he make it?" Tiva asked through her tears.

"We don't know. I can't help back to think back to when Lucky got hit. I swear I thought he was gonna pull through, but he took a terrible turn. I can't sit here and tell you I'm certain Junior will survive because nobody knows. Doss said it'll be another four hours before he can be moved."

"We was supposed to get married at the end of the month, momma. Can I go to him?"

"You can't, Tiva. Junior is breathing, but he's not responding. He's unconscious. Everybody involved is tryin' to stay off the radar for now. We'll get an update before morning," Naomi said as she eased up from her seat.

Naomi continued on towards the open area on Ponderosa's pristine first floor with her hands behind her back and her head bowed in deep thought. Losing Junior would have serious repercussions. Mendoza and DeeDee were on the verge of retiring and the crew needed all the experience they could muster because the business was getting more treacherous as time wore on. Carmella had been taken down, and for that, the family may have to answer someday. The Somalis were still unknown and there was no telling what would jump off with Asa Spade because he was still in a weakened state after battling Carmella, who was kicking his ass outright by all accounts before the family finally got to her if Naomi had to tell it.

Martha, meanwhile, was in the kitchen looking for a corkscrew so she and Twiggy could uncap a bottle of wine and watch a movie in the theater room when she saw her sister strolling by. Naomi seemed to be in deep thought to Martha, but there was much more to be read in her eyes. Her oldest sister wore a black sombrero that covered her head completely and had a pair of thin framed sunshades were covering her eyes. A white, tight-fitting denim outfit was plastered to her voluptuous body and she wore a pair of expensive knee length boots that were hidden by her jeans. Naomi was always dressed when she was awake. Unless she was under the weather, she was up and about and in a managerial state of mind each and every day. Running a ranch couldn't be this stressful in Martha's mind and she'd now resolved herself to getting some answers on this night as thunder began to rumble across the land from an approaching storm.

"Sis," Martha called out.

Naomi was startled from her thoughts as she eyed Martha. "What's up?" she asked.

"I should be asking you that, Naomi," Martha said as she sat the bottle of wine down and approached her sister.

Naomi looked off into the openness of Ponderosa briefly. For a while now she'd been feeling Martha. She knew her sister was paying close attention to her dealings and it was only a matter of time before Martha could withhold her thoughts before she erupted. That point had just arrived. Naomi thought briefly on what she would say before gazing her eyes back upon Martha.

"You got something you wanna say to me, sister?" Naomi asked calmly.

"What's really going on, Naomi? This here is more than just running livestock. Mendoza and DeeDee are in the streets and the apple didn't fall too far from the tree with Doss and Junior. And Dawk and my oldest nieces ain't just learnin' how to run a warehouse."

Twiggy emerged from the long hall at that moment flustered. "Martha, you takin' all day with wine, girl. The movie about to start!" It didn't take a scientist for Twiggy to figure out that she'd stumbled upon to something involving Martha and Naomi given the way they were standing eye to eye. She eased around the two and grabbed the wine off the counter.

"I'm about to share some things with Martha concerning the family, Twiggy," Naomi said lowly. "You want in on this?"

"Nahh. Thanks, but no thanks, Naomi." Twiggy said as she curled her lips and walked off, leaving Martha and Naomi behind with stunned looks upon their faces.

"Well, that's a new one." Naomi said, breaking the silence between her and Martha. "Follow me," she then said as she led Martha to the first floor observation room where she closed and locked the door and began to give Martha the lowdown on the family's most profitable form of revenue, which involved everything from drug dealing to murder-for-hire.

Tiva, meanwhile, was pacing the library floor when Siloam walked in and began rummaging through stacks of magazines in search of an editor she felt would give Jane Dow a chance at stardom. She could see Tiva out the corner of her eyes as she went about her business and could tell she was troubled. "You okay, Tiva?" she finally asked.

"Just a thang I'm going through," Tiva responded.

"Sometimes a 'thang' could be too much for one person to bear. Care to share?"

"Not really."

"Tiva," Siloam said humbly as she pulled out a chair and extended her hand.

Tiva sat down and Siloam sat beside her. "Tell me, please, what's going on with you?"

Tiva eyed Siloam with a blank stare. Discussing family business was a no-no. As much as she needed a listening ear, Tiva refused to engage Siloam in conversation.

"You know me and Junior have a history, right?" Siloam asked lowly.

"That was years ago."

"Yes. Years ago. You ever wonder why we never continued on with our rapport?"

"Not really."

"You're being curt with me and I understand. But you need to know that I know the man Junior is, Tiva. He's every bit his father, and for that? We could never be. You are the very thing Junior needs because you two are the same."

"What you mean, Siloam?"

"Tiva? I don't live in this house with blinders on. Mary and Regina are the truly innocent ones, but I know what goes on here. You, your father, Dawk and Bay are in the business that DeeDee, Mendoza and rest his soul, Lucky, was into when he was alive."

"You talk like you know everything."

"Not everything, but enough, Tiva. I figured out long before Serena and Kevin died what your parents were into. But you know what? I don't care about that. Your mother and father gave me life. I'm grateful for that."

"Why you never said nothing?"

"Because it isn't my place to do so, Tiva. I accept what goes on here the same way you accept what you do."

"The wedding may not happen."

"You can't think like that. For that to happen it would disrupt your life entirely. I don't think such a tragedy is in your future."

Tiva smiled at that moment. For as long as she could remember, Siloam was always an optimistic person. Optimism isn't a guarantee of one's survival, however; and as much as Tiva appreciated Siloam's attempt to comfort her, she knew Junior's fate rested on his fortitude to fight for his life.

Truths had come out on this day amongst some of the family. Secrets were revealed, judgments were nonexistent. Those in the know were now along for the journey's duration and the possible outcomes were understood. There was no room to shed tears should the unthinkable happen because everybody involved understood that the business outside of the ranch could lead to possible death.

THE HOLLAND FAMILY SAGA

CHAPTER TWENTY-SIX
TYING UP LOOSE ENDS

The day after the hit on Carmella found Rafael Gacha sitting in the backseat his Bentley watching as his plane cruised to a halt on the runway of Margarita Island. Two of his henchmen exited the plane with DeAngelo Spires walking in between the two as they descended the stairs. As he watched the men, Gacha placed hollow tip shells into a .9mm Beretta. When he was done loading the clip, he slid it into the gun and leaned back and rested his arm on the top of the soft leather as DeAngelo approached. "Mister Spires," he smiled, "what a great thing you have done for us, my friend."

"It wasn't by choice as you know." DeAngelo said meekly as he climbed into the front seat. "Are they o—"

"Wait a minute," Gacha said, cutting DeAngelo off as he picked up a remote control and turned the volume up on the stereo. "*Nunca lo encontrarás...siempre y cuando vivas... alguien que te ama...tan tierna como yo...*" *(You'll never find...as long as you live...someone who loves you...as tender as I do...)*

"I love Mister Lou Rawls's song, but this Spanish band has a much better version," Gacha laughed over the music as he tapped the backseats of his ride as if he were playing drums. "I met Mister Rawls once you know? Down here on the island when he was vacationing. What a wonderful time we had. He sung this song on the beach before me and a group of friends."

"Can I just have my—"

"Wait," Gacha told DeAngelo, my favorite part is coming up. *"Oh, yo no estoy tratando de hacer su estancia bebé...pero sé de alguna manera algún día...algún modo...te vas a perder mi cariñoso..."* (Oh, I'm not trying to make you stay baby...but I know somehow someday...some way...you're going to miss my loving...)

DeAngelo listened as Gacha sang along with the music, steadily tapping the headrests, adding to his anxiety.

"Okay, amigo," Gacha said halfway through the song, "let me give you back what you've given up so easily."

"It may have been easy on your part, but it wasn't by choice, Rafael." DeAngelo reiterated as Gacha's driver put the car in drive.

"Since when have we been on a first name basis?" Gacha asked seriously as his driver slowed the car to a halt.

DeAngelo turned and eyed Gacha in the backseat and said nervously, "I'm, I'm sorry, Senor Gacha. I meant no disrespect."

Gacha laughed at that moment. "I'm only kidding with you, Mister Spires," he said as he patted DeAngelo's shoulder. "Loosen up, my friend. Would you like some champagne during the trip back to my home?"

"No thank you. Can I just have my family back, please?" DeAngelo pleaded.

"I will take you to them right now." Gacha remarked as his driver pulled off once more.

The kidnapping of DeAngelo's two sisters and his mother down in Mexico City two months earlier by a crew of Gacha's soldiers shortly after they'd met up with Doss in Brownsville, Texas, had pushed the man into a corner. He'd been loyal to the Lapiente` family for years, but he'd grown lax on protecting his own family. Gacha knew exactly who to latch on to in order to get close Carmella and he'd picked the perfect mark in DeAngelo. Having his mother and two sisters run the risk of torture and death was more than he could bear and he readily chose family over friendship. He'd sabotaged Carmella's plane the night before she left and had given up Carmella's schedule.

DeAngelo rode in silence in the passenger seat as Gacha's driver wheeled his way through town. It was dead silent in the car now, a little unnerving for DeAngelo, but he didn't show any fear. All he wanted was his family back and he would retire from the business. Brazil was on his mind as Gacha's car slowed to a roll in front of a woodshed near the rear of the orange groves on his vast span of land.

Gacha and his driver hopped out the car and began walking towards the small wood shed. "What are you waiting on?" Gacha asked as he walked pass DeAngelo sitting in the front seat. "You want to see your family, no?" he asked as he patted his side with his gun.

DeAngelo looked around at the scenery surrounding him from the front seat. He was in a shady area with numerous wooden tables laced with remnants of oranges that had been picked a while ago. He slowly emerged from the car, leaving the passenger side door open, a way of telling himself and the men who were eyeing him coldly that he had plans on returning.

"Where are they?" DeAngelo asked Gacha meekly.

"There in the shed. You'll have to untie them. We'll wait here."

"I've done all that you've—"

"No need to speak," Gacha said, cutting DeAngelo's remarks short. "Your family is waiting on you. I told you, you would see them again so go."

Slowly, DeAngelo approached the wooden doors of the shed. He heard no sound as he grew near the entrance and he began shedding silent tears, realizing he'd reached the end of the line. His family was dead if he had to tell it, and he was now walking into his final resting place. He'd tried though; he'd tried to save his family, but the trust he'd put in his family's captors had been betrayed in the same manner in which he'd betrayed Carmella. DeAngelo looked back at Gacha as he stood before the wooden doors.

Gacha merely extended his hands, remaining silent as he eyed DeAngelo. He pulled one of the doors open slowly, and was relieved to see his mother and two sisters tied up and kneeling down on the dirt floor.

"Momma! I've come for you!" DeAngelo said happily as he removed the gags from his mother and sisters' mouths and untied them.

"*Por qué viniste aquí? No debería haber venido, DeAngelo!*" (Why did you come here? You shouldn't have come here, DeAngelo!) DeAngelo's mother said in horror.

"We are done, mother. We have enough money to live three lives. I've made us all rich." DeAngelo said happily.

"We are done, mother? Never have any words spoken been truer," Gacha stated calmly as he entered the woodshed with four of his henchmen following his lead, all of the men toting AK-47s and eyeing DeAngelo and his family coldly.

"*No! Por favor el señor Gacha. Ha hecho todo que pregunta! Tómeme! Deje a mis hijos ir, por favor!*" (No! Please Mister Gacha. He's done all you ask! Take me! Let my children go, please!) DeAngelo's mother pleaded as she held onto her daughters, who were crying their hearts out.

DeAngelo jumped up and stood before his family. "What is this?" he asked nervously.

"I told you, you would see your family again, my friend. I didn't tell you the rest, though, now did I? Your mother knows what else I have to ask of you all, Senor."

"What else do you want from me? From us?"

"Glad you asked. I want you all to die, my friend. Just to die," Gacha said nonchalantly as he and his men opened fire on the Spires family, riddling their bodies with multiple gunshots, nearly tearing them apart. When the smoke cleared, Gacha surveyed the damage and said, "Chop them up and cover their bodies with lime and bury them deep in the woods."

"Si, boss," one of the men replied.

The death of DeAngelo Spires had closed the chapter on the Lapiente` family. With their deaths, went the planned hit on Denver and the Sinaloas backed away, having lost one of their distributors. Those who remained behind in Mexico had no fight left in them; they were only warehouse workers who hadn't the strength to battle the Americans, let alone Gacha himself. The Boss of Bosses had brought about a swift end to the Spires family on behalf of his American counterparts and now, it would become business as usual for all parties involved.

****

"He's fortunate the bullet didn't travel downwards instead of upwards," Doctor Fitzgerald told Dawk as he operated on a comatose Junior inside JunJie's mansion in Paradise, Nevada.

"So he's gonna make it?" Dawk asked as he stood a ways off, watching the doctor use a scalpel and tweezers on Junior.

"By all measures I would say so. He is in the clear so far and things are looking up," Doctor Fitzgerald replied happily as he removed small pieces of shattered bone from Junior's clavicle.

"Good," Dawk said as he pulled out his cell phone to call Tiva, "his wife will be glad to know he's okay."

JunJie had flown down to Brownsville the night before where he picked up the Chicago Gang and transported them back to Las Vegas where medical attention was afforded Junior and the soldier from Fox Park. Junior's wounds were severe, but not life threatening. Before Doctor Fitzgerald induced a coma on Junior, he told Dawk that he could feel the tips of his fingers. Things were looking up.

"Our friend south of the border appreciates your work, Mister Dawkins," JunJie said as the two sat in his lounge area on the third floor of his mansion. "That hit has opened big doors for us."

"Well," Doss said as JunJie poured him a glass of vodka and orange juice, "I've done what I had to do for my family. That woman was causing major problems for all of us."

"She was an interesting person, though. A little disturbed, but she was intelligent and courageous. I have to give her that much credit. They will fight like cats and dogs over the route through Valle Hermoso now."

"Will it affect us?"

"Not in the least. We ship everything on those freighters I was able to obtain after the Onishi brothers', umm, their, sudden departure shall I say?"

"Anybody ever question you about that job?"

"If you mean the authorities then the answer is yes. But I have a contact on the inside. My alibi at the time checks out also and your gang's name is nonexistent."

"How connected is your man on the inside?"

"He's a federal agent, my friend. That's all you need to know."

"You have the FBI in your pocket I see. Well, that should keep us all a step ahead."

"There's nothing to worry about at the present time except for the health of your friend, Doss. We've won not only the battle, but the war itself. As of today, we are in the clear."

"Good. I have a feeling things are going to pick up on the drug side of things and the last thing we need is for the law to start sniffing around."

"The burden is mines to bear, my friend. You just remain safe. Your payment will be delivered within the week," JunJie said as he poured himself a drink. "And don't worry about Junior. Doctor Fitzgerald is a wizard," he ended.

Doss and JunJie were enjoying the success garnered on Carmella's hit in October of 2004. The job by far was a classic takedown. The authorities in Mexico were under the impression that Carmella had been hit by a rival cartel from within the country, although files garnered on the homicides had been forwarded to the F.B.I., who had an interest in the on-going drug wars south of the border.

Doss and the crew had left behind no evidence leading back to America, but he'd unintentionally ignited a fire along the way. It would be a spark that neither he, JunJie, nor Gacha had ever anticipated.

THE HOLLAND FAMILY SAGA

CHAPTER TWENTY-SEVEN
CHILLVILLE

"*Come on outside who wanna ride with these big boys...we got some big toys in the parking lot making big noise...we bring them hoes out like it's summer...blowing marijuana... while we rolling in that hummer...with no drama...*" The rapper Tela's song, *Bring them Hoes Out,* blared loudly from the opened sunroof of Dawk's Escalade the first week in November of 2004.

Things were back in order for Doss and the Chicago at this point. The crew was now back in full power in Saint Louis and they were now supplying Detroit, Milwaukee, and Cleveland as well, through increased shipments.

Asa Spade and his crew, meanwhile, were back in full control of Denver and also had cocaine in Idaho, Wyoming, North and South Dakota. The network was up and running at full steam once again; and without any more hits on the table, the big three got to spend more time back in Ponca City.

Junior had spent a week down in Vegas recovering and going through several surgeries. He was still recovering from the bullet wound that had left the left side of his body partially paralyzed, but Doctor Fitzgerald assured him that he would regain complete control of his extremities in six months or so as the wound healed. He was now living on the ranch and spending his days with Tiva, who was carrying twin baby girls, the two of them planning to marry in April of 2005.

Dawk, Bay and T-top simply loved hanging out in Ponca City; here they were celebrities, and they garnered no retaliation in their hometown; besides, the only person in Saint Louis that knew where the family resided was Junior, and he never spoke about Oklahoma to no one as for as they all knew and believed. Fun times were had, and on this cold November night in 2004 down in Ponca City, a few of the siblings were hanging out in the parking lot of Kaw Lake Park listening to music and just kicking back in the cold air.

Bay was sitting in her old school Lincoln with AquaNina sipping champagne with the heat on, the two of them making sweet talk and planning a trip to Oklahoma City to do some Christmas shopping with Tiva and Junior on Black Friday.

Dawk was beside the lake shore with Oneika. She was his sole woman now ever since his girl Jordan had hooked up Walee. It wasn't that long ago when Walee had told his father, grandfather DeeDee, Mendoza and Dawk that he would never like girls. Those thoughts quickly vanished, however when Walee hit puberty a year ago. Frequent wet dreams, porno-flicks and conversations with Dawk had piqued his interest. So much so he'd paid eighteen year-old Jordan Whispers a hundred dollars to have sex with him a few months back in late August. All the things he'd said he would never do, right up to paying for sex, Walee had done at age thirteen. He'd turned fourteen a month earlier and was now wide open in November of 2004.

Jordan was no better. At one point she was sleeping with Dawk and Walee, but Dawk cut her off because he was really beginning to like twenty-year-old Oneika Brackens. Dawk got around, having been with a few girls in the city, but Jordan wasn't someone he wanted on his team because of the way she carried herself now. She would let Walee handle her in some of the worse ways imaginable. Everybody knew it, but none of the siblings did a thing to correct it because they all felt Jordan, being four years older than Walee, should have known better.

The door on Dawk's Escalade flew open and the music grew louder. He turned and saw Jordan jump from the backseat and spit onto the ground.

"I told you not to shoot off in my mouth, Walee!" Jordan yelled.

"The fuck you doing? Get your Judy Jetson-looking ass back in this mutherfuckin car," fourteen year-old Walee yelled to eighteen year-old Jordan as Bay, Dawk, AquaNina and Oneika burst into laughter.

Walee couldn't get enough of Jordan, who liked having sex with him as well, but each time she went down on Walee, he erupted into her mouth without warning, something she hated. Jordan couldn't walk away though because hanging with the Holland family's children and sharing in some of the expensive toys they owned was too alluring. She spat onto the ground and wiped her mouth with the back of her hands and turned and faced Dawk's SUV. "Don't do that no more, man!" Jordan snapped.

"Alright," Walee sighed. "My bad, baby girl, but it's cold, come on back in and close the door. I ain't gone do it again."

"Walee, man, you say that every time! You play too much!" Jordan said as she walked back to the Escalade, got in and closed the door. Before long the SUV was bouncing up and down. Jordan was Walee's first, but she wouldn't be his last by a long shot as he wanted to sow his young oats to fullest extent possible. The youngest of Naomi's two sons was slowly turning into a player, but he'd rather call himself a ladies man.

Dawk laughed and turned back to Oneika. "What's wrong with your girl?" he asked.

"Man, she fall for that play every time. She might as well swallow and get it over with," Oneika said laughingly.

"That girl there weak-minded. Walee gone meet his match early, though, watch what I tell ya'," Dawk said as he and Oneika walked a good ways down the lake shore towards a stack of fallen timbers where they began building a bon fire.

After a while, everyone was out in front the huge fire Dawk and Oneika had built. The six family and friends were just hanging out having a good time, Dawk, Oneika and Jordan sipping brandy, Bay and Oneika dancing and Walee cracking jokes with everybody; it was just good country living down in Ponca City in late fall of 2004.

"Hey Bay, check my new dance!" AquaNina said as she began to do the butterfly, an old dance from the early nineties where a person would slowly move their legs in and out like wings. Bay watched and burst into laughter when AquaNina closed her eyes and wrinkled her lips as she danced.

"Girl, what is that?" Bay asked before she guzzled her champagne.

"It's called the butterfly, how I look?"

"You look ugly as fuck!" Walee yelled as he threw a snowball that crashed in AquaNina's face. Soon, an all-out snow ball fight got underway as the group began running around the darkened park.

****

"Damn, Kimi," Koko sighed as she lay back on the bed. "Girl, if people in the family knew what we were doing I would be so embarrassed."

"Me too, girl. But they ain't gone find out. It feels good though, don't it?" Kimi asked.

"It does." Koko sighed.

"You want me to do it again, Koko?"

"Yeah, but go slow this time. I really wanna feel it, Kimi."

Kimi leaned forward and Koko rose up from the pillows and the two sat face to face. Kimi placed the blunt in her mouth in reverse and blew her sister another strong shotgun, letting the smoke linger in the air as her sister inhaled deeply.

This was a private party the sixteen year-old middle daughters were having on this cold November night. Spoonie and Tyke were having a slumber party with a few of their friends from their softball team and the dozen or so twelve and thirteen year-olds had the theater room on lock. And what Kimi and Koko had planned couldn't be done on the ranch anyways as there were too many eyes around. A trip to the movies and then the bowling had become their story, but in all actuality, they'd scored a twenty-five dollar bag of weed from Jane Dow's parents and rented a suite in town.

Kimi and Koko loved to pamper themselves; this day was no different. The suite they were in had two king-sized beds, a large Jacuzzi, two thirty-two inch screen TVs and a wet bar. They'd stopped at Kentucky Fried Chicken and bought a fifteen piece box of original with cole slaw and macaroni, a two liter Pepsi and copped Ludacris' latest CD to go along with their burnt copies before parking their bodies inside the hotel.

The twins were kicking back in the plush room wrapped up in thick cotton robes with mud packs on their faces. They'd done their nails and were preparing to style one another's hair, but had decided to smoke a blunt. It was their first time getting high, and the feeling was indescribable. They sat on the bed giggling, enjoying the light-headed feeling the drug was producing.

"Turn the radio on," Koko said as she took the blunt from Kimi and took a few tokes.

****

Martha and Twiggy, meanwhile, were just entering the west side of Ponca City on Highway 60, the two having driven in from Salina, Kansas. The day Naomi had shared the family business with Martha, she was left a little stunned. She had an idea Doss was pushing drugs, but she never imagined him being a killer-for-hire and had trained her oldest nephew and nieces to do the same.

Naomi didn't go into full detail nor did she discuss jobs with Martha, she only told her that the business sometimes called for gunplay. Martha understood. She'd run the streets herself back in Ghost Town, but Naomi and her bunch were on an entirely different level. Martha didn't pass judgment on her family though; she actually respected the way Naomi balanced business and family.

When she was done talking to Naomi that day, Martha sought out Twiggy. She wanted to know why her friend wanted to not hear what Naomi had to say. The two went into Naomi's private room and Twiggy was nearly in tears when she told Martha that she wanted to die a free woman and a peaceful death.

Forty-five year-old Irene 'Twiggy' Charles was the last surviving member of her family. All of her relatives had died violently. Her brothers, Nolan and Peter Paul, having been shot to death in Jackson, Mississippi along with her nephew Simon, and her favorite brother, Albert Lee, was executed in Parchment State Penitentiary. Both of Twiggy's parents had died behind bars. Her mother was stabbed to death and her father had succumbed to pneumonia, although Twiggy knew he'd actually died of AIDS.

"You got your whole family, Martha. I just wanna enjoy life and watch these kids grow up. Help around when I can and just be a part of the family until my dying day," Twiggy told Martha back in October, which was a month ago.

Forty-five year-old Martha understood Twiggy's reasoning. And she herself had no direct involvement in the family's outside business at the time, but she was willing to get involved should it come to it. If Twiggy wanted to remain on the outside and just live amongst the family, Martha had no problem with it because in all honesty, Twiggy was family long before Naomi had entered the picture. The two would continue to drive for the family and enjoy life with the understanding that Martha may someday take a different path.

Martha was behind the wheel of her and Twiggy's rig as she and Twiggy cruised into town. She wore a cowgirl hat and had on a thick jean jacket as the heat had gone out in the truck. She and Twiggy were bundled up inside the rig eager to get home when Martha noticed her Sebring parked in front of the Holiday Inn Express.

"What the fuck is this shit here?" Martha asked perplexed as she pulled the eighteen wheeler into the hotel's truck parking area.

Twiggy looked and saw Martha's car. "Hey, who got your shit? Dawk or Bay?"

"It *better* be one of them and not who the fuck I *think* it is!" Martha exclaimed as she dialed T-top's number on her cell phone.

"Sup?" Tiva asked as she lay beside Junior in her bedroom.

"You got my whip, T-top?"

"Nahh. I'm home chillin' with Junior, girl. I can't move around in the shape I'm in."

"Where Kimi and Koko?"

"They said they was going to the movies and then hang out at the bowling alley. Why?"

"Never mind!" Martha snapped as she hung up her phone, grabbed her .44 magnum and she and Twiggy exited the rig and walked towards the hotel's front desk and obtained an extra key after arguing with the receptionist for several minutes.

"*How you ain't gone fuck...bitch I'm me...I'm the reason your got damn ass is up in V.I.P...*" Ludacris' song *Stand Up* was earsplitting inside one of hotel rooms as Kimi and Koko stood in the center of the room dancing. Kimi had a beer in her hand and Koko had just taken another long toke from the blunt straight to the head and she was just as lit as her twin. The girls were 'dropping it like it was hot', 'pussy-popping' and 'making it clap' inside the room as they danced in their robes.

"*When I move you move...just like that...when I move you move...just like that...when I move you move...just like that... hell yeah, eh DJ bring that back...*"

Kimi and Koko were both face to face pussy-popping when the door opened and in stepped Martha. She wrinkled her face when the stench of marijuana filled her nostrils as she scanned the room.

Kimi stopped when she saw Martha and Twiggy. Koko, however, had her back to the door and was steadily dancing. She saw Kimi staring at the entrance to the room. She pussy-popped up from her bent-over stance and asked, "What's wrong, Kimi? You look like you seen a—Martha!" Koko screamed when she turned around and eyed her aunt.

"What the *fuck* y'all doing in this room?" Martha asked loudly as Twiggy closed the door and turned off the music.

"Nothin, Auntie! We was just dancin'!" Kimi and Koko replied.

"Dancin! In ya' fuckin' drawls? Looking like you work in a strip club? Put your shit on!"

"Kimi and Koko y'all was supposed to be at the movies. What y'all doing in here?" Twiggy asked as she eyed the weed spread out on the table while inhaling the scent of the marijuana.

"Twiggy we was just dancin'. I swear." Koko stated anxiously.

"Look around this room, Koko! Look how y'all playin' yourselves." Martha reasoned, extending her hands outwards.

"How we playin' ourselves?" Koko asked in dismay. "It's just us two. Ain't no boys in here, no crowd or nothing, just us two. We was chillin', Martha! We could never do this at home! We just wanted to have a little party of our own that's all."

"Can I get a piece of y'all chicken?" Twiggy asked as she eased over to the table.

Martha placed her hands on her hips and eyed her friend in surprise. She'd just caught her nieces smoking and was trying to school them right, but Twiggy wasn't on the same page as Martha by a long shot.

"What?" Twiggy asked as she grabbed a napkin and picked up a chicken leg. "They could be doing a lot worse, Martha. And this is nothing like what we thought we would see. These girls ain't bothering nobody."

"Smoking weed at sixteen? How y'all was gone get back home?" Martha asked her nieces.

"We had like five hours left before curfew. We was gone be good. We had one beer and I was gone throw it away because I don't like the taste."

A lighter was soon heard flickering and the twins and Martha turned and saw Twiggy lighting up the blunt. She took a toke and choked and sat the blunt back in the ashtray as she pounded her chest. "What, what the fuck y'all smokin'?" she asked as she coughed repeatedly.

"We got that from Jane Dow people. They said it's called purple haze," Kimi answered lowly.

"This is some good shit! Here, Martha! Hit this one time," Twiggy said as she picked up the blunt and held it out for Martha.

"Twiggy this here ain't even much what we had in—"

"Fuck that! Hit this shit, girl!" Twiggy snapped as she held out her arm with the blunt in between her fingertips. "Look the fuck around! They chillin' big time!"

Martha eyed the room briefly. Food was laid out, Kimi and Koko had a wide assortment of cosmetics and lotions spread out to pamper themselves, the wet bar was ripe for the taking, and the Jacuzzi looked more than inviting; and seeing Twiggy choking off the weed after only a couple of tokes did arouse her curiosity as well.

"How often y'all two do this?" Martha asked curiously.

"This our first time," Koko answered, not sure what Martha was going to do.

"That's some good smoke, Twiggy?" Martha asked as she removed her hat and jean jacket.

"Girl, if you don't hit this weed I'm gone walk over there and slap fire from your ass!" Twiggy said before taking another toke, that one forcing her down into a chair. "Goodness gracious I ain't had one like this in years—*years*!"

Martha eyed her nieces, who now had smirks on their faces. "I'm a, umm, I'm a see, see what she saying."

Kimi and Koko stepped aside and watched as Martha took the blunt from Twiggy and hit it a couple of times. She held the smoke in, trying not to choke, but it was all in vain. She let out a loud cough, and took a knee as she pounded her chest while passing the blunt back to Twiggy, who took a toke of her own.

"What we gonna do now?" Kimi asked as she and Koko

stood staring at their aunt and Twiggy.

****

"*...When I move you move...just like that...when I move you move...just like that...when I move you move...just like that... hell yeah, eh DJ bring that back...*" Ludacris' song *Stand Up* was blaring from Kimi and Koko's radio once more as the two danced with their aunt and Twiggy while sharing another blunt.

Originally she'd set out to try and correct her nieces. Martha Holland, however, now found herself wrapped up in one of the hotel's complimentary robes dancing as if she were in a night club. She'd showered, removed her nail polish and now had her face covered with a mud pack and was preparing to give herself a French manicure while taking tokes and going so far as to pass the weed around to her sixteen year-old nieces as the four danced in unison, bouncing their shoulders as they dipped in one place while slowly turning around in a circle where they stood. This wasn't Martha's plan by a long shot, but Kimi and Koko really were parlaying and it was easy for Martha to get down with her nieces, who were taking her and Twiggy back to their younger days in Ghost Town with their antics.

Kimi and Koko, in Martha's eyes, when it got down to it, were the coolest of her nieces. They did their own thing and had their own style, a style Martha could relate to fully. Although being on the ranch, Martha hadn't really got down with Kimi and Koko, or any of her nieces for that matter, in this manner ever. Bay and T-top were different breeds. They were all about business most times and that was understood given the business they were involved in. Spoonie and Tyke were pure athletes and were interested in sports and sports only. Kimi and Koko, however, Martha, quickly realized, were fun-loving and laidback.

Apprehension and counseling was thrown away on this night as Martha had made up her mind that she would kick it with her nieces uninhibitedly. This wouldn't be a routine thing, however, and she'd admonished the twins to not let anyone in on what they were doing.

Kimi and Koko promised to do so and had also made up their

minds that what they were doing wouldn't become habit. With that understanding, a private party meant for two had turned into a gathering for four.

"This bitch here had a gun and was about to shoot your aunt the day we first met, yeah?" Martha said over the music as she pointed to Twiggy.

"Your ass robbed Chug-a-lug shit, girl. You had Ghost Town hot with your ass, Martha!" Twiggy laughed as she went and poured her and Martha a glass of Dom Perignon as they'd cracked open the wet bar fully.

"How y'all fixed that?" Koko asked as she began styling Kimi's hair, still gyrating to the music.

Martha went on and told her nieces about some of the things that unfolded when she ran the streets while she did her nails. She talked a good bit about Ne`Ne` also, bringing Regina's twin to life and giving Kimi and Koko profound glimpses into the life of a cousin they'd never met. The marijuana had Martha talking more candidly than ever before; she'd brought tears to Kimi and Koko's eyes as she went into detail about the events that had led up to Ne`Ne`'s death.

The story of Ghost Town was given to Kimi and Koko in explicit detail and they had newfound respect for their aunts and Twiggy, given all they'd been through before the family was reunited. Another blunt was rolled and the females went on to pamper one another; Martha had called Naomi and told her that she and her nieces and Twiggy were going to camp out at the hotel because the roads had become too icy to travel.

Dawk, Bay and Walee had made it home already, Spoonie, Tyke and their company was still hanging out in the theater room watching EPSN, so Naomi was comforted knowing her daughters were with her sister. The four females went on to have one of the most memorable times of their lives before returning home the following afternoon.

THE HOLLAND FAMILY SAGA

CHAPTER TWENTY-EIGHT
HERE ME OUT

While Martha, Twiggy, Kimi and Koko were unpacking from their overnight party down on the ranch, a meeting that would soon ignite that spark within the organization was being held 1,300 hundred miles away on the east coast.

"So what I'm asking for is four hundred thousand dollars to run a brief investigation into the on-going activities in Seattle, Washington. It is my goal to seek out those responsible for the deaths of Hayate and Isao Onishi. These two guys were on the verge of being apprehended by myself and agent Norcross here before they were murdered," forty-seven year-old Lisa Vanguard told the Senate Appropriations Committee as she sat before the gang of seven Caucasian males and one female Caucasian, all over the age of sixty.

"The funds were pulled on your investigation after the death of Hayate and Isao," one of the male Senators remarked.

"That was the first thing I said when this hearing began," Lisa responded in frustration.

"You didn't let me finish," the Senator said as he shifted in his seat and stared down at Lisa over his eyeglasses. "What evidence do you have concerning those involved in the Onishi hits if any at all?"

"None yet, but the monies allotted will allow me to conduct a secret investigation into the Onishi brothers' affiliates. I can do a loop-around and capture their murderers and take down an entire network that has filled their position."

"A loop around," the lead female Senator inquired. "Is the 'loop-around' a legal procedure?"

"I'll make it legal. Look, Senators, let's not drag this out. Hayate and Onishi have been removed by another organization—one more violent than we could ever imagine. Does anybody care about the citizens that are succumbing to the drugs being peddled on the streets of the Pacific Northwest?"

"If I'm correct, they're pushing hard to make drugs legal in that part of the country," another Senator remarked.

"Marijuana only. I'm talking cocaine and heroin here. That's still illegal last time I checked, sir."

"But you have no evidence. No proof that a criminal organization even exists," the lone female Senator remarked. "You were on to the Onishi brothers and had our full support, but they've been dissolved and you have, as has already been stated, no proof that another criminal network is in operation."

"And even if one does," another male Senator said, "an investigation of the magnitude that you're proposing as we all know, could take years and millions of dollars—not the four hundred thousand dollars you're asking for today."

"You know," Lisa said in frustration as she stood up and ran her hands through her cropped red hair, "I genuinely believed that by asking for a minimal amount of funding? I'd receive the grant unabashedly. I'm asking for funding to take, I admit, a shot in the dark. But, so help me God if I'm right," Lisa said as she smiled and looked down at her files. "If I'm right about this hunch, we would have uncovered, for the cost of what it takes to operate an aircraft carrier for an hour in the Persian Gulf, one of the biggest drug networks on the west coast."

"That hunch can be argued as speculation, Miss Vanguard," a Senator remarked. "Those aircraft carriers you speak of have a designated assignment—you, on the other hand, have no designated assignment. And taking, as you say, 'a shot in the dark' or operating on a 'hunch'—your own words mind you—isn't worth the return on investment—which could amount to a pile of beans."

Lisa began packing her briefcase at that moment. "Laddy," she said as she headed for the door.

"The Senate Committee—"

"Has ruled against my proposal for funding. I already know the outcome so save me the formalities, okay, Senator?" Lisa scoffed, cutting the female Senator's remarks short as she headed for the doors.

"Wait a minute," the female Senator said. "I come from the west coast—California. My colleagues in Oregon and Washington state have interests in what you're doing, or trying to do."

"So, I have the funding?" Lisa asked, getting a little excited.

"Not yet. You bring us back something. Anything. And you have my word that you'll get—"

"I don't think this deal is a good—"

"Just hear me out, Senator," the lone female Senator, responded, interrupted her colleague. "If Miss Vanguard can bring us a shred of solid proof on her own, I say we grant her what she's asking. All we have to do is park an aircraft carrier in the Persian Gulf for an hour? Something we won't ever do, but, but we'll find the money somewhere. Do you understand your end of the bargain, Miss Vanguard?"

"I do, ma'am. This will have to be done on my own time."

"We'll, we'll give you a start, though," the female Senator remarked.

"In what way?" Lisa asked as she returned to her desk.

"Several cases are still open in the south that I know of—I'll give you something to get you started. From there, you do your part. Bring us something—then you'll get your funds."

"We have ourselves a deal. But I must inform the committee that I will continue to pursue all avenues in order to accomplish my goal," Lisa replied.

"I can respect that," the female Senator remarked. "Don't give up."

"That's not in my blood. Thank you, Senator Feinstein." Lisa ended as she and Laddy exited the conference room.

****

The following day, Lisa was planning on flying to Massachusetts to meet with a powerful longtime Senator in hopes that he could pull some strings to get the Senate Committee to appropriate the necessary funds without her having to leave D.C. when Laddy walked in and threw a folder onto her desk.

"What's this?" Lisa asked as she picked up the folder.

"That's the Ben Holland case and the files on Leaky Faucet. Senator Feinstein threw us a bone."

"What are they doing on Capitol Hill?"

"Tryna get rid of us if ya' ask me."

"Well, I'm behind on this Ben Holland trial. But I tell ya' what? I'm so ready to leave Washington I'll go there and wing this one. Cancel my flight to Massachusetts, please. I doubt if the senator would even listen to what I have to say anyhow. How's that informant coming along on Leaky Faucet?"

"You didn't hear? The guy hung himself in his cell."

Lisa sat down in defeat. "My name should be brick wall. Brick-fucking-wall! When did this happen?"

"Last month—about a week after he was arrested. He left a letter detailing some things, though."

Lisa held her hands out and widened her eyes, signaling to Laddy that she was waiting to hear what the letter said.

"Mister Sweetwater, in his farewell letter, says that a woman named Carmella Lapiente` mentioned a man named Asa Spade. Something about Shorter Arms apartments and a Royal, a Royal Flush night club. Said umm, said this guy Asa Spade tried to kill Carmella Lapiente` at her home in Denver last year."

"Denver? Where the Holland retrial is to take place," Lisa said matter-of-factly as she chuckled.

"Exactly. And Misses Lapiente`, the woman involved in said war with Asa Spade—"

"Was killed fifteen miles south of Brownsville," Lisa said, cutting Laddy's remarks short. "Sweetwater was busted with three kilograms of cocaine last month during Operation Leaky Faucet. He was moving weight for our dead friend south of the border and decided to come clean before he checked out I guess."

"The operation is still on-going, but we have no further leads since our informant decided to take a dirt nap."

"Right. But old dogs can still hunt. We can look into some things while in Denver."

"You're gonna reexamine Leaky Faucet? Where will we start?" Laddy as inquistively.

"Carmella had one hundred and forty-four kilograms on hand when she was assassinated. Looks as if she was on her way to resupply her clientele and got cut off," Lisa replied as she scanned the contents of the folder, looking at the photos of the massacre that had taken place south of Brownsville. *"How does this puzzle work? And just who is this Asa Spade character?"* she asked herself.

Lisa then tapped the pictures of Carmella's lifeless corpse with her fingertips. "You did not die in vain, young lady. Your death will lead to bigger fish and I will fry their asses just as sure as my name is Lisa 'badass' Vanguard," she said out loud as she began looking over the files on a man by the name of Benjamin Holland, whose case she would soon be prosecuting in Denver, Colorado.

THE HOLLAND FAMILY SAGA

CHAPTER TWENTY-NINE
HOOK UPS

It was now May of 2005, a month after Junior and Tiva's wedding, which was a small ceremony held on the ranch, followed by a large gathering of the siblings' friends from town and the family from Chicago.

A month before the event, Tiva Holland-Cernigliaro gave birth to identical twins in which she named Malaysia and Malara Cernigliaro. They were slender babies; light brown-skinned like their mother, with jet black hair. They had their father's sexy lips and their grandmother Mildred's crystal blue eyes.

Malaysia and Malara, although resembling their parents slightly, oddly favored Spoonie and Tyke, just a lighter version of the two. And even though their last names were Cernigliaro, one knew right away that Malaysia and Malara were Hollands because the trademark birthmark was clearly on display under their left eye.

Everybody was excited over the new additions to the family, including seventy-four year-old DeeDee, who'd survived a life of crime to see eight grandchildren and two great grandchildren come into the world.

With the new additions, DeeDee hung up his hat. He wanted to be around for as long as possible to see his great grandchildren grow up. Five decades plus of life on the streets had come to a peaceful end for seventy-four year old Doss Dawkins Senior, who was still in good health and had an active lifestyle. He was planning on moving down to Ponca City for good in order to enjoy the twilight years of his life there on the ranch with his family.

There was a lot of activity around Ponderosa and over to the guest house this time of year. Mary was busy with her harvest, Naomi was closer to owning the land behind the family's property as it had matured in value, Tiva and her kids, Bay with her relationship with AquaNina, Dawk and Oneika, Siloam and the band she was managing, and of course, there was Kimi, Koko, Walee, Spoonie and Tyke.

The youngest five were all teenagers now; hanging together a few years back was unheard of when Kimi and Koko were the only teenagers out of the young five, but with age came a little maturity for Spoonie, Tyke and Walee. They could somewhat relate to Kimi and Koko, who now stayed on the go most weekends once they were done with their homeschooling.

The first time thirteen year-olds Spoonie and Tyke asked Kimi and Koko could they ride with them down to Oklahoma City, which was about two months ago, they were prepared to hear Kimi and Koko go off and turn them down. To their surprise, however, Kimi and Koko were happy to have their sisters tag along.

The trip had turned into a girls' day out where Kimi and Koko catered to their sisters' every need. Constant conversations about fashion from shoes to scarves took place the whole time. Kimi and Koko had even bought their sisters a week's worth of clothing each.

Spoonie and Tyke were changing clothes in different stores, modeling for their sisters happily. The moment was magical for Spoonie and Tyke, they'd seen a side of Kimi and Koko that they'd come to love completely, not because they spent money on them, it was because they had something real—big sisters who wanted them around. Big sisters who didn't mind spending time with them and being genuine, and to Spoonie and Tyke, the way Kimi and Koko treated them meant the world.

Kimi and Koko were coming into their own being as well. Ever since the day Martha had caught them dancing nearly naked over the Holiday Inn Express, they'd been on their best behavior. They were appreciative of the fact that Martha and Twiggy didn't tell their parents also. Through their actions, Kimi and Koko showed Martha and Twiggy that they were genuinely sorry for their actions. They could get a little rowdy at times, true enough, but they now knew how far to go with their behavior.

Amidst the activity swirling around Ponderosa, the young five descended the patio stairs pass Siloam and her band and climbed into Martha's Sebring and let the top down on this warm and sunny April morning. Everybody was gearing up for a show Siloam was putting on for her band later on in the evening, but before the festivities, the young five wanted to travel down to Oklahoma City and buy outfits as it was Easter weekend. Sales were on and high end fashions had to be purchased by all inside the Sebring. With the top down and music pumping inside Martha's ride, the young five caravanned off the land headed towards OKC, about an hour and a half's drive straight south.

Quail Mall was the place to be on Saturdays in Oklahoma City; and the shopping center was doubly packed since it was Easter weekend. The young five had hit up shoe stores where fresh Nike's, stilettos and sandals were bought. Macy's took up a grip and Toys R' Us Express was perused where a new basketball and football was purchased for Regina's son Tacoma. After making a trip to the car to offload bags, the young five returned to the mall for another round of shopping, but first, they decided to stop off in the food court.

While the group was waiting in line at Chic Fila, loud applauds were heard. Kimi looked over to the other side of the court yard and saw a crowd forming in front of Famous Cajun Grill.

"Who that is over there got all these people worked up?" Kimi wondered aloud.

"That might be that singer Narshea," Spoonie answered as she showed Kimi the flyer she'd picked up when the group first entered the mall that announced the popular singer's appearance inside Quail Mall.

"The southern sensation?" Kimi asked happily. "She got that song out call I do it right, or I do it well, something like that."

"It's called I Do It Well. Me and Spoonie love her music. Let's go see her." Tyke cheered.

"Shiit," Koko protested. "She cool and all, but I want my food."

"Y'all go 'head. I got it," Walee intervened, never looking back at his sisters.

Koko followed Walee's eyes over to the counter where a female stood ringing up items. The two girls before the register were placing their order, but the cashier was paying them no mind because she was too busy eyeing Walee, who was dressed fly in a baggy pair of white jeans, a fresh white t-shirt and blue and white Adidas. The platinum chain draping his neck set his outfit off completely. Walee had his grandfather's height and slim build. He was tall for fourteen, standing nearly six feet. Working the ranch had the dark-brown-skinned teen in shape also, and the two thick plats he wore left his handsome face, with his neatly trimmed, thin mustache, wide open to be admired.

Koko was all smiles as she watched the girl behind the register fumble with empty cups before walking off. She was cute, if Koko had to tell it; short and brown-skinned with short, curly hair, dark eyes and a nice smile. She was obviously a couple of years older than Walee, but Koko knew he'd been dealing with Jordan for a while so her age really didn't matter.

"Go 'head, playboy." Koko said as she smiled at Walee. "Handle your biz."

"I got this here," Walee said confidently as he smiled at the female and gave her a friendly wave. "I'm a get her name, number and a hook up for us, watch."

"Well, do your thizzle. Me and Kimi gone take Spoonie and

Tyke across the way to see this here singer. Get us a table 'cause we gone sit down and eat."

"Cool."

Narshea, (Narshay) meanwhile, although she smiled as she signed autographs and took pictures, was pissed to high heaven that 'Big Derrick' and Torre`, her record label's owners, had sent her down to Oklahoma City to make a couple of appearances. She had only planned on stopping over to Quail Mall to see what kind of jewelry was on hand and to get a bite to eat, regardless of what the flyer said, but she was quickly spotted by a group of females who practically worshiped her. A crowd soon formed and Narshea was now swamped with fans as her bodyguards held back the crowd. Getting into the groove of things, because she truly loved adoration, Narshea began handing out free tickets to her performance on the University of Oklahoma's campus the following Saturday.

Spoonie and Tyke made their way through the crowd with Kimi and Koko following close behind. The youngest were eager to get a hold of some tickets and return the following day to see one of their favorite singers perform, but when they reached the front, Narshea had given all of the free tickets away.

"Can we get an autograph?" Tyke yelled out. "Narshea! Narshea! Give me and my sister your autograph! We got all your music!"

"Thank y'all for comin' out! See me tomorrow on the Sooner campus!" Narshea yelled aloud as she backed away from the crowd.

"Hey! We asked you for an autograph!" Spoonie yelled aloud.

"Calm down, Spoonie," Kimi said. "She probably didn't hear you."

"She heard her! She was looking dead at us!" Tyke yelled. "Narshea, you ain't all that!" she then screamed.

Narshea heard the comment and turned back to the crowd and looked over in the four sisters' direction. "Look at you, okay?" she said matter-of-factly. "You drug your country ass down here to this mall to see me, okay? And now ya' mad ya' ain't got no free tickets to see me, okay? So yes, boo, boo—I am all that and then some!"

"We ain't come here to see you we came here to buy stuff!" Spoonie yelled.

"What the hell you all up in my face for tryna get free tickets then? Carry on!"

"You carry on! Ole hoola-baloola looking self!" Tyke snapped.

"I got ya' hoola-baloola ya' saucer eye heffas!"

"You ain't gotta be so mean to people!" Kimi snapped.

"Fuck you!" Narshea snapped as she mean mugged Kimi.

Kimi and Koko charged at Narshea, but two of her bodyguards stopped them both while the other bodyguard shoved Narshea behind the counter of the Famous Cajun Grill. "You ain't have to do that! I coulda handled them hoes!" Narshea yelled.

"You lucky they here or we woulda' kicked your ass with a smile on our face!" Koko yelled.

"Yea! Yea! Yea! Poof! Be gone ya' double mint groupies!" Narshea yelled as she danced behind the food counter, taunting the twins before she walked off.

"That's why we be burnin' all your music! We ain't never pay for nothin' you got! And when we get home we gone smash all your shit!" Tyke yelled, startling Kimi and Koko, who merely laughed aloud.

"And ya' looks good behind that fast food counter," Kimi added. "Your ass phony anyway! And nobody like ya' music! And this where ya' gone be workin' pretty soon if you keep treatin' your fans like that ya' booger nose bitch!"

"Alrighty then," Koko said, still laughing. "We are done over here. Let's go eat."

Walee was cracking up as he sat at the table watching his

sisters walk his way. Their voices were echoing throughout the food court just seconds earlier and people were eyeing them like they were all crazy as they headed towards their table.

"That's right we said it! Y'all stupid for lettin' her mishandle y'all! I wouldn't set foot on Sooner campus to see that ungrateful ass!" Kimi yelled out to no one in particular as she sat down.

Once the sisters were seated, they all noticed the table was void of food. "Where the order?" Koko asked.

Walee looked around. "Oh, here it come now," he said nonchalantly as he draped his arms around a couple of chairs and shook his legs with a smile on his face.

"Whaaat?" Kimi and Koko sang.

"You got table service, Walee?" Koko asked in surprise.

"I do my thang well," Walee said through a smile, quoting a line from Narshea's current hit single.

The girl who'd been eyeing Walee and another worker from Chic Fila sat their order down. "You got the number for me, baby girl?" Walee asked casually.

The cashier slid Walee a slip of paper with her name and number and walked off shyly as Walee's sisters mocked him playfully. "I told y'all," Walee said. "And this whole order on the house, ya' dig?"

"I dig ya', lover boy." Koko remarked.

The family was kicking back enjoying their meal when sniggling from a nearby table caught Kimi's attention. She looked over and saw two boys eyeing her and Koko.

"Something funny over here?" Koko asked.

"Me and my boy Chablis heard y'all takin' it to Narshea over there and thought it was funny," one of the boys remarked.

"Chablis?" Koko said. "Why your momma name you after a wine, boy?"

"He might be sweet?" Walee said before biting into his chicken sandwich.

"Nahh, cuz. You got me mixed up with somebody else." Chablis replied as he stared hard at Walee. "Ain't nothing sweet about me so let's get that straight right now, my dude."

"I'm just sayin', dog. They ain't gone talk to y'all."

"What? They can't speak for themselves." Chablis asked.

"Not while I'm around. We don't even stay in the OKC. And they got boyfriends back home anyway so y'all can go on and kill that noise."

"Walee, we ain't—we ain't got no boyfriends, y'all." Kimi told the boys.

Kimi thought the other guy with Chablis was cute with his smooth, tan skin and wavy hair. He was a little on the chubby side, but she and Koko were thick themselves; but even if they had stallion status like their older sisters, it didn't matter because Kimi and Koko, by all measures, were real down-to-earth when it came to dealing with the opposite sex and people in general. Looks really didn't matter all that much, especially to Kimi.

Koko thought Chablis was good-looking. He was a little shorter than she, but he was muscular like Dawk, brown-skinned like Walee and wore dreadlocks. His name didn't match his appearance in her eyes and that was turning her off somewhat as odd as it was.

"What y'all up to when y'all leave here?" Chablis' friend asked.

"Going to a concert." Kimi answered.

"Oh, y'all going see Narshea tomorrow?"

"Didn't you ask what we doin' when we leave here today, man? If her thing tomorrow how we goin' today?" Koko snapped.

"You ain't gotta get all technical with a brother," Chablis remarked.

"I ain't gettin' technical. I'm just stating the facts."

"You the nice twin," Chablis' friend said to Kimi. "How you

doin'? My name Udelle. I live down in Norman."

"You got to Oklahoma?" Kimi asked.

"Gone be a freshmen this fall. I'm majoring in meteorology."

"Udelle the weatherman," Kimi said as she smiled. "I can see that."

"Really? People think I'm weird for wanting to do that."

"I think you weird for wantin' to do that." Walee added as he got up from the table to use the restroom. "Y'all be ready when I get back."

"Now, look at him," Spoonie said through laughter.

"Umm hmm," Koko sighed. "Tryna play like he Dawk or somebody."

"Dawk? That's one of y'all boyfriends?" Udelle asked.

"That's our brother. You don't wanna meet him no time soon," Tyke said.

"I will eventually once I become a part of the family," Udelle remarked.

Kimi laughed and stuck out her hand and wiggled her fingers.

"What?" Udelle asked.

"The phone number, stupid," Chablis said as he grabbed his cell phone and looked over to Koko.

"We stay in the same house, boy!" Koko snapped.

"You know what? I don't like the way you be talkin' all sporty to a dude. You gone have to change your attitude if you ever wanna get with me."

Koko was smiling on the inside. She liked Chablis, but she'd decided to play hard to get just to see how far he would go to get to know her. "When she call your friend and talk to him—if she call—then you can talk to me."

"Me and him don't live together."

"Well, ya' better camp out over to his house then, soldier,"

Koko snapped as she got from the table and grabbed her bags. "Arrivederci," she ended as she walked away from the table, Spoonie and Tyke following her lead.

Kimi got up slowly and grabbed her purse and bags, noticing the look of disappointment on Chablis' face. "Don't worry," she said softly. "I'll call your friend."

"You think she gone hollar at me?"

"Like she been doing? Yeah."

Chablis laughed and said, "Yeah, she got me today. She cute though."

"Thank you." Kimi said as she walked away from the table. "Talk to you later, Udelle."

Udelle threw up a peace sign as he watched Kimi walk off. "I think I'm gone marry her someday, homeboy." he said.

"Look at you, man," Chablis said through laughter. "You don't know nothing about Kimi and Koko 'nem."

"Don't matter. Sometimes you just know, Chablis."

"Either way—you got the hook up dog," Chablis sang as he and Udelle pounded fists and continued on with their meal.

****

"Siloam? You comin' out to do the formalities?" Doss asked as he knocked on the threshold of Naomi's office, where Siloam was sitting behind one of the desks.

"Yes, sir. I just have to sign this check and I'll be out there."

Doss walked into the room and closed the door and walked over and stood before Siloam. He knew of her endeavors to assist Jane Dow in reaching stardom, but the five-thousand dollar check she was signing was a bit much in his eyes to pay a Rolling Stone magazine editor whom she hadn't met in person and had only been communicating with through email.

"Are you sure this guy is legit," Doss asked as he pulled a chair up and sat before the desk. "It's unusual for an editor to request monies from a new band."

"It really isn't, Doss. Rolling Stone gets solicitations from new bands all the time. Payola is a way to weed out the competition."

"Some of the hottest bands started from nothing, you know? They earned their keep through good music and making the right connections."

"You know someone inside the music business?"

"Not off hand. I guess I'm tryin' to tell you to not get your expectations up too high because they're con men all around us."

"Thank you for your concern, Doss. This project, though? This is very important to me. I see my younger self in Jane and I wanna see her make it."

"Does she want to make it?"

Thirty-one year-old Siloam Bovina bowed her head at that moment. For a while she'd been wondering if what she was doing was for fifteen year-old Jane's benefit, or was she living vicariously through a young woman who had youth and time on her side, something Siloam herself was short on as far as music was concerned. She believed her time had passed, despite her musical abilities, and in her heart she felt as if she was making the right move.

Jane Dow was real good with the drums and the guitar and had a strong voice, much like Siloam in the past. The only problem with Jane was the youngster's drug habit. Marijuana and liquor was her pleasure, and the monies she and her band made from playing fairs and bar-b-cue contests around the state of Oklahoma was all spent getting high. Still, Jane was one hell of a performer and Siloam felt that the world should know of this youngster's talent.

"If she can conquer the drugs she'll make it, Doss," Siloam said proudly. "All she needs to know is someone cares and has her best interests at heart, which I do. I admit, part of it is to see what I would've become, but Jane does what she does because she loves it—the music I mean. And that is the thing compelling me to invest my own money into this project."

Doss nodded his head, understanding Siloam's motives completely. The last thing he wanted, however, was to see Siloam, a woman he viewed as his own flesh and blood, be taken advantage of by anyone, including Jane. He had a feeling that Siloam would learn a life lesson dealing with this editor in whom she was sending her money to and he'd made up his mind that he would set aside $5,000 dollars to reimburse her should she be met with adversity from this purported Rolling Stones Magazine editor from New York City.

Siloam didn't have much in life, although hers had been quite an adventurous one. Doss and Naomi catered to her every need and she earned pay working the ranch, but for the most part, Siloam was a woman without many possessions at the present day and time, but Doss and Naomi had written her into the family's will. Siloam would be taken care of always and was given freedom to do as she pleased; and even though she could ask Doss and Naomi for anything within reason and receive it, she was the type of person who paid her own way and had earned her keep years ago.

For as long as Doss could remember, Siloam had always been a free-spirit, a person who lived each and every day to the fullest and made no plans for tomorrow. It was a flaw to a degree, but the flaw Siloam carried was innocent. She wouldn't hurt a soul and was optimistic always. To see her hurt, would hurt the hearts of the ones who cared for her; Doss was a man who cared, and he would aide Siloam wherever possible as she embarked on what he knew was the road to fame. What form that fame came in, Doss was uncertain, and it was also a chance that Siloam's dream would remain just a dream. Many have tried to achieve accolades in the music world, sacrificing health and family and chasing after a vision that remained just out of reach the entire journey. And in the end, they were left shattered souls with a wealth of bad memories, victims of scams and hurt feelings that would leave them bitter and envious towards those who'd actually made it.

Siloam was up against a stacked deck in Doss's eyes, but he'd been holding hands with death for nearly three decades. If he could survive in his world, then Siloam could surely survive in her world, especially with help from time to time from those who loved her; but it would be her journey, her experience, one to be watched from afar because it was truly an amazing thing to see Siloam, who had no stake in the matter, other than to see Jane Dow succeed, pour her heart and soul into a project she held dear to her heart.

"The family will be waiting out on the patio for you," Doss remarked as he stood up from his seat. "Now," he then said with a smile to lighten the mood, "we got two old men out there in my father and Mendoza, who are worse than the sand man at the Apollo. If Jane doesn't come correct, she'll get tapped dance off the ranch."

Siloam chuckled and said, "Trust me Doss—this little girl has a way with music. It'll be a performance to remember."

"Make me a believer today."

"Did Kimi 'nem make it back?"

"Yeah. The whole family waitin' on you. Come on out and emcee this thing. We wanna see what kind of a manager you are. See if you know talent," Doss ended as he walked out the room.

****

"Girl, I ain't know you get high and shit," Koko said as she took a toke off a thick blunt Jane had rolled for herself, the twins and Walee.

Jane Dow was a pudgy fifteen year-old standing barely five feet tall with hazel eyes and had short brown hair and a face full of freckles. She was a gorgeous Caucasian/Lakota Indian and a lifelong resident of Ponca City. She grew up on the west side of town in a trailer park close to where Dawk's girlfriend Oneika resided. Her parents were meth addicts who peddled marijuana from time to time and often spent weekends in jail on domestic violence charges.

Jane's home life was a dysfunctional one; music was her escape, right along with drugs. She often got high to deal with the constant arguing and occasional fights inside her home, but when she got high before she performed, she became entrenched in her music. She was a cover singer that could mimic everybody from Connie Francis to Evelyn Champagne King, and nearly any voice in between. Her idols were Billy Joel, Teena Marie, and the guitarist Slash from Guns 'N' Roses.

Jane had a lot of problems in her home life and it sometimes spilled over into her performances; acts that often left Siloam perplexed and equivocating the subpar presentations to her drug use. The two would often argue and Jane was hard to deal with sometimes for Siloam, but through it all, Jane knew what she had in Siloam and always tried to do her best. For a fifteen year-old with drug addicted parents and a drug addiction of her own, however, the road wasn't always an easy one to travel. With that aside, Jane Dow always did her best to put her best foot forward.

Taking the blunt from Koko, who was coughing uncontrollably, Jane took a toke herself and exhaled the smoke and said, "I been gettin' high since I was twelve. My momma, daddy and me got high one Saturday night watching a Oklahoma Sooner game and it was on after that."

"I wish the hell my momma would pass a blunt to me," Walee said as he sat atop his father's tarp-covered Camaro. "Y'all hear that caterpillar crawling," he then asked.

Jane, Kimi and Koko laughed aloud at that moment. "How the fuck you gone hear a caterpillar crawlin'" Jane asked through sniggles.

Jane Dow's parents had the fire weed. Marijuana they grew themselves inside their trailer home and dried until it was brittle and potent. All four were dazed off the blunt and had gotten the giggles off Walee's last remark.

"She said Oklahoma," Koko laughed. "Kimi you gone call Udelle? 'Cause I wanna talk to Chablis."

"Shit. I don't know what I did with the number," Kimi replied as she grabbed her purse.

"You lost the number," Koko asked in a panicked state.

Kimi laughed at that moment. "Your ass sittin' there playing hard to get. I knew you like that boy."

"Forget you," Koko snapped as she shoved her twin's shoulder.

"Y'all? I have to get over to the patio and set up," Jane said as she dropped the blunt and stomped on it to put out the flame.

The four hopped onto a golf cart and rode back towards the patio—it was the slowest ride ever. Walee was behind the wheel cruising as he texted the female he'd met at Chic Fila, Kimi and Koko dreaming about the boys they'd met and Jane Dow getting into her groove in preparation of her upcoming performance.

Back on the patio, the entire family was out mingling. The grills were going, a bar was set up and games of spades and dominoes were going. When the Holland-Dawkins family had a gathering there was no expense spared and the family entertained themselves to the fullest extent.

Walee and company rolled up, all four wearing shades to hide their low and red eye sockets as they disbursed amongst the family. Siloam soon emerged and began helping Jane set up. She noticed her slow movements and asked, "Jane, are you okay?"

"I'm fine, Siloam," Jane replied as she helped her three band mates set up the drums. "We going to California today."

"You're real good with that song," Siloam said, knowing full well Jane was high, but her mood was good so all was well. Siloam had seen this move before and each time, Jane was magical. She decided not to engage her in a conversation about drugs so as not to upset her and merely went about setting up the equipment.

"You got the camera set up, Siloam?" Jane asked calmly.

"All is set. The editor says for us to record a great performance and send it to him for review so he can do an expose` on the band."

"You think he'll be the one to give us a shot at the big time?"

"He says he knows people in the business, Jane. We do our best and we give ourselves the best chance. It's no guarantee, but we have to at least do our part."

"Not a problem." Jane responded calmly as she picked up her drumsticks.

About thirty minutes later, after Siloam had given her introduction, the family grew quiet as Jane took her seat behind her drum set. The sun had begun to set at that moment, coating the land with a picturesque orange hue as cattle prodded along and birds took the air. The adults in the family held onto their adult beverages while younger members sat at patio tables in total silence awaiting the performance.

Jane leaned over into her microphone, her head barely visible from behind the white and chrome drum set. "This song is one the coolest songs ever written to me," she spoke softly. "I umm, I wanna thank my mentor Siloam for puttin' this event together and it is a pure pleasure to play before you all today."

"Show us what ya' got!" Mendoza yelled aloud from his seat on the opposite side of the patio.

"I sure will, mister," Jane said as she nodded towards her guitarist.

A melodic tune was soon gracing the family's ears and everybody recognized the melody right away. "No singing," Jane said as the fifteen year-old Caucasian guitarist played his solo.

Everybody was eyeing Jane. She had a presence behind her drum set even before she began playing a single note. Siloam smiled proudly at her protégé as the guitarist's solo came to an end.

At that moment, fifteen year-old Jane Dow, who was high as all out doors, with a pair of shades covering her eyes and a red bandanna tied around her head, pounded her drums as the sun began setting behind her back. She leaned into her microphone and let her voice rip. "*On a dark desert highway...cool wind in my hair...warm smell of colitas...rising up through the air...up ahead in the distance...I saw a shimmering light...my head grew heavy and my sight grew dim...I had to stop for the night...there she stood in the doorway...I heard the mission bell...and I was thinkin' to myself this could be heaven or this could be hell...*"

"Now this is music at its best," Mendoza said lowly as he wrapped an arm around Francine and smiled proudly.

The entire family was awestruck hearing Jane Dow sing. The youngster had a soulful voice, and she'd chosen a perfect song for a perfect day. Don Henley, the original singer of The Eagles' song *Hotel California* would have to bow his head in appreciation upon hearing this female cover his song in a voice all to her own, yet in the same cadence as the original.

Siloam had set up a TV on the patio to record the footage and the angle she'd given Jane Dow was nothing short of spectacular. The camera was angled up to make Jane Dow and the band look larger than life on the TV screen as their images glowed in the setting sun's light. Everything about this performance radiated stardom, and young Jane was carrying the image Siloam was trying to present with total perfection and grace as she sang the chorus with her band and slid into the second verse as she pounded her drums.

"*Her mind is Tiffany-twisted...she got the Mercedes Benz... she got a lot of pretty, pretty boys...that she calls friends...how they dance in the courtyard...sweet summer sweat...some dance to remember...some dance to forget...*"

Naomi was nearly in tears watching such a graceful performance; one laced with soul and had her reflecting on all that had transpired in her life. Tiva sat cuddling Malaysia as Junior sat beside her, bouncing Malara on his leg rocking her to sleep.

Mary, Martha, Regina and Twiggy were reflecting on Ghost Town as they listened to Jane's performance. Loretta and Sandy Duncan loved rock and roll music. They were more Lynrd Skynrd, but they'd all heard mother and daughter jamming on some Saturday mornings to this song.

Bay saw nothing but the game in Jane Dow as she sat beside AquaNina reflecting on the hit against Carmella.

The image Siloam had given Jane Dow would become her signature. Her forte, although unknowingly, would become that of singing portentously to gangsters who were either living, or had lived the words in many of the songs she often chose to sing.

"Welcome to the Hotel California...such a lovely place... (such a lovely place)such a lovely face...they living it up at the Hotel California...what a nice surprise...(what a nice surprise)bring your alibi..."

Sweat poured off Jane while she sung, approaching the song's crescendo as she pounded her drums in harmony with the guitarist as he played the song out to its conclusion. The entire family stood up and clapped and cheered in appreciation as Jane eased from behind her drums and requested a bite to eat. It was fair to say that on this day, the entire family down in Ponca City had come to support Siloam and her vision for The Jane Dow Band.

****

"You on highway sixty?" Regina asked excitedly as she walked through Ponderosa towards the front doors with Tak at her side shortly after Jane's performance. "Okay. After you cross over the lake and pass the produce stand take the first left. Follow that road to the end and make another left and it's on the left. You gone see a bunch of cows before you get to the main gate."

"I'll be there, shortly," the voice on the other end said before disconnecting.

"You sure about this, Dimples?" Takoda asked, unsure about his wife's intentions.

"No. But it's worth a shot." Dimples sighed as she ran her hands through her hair. "God, I hope this works."

A few minutes later, Regina's guest arrived, pulling up to the front of Ponderosa in a black 2002 Ford Explorer. She and Tak greeted him and stood and talked for a while, the three discussing how they would make their appearance.

The family was all out on the back patio enjoying the night when Dimples and company emerged. Martha was shuffling dominoes and had to do a double take when she saw the man walking behind Dimples and Tak. She stood up and placed her hands on her hips and said, "Who in the hell invited this bum to Oklahoma?"

Family members looked and wondered who the man was standing with Dimples.

Mary was over talking to Francine when she eyed the man. Her mouth dropped open and she screamed aloud as she hopped up from her seat and ran down the patio stairs and turned around with a face full of tears.

Naomi ran and hugged Mary gently. "Mary? What's going on?" she asked.

"It's Reynard," Mary said through her tears. "Ne'Ne's daddy."

Naomi looked back over to the patio at the tall, muscular, bald-headed man with a grey beard and could see her nieces in his features. Forty-six year-old Reynard Jacobs greeted the family with kind handshakes and a warm smile on his face.

Dimples had found her father with the help of The Lost Orphan Committee. He was living in Itta Bena, Mississippi and was the head coach of the Mississippi Valley State football team where famed NFL wide receiver Jerry Rice once attended. When he and Dimples talked over the phone he told her he had one daughter, who was married and was married himself, but separated at the time.

Martha hated Reynard on sight. She let her position be known by telling him to his face that he wasn't welcomed.

"I understand your animosity, Martha," Reynard responded gently, "but it is Mary's decision as to whether I should stay or leave, and even then, my daughter has welcomed me."

Martha wiggled her finger in Reynard's face in protest. "My niece doesn't live on this land. We do—and we got every right to throw you out on your ass. You got some nerve, Reynard!"

"It's okay, Martha," Mary said, trembling as she climbed the stairs with a face full of tears.

Reynard smiled and walked over to Mary and extended his hand. "Mary, it's so good to see you."

"We lost one," Mary cried.

"I know. Regina told me all about it."

"This wouldn't have happened had you been there!" Mary screamed, as the family stood by in silence. "You show up almost thirty years later and all you have to say is it's good to see me?"

"What else can I say? What could I say?" Reynard asked through heartfelt conviction.

"You could apologize for running out on ya' family ya' bum!" Mendoza yelled aloud.

Mendoza's outburst had basically set the tone for Reynard's visit. None of the family liked him because they all knew his story. He'd lied and denied his offspring. Everybody on the Holland ranch was all about family, and what Reynard had done didn't set well with no one—even if what he'd done had transpired years ago.

"Don't you go takin' what I said personal, now," Mendoza added. "It was just an observation."

Ignoring Mendoza's remark, Reynard grew nearer to Mary and said, "I'm sorry about what happened to Rene. Mary, I was a young, scared boy three decades ago, but I've learned how to be a man. Whatever way you feel, I'm sorry. I'm sorry for everything I ever did."

"She would still be alive if you hadn't denied us! You forced us away! Forced us to a place that took my child away from me!"

"She was my child, too, Mary. Don't you think my heart feels pain?"

"You never knew her!" Mary yelled as she charged at Reynard and began swinging at his face.

Reynard reached out and grabbed Mary and all hell broke loose. Dawk was the first to pounce on him and Martha quickly followed. Reynard was a big man, 6'3" and a solid two-hundred and thirty pounds. All the muscle and strength he possessed couldn't ward off two members of the Holland family, however; a few tables were knocked over and the family scrambled to break up the melee.

"Don't hurt my daddy, Dawk!" Dimples yelled. "Please don't hurt him!" she cried.

Mary assisted with Tak, Twiggy and Siloam, pulling Dawk and Martha off Reynard and separating the three.

"Regina what were you thinking inviting this man to our home?" Mary yelled through her tears.

"Momma, I just, I just wanted you to see him. You two have to talk."

"We were fine the way we were, Regina!" Mary screamed. "Bringing this man here has opened wounds in me that'd healed years ago! Years ago and I can't stand it! I can't stand the sight of this man!"

"It's not his fault Rene died, momma."

"Yes it is! You don't understand!" Mary cried as she pointed towards Reynard. "This man is a liar! He started out lyin'! And it cost you and I to lose some one we both loved! Accept him if you want to! I can't and I refuse! I want him gone from here!" Mary ended as she ran into the home.

"Daddy, I'm sorry. I'm so sorry," Dimples remarked as she handed her father a napkin.

Doss walked over and stood before Reynard and said, "Regina, if you want to see this man, do so over to your own home. Your mother isn't ready to have any dealings with him," he ended as he eyed Reynard coldly and walked off.

Dimples was embarrassed. She'd hoped and believed that reuniting her mother and father would be a good thing, but her dream had been shattered. She understood her mother's pain, but she wanted to know and love her father and her sister. She apologized to the family and escorted Reynard to his car.

"I tried, Regina," Reynard said sadly. "I did what you asked, but it didn't work, baby."

"We still have each other, though. Right, daddy?" Regina asked meekly as she wiped tears from her eyes.

"Right," Reynard replied lovingly. "I'm going back to my hotel. You wanna have breakfast in the morning so we can talk?"

"I would like that, dad." Dimples said as she leaned in and hugged her father tightly.

A rapport would soon begin with Dimples and Reynard and it would develop further over time. Mary, however, remained distant. She'd apologized the following day for basically starting the melee, but that was about as far as she went. She remained free and clear of Dimples and Reynard's relationship, only speaking politely to him on occasion whenever he called the guest house to speak with Dimples, who'd met her sister down in Texas in the month of July and seemed happy having found her father after nearly thirty years.

The rest of the family, however, never even thought about Reynard, nor did they care for the man, but because Dimples accepted him, they remained cordial the few times he'd returned to Ponca City for a visit with his daughter and grandson.

CHAPTER THIRTY
TEXAS CAKE AND CREAM

"*Dios, no dejes que me o Simone morir esta noche.*" (God, don't let me or Simone die tonight.) fourteen year-old Peppi Vargas said to herself as she rode in the backseat of a rental car with Toodie and Simone Cortez, the three riding south on Interstate-45 through the town of Aldine, Texas, headed towards Houston on a rainy August night in 2005.

Shortly after Carmella's death, just over ten months ago, fourteen year-old Pepper had begun living under harsh conditions in Fox Park. She and sixteen year-old Simone Cortez were basically fending for themselves on Ann Avenue by selling any and all drugs they could score to turn a profit, and an occasional pawn shop robbery. The two were jam tight, practically inseparable, and they had each other's back through thick and thin because when it got down to it, all they had left were each other; in spite of their survival instincts on the streets, Simone and Pepper were still young, and therein lay their conundrum. The two felt as if they had to listen to Toodie because they'd been under her for some time, before Carmella had been murdered and well afterwards.

Twenty-four year Kathryn 'Toodie' Perez, now the last remaining leader of a once prosperous drug organization, was now getting money by any means necessary, using Simone and Pepper at will in her endeavor to remain on top of the game.

When Carmella went down in Mexico, the cocaine had been shut off completely to the click in Fox Park.

Ann Avenue had gone from brick sellers to the bottom of the rung, barely able to sell quarters on the streets let alone ounces and kilos. Cocaine was hard to come by now that the lead supplier was out of the picture. To add insult to injury, the Chicago Gang was in control of the streets and there was little Toodie could do about the matter because she hadn't the muscle. Starving was not her style, however; Toodie was used to having things—the best of things. The disdain she had for the Chicago Gang was still in her heart, but her survival was now top priority. She would deal with the crew from Chicago soon enough. Carmella's home in Crestwood was now hers; and she still had several cars, and a little bit of money stashed, but the hustle wasn't coming in as fast and as large as Toodie had been used to during the time Carmella had things pumping.

As Toodie drove down the highway, her phone began ringing. She looked down at the screen and saw a number she didn't recognize that had a Missouri area code. It was the second time in three days she'd gotten the call, but she never bothered to answer because she didn't know the number and whoever the person was that was calling on the other end never bothered to leave a message. She sent her phone to voice mail and continued her drive towards Houston.

Riding behind Toodie's rented PT Cruiser, in a Buick Roadmaster, was twenty-six year-old Bahdoon 'Q-man' LuQman and his three man crew. Q-man was a man that had burned bridges. When Carmella cut the price per kilogram, he'd cut off his supplier from New York. After her death, he returned to his old supplier and business was good for a while. Q-man, however, had become accustomed to getting cocaine on the low. Carmella had spoiled the boys from Minneapolis; and rather than pay full price, the Somalis had decided to rob their connect out of forty-two kilograms he'd had in his stash house and had taken five lives in the process. They'd fucked the game up for a brief minute over in the Bronx and could never return to New York City.

Q-man soon clicked up with Toodie, and for a while they

broke bread with the stolen cocaine; but now that the kilograms had all been offed, this newly-formed band of armed jackers was after a new target located down in Houston, Texas.

Not having a legitimate connect and the refusal to pay the going rate for a kilogram of cocaine had brought about a deadly alliance between Toodie and the Somalis. Game didn't stop. And even though Toodie had lost a sister and her best friend to the game, she was still deep into the mix and had taken on a new occupation. She drove down the highway as rain whipped about, the windshield wipers on the PT Cruiser working overtime to keep the windows free of water as they seemingly mimicked the words *'goin' kill 'em...goin' kill 'em...goin' kill 'em...goin' kill 'em...'*

Everything was all set up on this night as Toodie rode into Houston and traveled to the north east side of the city and entered the Fifth Ward where she and her crew were to meet up with their contacts. She pulled into the back parking lot of Phillis Wheatley High School shortly after midnight and parked beside a 1986 two door Delta '88.

The tinted window on the driver's side rolled down on the car in the rain, which had turned into a light drizzle, and Toodie laid eyes on Pancho Vera and Cesar Guerrera for the first time in nearly two years.

Twenty-one year-old Pancho Vera, who went by the nickname Dead Eye, because of his droopy left eye, and his partner in crime, twenty-one year-old Cesar Guerrera, who everybody called Big Bounce because of his six foot tall, three hundred and fifty pound frame, were Carmella's Enforcers down in Houston.

Dead Eye and Big Bounce distributed cocaine throughout Texas, Arkansas and Louisiana for Carmella during her time; but they, too, had been on hard times since the woman's downfall. They knew all that was going on down in Texas, who got busted, who was ratting, when Carmella's next package was coming in, and how much money each city was supposed to bring in. Dead Eye and Big Bounce often hung out in Fifth Ward where they ran a trap house, selling bags of marijuana being that their cocaine connect had went away with

Carmella's death.

Itching for a major come up, Toodie's call a month ago had landed in Dead Eye and Big Bounce's lap at the right time. They knew all the big suppliers in Houston because they'd once supplied the clicks. With a chance to make off with a big score, Carmella's former Enforcers jumped on the Texas cake and cream bandwagon and agreed to help set up two dealers they'd once sold kilograms to.

Q-man exited his ride and walked in between the cars and the group went over their plan one last time before they set out to do their jobs. A big time dealer down the road in the Fifth Ward, known to store bricks by the dozen in his trap was to be hit by Q-man and his crew, along with Dead Eye, who'd set up the sting. Big Bounce would ride with Toodie, Simone and Pepper over to a home in River Oaks and pull a kick door on another dealer who was rumored to have a safe full of money tucked away in his mansion. The crew dapped off and hopped into their rides to get their plans underway.

Pepper sat in the backseat beside Simone in silence as she rode listening to the music and inhaling the potent marijuana Toodie and Big Bounce toked on as they cruised towards River Oaks, one of the wealthiest neighborhoods in the country with homes ranging from one million to twenty million dollars. The guy the crew was planning on robbing was a married man in his mid-fifties and had been the main supplier to the city of San Antonio, Texas for years. His eight million dollar two-story Swedish-style home sat on a golf course beside a thick groove of trees. The man did no business in Houston, hadn't harmed anyone in years and had retired from the game with his riches when Carmella was gunned down in Mexico last October. The fact that he had no body guards and lived alone with his wife made him a perfect mark for Toodie and her bunch, who only wanted an easy lick that would go smoothly and with as little hang ups as possible.

The PT Cruiser turned into the River Oaks Golf Course, passing a guard shack that was empty and began winding down the road. The homes here were pristine, to say the least. Large, exquisite structures that sat back from the road, some hidden by tall pine trees, dotted the hilly landscape and they were all unique in design. When Toodie rolled up on the brown two story home sitting beside a tall grove of trees with a fountain out front, she knew she'd found the place she was searching for. The address on the custom-built brick mailbox confirmed the location and she wheeled the car up the narrow concrete road leading to the home's three car garage with the PT Cruiser's headlights off.

Under the darkness of night, Toodie and the gang exited the ride with guns in hand and ran along the right side of the huge mansion towards the back of the home where she, Simone and Pepper hopped a small iron gate that led to the home's swimming pool area. They climbed the theatrical-style stone stairs without making a sound and approached one of the French doors just as a searchlight began gleaming, lighting up the entire area. The lights went out several seconds later when Big Bounce pulled the circuit breaker, signaling Toodie that it was safe to enter.

A crowbar wedged in between the patio door's hinges forced it open and Simone entered with a twelve gauge that had an illuminated flashlight duct-taped to the top of the barrel. Big Bounce joined the crew with another twelve gauge and led the group through the home towards the stairs where they met the man of the home in the stairwell. The man had a .357 revolver in his hand, and when he aimed it, Big Bounce blasted him in the chest and he tumbled down the stairs, his body now resting on the mid-drift.

"Stay here, Peppi. Simone let's go," Toodie said as she and Big Bounce climbed the stairs and ran towards the room where they heard screams emanating from the man's wife. The three entered the room where Toodie grabbed the woman, knocked the cell phone from her hands and forced her to her knees. "The safe? Where's the safe?" she yelled in the darkness as she checked to make sure the woman hadn't called 9-1-1.

The woman was scared beyond words. She crawled over to a large walk-in closet and opened the door and lay face down on the carpeted floor, readily complying with her assailants. She was pulled back up by Toodie, however, who forced her inside the room and hissed, "Open this mutherfucka before I blow your brains all over the place!"

"Please don't hurt me," the woman begged as she slowly twisted the knob on the four foot tall safe until it clicked.

Toodie and Dead Eye shoved the woman away from the open safe and began placing stacks of hundred dollar bills into a satchel along with diamond necklaces, ruby and diamond rings and a small packet of loose diamonds.

Simone, meanwhile, was rummaging through boxes on the dresser, picking up on a couple of large diamond rings and an expensive diamond-crusted watch. A gun blast to the back of the woman's head ended her life and Toodie and Big Bounce emerged from the walk-in closet and trotted out the master bedroom's double doors with Simone trailing.

Pepper, meanwhile, as she stood on the stairs with her .380 clutched tightly in her right hand, had watched in silence as the man Big Bounce had shot just a minute ago died before her very eyes. She'd seen death up-close before, the day her mother died and the day Phoebe had been killed, but each time it was a brand new experience. The man had asked her for help, but she said nothing. He'd pleaded for her to help his wife, but she did nothing, only standing by and watching in silence as the man died before her very eyes. Pepper was shaken from her trance when she saw and heard Toodie descending the stairs and all four left the home and rode calmly off the golf course.

****

"So my man here from Dallas looking for that fire connect, ya' feel me," Dead Eye said as he sat beside Q-man inside a trap house of some long time acquaintances of his.

Two black men sat on a sofa opposite Q-man and Dead Eye with a lone female who was rolling a blunt as she paid little attention to the conversation at hand. It was just a routine deal at the dope house between her man and his customers as far as she was concerned. Q-man's crew had guns drawn and was standing beside the wooden shotgun house as lookouts.

"You say he want three of them thangs?" one of the men asked Dead Eye in a calm manner back inside the living room.

"Yeah, homes. You know my word good. We been doing business for a while now. I lost my connect, but it ain't nothin' for me to turn my people on to some real shit, ya' know?"

"True dat. Show me some loot," the dark-skinned slender man replied as he sat on the edge of the sofa eyeing Dead Eye and the man who called himself Q-man.

"I'm sayin', where the product, homes?"

"Don't worry about that. You know the routine, Pancho. Cash up front, my nig. We talkin' sixty stacks, dog, and that shit mean something. Let me see it."

Q-man leaned forward and said, "Yo, Panch, just go 'head and pay dude up front. What? We gotta wait here 'til you go get the work, my dude?"

"You pay me, you get what you ask for, cuz. Panch know the play."

"I know the play, homes," Dead Eye said as he leaned down and unzipped the duffel bag situated between his feet.

"Yo," the man sitting opposite of Dead Eye said to his comrade, "get them thangs ready so we can make this deal and stab out."

"Yeah, do that," Dead Eye said as he came up with a Mini-14. "Get them thangs so we can make this deal and stab out."

Q-man drew down with a Mini-14 of his own and all three occupants inside the house eyes grew wide as they stared down the barrel of the guns being wielded on them by their assailants. "You know what it is, dude," Q-man said. "Get us what we want and we out."

The man eased up from the couch eyeing Dead Eye coldly. "You wanna go out like this, Panch?" he asked.

"I wouldn't be here if it didn't plan on it, big dog," Dead Eye replied as he blasted the man's girlfriend, killing her instantly. "Now you know for certain I ain't fuckin' around, homes."

Q-man opened fire on the two men and he and Dead Eye ransacked the place as they lay dying on the living room floor. They bagged all of the product in under two minutes and left the home and jumped into Big Bounce's ride where Q-man's soldier sped away from the scene, leaving behind three dead bodies inside the home. The band of bandits had come up on a lick that netted them $160,000 dollars in cash and thousands more in jewelry along with nine kilograms of cocaine collectively.

This would become Toodie, Q-man, Dead Eye and Big Bounce's main hustle for a while; they would travel from city to city and rob the very people they'd once done business with, people who'd trusted them and unwittingly let their guards down given their past history. With that aside, Toodie still had it in for the click in Saint Charles. When she was able, she would reach out and touch them once more.

CHAPTER THIRTY-ONE
LATCHING ON

"One by one by one, they've all stood before your very faces and told you what they were coached to say by the defense. Friends of Benjamin Holland would never condemn that man because they've all been a part of what he's been perpetrating from day one. Friends, lovers and others all came together and sold this courtroom pure fallacy."

Lisa Vanguard was in the final phase of her closing arguments in the Ben Holland murder retrial case over in Denver, Colorado in early August of 2005, just a few days after Toodie and her bunch had begun their terror campaign down in Houston.

Lisa had somewhat prepared for the case over the last few months, but her mind was really elsewhere. She wasn't giving her best effort either, and she knew it; the defense was really winning the case outright, but Lisa had an ace up her sleeve that she was preparing to use on the defense the following morning to prolong the case, if only to extend her stay in Denver to further investigate another case she was developing. She was constantly agitating her opponent, whom she'd had a history with, by trying to persuade the jury through the use of overstatements and subtle implications. Lisa's last remark had forced a sigh from her opponent's lips as he slid back in his chair.

"Objection again, your honor," Dante` O'Malley, the pepper-haired lawyer for Ben Holland said in an aggravated tone as he rose slowly from his seat and shot a look of disdain towards Lisa Vanguard. "The prosecution is…"

"Operating on mere speculation," the judge groaned, having heard Dante`s objection too many times to count.

Lisa ran her hands across her forehead, placed her hands on her hips and continued with her closing arguments. "Men and women of the jury," she said, trying her best to hide her frustration, "the evidence I have presented today is fact. You've seen the footage of Mister Holland gunning down two men inside of New Orleans' International Airport. Damenga and Alphonso Lapiente` were both known peddlers of massive amounts of cocaine. Their sister Carmella was gunned down October of last year in Mexico with a large quantity of drugs in her possession. The defense even admits it. This case is a classic example of revenge over drugs, not because one, Anastasia Gordon, was gunned down and the defendant had an epiphany that he should go after the men responsible. Chivalry is dead! Vigilante justice is illegal! The hard truth is that Ben Holland killed two men in cold-blood. Remember that as you debate whether this man," Lisa said as she pointed to Ben Holland, who sat beside his lawyer with a calm look upon his face, "that this man killed two people and has already been convicted of the charges. Why are we debating water under the bridge again? I ask that you find Mister Holland guilty once more of first degree murder and uphold the sentence of life behind bars without parole. I thank you all for your time," Lisa ended as she backed away from the jury and took her seat.

"Court will convene for recess where the jury will begin deliberation until a verdict is accomplished," the judge said as the courtroom began clearing out.

Later that night, Lisa and Dante` met up in a dimly lit restaurant in downtown Denver where she and Dante` tried to reach a deal over dinner, but there was much more to their meeting.

"When I heard Lisa Vanguard was prosecuting this case I grew scared. But I couldn't let that fear be shown to my clients," Dante` said as he poured Lisa a stem glass of white wine.

"Why were you scared? Thought I was going to bring up our little fling down in D.C.?"

"It wouldn't have surprised me if you would've managed to get that in doing your closing arguments and take us both down."

Lisa laughed at Dante`s remark. The two had a brief affair in D.C. in 1998 when Dante` was in town defending a congressman who'd been accused of killing his young lover. Her remains were found in a park on the south side of D.C. in a park and the congressman was under suspicion. The case was a brutal one that lasted nearly a month, but Dante` would eventually get the congressman off when it was discovered that his mistress was the victim of a serial killer lurking about in the D.C. area. The Massachusetts defense attorney had met Lisa Vanguard inside a cop bar in Georgetown, and the two hit it off with the understanding that once his case was concluded, Dante` would return home to his wife.

"How's Olivia?" Lisa asked before she sipped her wine.

"Doing great. She's resumed practicing, you know?"

"Defense attorney?"

"Yeah. Also family law. But enough of her, it's really good to see you, Lisa."

"Same here, Dante`. You wanna fuck before I win this case tomorrow?" Lisa asked calmly, just as easily as if she was asking Dante` to pass the napkins.

"You're still the same. Blunt and to the point," Dante` chuckled. "I would love to bang that tight little cunt of yours, but I'm faithful now. Have been since we ended our affair back in ninety-eight."

"My ass!" Lisa laughed. "Your name is synonymous with the word cheat."

"Okay. So I fucks around on my wife from time to time. Who gives a rat fat ass, really? I'm a sleaze ball, Lisa. You all of all people should know that. And I'm catching a boner over here that I would just love to penetrate you with for old time's sake."

"Well, what's stopping you?"

"I don't know," Dante` said as he leaned back in the booth. "I guess this here case is bringing about a change in me. Whether my client is found guilty or not, he and his friends are inadvertently forcing me to reexamine my personal life."

"I'm drying up over here listening to you, mister."

"Well, get drier," Dante` said through laughter. "I have every intention of winning this case. And as of right now, the defense is winning."

"Not for long. Not when I bust this thing wide open with new evidence," Lisa said as she slid Dante` several photographs.

"Who are these people?" Dante asked as he eyed several photos of Ben Holland talking to two men.

"That would be Swanson Gautier and Isaac Montgomery."

"Please elaborate," Dante` said, never making eye contact with Lisa as he was too busy staring at new evidence that could derail his entire case.

"You're slacking in your old age, man. Those are two of America's most wanted detectives. Ex-narcotics detectives down the city New Orleans. Just as you have linked Sherman Davis to corrupt cops in Memphis, Tennessee? I've managed to come up with a little link of my own. What's Ben Holland doing talking to two cops wanted by my agency?"

"I knew you had something up your sleeve. You've been slick ever since I've known you. Lisa, Ben Holland has paid his dues. And you know damned well the man was provoked." Dante` said lowly as he sipped Scotch on the rocks.

"Ben Holland was in with Damenga`, Dante`, and you know it. And I know damned well he was in that house where Carmella was shot and left for dead. You came out lying from the get-go."

"I've told no lies. I only stated the evidence presented by

prosecutors to tell my own story, which is the truth I might add."

Lisa leaned back and said, "Carmella wasn't busted with nowhere near ten thousand pounds of cocaine, so there's your first lie."

"I was wrong about that?" Dante` asked with a smirk on his face.

"You know damn well you were wrong," Lisa stated matter-of-factly. "Carmella had one hundred and forty-four kilograms on a truck registered to some bullshit tomato company in Valle Hermoso, Mexico. I could've nailed you for that lie, but I felt it would help my case. And when I present these pictures your little lie will backfire."

"That won't hold water. I can easily claim a miscalculation in weight being that I'm not a drug dealer. That won't be a problem."

"Everybody that testified for Ben Holland knows damned well he was in that house in Memphis. They sat there under oath and flat out lied. Everything I said about Mister Holland was true and you know it."

"Okay," Dante` sighed. "Let's get on with bargain barrage. My client is prepared to pay a fine of two hundred thousand dollars to plead guilty to passion-provoked manslaughter."

Lisa laughed. "A fine," she asked as she leaned back in the booth. "That sounds more like a bribe. You offer me a bribe, Dante`?"

"Not a bribe, Lisa—a deal. I know you need funding for your investigation in the North West. The Senate Appropriations Committee has steadily been denying your requests for more funds, so you can't move a muscle. And as long as the republicans are running things in Washington, you'll never get those funds. Let me help you—but you have to help me."

"I don't need your help in that matter, Dante`. And this little bribery attempt will be made known to the court-of-law."

"You won't say a thing because I have more dirt on you than you could ever imagine. And let's not play the 'I got your ass game', okay? Let's not pussy foot around here, Lisa—because I'm talking real numbers. Three hundred thousand dollars." Dante` stated lowly, knowing Lisa was hard pressed for funds.

Lisa paused and drew back in her seat again and stared hard at Dante`. She then leaned forward, resting her elbows on the table. O'Malley could see he had touched a nerve within the woman, so he upped the ante even further. "Four hundred and seventy-five thousand dollars," he said calmly. "That's more than enough to conduct your investigation. You want funds so your case in the Pacific North West can get made? Here's the money you need on a silver platter. Now, you can show those pictures tomorrow and keep a penniless man behind bars, or you can let him go free and pursue much bigger fish."

Lisa got up from her seat and sat next to Dante` and leaned over and whispered in his ear, "Who will know about this agreement?"

"Only you and I. But I have to have those pictures, and the negatives." Dante` replied in a whisper.

Lisa thought for a minute. Dante` was giving her the fuel she needed to light the fire she had been trying to ignite. She could easily hide the money in a separate account and conduct her investigation into drug activity back in Seattle without reporting back to the Senate Committee, and once she had enough evidence, she could report back to the group of Senators with enough evidence to garner an even bigger budget and bust her case wide open.

Lisa Vanguard was the type of woman to finish what she started. She was intrigued over the circumstances surrounding the case she was working in Seattle back in 2002 and she wanted to see just how far-reaching the drug activities of the Onishi brothers extended and to also uncover the people who were behind their deaths.

The woman's mind was working overtime. Drug smuggling and murder under the guise of legitimate business, hired assassins, and a murdered policeman—the possibilities swirling around the case she'd been shoved off of back in Seattle were just too hard to resist and she wanted back in on the action—with or without the approval of her superiors back on the east coast. The ends would justify the means was her thinking, and without giving it a second thought, Lisa forged a deal to allow Ben Holland to go free—upon the condition that she received her payoff upfront. Dante` had a blank check written by a rap mogul by the name of 'Big Derrick', a friend to Ben Holland. He filled in the check for the agreed upon amount and handed it to Lisa. Lisa in turn handed over the photos and the two shook hands.

"You will get the negatives when the money goes through. I trust it's good?"

"I can guarantee that the money is good. You just be sure to send me those negatives. No copies. I want the originals."

"You'll get what you ask for, Dante`," Lisa said as she waved the negatives in front of O'Malley. "So long as the check clears. I mean, we aren't talking peanuts here. And for all I know you could be bullshitting me to get me to let your client walk free."

"When the check clears, as I know it will, you just make sure you hand over the negatives."

"We got ourselves a deal. I'm trusting you, Dante`. I want to blow this case up in the North West more than anything." Lisa stated just as her cell phone rang. She answered and remained silent for a minute. "Where are you now, Laddy?" she then asked. "I'm on my way. Sorry, Dante`. We'll have to end dinner early, but if you're ever in D.C. give me a call. I'm always up for a good lickin' and stickin'," she ended as she slid out of the booth, leaving behind a blushing Dante`.

****

About an hour later, Lisa was standing outside a defunct night spot named *Glitz* with life size photos of a dead woman named Desiree Abbadando. One of the photos was laid out in the exact spot where the woman had been lying on the night she was killed nearly two years ago back in October of 2003. The investigating officer was on hand, and he'd filled Lisa and Laddy in on what witnesses told him.

"So, this woman was killed by a sniper shot?" Lisa asked as she walked around the picture, looking down at the image.

"Yes, ma'am. That is what we believe because witnesses say the shot came from nowhere," the detective answered.

"Shots do not originate from nowhere. And please, call me Lisa. Ma'am sounds so amateurish and makes me feel, it makes me feel old."

"Yes, Lisa," the Hispanic officer said. "But no one knows where the shot came from."

Lisa only shook her head over the detective's last statement. For some time now, she'd been encountering low grade gumshoes that half-assed did their jobs. She understood many of the people killed on the streets were criminals, and investigators would rather go after those who preyed upon innocent civilians, but a crime was a crime was a crime in her eyes. It all led back to keeping the community safe in her mind.

"If Desiree was standing here," Lisa said as she turned her back to the picture and looked forward, "if she was here when she was shot and fell backwards to the left, then the shot had to come from her right side. I'm guessing, because the bullet that sliced through Miss Abbandando's skull entered her right cheek and exited at the base of her skull on the left side on a downward angle."

At that moment, Lisa and Laddy both looked across the street towards a three story office building that anchored a dentistry on the first floor. They turned to one another and nodded their heads simultaneously as they began walking towards the building.

"What are you going to do with these pictures?" the detective asked.

"Leave them with my aides, will you, please? Thank you officer, you've been more than helpful. We'll call you if we need further details."

Lisa and Laddy crossed the intersection and walked around to the back of the building where they came upon a ladder that led to the roof. Once atop the building, the two pulled out small flashlights and began looking around under the moonlit sky.

"It's been nearly two years since this homicide. What are the chances we find something?" Lisa asked excitedly. The woman simply loved her job. Poking and prodding to find the truth was her specialty on any given day.

"I'd say the chances are slim and next to naught." Laddy answered dryly.

"You have to have more faith than that, young man."

"Faith doesn't crack a case, Lisa."

"You're right, Laddy. But," Lisa said as she approached the edge of the building where a clear view of the entrance to *Glitz* was situated and knelt down and began feeling around. "Hunches sometimes do," she finished as she pried up a rusted and bent 7.62 millimeter shell from the roof's asphalt and showed it to Laddy with a smile on her face. "I'm a bad son-of-a-bitch."

"Seven, six, two," Laddy said as he eyed the shell.

"The same kind used in the Onishi hit up in Seattle coincidentally." Lisa said as she looked down on the angle taken by the sniper. "Another good shot. And it's similar to the shots taken on Hayate and Isao. What are the chances," Lisa asked rhetorically as her eyes glazed over. "What are the chances these two cases are connected?"

"We have more you know?" Laddy said, shaking Lisa from her thoughts.

"What else have you?"

"Well, umm, I'm thirsty," Laddy said as he tucked his hands inside his silk slacks and smiled down at Lisa.

"Lush," Lisa chided. "Okay, let's find a bar and you lay it out for me."

"How's about The Royal Flush?"

"The Royal Flush?"

"Yeah. It's where one suspect in this case, a man named Asa Spade is headquartered."

"Not a smart move, Laddy. These people are sharp, and we both look like a couple of sticks in the mud. I have a case to work in the morning also and I'm not going to change into a costume and sit in a potential suspect's night club and map out his shit. He'll pick us out like a rotten tomato sitting on a grapevine. Let's go."

"Where?"

"Where we can be alone."

"Oooh. I like the sound of that."

"Don't get your hopes up too high, lover boy. I like them hard and big, not soft and small."

"You saw me getting out of a cold shower once and you won't let that down will you?"

"You had your shot and you blew it, Kemosabe. It dried up on your ass. The hot box doesn't like to be teased, nor can it function properly without proper lubrication. She has to be excited, that's the only way maximum pleasure can be achieved," Lisa remarked as she backed down the ladder.

"Cock tease."

"Limp dick," Lisa retorted as she jumped down the remaining three ladder rungs and walked over to her and Laddy's Nova.

A near-empty, yet cozy lounge inside the Sheraton Hotel where Lisa and Laddy were staying was the perfect spot to lay out all the evidence Laddy had collected the four days he and Lisa were in Denver. While Lisa was working the Ben Holland case, she had Laddy looking into the background of a man by the name of Asa Spade in order to see what he could dig up on the man, and what Laddy had uncovered was nothing short of magnificent.

Lisa walked around the pool table where numerous pictures were laid out as she sipped on a Budweiser beer and entertained a shot of Jagermeister. Pieces of a puzzle were being put together, but Lisa was only scraping the surface. With that aside, the train had left the station with what lay on the table.

Laddy and the rest of Lisa's aides had taken photographs of Asa Spade. His face and real name was now known, having been confirmed through arrest records down in Las Vegas. There was an Asian woman and a black woman that had been photographed as well outside of *The Royal Flush* and their photographs were on the table also.

"Who are the two women you photographed at this club, Laddy?" Lisa asked.

"Don't know. But we trailed them over to Shorter Arms apartments where they disappeared behind some buildings. We felt we would get made if we tailed them any further so we laid low."

"Okay. What did they do?" Lisa asked as she picked up a couple of photos of three Asian men exiting a small jet.

"I don't know what they did back there," Laddy replied.

Lisa shook her head in dismay. "You remind me of the lames I have to—"

"They left," Laddy said, cutting Lisa's remark short once he realized the full scope of her question. "The two women left in a blue Tahoe and we tailed them one hundred miles or so north to Loveland Airport in Fort Collins where they met up with three Asian guys and a black guy. Here's the photo of the group together where the Asian woman handed over a black satchel."

Lisa downed her shot of Jagermeister and said, "The drop off."

"We believed so at the time, but we didn't have probable cause to pull the two women over and do a search when they left the airport and we didn't want to risk letting them know we're on to them. What is known is that heavy drugs are being moved inside Shorter Arms by some gang. A blood gang called the Bounty Hunters. That information comes from the Denver police department, but we can't get close enough to verify."

"Asa Spade is listed as a lead member of the Blood Bounty Hunters down in Vegas. There's a tie-in to this crew in Shorter Arms."

"Exactly. But the few days we've been watching Shorter Arms, Asa Spade hasn't been seen there. He has to have someone down in Shorter Arms doing the dirty work. What we have is the two women going in, an empty space at that point, because we don't know who the go-between is, nor can we identify him or her, and then we have a possible drop off to the suppliers in Fort Collins. We're at the threshold of a criminal organization if you ask me."

"Yes we are," Lisa said as she stared hard at the images of the three Asian men and one lone black man.

"Who are these silk suits that got off the plane?" Lisa asked as she eyed the photos.

"Those are the men the two women met at the airport. They received the payment is our best guess."

"Where did this flight go? The three Asian guys and the black guy? What was their listed flight plan and names?"

Laddy poured a shot of Jagermeister for himself, gulped it down and pounded his chest.

Lisa was under the impression that Laddy had come up short. He always grew nervous when he felt he'd let her down. "You have to go back there and get those flight plans, Laddy."

"You doubt me?" Laddy said with a smirk.

"You have the names and the flight plan?" Lisa asked, barely able to contain her joy.

"That cough was sincere. That drink is potent as the fuck. But I did good, Lisa. When our Asian friends took off, me and a couple of guys went in and obtained the flight records. The only name for certain is the black guy. His name is Finland Xavier. We ran a check on him and he's a lawyer in Chicago that operates a trucking company called Midwest Express."

"Do we know the businesses this Midwest Express deals with?"

"We do. Looking at old tax records, there's a warehouse in the Bedford section of Chicago that accepts freight from a guy named JunJie Maruyama based out of—"

"Seattle, Washington," Lisa said, cutting Laddy's remark short. "Maruyama? Let me guess—that's an Asian name?"

"Damn sure is. You may be right about another Asian gang moving in on the Onishi brothers."

"I may be. But for all accounts, this could all be legitimate business between these people, Laddy, and just coincidence. We need more proof to get funding from the committee back in Washington."

"But the drop off can't be ignored. We have two women who we believe are the money handlers for Asa Spade leaving Shorter Arms and meeting with these men and handing over a satchel believed to contain drug profits."

"Three Asian men, a black lawyer and a former pimp from Vegas are caught up in the mix," Lisa said as she eyed the photographs. "In order to gain ground on this case, Laddy, we need to get somebody in this organization to flip. Hmm. Eeenie…meenie…miney…mo," Lisa said as her forefinger darted back and forth across the photographs, "catch an… informant…by…the toe. Let's take a trip to Vegas and see what we can dig up on Montoya Spencer, Laddy," Lisa finally said as she scooped up the photographs.

"But, we haven't the funds to continue on," Laddy retorted. "All of this was done during the case we're on now—which is scheduled to conclude the moment the jury hands down a verdict."

"They will reach a verdict tomorrow," Lisa said, happy she'd made the deal with Dante` O'Malley earlier in the night. "And after the verdict in the Ben Holland trial is read tomorrow? We'll begin looking into this guy Asa Spade and see if there's a connection between him and the Asians from Seattle."

When court reconvened the following morning, Lisa couldn't wait for the verdict to be announced. She had planned on presenting pictures of Benjamin Holland talking to two cops who were on the lam, but the deal she'd made with Dante` the night before, coupled with all the evidence Laddy had accumulated the five days or so she was in town, had pushed all those plans aside. Benjamin Holland could've flown out of the courtroom with gold wings for all she cared. The woman was onto something big and she knew it. Once the verdict was read, Lisa and her staff exited the courtroom amidst cheers for Ben Holland, sliding pass his friends and out of his life for the time being because she was now on the trail of much bigger fish, namely a man by the name of Montoya Spencer who went by the alias of Asa Spade.

CHAPTER THIRTY-TWO
THE MIDDLE MAN

"What that boy doing 'round that corner," twenty-five year-old Dougie asked as he sat inside a blue Tahoe deep off inside Shorter Arms.

Dougie ran shop over in the apartment complex for Asa Spade. A lifelong criminal who'd done his own fair share of crime from robbery to murder, Douglas 'Dougie' Hunt had been running trap houses since he was teenager; but he was a step above now. The gangster never touched the dope. He only collected money at the end of the day and transferred it over to Xiang and Francesca once he and his crew got their cut. Dougie was unknowingly the missing piece to Lisa Vanguard's puzzle.

Everyday shop was open, Dougie would sit across from the dope house in his Tahoe and watch traffic. A soldier would text him a number and Dougie would keep a mental count on the money earned. Soldiers were up and down the block for protection. The war against Carmella, in which his cousin Percy, his homegirl Ponita, and nearly a dozen soldiers had been murdered, had taught Dougie certain methods of operation when it came to moving major weight.

He now had three gunners around him at all times while sitting inside his Tahoe that was parked among the other cars in the complex. And whether it was eight, or eighty degrees,

Dougie never moved from his spot until it was time to count cash. He let the youngsters, who were infatuated with being in a gang, handle the dope. The boys knew to come correct each time because Dougie had made an example of one sixteen year-old who'd come up short on sales by breaking both his legs with baseball bat and fracturing his skull.

Dougie watched everything that went down in his spot as he called shots. The youngsters looked up to him, believing they were Blood Bounty Hunters for real, but it was just a name Dougie had laid on the crew to garner more respect. He was beyond gangbanging, but if that's what it took to keep the crew in order, he would run with it; he had all the boys in the crew believing they were in a gang, but they were mere pawns on the low rung of the ladder.

"Yo, blood? I said what that boy doing 'round the corner?" Dougie asked again with a little more force.

"He going get the fish sandwich you asked for," one of Dougie's soldiers replied.

"It shouldn't take that long on no fish. Go get that nigga and bring his ass back to the house, but if he up in that li'l broad face in that store? Call me and I'm a smack the shit outta his ass when he get back 'round here," Dougie snapped as he leaned back and raised the window on his ride.

Just then Dougie's cell phone rang. "What up, big dog?"

"What it look like over there?" Asa asked as he sat at his desk inside *The Royal Flush*.

"We 'bout done. Moved seven 'nem thangs."

"Alright. Alright. I'm gone have the girls swing through in about two hours." Asa Spade responded in appreciation.

"We be ready. They got the new burners?"

"Yeah. That's what I call to tell you. Lay off this line unless you absolutely need me before they get there and dump it and use the new ones once you get those new ones in."

"Gotcha," Dougie replied as he ended the call. "Hey," he them called out to his soldier, "forget about that call. Just go get that boy."

****

"We can't see everything from here. Who's the guy in the Tahoe?" Lisa whispered to Laddy as the two hid inside of a dumpster that gave only a partial shot of the activity unfolding outside of what they believed to be a dope house in Shorter Arms apartments.

For the last four days, Lisa and Laddy had been photographing a man they believed was the go-between for Asa Spade and the drugs he ran. They weren't certain, however, because the man rarely moved from his location once he parked in the driveway across the street from the alleged dope house. He would sit there for hours and occasionally get out to stretch his legs, sometimes while texting on the phone.

"I believe that's our middle man," Laddy answered. "We have his picture. Maybe we can take it down to the station and see if we can get an identification from a jailhouse snitch?"

"That may work. Or maybe the vice squad down in Vegas knows something."

"Do we have enough time to make that trip? We're supposed to be up in Philly, you know?"

"Don't remind me. Who in the hell gives a fuck about a bunch of teenagers boosting clothes from a department store? Shit, I'll steal from their asses myself if the opportunity presented itself. This is way more important than a crew of shopping mall thieves."

"I agree, but the question still stands."

"Let's wait a while longer and then we'll head down to Vegas and see what we can dig up on this guy in the Tahoe before we fly back to Philadelphia."

Lisa was bulldog of an agent. She was also defiant. Her superiors back in Washington now had her undercover buying stolen merchandise from a group of females who boosted clothes, jewelry and shoes from high end fashion stores in the Philadelphia area, which wasn't a part of the deal when Senator Feinstein handed her the Ben Holland case. She was about to crack the Philadelphia case wide open as it was a chip shot given her caliber; but during her down time, she and Laddy took flights to Colorado to spy on certain members within Asa Spade's organization.

If Lisa were on the tail of Asa Spade full time, she would've made much further progress, but being that she had no authority to even be investigating the case in Denver, Colorado, she could only make minimal headway in the on-going case that was of her own doing. It would take quite a bit of time for her to unravel the puzzle, but the three times she and Laddy had returned to Denver since the month of August, they'd gain some ground. They'd identified the two women who were the possible money handlers for Asa Spade as that of Xiang Nyguen and Francesca Aranello; and on this trip, they believed they'd obtained photos of the middle man, whose name was still unknown.

The money given to her by Dante` O'Malley in a deal she'd made over the Ben Holland case was fueling Lisa's rogue investigation and she knew she only had until the money ran out to put the case together and bring solid evidence before the Senate Appropriations Committee lest her investigation be for naught. With only one roll of the dice, Lisa knew she had to pick her battles wisely. She and Laddy remained crouched inside the dumpster under the cold night air for another hour, watching in silence as activity unfolded in Shorter Arms before they left the area and began making plans for a flight down to Vegas to see if the guy they'd photographed had any connection to Asa Spade. Had Lisa and Laddy remained in position for just an hour longer, they would've made the connection between Xiang and Francesca, Dougie and Asa; but their limited time frame had unwittingly let that fact go unbeknownst for the time being.

****

Meanwhile, over in Saint Louis, eighteen year-old Simone Cortez and fifteen year-old Peppi Vargas sat at a wooden dinette table eating teriyaki chicken wings inside their new apartment that sat across from Fox Park on Saint Louis Street. The two were more than friends now, breaking bread together and hustling side by side had blended them into sisters. They'd made a big come up with Toodie pulling licks over a two month period, and moving out of the apartment on Ann Avenue had done wonders for Pepper. She'd come into her own the time she spent with Toodie, Q-man, Dead Eye and Big Bounce, and having her own place had elevated her confidence, bringing her out of her shell completely.

Simone and Pepper both jumped ship on Toodie and her boys on the last jack play because Dead Eye and Big Bounce had gone off the deep end. The click was robbing a house in Indianapolis when Dead Eye decided he would rape the man's wife; but that was only the beginning. The man's four year-old daughter was forced to watch as her mother was sexually assaulted and then shot dead. The little girl watched in horror as her father was murdered before she was killed herself. The sounds those people made, the little girl's screams, the mother repeatedly asking Dead Eye to take her daughter out of the room before he did his deed while the man's cries of mercy for his family fell on deaf ears, left Simone and Pepper shocked and stunned. They'd never seen such treachery and wanted no part in the raping and killing of innocent women and children.

Dead Eye, Big Bounce, Q-man and Toodie often made Pepper and Simone sick to their stomachs over some of the crimes they committed, and at the same time, it gave them deep insight into Toodie and her friends' attitude when it came to the game and neither liked what they'd seen. Toodie, Dead Eye, Big Bounce and Q-man were the type that killed their own friends, belittled people in public and cared about no one and nothing but themselves; they weren't for crew, which was the very thing Carmella had stood for when she was alive. And it would be for that reason and that reason alone, that there would always be a certain amount of animosity lying just below the surface of what was once a well-oiled machine. Carmella's death had severely deteriorated the gang in Fox Park. Toodie was trying to keep things in order, but most of the click was now scattered and fending for themselves; doing whatever needed to be done in order to survive.

With Simone on her side, Pepper was prepared to make some major moves of her own on the streets of Saint Louis. Simone may have been older, she'd even schooled Pepper on the game, but Pepper was far more intelligent and had a more ambitious drive and had been taught well by Carmella the three years or so she'd spent with the woman. She was scoring a half kilo on her own and was now looking to form her own crew with the help of Simone, her partner in crime and sister from another mother.

Simone sat across from Pepper chomping down on her wings. She made eye contact with her friend and nodded towards the living room where Dead Eye, Big Bounce and Q-man were parked on the couch playing Pepper's Playstation.

"I wish she call so they can get the fuck on," Pepper said, loud enough for the men to her speaking.

Q-man sucked his teeth and shook his head. He was ready to get gone himself; but Toodie had gotten herself locked up a week earlier when she was busted with a half-ounce of crack cocaine in the drive thru of the McDonald's on Jefferson Avenue and he needed to be around to catch her call.

Dead Eye and Big Bounce were looking for another score so they could get Ann Avenue pumping again and they was hoping Toodie could put them up on a lick. They'd scoped out Pepper's supplier, a Mexican named Malik Gomez, who lived on the opposite end of Fox Park, but they quickly understood that 'The Gomez Boys', as Malik and his crew were known by on the streets of Fox Park, didn't fuck around. Malik and his crew were strapped at all times, vacated the area when they sold out and nobody knew where they went when they left Fox Park.

Malik and his boys were hard to get to, and unbeknownst to the crew on Ann Avenue, they were affiliated with the Chicago Gang. Malik's suppliers were unknown, and as far as everybody in Fox Park knew, he was the man.

"Yo, we gone handle that tonight." Simone yelled out to Q-man.

"Somebody need to. Her ass riding 'round like it's all good," Q-man replied. "Look, soon as I talk to Toodie I'm gone."

"Yeah. Soon as we talk to Toodie we gone," Big Bounce repeated seriously.

"Well, why ya' here how about getting your foot off our coffee table?" Pepper said as she leaned back in her seat and looked out into the living room. Big Bounce grunted as he removed his thick calf from the circular glass table and sat up in his seat.

These were dangerous men Pepper and Simone were dealing with—murderous vultures with numerous bodies under their belts, but the girls were holding their own. Pepper had upgraded her artillery from a .380 to a seventeen shot Glock .9 and was prepared for whatever; Simone was a twelve gauge fanatic. She never left home without her fifteen shot semi-automatic twelve gauge, a weapon she affectionately called Roscoe.

For the most part, everybody from Ann Avenue got along because they were all involved in the same occupation and had a vested interest, which was the almighty dollar. Conversations were kept to a minimum because outside of cash, the crew had nothing in common. They could care less what went on outside their joint business ventures.

Nearly an hour later, Simone's phone rang. "Her she go, y'all."

"Yes!" Pepper exclaimed. "Now they can get up out our spot."

Simone accepted the collect call and Toodie didn't even acknowledge her; all she asked was Q-man over to the house.

"Hello to you, too," Simone said as she pulled the phone from her ear and handed it to Q-man.

"Yo?"

"You talk to our boy?"

"Nahh. That's why I was waiting on you. I need a number on dude."

"It's the same one. You got a new burner so he don't know your number and he ain't gone answer. All that time I kept gettin' those unknown phone calls from Missouri and it was him. Who woulda figured?"

"That's what we needed though. How I get in touch with dude?"

"Leave a message and he gone hit you back. Give your number to Simone, too, so she can pass it to me. We need to stay in touch and set something up for when I get out next year."

"Next year?"

"Yeah, man. Bitches got me dead right comin' out the drive thru. I'm gone take a thirteen month plea on possession, but I be out in about ten or eleven. It's cool. I need to sit my ass down for a minute because shit was gettin' outta control."

"Alright. We gone hold your bread unless we need it."

"That's cool. How them li'l girls doing?"

"They some g's. Make ya' wanna bust they head sometimes, but they real with it. They should be 'round when you get out."

"This our deal, though. I don't want them involved in our business on that level. We take care our end we back where we were before my girl got killed last October."

"That's what's up. I'm gone call dude before I leave out for the Ap. He might be in town and I could link up with 'em and get that info firsthand."

"Do that. And when I get out it's on."

"Your fam from down the road say you know something?" Q-man asked, a coded question in which he was asking Toodie did she know of a good lick for Dead Eye and Big Bounce.

"You would have to come see me for that, homeboy. I ain't talkin' like that on this wire. Just roll like you been rollin'—but stay off the radar until I get out. We gone be paid I'm tellin' ya'."

"You know your word good with me. I be here. Hollar when you touch down."

"Si. Tell them boys beside you to do the same. Everybody

maintain. Let me hollar at that girl before this phone cut off." Q-man whistled to get Simone's attention as he held out the phone.

"Yeah?" Simone asked.

"You took care that?"

"Tonight."

"Cool. I got you on the visitor's list so see me when you get done and bring that phone number he gone give you."

"Aite," Simone said before she hung up the phone.

Later that night, Pepper and Simone left their apartment and began making their way through the back alleys of Fox Park. It was after one in the morning on a star-lit, crisp and cool night as the girls walked side by side, Simone with her twelve gauge draped across her shoulder and Pepper clutching her Glock 9. Broken glass and trash littered the alley ways the two walked down as they approached the block where they posted up inside an empty apartment building.

"I been thinking about coppin' some wheels, Simone," Pepper said lowly as the two knelt on opposite sides of a hollowed out window in the living room.

"Yeah? What kind?"

"A Mazda. A black one with the suicide doors. I forget what it's called."

"You want the RX eight? That's hot."

"It is ain't it? I want a motorcycle too, but that's gone be too much. I'm definitely gone score that ride though watch." Pepper said as she lit up a blunt and the two smoked and continued watching the block for their intended target.

Simone and Pepper were waiting on the manager from McDonald's. Toodie had put the word out that the lady had snitched on her a few days after she'd gotten busted in McDonald's drive thru. The woman had been caught inside the store with cocaine Toodie had sold her a week earlier and narcotics agents had set up a quick sting and had taken her down.

Simone and Pepper waited for about an hour until the woman's '05 Camry pulled up in front her apartment. She climbed out of her ride in her McDonald's uniform and while she was putting the key in her front door, Pepper and Simone emerged from the empty apartment beside her home and ran up on the woman. She turned around and screamed when she saw the guns aimed at her, but quickly went silent when blasts of fire lit up the night and hot lead began penetrating her head and torso. She slumped down against her doorway and fell over on her side as Simone and Pepper trotted off and disappeared into the darkness.

"You get the car, I'll get a motorcycle for us," Simone said as she jogged beside Pepper.

"Deal." Pepper replied casually.

A favor was done for Toodie, a favor that would keep Pepper and Simone in good standing with her and her boys for the time being, but in all actuality, the two teenagers were looking out for themselves; Pepper was moving a little weight, and the last thing she needed was to have a rat in the neighborhood. The murder of the neighborhood snitch had given Simone and Pepper big stripes in Fox Park; their names were now ringing and their clientele would only increase over time.

CHAPTER THIRTY-THREE
NEW VENTURES

"I'm tellin' ya right now, if they choose Texas, Kansas State or Kansas? Momma, you should cut off their inheritance with the quickness!" fifteen year-old Walee snapped as he assisted his father with the grilling of chicken and ribs on the family's patio.

It was the weekend of July 4th, 2006 and all was going well for the Holland-Dawkins family on and off the ranch. The Chicago Gang had been trouble-free since the hit on Carmella, even gaining a strong foothold on Fox Park. Cocaine was moving smoothly, murders had subsided and most of the crew was stacking money and seeking out new ventures.

Malik Gomez, one of the crew's most trusted soldiers, had teamed up with Doss and Eddie Cottonwood. Doss and Eddie had bought the old cleaners across the street from *Connections* down in Saint Charles and was preparing to open up a night club. Doss often talked with Asa Spade over the phone and had gained insight on how to run the business. He'd also hired Malik, who'd started his own renovation company, and gave him the job of renovating the old three story early 1940's structure and transform it into one of the most happening spots in the Saint Louis area.

Dawk, Bay and T-top had given their mother money to open a large entertainment complex back in Ponca City. The old bowling alley had been ripped apart by a tornado in October of 2005 and that left little by way of entertainment because the owners of the bowling alley had decided against rebuilding the place. The big three had designed an entertainment complex that featured seven movie screens, a bowling alley, large game room and a skating rink; a $1,000,000 dollar investment of their own, with all the investment money having been gained from the streets that would be run through the family's upstart company titled *Holland-Dawkins Enterprises, LLC*.

The formation of the new company had put Naomi back into the business of corporate lawyer, which was her expertise. She'd filed all the paperwork, obtained the necessary permits and it was easy for her to persuade the city council to give her the contract because the family was highly favored in the city. While she was brokering the deal on her oldest three's venture, Naomi had also closed the deal on the land behind the Holland Ranch that her neighbor once owned. Approval rested on the city council's approval, who weren't scheduled to resume hearings until after November elections, but Naomi was already assured that the land would be hers and she was first on the city council's docket.

Siloam, meanwhile, had indeed taken a loss on her dealings with the editor from Rolling Stone magazine. The man had been fired from the company years ago, but had been using false ads online to scam up and coming bands out of their monies. It was a hard lesson for Siloam, but when Doss reimbursed her the money, she was put at ease. She was now touring with Jane Dow with the hopes of breaking out into the mainstream with a hit of their own.

Mary's Produce was the name of Mary Holland's new company. The forty-seven year-old woman's business had soared onto the shelves of grocery stores in Ponca City, Oklahoma City, Tulsa and Stillwater, Oklahoma. Fresh onions, collard, mustard and turnip greens were her specialty. Mary had even purchased two refrigerated trailers with her, Ne`Ne` and Dimples' images on the sides of the trailers. It was a fascinating thing to see Mary's trailers riding off the land with her image, along with those of Ne`Ne` and Dimples plastered onto the side. Ne`Ne` and Dimples were smiling brightly while displaying a basket full of greens and onions as their mother stood in between them with her arms around their shoulders with her gorgeous smile on display. The trailers were being pulled by Martha and Twiggy most times as they were still trucking for the family and earning better than average pay.

DeeDee had finally moved down the ranch and it was a pure blessing for the aging gangster. He got to see his grandkids and great grandkids every day, had a garden of his own, and often worked alongside Walee, Spoonie and Tyke down in the poultry yard. DeeDee's past was behind him, he was now a grandpa living on a ranch on Oklahoma, something he'd never even dreamed when Naomi first set up in Oklahoma nearly fifteen years earlier.

Mendoza and Francine, meanwhile, were still going strong. Francine often got sick when she was home in Cicero, so she and Mendoza often spent weeks at a time on the ranch as it was therapeutic with its fresh air and organic cuisine. Francine often joked that Mendoza was making her sick on purpose so he could take her to Oklahoma where he could spend time with DeeDee, his lifelong friend.

Mendoza always laughed it off, but his wife's illness was really bothering him. Something about Cicero was making her ill, but he couldn't quite put his finger on it as of yet. Through his many smiles and jokes, it was fair to say that Mendoza had suspicions, suspicions that only he and DeeDee would discuss from time to time, but neither would ever imagine, as it was too gross and treacherous to even fathom. The two old Mafioso often sat and observed life unfolding before their eyes, and by all accounts, life was good, save for a few things involving Francine's illness that left them wondering some days.

Everybody was doing well summer of 2006. The family was prodding along, growing and prospering and many decisions had been made over time. On this July 4th holiday, another decision was about to be made and a couple of milestones were about to be reached. Seventeen year-olds Kimi and Koko were preparing to go to college and Bena and Tiva's 21st birthday was just under a week away. It was a big deal on the ranch this holiday.

Bay and T-top were nonchalant about their birthdays. They'd gotten their gift a while back when the deal was sealed on their entertainment complex. Tiva was happy with her marriage and Malaysia and Malara were thriving on the land. Bay and AquaNina were still hot and heavy and getting along well. They'd leased a condo down in Oklahoma City and were planning to form a civil union. It wasn't much more Naomi's oldest daughters could ask for, so they'd reserved their day and gave the floor to Kimi and Koko.

Naomi's middle daughters were locked away in their mother's private room preparing to announce their decision on which college they would attend. Members of the family had money on the line over which college the twins would choose. Rumor had it that Northwestern, their mother's Alma Mater, was in contention, along with Ohio State and the University of Kansas.

Doss was worried. The last thing he wanted was for his middle daughters to attend Northwestern. With Kimi and Koko being based in Chicago where he was widely known, they would need protection around the clock. His oldest three would have to move there with them, thereby disrupting their lives and the business they had going on in Saint Louis. Malik and Jay-D could fill in from time to time, because that was all the people Doss really trusted, and protecting his family was first and foremost for the man.

The family was all out on the patio mingling, placing bets and discussing possible arrangements for Kimi and Koko's protection while Jane Dow and the band cued up their instruments for the impending celebration when the twins emerged from the home with a slip of paper. Everybody grew quiet and stared as Kimi and Koko walked over to Naomi, who sat beside Francine and Mary, and handed her a sheet of paper. Naomi opened the paper, scanned it and asked, "Are you two sure this is where you want to go?"

"We've thought it about long enough and given our obligations to the family," Kimi said, "we think this is the right choice, momma."

"Fine. I don't like it, but it's you all's decision," Naomi

sighed as she waved her hands, ushering her daughters away.

When Kimi and Koko left the patio, Naomi resumed talking to Francine and Mary. Francine had a look on her face that could freeze lightening. Mary looked confused. Doss was waiting. DeeDee and Mendoza were waiting—everybody was waiting.

"Where they going, already?" Dawk yelled aloud.

"Oh, they said they going right down the road to the University of Oklahoma," Naomi said matter-of-factly as she eyed Doss with a wide smile.

Doss leaned down and pumped his fists. "Yes, sir!" he yelled aloud through laughter.

Dawk stuck his hand out to Junior, who slid him a C-note. "Shoulda known they wasn't going too far," Junior said, having bet on Ohio State.

"This here a family thang. Kimi and Koko know what's up without even being told," Dawk replied as he tucked the money into his jeans.

Kimi and Koko had been discussing what college to attend for some time. The University of Oklahoma was perfect for them. Their boyfriends, Chablis and Udelle were sophomores there; Bay lived just up the road in Oklahoma City, about twenty miles or so from Norman, Oklahoma where the campus was located. They could travel home on weekends or just kick it with Bay whenever they wanted.

On top of that, they could still help their mother out in the family business. Kimi and Koko were both planning to earn degrees in corporate law like their mother, and they were going to take minors in accounting to further develop their skills when it came to washing dollars.

Kimi and Koko didn't understand fully their importance to the family or the scope the criminal activity that actually went on; all they knew was that they would be much more valuable if they were to remain close to home so as to be able to continue on the path that their mother had placed them on while still being able to maintain a certain amount of freedom while remaining close to their family.

The twins were peeking out the French doors on the patio, reveling in the family's jubilance and were unable to contain their joy. They ran out onto the patio into their father's arms and hugged him tightly as Jane Dow began playing Kool and the Gang's song *Celebration*.

"Daddy, we thought hard about having grandpa condo to ourselves!" Koko exclaimed.

"Yeah, right," Dawk said. "I woulda been their every night. Here," he then said as he handed Koko a hundred dollar bill. "Junior bet on Ohio State."

"Buster!" Kimi yelled aloud to Junior, who only smiled and walked off as he began texting on his cell phone. *No dice on Chicago. That's off the table.* The text read.

Get at us when you can so we can work it out. A text read back before Junior deleted the messages and returned to the celebration.

While Junior was walking up the stairs back to the patio, a horn was heard blowing wild and loud. The entire family turned and looked and saw a candy apple red 2007 Maserati Quattroporte sitting on 23" inch chrome wheels being driven by Martha. The car was a four door luxury coupe valued at over $145,000 dollars.

Koko grew weak-kneed. She had to be helped to her feet by her father while Kimi ran down the patio stairs and stood before the car and stared as she covered her lower face. She looked at the car, then back at her mother who was all smiles. Kimi did that routine repeatedly as Koko wobbled over to the front of the car and stood beside her sister and the two shed tears as they stared at the immaculate vehicle. The car was dressed in white leather, wood on the door panels and steering wheel, Bose sound system, TVs in the headrests and a personalized tag that read *DA-TWINZ*. "

"Koko! They got it! They got it!" Kimi yelled excitedly as she jumped up and down with watery eyes.

"I don't believe it! Oh my god," Koko whined as she stepped

back and stared at the vehicle in awe.

Kimi and Koko had merely shown their mother and father a picture of a car they thought was beautiful on-line nearly a year-ago, but Naomi and Doss, ever proud of their middle daughters, made it happen on July 4th and the twins were thrilled to tears. The summer of 2006 was the best on record for seventeen year-olds Kimi and Koko, who'd completed their homeschooling and were now embarking on careers that would solidify their positions within the family for years to come.

CHAPTER THIRTY-FOUR
THE FIRST COLLAPSE

"The medicine. It has to be the medicine that is making me nauseous, Mendoza." Francine said as she rode beside her husband holding a plastic bag.

It was a month after Kimi and Koko's decision, August of 2006. Seventy-five year-olds Mendoza and Francine were on their way to the hospital to have more tests run on Francine because it seemed as if her cancer was metastasizing and coming back in full force despite her double mastectomy several years earlier.

"That may be it," Mendoza said as he grabbed his cell phone and called Junior over to *Eastside Bar*.

"Grand dad, how's everything?"

"Not good. Shortly after you left, your grandmother fell ill and started vomiting all over the place. I'm headed to Mount Sinai right now to have her admitted again."

"I'm headed that way." Junior said as he got up from his stool behind the bar counter and signaled Eddie.

"No, no, son. I have it under control. Besides you have that other thing."

"No. Grand dad, I want to be there. Last time I stepped out on my family, my father died. I'm not saying that is what will happen to grandma, but I'm coming to the hospital. I should be there."

"Well, I guess so. Can somebody cover for you down in Granite City?"

"Yeah. Eddie and the guys can cover for me."

"Okay. We'll be in the Cancer Center with your mother's doctor."

"Okay. I'm on my way, grand dad."

Junior left Eddie in charge and headed out to meet his grandfather and grandmother at the hospital. Eddie, meanwhile, remained behind for another hour securing *Eastside Bar* before he hopped into a rented U-Haul truck with Jay-D and headed south towards Granite City, Illinois where he was scheduled to meet Dooney and Malik at the crew's safe house to unload twenty kilograms of cocaine.

"So what's up with this rap business you and Dooney supposed to be startin' up, Jason?" Eddie asked as he drove south on Interstate-55.

Jay-D sucked his teeth and leaned back in the passenger seat. "Dooney keep bringin' these ole fake ass gangsta rappers' CDs 'round the crib wantin' me to listen to that wack ass shit. Talkin' 'bout, 'dog we gotta go 'head and get the label started so we can sign these niggas'."

"They ain't that bad are they, li'l brother?"

"Shiit. Niggas be talkin' bout how many bricks they moving, niggas they done popped on the streets, how the feds be all up in they shit."

"That's some real talk, though. And that gangsta rap be sellin', li'l brother."

"It do, but them niggas Dooney sendin' at me ain't got a clue how shit really work. And if they did, or do, I don't want that shit being talked about while we off into this here game. That's a case waitin' ta' happen. Ain't gone do nothing but draw heat."

"I can dig it. Keep at it though, this game ain't forever."

Eddie said as he turned up the radio and continued on down the highway.

Four and a half hours later, Eddie was pulling up to the crew's safe house in Granite City. The neighborhood where the house lay was in quiet suburb consisting of newly built one and two story single family homes with paved driveways, lush green lawns and two car garages. People rarely ventured outside in this neighborhood and that worked out well for the Chicago Gang.

Malik and Dooney emerged from the one story home while Eddie was backing into the driveway and they greeted Jay-D. "Dog, got this tight producer over to the Lou, man. His CD in the car. We can check it out after we done unloading," Dooney said happily.

"Man, you and them wack as niggas you keep stressin'," Jay-D snapped as he raised the door on the U-Haul. "Fake ass wanna be ass no rappin' ass niggas."

Malik laughed and said, "We was listening to the tracks on the way over here, homes. They pretty good. You should listen."

"See? That's a man that know talent like myself. I should be an A and R rep."

"More like a BS rep," Jay-D quipped as he grabbed a small box containing five kilograms of cocaine. Jay-D, Malik and Dooney followed and the product was unloaded in a matter of minutes and Eddie quickly began situating the cocaine inside a closet in the master bedroom of the two story home.

"Y'all go on out," Eddie said. "I got it from here. I be done in a couple of minutes and we gone go get Nancy from the hair salon."

"Your daughter live in the salon," Jay-D said as he headed for the bedroom door.

"Eh, ever since she learned they had people that can braid her hair without ripping it from her scalp she been a happy camper. She done seen the light," Eddie said with his hands on either side of head and sounding like a preacher.

"Whatever, reverend cocaine," Jay-D replied as he left the bedroom and exited the home.

A few minutes later, Jay-D, Dooney and Malik were sitting in Eddie's Tahoe listening to a sample of music from Dooney's new-found talent. Jay-D was nodding his head slightly in appreciation of the instrumental he was listening to, which was a sampled track of the Isley Brothers' song *For the Love of You*. The beat was mellow, with Ron Isley's soulful, *"yeah... well, well, well...yeah, heh..."* looped over a smooth bass line.

Dooney took notice of his brother and Malik's head bobbing from the back seat. "What I tell ya', Jay-D? That boy got some work with 'em!" Dooney said aloud the music as he began tapping his feet and bobbing his head.

"He aite," Jay-D replied casually, not wanting to fully admit that the dude's track was the tightest piece of music Dooney had ever come across. "What this nigga name?"

"His name Alonzo Milton. I ran into 'em over to Bangin' Heads where Nancy get her head tightened up."

"Okay. We gone, we gone hollar at ole boy later on when we grab Nancy, then. See what else he workin' with."

Dooney began bucking in the backseat. "We gone be some legit rich niggas!" he exclaimed.

Jay-D smiled and shook his head. "That's a fool back there," he said. "Malik, how the cleaners Doss 'nem bought comin'?"

"You don't see me workin' that joint, homes? We guttin' the inside right now. That's gone be the hottest club in the Lou when we done."

"And it's right on our block, nigga!" Dooney snapped. "We get this label poppin' we can do live shows ya' smell me?"

"The hottest club, huh, Malik? How long before you able to get that thing poppin', fam?" Jay-D asked.

"Well, with just me and three other guys right now? I say two years."

"Two years?" Jay-D asked as he sat up in his seat. "Nigga, we ain't even guaranteed to be here tomorrow let alone two—"

"Yoooo," Dooney yelled over the music from the backseat as he pulled down on his fitted baseball cap. "Rollers!"

Jay-D and Malik looked up to see four patrol cars speeding up the block. They then turned to the rear and saw four more cars speeding there way with flashers blaring. Before Jay-D, Dooney and Malik could even react, the Tahoe was surrounded by eight officers while eight more patrolmen stormed towards the front door and knocked it off its hinges with a small battle ram.

"Police search warrant! Search warrant! Search warrant! Come out with your hands up! Hands up! Get down! Get down! Get down!"

Eddie had just finished stashing the cocaine when he heard the officers entering the home. Remembering the last raid, and Doss's orders, he grabbed his .9mm from his waistband and calmly stood beside the bed with the gun at his side. An officer peeked around the corner and saw Eddie standing beside the bed with his gun and aimed his weapon. "Freeze, mutherfucka or I will shoot you and kill you!" he yelled. "Drop the gun, turn around and raise your hands in the air!"

"I done heard that shit before, man. If I'm going to jail, I wanna be certain the law takin' me in and not some cowboys. Show me the search warrant," Eddie said calmly.

"Drop your weapon!" the officer yelled.

"Show me the mutherfuckin' warrant!" Eddie retorted as he held his gun at his side with his finger on the trigger. The officer fired a single shot that hit Eddie in the left leg. He fell up against the dresser, shattering the mirror before he crashed to the wooden floor screaming in pain.

Another officer ran up and knelt down before Eddie as he lay crumbled on the floor and shoved a search warrant in his face. "Sergeant Young of the Granite City Police Department—search warrant you son-of-a-bitch! Get paramedics here for this guy A-S-A-P!" the aging sergeant ordered. "Was it worth it, son?" he asked as he checked Eddie's wound.

"You don't know my struggle, man. I couldn't be happier,

mutherfucka," Eddie hissed as he clutched his wounded leg. "Where my people?" he asked as officers began searching the entirety of the home.

Back outside the house, Jay-D, Dooney and Malik were kneeling in the grass on the front lawn while a German shepherd sniffed the interior of Eddie's Tahoe. "Ain't shit in there, bitches!" Jay-D yelled.

"Yo, man! We was just listening to some music! What's all this harassment and shit?" Dooney questioned.

"Found twenty kilograms inside the house! Tip paid off!" an officer yelled aloud.

"You wanna keep talkin'?" the officer asked through a smile as she pulled her K-9 from the interior of the jeep.

Jay-D looked up at the officer and uttered one word, "Lawyer," he said calmly before he spat in the grass.

"Lawyer," Malik said.

"Lawyer," Dooney followed as the three invoked their right to remain silent.

CHAPTER THIRTY-FIVE
PREPLANNING

"And no one said a thing after the bust?" Mendoza asked Doss as the two walked through a large Recreational Vehicle sales lot in Bloomington, Indiana, a week after the bust down in Granite City.

"Nobody talked. The charges against J-Day, Dooney and Malik were dropped because none of the officers can verify that they were in the home and they denied knowing anything under questioning."

"What about our guy Eddie?" Mendoza asked as he paused in front of a 2006 Challenger RV priced at $550,000 dollars.

Doss shook his head as he eyed Mendoza. "It's not looking good for Eddie. He's gonna have to take the rap and he understands that. He was busted with twenty kilograms. Finland is working his case since he was busted on the Illinois side of the border. He tried to get Eddie a bail, but with that amount cocaine?"

"The judge viewed him as a flight risk," Mendoza answered as he opened the door on the white and tan RV and peeked inside the vehicle.

"Finland said this sting wasn't done with the best of precision. The officers acted on a tip, but they have our guy in possession of the cocaine and he's been charged with intent to distribute, so it's serious business."

"Someone has dropped a dime on us, Doss."

"There's no doubt about that. The only question is who is behind it."

"Could be somebody in the neighborhood where the stash house was located, or it could be someone close to home." Mendoza said as he climbed inside the RV and sat in the driver's seat. "This is a really nice machine."

"You think one of our guys is behind this?" Doss asked as he climbed the stairs and entered the luxurious RV and looked around impressed.

"I don't know yet," Mendoza replied. "Coulda been anybody to be honest. We just don't know."

"The only thing good about this situation, if anything good can be said about it, is the fact that the feds aren't involved. Eddie is facing state charges, but he can still get up to twenty years."

"It is a good thing, il mio amico. Had the federal authorities gotten involved they would've been so deep into this thing of ours it would've all come crashing down. With that aside, since we know the feds aren't on our backs, sometimes the best thing to do during a storm is to get right out there and stand in the middle of the shit and take a look around. You can better understand what you're up against."

"But you can also get your ass blown away."

"Depends on the storm, sometimes it looks worse than what it really it is." Mendoza said as he got up and walked through the RV, which had a fully equipped kitchen, a living room, two king-sized beds, a bath and four 17" LCD TV screens scattered about.

"Are you saying we should return to business as usual because this isn't as big a deal as it seems?" Doss asked as he trailed Mendoza inside the RV.

"That's exactly what I'm saying. Not right away, though. We want those plotting against us to think we aren't on to them.

Which we really aren't, but they don't have to know that. We keep operating, the people responsible for tippin' off those cops will play right into our hands." Mendoza said casually as he sat down on a leather sofa and crossed his legs. "You know, Doss? One of my first jobs, my umm, my first contract was against my own boss?"

"I've heard about that. Albert Anastasia back in nineteen fifty-seven." Doss said as he sat down beside Mendoza.

"Forty-nine years ago. The guy was a man who trusted me, he was, he was like the father I never had you know? But I stabbed him the back. I nearly got Zell's ass, too. But Zell's situation taught me a lesson."

"That lesson being?"

"That people like myself, people like myself will always be around. Back biters, betrayers of trust who will kill anybody, anybody for loyalty's sake. It's something I'm not proud of, but I can honestly admit to. Others, though, others will not admit to such treachery."

"Our loyalty has been betrayed," Doss said. "By who?"

"You wouldn't believe me if I told you, son. I don't even believe it, but if I'm correct in my assumptions, this will have to be my deal, and my problem to rectify. My own situation that will be handled by me in due time."

"You old mobsters love to talk in riddles. I wonder what's going on in that wise mind of yours."

"I'm not too good with analogies, but understand me when I tell you that my mind is struggling to overpower my heart. I do this for this thing of ours, because I've always been loyal to those I love—for the most part."

"We all have been loyal."

Mendoza smiled at Doss and said, "You and your family, from your father on down to your oldest three children are the epitome of loyal, Doss. Me? I've stabbed one man in the back and nearly did the same thing to another man who trusted me."

"You're talking about Zell," Doss replied lowly, now with

full understanding that he was in the middle of being handed down decades of wisdom from a man who'd spent his entire life inside La Cosa Nostra.

Mendoza nodded his head up and down slowly to say yes. "When Zell forgave me for staging a coup back in ninety-two, because my ass should've been killed the night he put two and two together, when Zell forgave me, I told myself that I would be forever faithful to the crew he put me in charge of. I would love them all unconditionally and do whatever I needed to do in order to teach how important loyalty is to a crew's survival. Quattordici anni," (Fourteen years,) Mendoza said seriously in Italian as he stared Doss directly in the eyes. "Fourteen years. I've stayed true to my word for quattordici anni. I'm one of the last of my kind in this thing of ours to stay true, son, but my heart is heavy on this day, because I foresee something in the future and I don't think I'll have it in me to do what's right should it have to come to that. And it is for that reason, and that reason alone, that I'm, I'm going to remove myself from the business, Doss."

"Are you ready to step down completely, Mendoza?"

"I am, son. You will run this thing of ours. I umm, I want your children to be the underbosses."

"What about Junior?"

"Junior will have his place amongst us as well, il mio amico. Before I retire though, I want you to join me and my wife for dinner inside our new home." Mendoza said as he stretched his hands.

"New home?"

"Yes. I'm going to buy this RV to go along with the ranch I've bought over in Montana and park it on the land until we build a home there. These two deals will become the first phase of my last big deal, il mio amico. And this deal," Mendoza said seriously as he leaned forward and eyed Doss. "Ask not what I do, because the why will be understood soon enough."

"One of those Italian things I assume."

"An Italian matter it is, my friend. I'm preplanning for my

final stages in life."

"You're healthy, Mendoza. You'll be around, my friend."

"That is the thing that worries me, Doss—the fact that I'll be around." Mendoza said somberly as he looked to the floor. "How's the hunt for those Somalis going," he then asked lowly.

"The Somalis," Doss said as he leaned back and rubbed his chin. "We haven't a clue where those guys are located. They've dropped off the radar. All we have is one photo and no name to put to the picture."

"We have business here in Chicago, up in Milwaukee and over in Detroit. Saint Louis is a dangerous place now, son. My final order before I step aside is to cut back on the shipments to Saint Louis until we find those Somalis. What other business have we have down there? Will our boys in Saint Louis continue to eat with a decrease in cocaine?"

"Yeah," Doss replied. "Jay-D getting ready to invest in this rapper guy and he has Eddie's football pool to run. That usually nets about ten grand a week during the football season. I have Malik working on the club I plan on opening, so he and a couple of our guys are earning pay there. Can't speak for the foot soldiers. We cut back in Saint Louis I reckon we can break the product down, but I hate to go back to selling crack and ounces."

"It is best for now, Doss. Until, until Eddie is sentenced and we find those Somalis, I think it's best we cut back in Saint Louis. There's a stink in the air in Saint Louis and I don't like it one bit. I see clouds, my friend. I want you to be careful. Stay on guard and keep your family close. Heed my warning."

"I most certainly will," Doss remarked as Francine and the salesman climbed inside the RV.

"What's the big deal with this RV and the ranch? Can you at least tell me that?" Doss asked.

"I want to leave something to my great grandchildren, Doss. My family is nearly done with this business," Mendoza said as he got up to greet the salesman. "In due time, the business will be all yours."

"We have the paperwork all ready, my love," Francine told Mendoza. "Doss? Your're gonna ride down to Ponca City with us? We're going to see the family, but I just can't wait to see our great grandchildren."

"Sure, I'll ride. This is really nice. I'm sure Junior will be glad to see you both as well."

Mendoza chuckled as he walked towards the front of the vehicle. "I'm sure he will, Doss. And I can't wait to take him and his family to Montana to show them the land we've brought. It's fifty acres of lush, green grass. I may buy some horses."

"Sounds like you and Francine are going to enjoy the good life in your latter years."

"We are. We will. And my great grandchildren will have something to remember me and Francine by when they get older. Something to be proud of for being a Cernigliaro—them and Tiva both. Remember, Doss, be careful in Saint Louis. Watch out for the Somalis," Mendoza said as he extended his hand towards the salesman. "Let's make ourselves a deal, my friend," he then said to the salesman.

****

"Goodness gracious! This is the biggest monstrosity I've ever seen in my life! You drove this gigantic thing all the way from Indiana, Mendoza?" DeeDee asked as he walked around the Cernigliaro's newly purchased RV three days after Mendoza, Francine and Doss had left Indiana.

"Sure did. And I'm on my way to Montana in another week. And guess what? Your ass is ridin' with me and Francine."

"I'm not ridin' with your old ass in this thing," DeeDee quipped. "Shit, I don't know about you, but I plan on being around to see my family grow up."

"You have to come. It's important that you come."

"Why?"

"I want to show you something."

"I've seen the ranch you brought up there. Ain't nothing new for me to see."

"When I say show, I mean from a conversational standpoint. This is important, il mio amico."

The look on Mendoza's face was a signal to DeeDee. The two aging gangsters had a rapport going concerning matters inside the organization they once ran and the issue that had been troubling Mendoza was obviously still on his mind in DeeDee's eyes. What the two gangsters knew was something unfathomable, a perpetrated act that would leave a bad taste in the mouths of many should it prove true. Mendoza was covering all bases, and he'd counseled Doss, but he had reasons for not revealing all he suspected to key members of the crew and DeeDee understood. Mendoza Cernigliaro, the last loyal Italian inside Twenty-third Street Mafia, was laying everything on the line, willingly putting his own life in danger and testing his own heart for crew.

DeeDee had his orders—if Mendoza failed to do what needed to be done should that day ever arrive, he would have the green-light to end his friend's life on his own ranch in Montana. What lay ahead for these two gangsters, would be the ultimate test of loyalty, and a true assessment of friendship. The legacy of the Chicago Gang's storied criminal history would be at stake. DeeDee and Mendoza would have to make tough decisions in their waning years that would leave a hallmark for those who will follow, basically instituting in a new form of loyalty. They would lay the foundation for a new way of doing business for those who follow in their footsteps. A most treacherous way of maintaining a crew's survival for those who had the gumption and determination to live a life of crime during these ever-changing times.

THE HOLLAND FAMILY SAGA

CHAPTER THIRTY-SIX
TAPPED

"She's been snooping around, asking questions, and she has names," Special Agent Daniel Jarkowski told JunJie Maruyama as the two sat inside JunJie's office on the first floor of his home located on Mercer Island, just west of Seattle in late September of 2006, just over a month after Eddie was busted in Granite City, Illinois.

"How long has she's known of Montoya Spencer?" JunJie asked as he slid a stack of hundred dollar bills across his desk; payoff to the rogue agent for the information he'd given up.

"For about a year is what she told me. She went down to Vegas and members of the vice squad gave her all the goods on your guy and his associate Douglas Hunt. She's on their ass something good if you ask me."

"Indeed she is, my friend," JunJie replied, never looking up from the copied files of Lisa Vanguard's mounting case against Asa Spade and his crew. "She has their background, does she know of me?"

"Not yet—but she's a bulldog. She won't stop until she connects all the dots."

"Where is she now?"

"Back in D.C. trying to raise more funds to get back out here on the west coast. And she will get it given all the evidence she has against your man."

"Did Asa Spade ever talk to this agent?"

"She's not going to approach Montoya until she's ready to make the bust. I suggest you have your guy lay low. Lisa has surveillance photos and has raised suspicion that Montoya Spencer is running a criminal enterprise. She will go before a grand jury in Denver shortly after getting her funds in order to bring charges against him for conspiracy to run a criminal enterprise."

"Will there be any witnesses that will testify during the grand jury proceedings?"

Agent Jarkowski chuckled slightly and pulled a small notepad from the inside pocket of his suit jacket and wrote down a name. He turned the paper facedown, and when JunJie reached for it, he pulled it back. "This here name is worth more than five thousand dollars, Mister Maruyama," he said seriously. "This name will send shockwaves throughout your organization."

"How much more are you asking for the name?" JunJie asked as he stood up from his desk and tucked his hands inside his silk slacks.

"Twenty-thousand dollars."

"That's all? You could've gone much higher, my man." JunJie said as he walked over to his safe.

While JunJie had his back turned, Agent Jarkowski went and stood behind him. The hard metal pressing against him alerted JunJie to the fact that a gun was placed to his back. He turned around and looked down at the chrome piece Jarkowski was gripping and then eyed the man with a surprised look. "Can't trust anyone in this fuckin' business," he said lowly.

"Ain't that the truth," Jarkowski sighed. "See, umm, this has been in the works for some time now, Mister Maruyama. Lisa is on to your crew—it'll only be a matter of time before she gets to you. She gets to you, she gets to me and I can't allow that to happen. I've opted to jump ship because of the betrayal taking place within your organization."

"Who was it that sold me out?" JunJie asked angrily.

Agent Jarkowski leaned forward and whispered a name into JunJie's ear. Upon hearing the name, JunJie yelled aloud and rushed Jarkowski, but he wasn't quick enough to dodge a single round from a .9mm that slammed into his chest. He fell forward and Jarkowski kicked him over onto his back and knelt down beside him as he coughed up blood.

"I've been doing my own little investigation, my friend," Jarkowski said calmly. "Take a look at this photo. As you can see, I'm not bullshitting when I say betrayal," he said as held up a picture of Lisa Vanguard talking to an individual JunJie was more than familiar with in the business. "Your whole crew is going down pretty soon. Starting with you," he ended as he stood up and shot JunJie in the chest a second time before he stepped over his body and emptied the safe completely, walking out of JunJie's home with over one hundred thousand dollars in cash.

****

Twenty-nine year-olds Phillip Tran and Grover Kobayashi had just returned home from *Goddesses*, the strip club JunJie owned, a few hours after JunJie had been shot. The two headed straight for JunJie's office with the days earnings, but were shocked to see the man lying on the floor before an empty wall safe.

Phillip ran over to his father yelling aloud in Japanese as Grover dialed an ambulance. JunJie had held on long enough until his son and godson made it home for the night. He knew he was in bad shape, so he quickly gave an order to Phillip and pointed up under the desk before passing out. Phillip looked up under the desk and began feeling around.

"I'm calling—" Grover was interrupted by Phillip when he scrambled and covered his mouth. He then placed a finger to his lips and the two left the home, Grover dialing 9-1-1 as the two walked out the to back side of the home and went and stood before the swimming pool.

"You were going to call Asa once you called paramedics, right?" Phillip asked lowly as he looked around, certain he and

Grover were going to be raided by the feds at any second.

"I was. You think we can we trust him now?" Grover asked.

"He's all we have for now. Maybe he can get in touch with Chicago." Phillip said. "Son-of-bitch! How did they get on to us?" he asked aloud just as the ambulances pulled up to the front of the home.

JunJie had all the contacts, but he was obviously out of commission for the time being and may never be the same if he were to even survive his ordeal. Grover was able to reach Asa Spade; and quickly, the pieces had come together once they'd discovered who was the odd man out in their organization.

The best thing for Phillip and Grover, they both knew, was for them to skip town for the time being, despite JunJie's condition. They left word with Asa Spade so he could contact Chicago, and while the paramedics were stabilizing JunJie, they gathered important documents and left the home. Phillip and Grover were so enraged over the things they'd uncovered they didn't even bother to ride to the hospital with JunJie, who was now near death. They had to make serious moves now in order to save the entire network.

THE HOLLAND FAMILY SAGA

CHAPTER THIRTY-SEVEN
THE DOMINO EFFECT

"AquaNina talking about getting married now, girl. Can you believe that, Tiva," twenty-one year-old Bena asked her twin.

It was just minutes after Phillip and Grover had discovered JunJie shot up inside his home. Doss was down in Saint Charles walking through the hollowed out walls of the old cleaners on the corners of Elm Street and Lindenwood Avenue that he was renovating and transforming into a night club as Bay and T-top trailed him closely.

"Y'all gonna do it, Bena?" Doss asked as he walked along the first floor.

"I want to, but man, we have problems as it is with her parents and other people trippin' on our lifestyle, daddy."

"Can't worry about what people say, Bena." Doss replied. "As long as this family approves of you and AquaNina that's all that matters. Her parents will come around."

"So you approve, dad?" Bena asked nervously.

"Do you love AquaNina?"

"I do love her, daddy. She makes me very happy." Bena responded with a beautiful smile on her face as she grabbed her father's arm.

"Well, I guess I'll get to walk my oldest daughter down the aisle."

"Oh that," Bay said as she backed away from her father shyly.

"What?" Doss asked.

"Well, I was, I was thinking about letting grandpa walk AquaNina down the aisle. I'm gone be standing at the altar."

Doss stepped back and placed his hands on his hips and eyed Bay. "Are you serious? What am I supposed to be doing while your grandfather father is walking 'Nina down the aisle?"

"Wishing me and 'Nina well from the front row?" Bay asked.

"I ain't sitting nowhere wishin' nobody well if I ain't walking. I'm not gone even attend the thing." Doss chided.

Bay and T-top laughed aloud at that moment. "You don't understand their relationship, daddy." T-top said.

Doss eyed his daughters with a puzzled look. "What am I missing here? Why can't I walk you down the aisle, Bena?"

"Daddy," Bay said as she walked up and hugged her father, "I would be honored if you would give me away, but it's the father of the bride's responsibility to give the bride away to the groom. And since AquaNina's parents disapprove of our relationship, she wanted DeeDee to do it. I tried to persuade her to let you do it, but the slick pimp stood in the way."

"Okay? But why is 'Nina walking down the aisle and not you?"

Bay and T-top laughed again. "It's the father's job to give— the bride—away—to—the—groom," T-top said slowly.

Doss reared back and rubbed his chin in deep thought as he stared at his daughters, trying his best to decipher what Tiva had said to him. "It's the father's job to give the bride away to the—ohh! Ohhh," Doss said as he snapped his fingers. "Bena, you the, you—"

"The groom," Bay blurted out as she eyed her father, a little disappointed in his lack of understanding of her and AquaNina's relationship.

"Don't be eyeing me like that now," Doss said as he raised his hands up even with his shoulders. "It ain't like I go around seeking details of you and 'Nina's, you and 'Nina's—"

"Sex life?" Bay finished.

"That's right," Doss responded, a little embarrassed over his lack of insight.

"Don't worry, dad. You can walk Kimi down the aisle." Bay said as she hugged her father briefly and kissed his cheek.

"And who is Kimi marrying?" Doss inquired.

"Udelle. And Koko gone marry Chablis." Bay joked.

"I can see Udelle and Kimi getting married, but Koko ain't ever marrying Chablis," T-top said. "That boy act too stupid sometimes."

"Who are Udelle and Chablis?" Doss asked.

Bay and Tiva laughed again. "Daddy," Bay said. "You met Udelle and Chablis like four times this summer already."

"Udelle? The weather man?"

"Yeah. And his friend Chablis," Tiva answered. "They met Kimi and Koko a while back at a mall when they got into that argument with that singer Narshea."

"Chablis is a little silly-minded. He has some more maturing to do. Udelle all right, though," Doss remarked. "That boy knows his stuff when it comes to weather. He told me one day when we standing outside, he said, 'it's gone rain tomorrow, Mister Dawkins'. Wasn't a cloud in the sky. I asked him how he know and he said it was getting hotter, that meant a cold front was coming through and it was pushing all the hot air ahead of it. Sure enough, the next day it rained all day. That boy got a bright future of he's able to predict like that."

"That ain't the only thing he be pre-dicking," Tiva said lowly as Bay sniggled and bumped her side with her elbow.

"Excuse me?" Doss said as he looked back at his daughters.

"Nothing, just thinking out loud. Where were we?" Tiva asked in a polite manner.

Doss eyed his daughters for a second before he turned around and stared at a large open space at the rear of the building on the first floor. "This here is where the first floor bar will be set up," he said, going on with the plans he had for the club. "Now, when people enter in through the V.I.P. section, they could walk along the wall and climb some stairs and walk behind the bar and head up to the second floor. The third floor will be for the crew and the crew only. I want an office up there where we can discuss business and pack heat." he said as he and his daughters continued walking around the place.

****

Asa Spade, meanwhile, was speeding back to his home in Boulder, Colorado, about an hour northwest of Denver. He'd talked to Phillip Tran about thirty minutes earlier and was aiming to call Doss, but Doss's number was locked away in his second burner, a phone he hadn't used in a while. Asa also now knew a federal agent by the name of Lisa Vanguard was on to him courtesy of Phillip and Grover. It would be a meeting Asa Spade wanted to make sure he would miss to for certain. He'd encountered the court system in Vegas back in 2001 and he knew if he were to appear in court under a federal indictment, he would never see daylight again given his past run-ins with the law. He was aiming to skip town with Xiang, Dougie and Francesca, all of whom were riding with him on this day.

"I'm not a distributor, Xiang," Asa admitted as he wheeled his BMW up U.S. Highway 36, headed towards his mansion in Boulder. "It was a good run, but this business ain't for me. Not on this level anyway. A few kilograms here and there I thought I could handle, but I got us in over our head. We been warring and dodging the law for the last four years. I done had enough of this shit!"

"Where we going, baby?" Xiang asked calmly while rubbing Asa's shoulder.

Asa had not a clue where he was headed once he left Boulder, but people were talking. If he were to have a day in court, he would be looking at thirty years minimum—time he couldn't do—time he didn't want to do. "I don't know where we going, Xiang. I really don't wanna head to this house, but I can't leave Doss in the dark about what's going down. I knew it from day one," Asa said as he shook his head in disbelief. "And they trusted the guy," he said in disbelief as he sped up the highway.

Once he reached the home, about thirty minutes later, Asa ran up the stairs to he and Xiang's bedroom and rummaged through his armoire and grabbed his phone and the memory card that went with it. His phone was powering up when he heard Dougie yell aloud, "Yo, Ace! Feds in town! The feds!"

Asa looked out his vista window and could see a S.W.A.T. team wagon trailing four unmarked cars, all five vehicles speeding up the gravel road leading to the home. The phone had just powered up and Asa was preparing to text just as the federal agents approached the front door. *"Come on, Ace!"* Asa Spade said to himself as he searched for Doss's numbers.

Dougie and Francesca were running out the back door of the home, but they were quickly greeted by federal agents toting semi-automatic rifles. They dropped to their knees and surrendered and were quickly handcuffed and escorted through the home back towards the paddy wagon.

Xiang, meanwhile, had run into the bedroom to be with Asa. "We fucked up," she said somberly as the federal agents were heard traveling up the stairs.

"Federal agents! Show yourselves! Federal agents come out with your hands up or we will fire! Surrender or we will fire!" the men were heard yelling aloud and at random.

"Asa!" Xiang said lowly. "What, what are we going to do?"

"We're gonna go our asses to jail today, Xiang. A pimp can't get a break," Asa said solemnly as he flushed the memory card down the toilet. He and Xiang exited the bedroom with their hands in the air just as four S.W.A.T. team members entered the room. Knees planted in their backs and on their back of their heads brought about the reality of the situation to Asa Spade and Xiang Nyguen as they eyed one another while being handcuffed.

There was no need for explanation. Asa and his crew knew what they were up against. Someone had ratted them out to the feds and they were about to take a fall. The only thing good about the matter was the fact that Asa Spade knew he hadn't been busted with any drugs. The home was clean, save for a few semi-automatic handguns and rifles, and the memory card with his cohorts' phone numbers had been flushed away.

Still, the weight of the matter was more than enough to keep Asa spade behind bars for quite some time fighting whatever charges lay ahead. On top of that, he knew the feds had a witness. His only hope was that Doss would receive the message he'd sent and act quickly; thereby giving him at least a chance to see daylight again.

****

"Two hundred and twenty-nine, two hundred and thirty. Just as our informant said," Laddy huffed as he jumped down from the rear of an unmarked trailer that had been seized at one of the docks behind JunJie's warehouse located at the port of Seattle.

"That guy was a gift basket. You think we should put him protective custody?" an agent asked Laddy as he removed his latex gloves.

"No. Lisa said he has orders to avoid everybody within this organization. And I'm sure Mister JunJie's getting shot will pause all activities and no one will ever suspect the guy. We'll leave him on the streets and see what else he decides to bring us."

Lisa had acted on information she'd received a while back when she cornered her informant in Chinatown-International District just outside of downtown Seattle. The information she'd been given a few months back had led to one of the biggest cocaine busts in Seattle in years. Two hundred and thirty kilograms of uncut cocaine, its origin unknown, but its ownership had been relegated to JunJie Maruyama. And Lisa was only just beginning. She had Laddy, several of her aides, and a dozen federal agents in charge of the bust on the port while she was paying an old friend a visit.

****

Special Agent Jarkowski was shredding documents in his office when he heard someone yell aloud, "Jerkoffski! What're you doing over there?"

Jarkowski looked up and saw Lisa Vanguard and several agents from the Seattle branch of the F.B.I. standing behind her. His white skin grew flush and sweat formed on his temples as he shoved several more documents into the paper shredder in a hurried manner.

Lisa laughed as she entered the office, the three agents behind her following as they held their guns on Jarkowski. "You have been a pain in people's ass ever since Hayate and

Isao were killed," Jarkowski said as he stood behind his desk. "What the hell do you want from me now?"

"You have the right to remain silent," Lisa said as she began citing Jarkowski his Miranda rights, the area between her legs getting moist over the excitement of capturing a rogue cop red-handed. "Anything you say can and will be used against you in the court of—"

"Spare me the legal bullshit speech, alright? What is this concerning?"

"Need I tell you?" Lisa asked seriously.

"I've done nothing wrong. I can't accept you reading me those rights because I'm innocent of whatever it is you're accusing me of."

"Explain this," Lisa said as she threw a duffel bag full of crisp hundred dollar bills onto Jarkowski's desk and pulled out her .9mm handgun. "We found this in the trunk of your car a few minutes ago."

"You had no legal right to search my car."

"If you say so—but the question still stands—if you care to answer."

"Casino winnings," Jarkowski snapped.

"Is that right?" Lisa asked as she turned to the agents standing behind her and shook her head. "Can you believe this guy?" she asked as she pulled out a tape recorder.

Jarkowski watched curiously as Lisa held the small recorder up and pressed play.

"Can't trust anyone in this fuckin' business," a voice was soon heard by all inside Jarkowski's office.

"Ain't that the truth? See, umm, this has been in the works for some time now, Mister Maruyama. Lisa is on to your crew —it'll only be a matter of time before she gets to you. She gets to you, she gets to me and I can't allow that to happen. I've opted to jump ship because of all the betrayal taking place within your organization."

"I planted that bug in JunJie Maruyama's office to catch him discussing illegal activities. Imagine my surprise when I heard your voice on the recordings!" Lisa said in a jubilant manner. "Shall, shall I keep going? Right up until the time you shot the man?"

Jarkowski was crushed. Lisa was more clever than he'd anticipated. He knew what else was to come on the tape. In minutes, everyone would hear the shots fired that he'd lodged into JunJie. The once respected and decorated agent had been caught, on tape no less, consulting with a purported criminal master mind and had attempted to take his life.

"He's in a coma now," Lisa said. "But whether he dies or not, we got your ass nailed to the cross." Lisa said matter-of-factly as she patted her gun against her pants leg. "You were right, you know, Jarkowski?"

"About what you bitch?"

"About me getting those funds. The bust on the docks, even the capturing of Asa Spade will not compare to this arrest. Your apprehension, sir, will show the Senators just how badly my investigation needs funding. I thank you for that. Take him in," Lisa ordered.

As the officers approached, Jarkowski, not willing to accept what his future had in store, looked down at his own service weapon that was laying on the desk.

Lisa followed his eyes and she need not be a psychic to know what the man was contemplating. "Daniel, don't you do it!" Lisa screamed as she aimed her weapon. "Don't you fuckin' do it!"

Jarkowski was going for-suicide—death by cop. He couldn't face the music, nor did he want to. He went for his weapon and Lisa and the three agents opened fire, releasing a hail of bullets that had ended Jarkowski's life before he'd ever gotten off a round. He fell forward onto his desk and died instantly, thereby bringing an end to what was once an illustrious career inside law enforcement. Lisa didn't discriminate. All outside of the law had to be taken down in her eyes; and as far as she was concerned, Special Agent Daniel Jarkowski was no more than a common criminal who'd refused to face his own demons.

"Well," Lisa said as she breathed heavily, "call, call internal affairs so we can give a full report."

****

While all the activities were unfolding out west, Doss, Bay and T-top were emerging from the club in Saint Charles and had met up with Dawk and Junior inside *Connections*, which was directly across the street from the club.

"Hey," Junior said. "It's dark out. It'll be three, four in the morning before we make it back to the ranch."

"I know, but it'll be a few weeks before we head back this way and I wanted to leave some instructions with Malik. Where he went?" Doss asked.

"Him and Jay-D had a quick sell back in Fox Park. I figured we would be leaving soon so I just sent them down there," Junior replied as he checked his vibrating phone. "Everybody ready?"

"Yeah. I guess I can call Malik when I get back to the ranch." Doss replied. "This is Kimi and Koko's first week home from college. I got 'em a couple of gifts for their sophomore year my wife keeping hidden. I'm really looking forward to seeing my babies. They're growing before my very eyes." he then said proudly as he tapped the counter.

"I can't wait to see my babies either," Junior remarked as he thought about his two beautiful daughters. "You guys go ahead. I'll lock up."

Doss, Dawk and Bay hopped into one of the family's Suburbans and T-top climbed into the passenger seat of her CLK and waited on Junior. When he hopped into the driver's seat, the crew all pulled away from the curb and began making their way down to 1st Capitol Boulevard, the main street that led to the interstate.

"Dang! I wanted to tell Bay about this store on First Capitol Boulevard that sell them seven for all mankind jeans she like," Tiva said as she grabbed her cell phone. "Shoot, my battery dead. Baby, let me see your phone," she requested.

Junior was reaching for his phone when he saw red flashing lights in the rearview mirror. "Hold up, let me let this ambulance by, baby."

At the same time, Doss's cell phone had vibrated, signaling he had a text. He looked down and recognized Asa Spade's number, but before he could read the text, he caught sight of an ambulance headed his way with the lights flashing. He pulled over to the side of the street to let the ambulance pass, never noticing that the side door was open on the vehicle.

Bay and Dawk were inside the Suburban with their father waiting for the ambulance to pass also when it came to a halt beside their ride. At that moment, Doss recognized the play. He leaned over and shielded Bay as bullets began penetrating the SUV, shattering its windows and flattening the tires on the driver's side.

Dawk hopped out the back passenger seat of the ride and scrambled to the back of the Suburban and opened fire with a .45 automatic from the rear driver's side. The shooter fell forward, landing inside the ambulance, but was quickly replaced with another one, who continued firing on the SUV from just yards away.

Tiva was going berserk amidst the gunfire. She grabbed her Glock .45 and was attempting to hop out of her ride to help her family, but Junior was holding her back.

"Tiva, stay here with me! They'll kill you!" Junior yelled.

"Fuck that!" Tiva screamed. "Let me go, mutherfucka," she yelled as she snatched away from Junior and hopped out of her CLK and opened fire with her .45 automatic, hitting the rear of the ambulance and shattering the back windows.

Together, Dawk and Tiva were able to ward off the ambulance. It sped off rapidly while sporadically spraying gunfire, but its close proximity to the Suburban left no doubt as to what they were about lay eyes upon because the bullets that rained down on the family's SUV couldn't have possibly missed. Only a miracle could've prevented that scenario, but the streets, they knew, were unforgiving.

Dawk and T-top ran towards the Suburban in desperation. Smoke was pouring from the hood and all its windows were shot out. The AK-47 spray had shredded the SUV and left it tilting to the left in a critical gangster lean. Dawk opened the door on the driver's side and was hit with a sight that would be forever etched into his psyche.

At the same time, Tiva had pulled the passenger side door open, and what she saw was nothing short of horror. Her father lay atop Bay, his brains spilling out onto Bay's back as she lay underneath her father, her body convulsing uncontrollably.

Dawk gently pulled his father back and looked him the eyes. Doss had been sent into the afterlife. He lay with his back against the front seats of the SUV with his eyes and mouth wide open and a surprised look frozen onto his face.

"Dad," Dawk said as he hid his face in one arm on side of the Suburban, tears forming in his eyes as he pounded the top of the vehicle with his balled up fist.

Tiva was weak. She stared at Bay and clutched her twin's hand tightly and wept. "I' sorry, sister," she cried. "Bay!" she yelled. "Bay!"

The Holland family had been blindsided with a blow to the chin that left them weak in the knees. Doss Dawkins, Boss on the streets, and patriarch on the ranch in Oklahoma, had been murdered in a cold-blooded ambush.

Bena Holland, arguably the family's most prolific assassin, had a bullet lodged in the front of her skull and was near death, barely clinging to life. Doss was able to cover his daughter, and he'd absorbed the bulk of the bullets that'd ended his life, but Bena was still critically wounded in the shooting.

Dooney and Eddie's daughter, fourteen year-old Nancy Cottonwood had run onto the scene after hearing the gunshots from inside their home on the opposite end of the block and they quickly assisted Dawk and Tiva with Bena by pulling her from the front seat and laying her down on the sidewalk. Dooney removed his jacket and covered Bay's body while

Tiva applied pressure to her head wound.

"I called nine, one, one. Help is on the way," Junior said as he stood over Bay. "Dawk, how's dad?"

Dawk only shook his head as he began removing his father's watch, wedding ring and wallet. "I'm gone call home and tell my momma what happened," Dawk said somberly. *"Who the fuck did this?"* he asked himself as he searched the Suburban for his father's cell phone.

THE HOLLAND FAMILY SAGA

CHAPTER THIRTY-EIGHT
THE FAMILY SECRET

"If we add four more cattle to this trailer and take one off the second trailer, and do that four times with the remaining trailers, it'll all balance out on paper because the listed weight will match the head count on the bills of lading," Naomi told eighteen year-olds Kimi and Koko, the three of them shuffling papers and entering data into two laptops as they all stood behind their mother's desk inside her office on the second floor of Ponderosa.

A satchel of money belonging to Dawk, Bena and Tiva, $36,000 dollars in total, was in the process of being funneled into the family's legitimate ventures for the week. Kimi and Koko were becoming expert money launderers, but Naomi was the crème de la crème when it came to washing dirty dollars clean. She could tally hundreds of thousands of dollars in her head, multiply, subtract and add figures in rapid succession and keep an accurate account of the family's assets and liabilities on a daily basis. She was a force to be reckoned with, and Kimi and Koko were walking directly in her footsteps.

A ringing phone caught Naomi's attention and she walked over to the mantle above the fireplace inside her bedroom and grabbed her cell. She saw Doss's number on the screen and answered only to hear Dawk's voice on the other end.

"Momma," Dawk said lowly.

Naomi could hear sirens and walkie talkies going off in the background and she was hit with an ominous feeling, the tone in Dawk's voice was dead giveaway also.

"Where are you, son?" Naomi asked anxiously.

"I'm in Saint Charles, momma. Got umm," Dawk choked back tears as he watched coroners removed his father's lifeless corpse from the Suburban and place him inside of a body bag. "Dad and Bena got hit tonight. Bena still holding on, but dad, dad didn't make it."

"What?" Naomi asked in disbelief.

"Momma, they killed daddy tonight," Dawk said somberly as the full force of the situation's reality hit him head on. He'd just loss his father and his sister was on the verge of death.

Kimi and Koko heard Naomi's voice of concern and looked up from the desk in time to see their mother lean forward as if her heart was weighted down.

"Momma, what's wrong?" Kimi asked as she walked over to her mother, Koko following close behind. "What's wrong, momma?" Kimi asked again.

"Get me Martha," Naomi said as tears flooded her eyes.

"Who's that on the phone?" Koko asked as she snatched the phone from her mother's hands. She eyed the number on the screen, placed the phone to her ear and said, "Daddy, you okay? Daddy, this Koko. You okay?"

Dawk heard Koko's voice and he couldn't find it within himself to give her the facts. He ended the call and went and sat in Tiva's car as Dooney and Nancy stood beside him.

"We got you, big dog," Dooney said as he patted Dawk's shoulder.

There were no words of comfort for Dawk at this moment. He leaned back against the head rest, placed a hand over his closed his eyes, and screamed a loud, angry scream before sitting upright and pounding the steering wheel and kicking about wildly inside the car.

****

Back inside Ponderosa, Naomi, with tears streaming down her face, stared at Kimi and Koko. "Where's Martha? Get Martha for me?"

"Momma, what happened?"

"I said get Martha, dammit!" Naomi yelled as she snatched the phone from Koko's hands and turned and faced the mantle.

"Momma, no!" Kimi said as she hugged her mother from behind. "No," she cried, sensing the tragedy that was beginning to unfold.

Naomi turned and faced her two daughters and hugged them both as she looked to the ceiling, tears pouring down her face, lips trembling, but all the while trying to be strong.

"What, what happened?" Kimi asked sadly. "Where Bay 'nem?"

Naomi, in a gentle manner, eased out of her daughters' grip and walked forward, her back to Kimi and Koko to hide her pain. She placed her hands on her hips and bowed her head to the floor in disbelief. Her husband had just been killed and her oldest daughter was near death. Who was responsible was a question she had, but securing the family was the most important thing. Just as she turned to face Kimi and Koko, there was a knock at the door of the master suite.

Naomi answered and saw Martha standing before her with a face full of tears. Tiva had called from Mercy Hospital in Saint Louis and had given her the news and she ran out of the theater room up to Naomi's room. No words were spoken as Naomi leaned into Martha and hugged her neck tightly.

"I want in," Martha said as she rocked Naomi's body. "I can't let nothing else happen to my family."

"We got hit tonight," Naomi said somberly.

"I heard. But you heard what *I* said, right? Let me in, sis."

Naomi led Martha back into the master suite where Kimi and Koko were standing in the center of the room fumbling their hands. They'd called their father's phone, Dawk, Bay and Tiva's phones also, but neither picked up. Seeing Martha trailing their mother let them know something serious was going on because no one inside the bedroom had even notified her. The look on Naomi's face told her daughters that they'd better not ask what happened again and they should leave immediately, only their legs wouldn't allow them to do so; they had to know.

"Get everybody together," Naomi told Kimi and Koko as she walked towards her desk. "Call Regina and Mary and have everybody wait for me in the theater room."

DeeDee entered the bedroom while Kimi and Koko were headed out, his presence only adding to their anxiety. The twins knew something serious had gone down, they just didn't know who was involved, nor could they ever imagine the scope of the tragedy. They left to fulfill their mother's request, rounding up the family in order to sit and wait on news they were sure was more bad than good.

"Who told you two?" Naomi asked as DeeDee locked the door.

"Tiva called me," Martha said through her tears. "She said Bena undergoing surgery for a bullet to her skull. Doss, Doss was killed instantly, Naomi."

DeeDee stood with his head bowed. "Junior said an ambulance pulled alongside the Suburban and opened fire. They were gunning for the jeep."

Naomi sat down at her desk and crossed her legs and looked towards the floor. "Who would have the ability to touch us in this manner, DeeDee?" she asked as she rubbed her forehead in anguish.

"We've all but wiped out Carmella's crew," DeeDee answered somberly. "My first hunch would be the Somalis, but they would have had to have had help. How would they know to hit us on this day? We weren't even operating. Doss was only looking into the night club he planned on opening."

DeeDee's cell phone rung at that moment and he answered. "How are you, il mio amico?" Mendoza asked.

"Not good, my friend. This is a big deal."

"Tiva called me. I know everything. Me and Francine are flying out of Montana in the morning. That thing? Now's the time."

"You sure?"

"I've made a miscalculation, Doss. This has to end soon."

"We'll talk when you get here," DeeDee said before hanging up the phone. "The Cernigliaros will be here tomorrow, Naomi."

Naomi only nodded. "I have to tell the children. How," Naomi said as she covered her heart with her hand. "How in the world can I tell the family this news? What, what will I say?"

"Me and DeeDee will stand with you," Martha said. "And anything, *anything* you need me to do to set things straight I'm on board. I don't want to hear no objections, and I have to know everything you two know—and I'm not taking no for an answer."

"Nobody's going to deny you, Martha. We'll bring you up to date later," Naomi responded calmly through her tears. "I've lost my husband, and Bena is barely clinging on to life."

"Everybody responsible for this calamity will answer eventually," DeeDee said lowly.

"They will, DeeDee. But now isn't the time. Let's go tell the family the bad news." Naomi said as she eased up from her seat, grabbed a couple of medium-sized gift-wrapped boxes from underneath her desk and led the way down towards the theater room.

****

"What's going on?" Dimples asked as she walked into the theater room with Tak and her son, Tacoma following. "Kimi what's going on?"

Kimi and Koko couldn't hold back their tears after gathering everybody together; there relentless crying had the family on edge. Mary kept asking her nieces what happened, but they honestly didn't know, and Kimi and Koko weren't going to speculate. They sat on the front row inside the theater room dabbing their wet eyes as the rest of the family speculated on the contents of the impromptu meeting.

Walee was on the row behind Kimi and Koko. He didn't have a clue what this meeting was all about, but it wasn't right in his eyes. He sat quietly with his arms around Spoonie and Tyke, who sat on either side of him fidgeting their hands and crying in silence, their tears brought on by Kimi and Koko's incessant weeping.

The family was all trying to figure out the reason for the meeting, the young five all shedding tears, when Naomi, Martha and DeeDee entered the room. DeeDee sat on the second row beside Tyke while Martha went and sat beside Mary. Naomi went and stood before the group, her eyes scanning the room, looking down upon her family, knowing very well their lives would be forever changed in just a few moments.

Kimi and Koko eyed their mother as she stepped forward and handed them each a box. "Doss, umm, Doss wanted Kimi and Koko to have these gifts." Naomi said aloud, silencing the family and forcing their eyes to the front of the room where she stood.

Kimi and Koko eyed one another confusedly before they opened the boxes and discovered they each had received a number eighteen Oklahoma Sooners jersey with their names on the back engraved in diamonds. Koko smiled over her gift as she wiped her tears. Kimi looked up to her mother and thanked her lowly.

"He really wanted to you two have those, Kimi." Naomi said through a smile.

"Where is he?" Koko asked as she began heaving.

"Family," Naomi said as she eyed the group.

DeeDee began welling up at that moment. When Martha leaned forward and hid her face and began heaving, Mary began crying; she now sensed that this meeting was bad—all bad.

Twiggy sat to the back of the room by herself praying, praying that what she felt in her heart was only an assumption, but when she heard Naomi say aloud, "Doss was killed tonight in Saint Charles, Missouri," she screamed aloud, as did others in the family.

Spoonie and Tyke stood up and covered their lower faces. Regina was stunned to silence. Martha screamed aloud at that moment. "Bay!" she yelled.

"What? What happened to Bay?" Kimi asked. Bay was Kimi's heart. To hear her sister was involved unnerved her severely. "What the fuck going on?" she blurted out.

"Bena is in the hospital undergoing surgery," Naomi answered in frantic state of mind. "She was shot alongside you all's father tonight, but she's still holding on!"

"I knew it! I knew it! I knew it! Oh my God," Koko cried as she leaned forward, her eyes squinted and her mouth wide open. "They was never going to Chicago!" she screamed as she fell forward out her seat, dropped to her knees and planted her head to the carpeted floor.

Kimi sat in silent disbelief. Naomi saw her wobbling in her seat and ran and grabbed her before she passed out. "Bay gone die, momma? Who shot my daddy?" Kimi asked as sweat mixed in with her tears.

Seeing her family is disarray drove Naomi over the edge. She hugged Kimi tightly, raised her right fist and yelled aloud, "God, give us strength!"

The entire family broke down at that moment inside the theater room; everyone was shocked, saddened and afraid of the future as reality hit home. Doss was dead, and Bena was near death. Walee went and sat in the corner and covered his eyes as he leaned back in seat, his body heaving uncontrollably and his heart numb. DeeDee had a tight grip on Spoonie and Tyke, who hid their faces in his chest.

Twiggy felt every ounce of the family's pain. Having lost all of her relatives, she'd experienced unbridled tragedy, but she wasn't as close to her father as Naomi's children were to Doss.

Her heart truly went out to the family as she eyed Martha, knowing full well her friend would surely enter into the family's outside business from this day forth.

Siloam thought back to the day Serena and Kevin died. This matter, however, was far worse. The ramifications would last a long time, maybe forever even, because everybody loved Doss. And if Bay were to die—Siloam could go no further with her thoughts. She had to get up leave the room. She ran through the house, out the front door, only wanting to scream to the top of her lungs because she was hurt that the family was hurting all over again because she knew their history—their full history.

Regina could relate to her cousins' pain also. The day she learned Ne`Ne` had been killed came flooding back on her; she knew the pain all too well. She got up and tried to console Walee, but he brushed her away. "Let me deal with it, Dimples," Walee said painfully, trying to be strong. Regina didn't budge, however, she wrapped her arms around her cousin and just sat with him and cried.

"What were they doing in Missouri?" Mary asked through her tears.

"That's not important, Mary." DeeDee remarked, choking back tears.

"I'm not talking to you, DeeDee! I want an answer from Naomi as to why Doss and my niece were shot? Where's Dawk and Tiva?"

"Dawk and Tiva are fine," DeeDee responded.

"Again! I am not talking to you, DeeDee!" Mary cried. "Naomi, what's going on?"

"This isn't the time, Mary." Naomi said as she soothed Kimi and Koko.

"It's never the time," Mary said as she stormed out of the theater room. "Living here is no different than Ghost Town!" she screamed.

"What the hell is wrong with you?" Naomi screamed at Mary. "You pick now to condemn the family for something someone did to us? You judge us, Mary?"

"I'm not judging anyone, Naomi! But you've been hiding things from the family for years and this is the end result!" Mary said as she extended her hands outwards towards her heartbroken family. "If only we would've known from the beginning! If we would've known, it wouldn't be so devastating! I knew what Martha was in Ghost Town! Knowing doesn't ease the pain, but it helps," Mary said from the top of the stairs. "It helps. We're all family here. We deserved better, sister. This was fair to no one," Mary cried as she left the room.

****

"Toodie y Q-man sigue con que mierda mierda. Que ha ido a parar aprender aún fucking con que la gente de San Carlos." (Toodie and Q-man still with that fuck shit. They gone learn soon enough to stop fucking with them people in Saint Charles.) Pepper said as she and Simone sat side by side on their sofa inside their apartment in Fox Park watching the news.

The news report was a short one describing the murder of a unnamed man, and another person, a female, was reportedly in critical condition. Pepper and Simone didn't know of Toodie's plans on this night, but they knew she was the one who'd set up the hit, because getting back at the people who'd killed her sister Phoebe and Carmella was all she talked about since she'd been released from jail three weeks earlier, and when Q-man and a boy out his crew came down from the Ap and clicked up with her and Dead Eye and Big Bounce, both friends knew something was about to go down.

Pepper and Simone had been steering clear of Toodie and her bunch, only wanting to get money as Malik was the fire connect. Toodie had asked Pepper to jump back on her team, but she refused, telling Toodie she was now doing her own thing. Pepper was no dummy. She knew Toodie resented her for not jumping on board, so she was always on guard. As she sat watching the news, Pepper was hit with an ominous feeling all of a sudden—one that told her she had better make a move and do it quick.

"Se ha ido de este hit, Peppi. Nos han ido a la herramienta y

a ser listo para lo que sea." (They gone hit back for this, Peppi. We gone have to tool up and be ready for whatever.) Simone said as she put her feet up on the table.

"Like the fuck we is," Pepper said as she hopped up from the couch, knocked Simone's legs down and ran upstairs.

Pepper sensed the Grim Reaper's sickle coming for her on this night. She saw flashes of her and Simone getting shot up in the living room by Toodie and Q-man while sitting on the couch and was propelled to act. Whether it was a severe case of paranoia or not, Pepper wasn't the one to test fate.

Simone followed Pepper upstairs, and when she entered her room, she saw Pepper grabbing stacks of money out of a shoe box and placing her Glock .17 into her waistband. She seemed to be in a hurry as she went about her room grabbing jewelry, cell phones, extra gun clips, a sack of weed and a few under garments.

"What you doing, girl?" Simone asked Pepper casually.

"What it look like? I'm gettin' the fuck from 'round here for a while. Niggas is gone be going buck wild after this one and I don't want no part of that shit. Go get your stuff!"

Simone merely eyed Pepper as she walked around her room, making sure not to leave anything of value behind. Pepper had a nice wardrobe consisting of the best name brands going from shoes to shirts, but she could easily replace those, her life, however, was the only one she had and she wasn't about to play around with it. *"Simone! Consiga su mierda o estoy sin mojar tu asno!"* (Simone! Get your shit or I'm dipping without your ass!)

Simone threw her hands up and eased over to her room and gathered up her twelve gauge and bullet shells along with her money stack and she was all set to go. She returned to Pepper's room and saw her sliding a clip into a Heckler and Koch MP-5 submachine gun.

"When you get that?" Simone asked.

"Got it right after we killed ole girl from Mickey D's. You got all your shit?"

"I been ready."

"Cool. Let's dip on these hoes. Toodie 'nem think they gone catch us slipping, but I ain't the mutherfuckin' one to end up on the fuckin' news," sixteen year-old Pepper said as she and Simone jumped down the stairs and trotted out the home and hopped into Pepper's 2005 four door black Mazda RX-8 on chrome wheels.

"Roll one up for when we hit the highway," Pepper said as she peeled out from in front of her and Simone's apartment.

Pepper bent a few corners and pulled up in front of Malik's dope house on the opposite end of Fox Park where she saw his work van out front and several workers standing on the sidewalk. She then eyed a dude she knew had power in Malik's crew, a dude everybody called Jay-D. "Yo," she called out. "Where that boy at?"

"Ain't nothing shakin'," Jay-D responded. "You know like I know you wanna get the fuck from 'round here," he added as he held onto a thirty shot .226 rifle.

Pepper wanted to tell Malik that she would be out for a minute, but she decided against it and pulled off. The tension was ratcheting up in Fox Park and all was on her mind now was getting out of the 'hood. She was headed towards Jefferson Avenue when she spotted Toodie's Navigator approaching from the opposite direction.

"Shit!" Pepper hissed as she watched Toodie extend her hand out the back driver's side window to flag her down. "Get Roscoe ready, Simone," she said as she opened the sunroof.

"Si," Simone replied as she pulled her twelve gauge up from between her legs and racked it.

Pepper slowed beside Toodie's Navigator facing the opposite direction and scanned the inside of her jeep real quick. Dead Eye was behind the wheel. Big Bounce was in the front seat and Q-man sat in the back beside Toodie.

"Sup, Toodie?" Pepper asked as she gripped her Glock.

"Where you headed, girl?"

"Going check this thing out across the way."

"Where 'cross the way at?"

"Now you dippin' all up in mines," Pepper remarked as she eyed Toodie.

"See you? You make a bitch wanna fuck you up out here."

Pepper didn't respond. She only eyed Toodie, watching her motions to make sure she didn't up with a weapon. Arguing wasn't her thing. She now knew where she stood with Toodie so there was no need to say another word. Toodie wasn't about to buck though; she was high off her blunt and kicking back in her ride just cruising the neighborhood with her boys. She'd put in work earlier and wasn't up for more gunplay, not with Pepper at least, not right now.

Simone emerged from the passenger side at that moment and said, "Yo, you got something to say, say it so we can be out and handle our business."

"Whatever, chick. I ain't trippin' with it. Y'all heard what happened tonight, though?"

"We saw it on the news." Pepper responded, her eyes steadily scanning the interior of Toodie's whip for any sudden motion.

"Them Gomez boys y'all been scoring from? They clicked up with the Holland family over in Saint Charles. That's who been running shit over there. Anybody on Gomez team gone get dealt with soon enough," Toodie said as she stared down into the interior of Pepper's Mazda. *"Peppi, quién puede con?"* (Peppi, who you rolling with?)

"Hablamos cuando vuelva." (We talk when I get back.) Pepper said as Simone jumped back into ride and she peeled out. *"Cómo Toodie sabemos todos que la gente apellido?"* (How Toodie know all them people last name?) Pepper asked Simone.

"Ella debe haber alguien en el interior." (She must have somebody on the inside.) Simone said as she lit the blunt she'd rolled. "Where we going, Pep?"

"I got a safe house about an hour north of here in Louisiana,"

Pepper responded as she cruised pass McDonald's and jumped onto Interstate-44.

"Damn, you just full of secrets ain't ya'?" Simone asked as she took a toke off the blunt and passed it to Pepper.

"Me han enseñado por uno de los mejores, Simone. Uno de los mejores." (I been taught by one of the best, Simone. One of the best.)

****

"I told you we shoulda bum rushed her shit right after we hit Doss." Dead Eye said as he eased up the street. "She gone side with them mutherfuckas over there in Saint Charles if she get the chance."

"Pepper ain't on nobody side," Toodie responded casually as she sunk back into the seat.

"While they gone y'all wanna run up in they spot?" Big Bounce asked.

"You ain't saying nothing, esse." Dead Eye responded. "Let's do it."

"Q, what's up with your man taking one for the team?" Toodie asked as Dead Eye wheeled her jeep through the neighborhood, the entire click scanning the area for potential retaliation to their hit in Saint Charles while armed to the teeth with AK-47s.

"Hard-headed. I told 'em stay out the door. His mom's coming down to claim his body in the morning. It's nothing. We gone hit Pepper shit or what?"

"Nahh," Toodie responded. "They ain't got nothing in there. That li'l bitch ain't dumb. She took all her shit and gone lay low for a minute. We'll deal with Pepper when the time comes —if it comes. Bend the block on them Gomez boys"

When Toodie and her click neared Malik's trap, they all saw right away that the set was on lock. Malik had soldiers up and down the street two blocks out. It would be suicide to ride down through his set so Toodie had Dead Eye turn off three blocks down and they left Fox Park and headed over to

Toodie's house in Crestwood to kick back and plan their the next move.

CHAPTER THIRTY-NINE
THE UNSAID TRUTHS

Naomi sat on her patio with Martha beside her the evening after breaking the news of Doss's death to the family. The sisters had a long discussion with the young five, Naomi and Martha consoling them and explaining best they could that their father was involved in illegal activities, but to not let what he did on the streets inside other states distort the man they knew in Ponca City.

The family secret could was now out in the open, no longer hidden from any its members, save for Tacoma, Malyasia and Malara, who were too young to comprehend. Naomi had made the decision to come clean with her children in order to allow them to come to their own conclusions concerning their father and his sudden death. Lying would only perpetuate matters in her eyes so she gave her children the hard truth—their father was a gangster—and Dawk, Bena and Tiva were a part of it as well, and still were. She didn't go into detail what all Doss and the big three were involved in, only telling them to think back to the life Martha lived in Ghost Town, envision her stories, and to multiply those stories several times over.

Knowing their Aunt Martha's history, the young five understood right away what their mother was conveying—their father sold drugs and killed people for a living. It was a bitter pill to swallow, especially for Walee, who'd held his father in high esteem. The sixteen year-old was conflicted. He loved his father, but was disappointed in the things he'd done.

Walee couldn't be mad though; he'd never seen that side of his father. All he had was a daddy that loved him; and that would be the way he would remember and honor his father. What his father did off the ranch was his business in Walee's eyes. He loved his father right or wrong, had forgiven him, and he would miss his father very much, but he told himself he would do his best not to become the man his father was when he was alive.

As far as Dawk, Bay and Tiva were concerned, they had always been rowdy, but Walee never knew the full scope of the depth of gangster his oldest brother and sisters possessed and adhered to. He admired them in a way because they, too, had never put that side of their life on display, save for a few fights here and there around town. The big three got a pass also from Walee. His only wish was that Bena would pull through so he could tell her how much he loved her, something he hadn't said to his oldest sister in quite some time.

Spoonie and Tyke had nothing but glowing memories of their father. Their father was a man who coached their softball team, helped out in the design of the park where they played, and had encouraged them to be the best at whatever they did in life. He was their friend. A man who watched ESPN with them every night he was home, even though he wasn't a huge sports fan, and he never grew bored. When they wanted their room decorated in Disney characters when they were younger, they remembered their father agonizing over finding the right color paint they wanted. When they became vegetarians, it was their father who made certain they had a delicious meal whenever he grilled out.

If Spoonie and Tyke had to tell it, their mother was wrong, their father wasn't a gangster—he was their best friend, wish granter and protector. They forgave him for his transgressions without hesitation and would miss him dearly. As far as Dawk, Bay and Tiva were concerned, Spoonie and Tyke were prepared to battle those who'd hurt their sister. They were angry at the people who'd hurt Bay, not their family.

Kimi was heartbroken. She was ashamed of her father for personal reasons. How would her friends in college view her was her thinking. She had a boyfriend she loved, and a host of friends who held her in high esteem. What would she tell her friends when they learned her father was dead and they asked how did he die? She was angry at her father for getting killed, as selfish as it was.

Kimi, however, knew all along what the deal was with her father. Had known for some time, but she'd chosen to look at the situation through veiled glasses. That was her fault. And by going along for the ride she knew she had no one to blame but herself. Her daddy was a gangster. So what? *'Don't ask me about it. Just know he's dead and I loved him more than I love myself'*, was a statement she was rehearsing over and over again in her mind because she would never reveal the truth about her father and the business she had resigned herself to for family's sake. As far as the big three were concerned, they had it in them along, Kimi knew, she only hoped that Bay would survive so she could shadow her sister, not in her occupation, but to help her heal and just to let her know that she loved her with all her heart.

Koko, like Kimi, had an inkling that it was much more to her father's story. She was mad at everybody from Mendoza to DeeDee to her mother. They'd lied, but did they really? Because she'd known the unsaid truth for a good while; she knew through observation. Washing dollars? And where was the money coming from really? She'd seen the numbers just like Kimi and they weren't adding up by any means.

From her grandfather on down, Koko understood that she came from a bloodline of criminals. What they did and had been doing she could accept, she just didn't want to be lied to anymore, because if she was going to continue on in the family business, she wanted to know all that was going on, if only to be able to better deal with troubling times like these; knowing was a must for Koko, it was the only way she could be able to handle her responsibilities. She had more conversing to do, she knew, and her way in would be through her Aunt Martha.

Dawk, Bena and Tiva were some slick ones, beasts in her

eyes if they were able to keep up with Mendoza and his kind. Koko wasn't ashamed of her family in the least, she was proud that they'd put it all on the line in order for them to live a life many only dreamed. The consequences were heavy, but Koko believed that this would be the last time her family would ever have to experience such tragedy because everything was now out in the open. And as far as her mind could see, the Holland-Dawkins family always rode together, right or wrong. Whatever it took to stay on top, Koko would be down for it, forget everything else.

Besides aiding in the burial of her father, Koko was hoping that Bay made it through; she wanted to tell her sister that she wasn't mad at her and she would never judge her for actions. The words, 'I love you' were ready to pour from her lips. She just had to tell Bay how much she loved her, because she hadn't gotten the chance to say those three words to her father before he'd left the ranch and she would never be able to tell him again. What Koko had taken from this tragedy was to never take a day for granted. She was the last one to leave her mother and aunt's presence, expressing her love before she and Kimi gathered Walee, Spoonie and Tyke and went into their father's private room to listen to his old albums and reminisce about the good times while beginning to deal with the reality of the tragedy at hand.

Naomi watched as Koko left the area and turned to Martha. "Tiva called me right before we came out and talked to the children," she said as she poured a glass of wine. "They're going to induce a coma on Bena for a day and try and drain fluid off her brain to help with the swelling. We're all leaving in the morning to go there to Saint Louis."

"Where's Dawk?"

"I had a talk with him earlier. He's at a hotel in Saint Louis waiting to meet with the Asians. Junior and Tiva are at the hospital," Naomi answered just as Mary emerged from the home and walked towards the table.

"Mary told me in the kitchen she was ready to talk," Martha said as she crossed her legs and eyed her sister meekly approaching her and Naomi's table.

Mary sat before Martha and Naomi and said, "I want to apologize for the things I said last night. I was out of line given the circumstances."

"We're all feeling the effects of this situation, Mary," Naomi replied. "The thing is, I did what I did to keep you all safe here at home. And I never meant to lie to you directly. I erred."

"That's not the thing that bothers me, Naomi," Mary said as she eyed Martha briefly. "When we were in Ghost Town, my daughters, especially Rene, Rene wanted to be just like Martha. We both did the best we could to keep them away from the street life and we were fine right up until the night I was shot. Ne'Ne' would still be alive maybe, if it weren't for this girl Latasha Scott. She was stealing from people's homes in the next neighborhood and Rene and her friend Sandy got caught up in something they had nothing to do with."

"What's your point in all this, Mary?" Martha asked.

"I would like to know why you willingly put your children into harm's way, Naomi? What was the reasoning behind allowing them to enter a life of crime?" Mary asked sincerely.

"Doss was involved in a dangerous occupation, Mary—one that required complete trust of those closest to him. When he asked me, I was reluctant, but if you know the big three, they're every bit their father. They are the only ones involved in the things happening outside of Oklahoma." Naomi replied, refusing to give up information on Kimi and Koko's role in the family business.

"What are you going to do now?"

"If you must know, we're still in the middle of something. We still have enemies laying in wait and unfinished business with some of our associates. It will be business as usual for those involved after things settle down."

Mary leaned back and looked to the ground. "This is not the life I believed in," she said as tears formed in her eyes. "You have something beautiful here and this is what you do?"

"What do you want from me, Mary? You want us to back away? Fold up and let it end like this?"

"I don't know what I want, Naomi. I wish I would've never learned the truth, that's all. I feel let down by it all. I liked my naivety, it made everything make sense."

"I'm giving you the truth now, Mary. Take your blinders off and throw them away because life isn't always wrapped up and tied into a neat bow and kept tidy and trouble-free. Some of the family is involved in illegitimate finance and have been for some time. That can, and will change, but not until we accomplish our goals, which is to finish what our enemies have started. There's your truth up-close and personal. I understand your anxiety, but we have to get a hold on things and make it right for our associates before we're done with the business. If you don't like the truth, if you feel threatened, then you're welcome to leave, but I hope that you stay. Nothing will happen to you here."

"Naomi," Mary said as she reached out and grabbed her sister's hands, "I have nowhere else to go. Ponca City is where I belong. This is where my family resides, and I'm here for them. I just, I just need time to accept the reality of the situation. Give me time."

"Take all the time you need. Just know, that we're planning to get out someday, but there's unfinished business that has to be addressed first before we can."

"I don't want to know anything unless it threatens our family here. What happens off the ranch isn't my concern. That's the conflict here!" Mary then blurted out as she stood up from her chair and rubbed her forehead in frustration. "It *is* my concern because family is involved! I don't wanna another day like this!"

"That's something I can't promise, Mary. But I'll do all within my power to prevent it from ever happening again."

Mary was in an emotional upheaval state. It was hard for her to accept that some of her relatives were criminals. The only thing that made it easier to digest was the fact that Martha had lived the life once so she could somewhat understand. Still, it would take time for her to come to grips with the reality that had been thrust upon her and the rest of the family. She apologized to Martha and Naomi before walking away, stating that she was going to the guest house to be alone until it was time to leave for Saint Louis.

"She'll be okay, sis," Martha said lowly as she watched Mary riding off in a golf cart.

"Mary's a humble woman, Martha. Too humble at times, but that's what I love about her. She helps keep everything in perspective without even knowing. Let's get ready for this meeting and then we'll spend time with Bena and get my husband's burial plans together."

"Let's do it," Martha replied as she got up and followed Naomi into Ponderosa. "Twiggy gone drive the truck over to the Lou for us, by the way," she added.

"Good. DeeDee and Mendoza are headed to Cicero tonight. Let's hope everything works out with the moves we're going to make pretty soon." Naomi ended as she entered the home.

****

The Millennium Hotel in downtown Saint Louis was ripe with activity in mid-September, two days after Doss's assassination. Naomi and Martha exited an airport shuttle van and walked amongst the dozens of Saint Louis Cardinals and Rams fans, both sports teams having home games this weekend, and were greeted by Dawk, Malik and Jay-D in the lobby.

Dawk hugged his mother and introduced his most trusted Enforcers to his family and the group hopped onto an elevator and rode up to the quiet 22nd floor of the hotel where they met Junior, who led the way to the suite at the end of the hall.

"These guys are scared as shit, family," Junior laughed. "I never seen nothing like it."

"Did you talk to them?" Naomi asked.

"I ain't say nothing to the guys. They're too distraught. Maybe you can sort this thing out."

"That I can and will do," Naomi said dryly as she and her group followed Junior down the hall.

The door opened and Naomi laid eyes on two Asian men sitting opposite one another on the beds who she knew to be named Phillip Tran and Grover Kobayashi. Malik and Jay-D remained outside and Naomi, Dawk and Martha trailed Junior into the room.

The men looked devastated in Naomi's eyes. Disheveled suits and weary eyes complimented wild heads of jet black hair, and empty bottles of beer were all around. There was a musky smell in the room and cell phones were all over the place.

"We've been here for an entire day," Phillip said as he stood up and extended his hand towards Naomi, introducing himself and Grover.

"Junior says you two have a problem?" Naomi asked as she stood before Phillip and Grover.

"My father is near death. We can't see him because the feds are all over Seattle. We don't know all that they know and we have no one else to turn to."

"Your father is?"

"JunJie Maruyama. He was shot by a federal agent the same day your husband was killed and is in a coma."

"What is it that you want from us? We're still sorting things out here on our end."

"You have to put us up for the time being. We need shelter until we can sort things out with our guy south of the border."

"How will this affect our standing with Mister Gacha?"

"It won't. We will carry the burden for the time being. We just have to know who else who we can trust because Asa Spade is on his way to prison on a racketeering charge. There's no one left in our crew but us."

"What's with the cell phones?"

"We've been trying to contact you since my father was hit. We used every number. Got a call back from your son, Dawk, and he set this meeting up." Grover remarked.

"We're going to need those," Naomi said as Martha grabbed a plastic bag and went about picking up the cell phones.

"We'll get rid of these for y'all," Martha said as Dawk gave Grover two new phones.

"Use these for now, here's the numbers," Naomi said as Dawk handed over the phones. "I have a home in Cicero where I can set you two men up. It is furnished, clean and very relaxing. My son and his crew will drive you there and I'm going to have to ask that you two remain inside. Don't venture out until our arrival."

"How long will it be before you return to Cicero?" Phillip asked.

"It'll be at least a week. We have to bury the head of our family. Then, we'll sort everything out and began making amends," Naomi said as she placed her hands together and bowed slightly, her way of honoring the Japanese men.

"Thank you for this. We will never forget this," Grover said calmly.

"It is our pleasure. We have much more business in the future, but as for now, we must all fall back." Naomi responded.

"We're all on the same page here, Naomi." Phillip said as he extended his hand. "We're ready when you're ready, young Doss."

"You know my name is Dawk, right?"

"I know. You just remind me of your father with your demeanor. I meant no disrespect."

"None taken. Let's move," Dawk replied as he led the way out the door.

"Okay, Junior, Martha, let's get on with the get on. I've been holding back tears for the past two days, but I feel them coming on as I speak." Naomi said. "I hope Bena gets through this ordeal unscathed."

"You ladies go ahead," Junior said. "I gotta use the crapper. The bathrooms at Mercy hospital are the filthiest."

"Don't forget to wipe," Martha joked as she and Naomi headed out the door. Once the door closed, Martha couldn't hold back any longer. "You think this plan is going to work, sis?" she asked lowly.

"It has to, Martha. The Asians' asses are on the line and we owe it to them to make things right in order to keep our ship afloat. The people working against us aren't the brightest, you know? We smelled them coming, but they caught us off guard. Now? We will play a game of bowling ball—and knock them all down at the same time and leave no room for a spare."

****

"Okay," Dawk told Phillip as Malik wheeled Jay-D's Navigator down Interstate-70 towards the airport. "These are your flight tickets and we have you two set up at the Ritz Carlton in Chicago. Lay low until you get the call and you'll get back at your man for what he did. My grandfather and his friend will handle that other thing."

"You think they'll buy it?" Phillip asked as he combed out his hair and straightened his suit and tie.

"Greed blinds people, my man. Y'all just lay low and let us work this magic. Asa Spade? Where is he?" Dawk asked.

"He really is locked up, Dawk," Grover answered as he tied his tie and splashed cologne onto his face and wrists. "The feds were knee deep in his ass. He may walk if our plans go accordingly, but he will have to sit for a while. Him and his entire crew."

"Good luck to the guy. It was stand up what he did when he sent that message to call you two."

"It was, my man," Phillip replied. "Helped put us on the offense. We'll stay out the way and wait on your family's call." he ended as he and Grover enjoyed a leisurely ride to the airport in order to catch a flight to Chicago, where they would await their next move.

CHAPTER FORTY
HOLDING ON

Naomi walked slowly, seemingly in slow motion, through the pristine halls of Mercy Medical Center with her head bowed, a ten gallon hat covering her head and a dark pair of shades covering her eyes as tears had begun streaming from her eyes the moment she'd left the meeting with Phillip and Grover.

For two days she'd been the one leading the way for the family. On the phone constantly with Tiva getting updates on her oldest daughter's condition, lining things up with DeeDee in order to clean house, having heartfelt talks with each of the young five, sitting for hours with Spoonie and Tyke, who'd been crying off and on ever since the night she'd broken the news. All the pain she'd been carrying with her since the night she'd received that phone call was pouring out of her heart like a waterfall—and this was only the beginning of her sorrow, she knew.

Martha and Junior were tailing Naomi as she approached the double doors leading into the intensive care unit. She pushed them open slowly and the entire group of family and friends came into view—and they were a beautiful sight to see—all of them were such a beautiful and consoling sight. Tiva, Kimi, Koko, and their boyfriends Udelle and Chablis, Walee, Spoonie, Tyke, Mary, Malaysia, Malara, Regina, Tak, Tacoma, Twiggy, Siloam, Flacco, Oneika Brackens, Jane Dow and oddly, Reynard, who'd flown in to comfort his daughter and grandson, were all present, sitting in chairs, standing and sitting on the carpeted floor even. They'd taken over the waiting area, had set up camp for the moment and were all praying and pulling for Bena to pull through.

Naomi went and stood amongst the group and they all formed a circle around her as she broke down into tears. The family hugged one another tightly and stood in a circle in total silence, some batting the tears from their eyes as they looked to the ground in disbelief. Bena had been shot in the head and was clinging on to life. It was a hard reality, but together, they knew they could be strong for Bay and help her through the most difficult time of her life.

As the group stood in silence, Kimi looked up and saw the doctor and his staff approaching. No one except for Tiva had seen Bay, and by all measures, it wasn't a pretty sight because she simply couldn't, or wouldn't describe what she'd witnessed.

"Momma," Kimi said through her tears, "there's Bena's doctor."

Naomi turned and eyed the man and stepped forth from the group. "Bena's family," the man said lowly. "You are?"

"I'm her mother. My name is Naomi Holland-Dawkins."

"It's nice to meet you, Misses Dawkins. I'm Doctor Obadiah Wickenstaff—lead Neurosurgeon here at Mercy Medical Center."

Naomi had heard the name Obadiah Wickenstaff back in 2002 when she'd first visited Lucky shortly after he was shot by Carmella and she'd never forgotten the name. She had wondered back then what race would a person by the name of Obadiah be; now she had her answer, she only wished it were under better circumstances.

Obadiah Wickenstaff was a seventy year-old Native American belonging to the Lakota Indian tribe in South Dakota. He was one of the first Native Americans in the United States to earn a degree in Neurology thirty-five years ago from

Harvard School of Medicine, the number one medical school in the country with a $3 billion dollar endowment. He'd been practicing for nearly four decades, had written numerous articles on brain activity, was once president of the Board of Medicine and had sat on three Senate committees to discuss healthcare reform in the nineties. He was a heavy weight in the medical field and respected worldwide, and eighteen year-old Bena Holland was now under his care. When Naomi shook Obadiah's hand, she was hit with a calming force. The doctor's hands were as soft as marshmallows. They were well-manicured also and Naomi loved that and much more about the good doctor.

"How's my daughter doing, Mister Wickenstaff?"

"Please, call me Obadiah. I'm Lakota. What tribe are you?" the tall, tan-skinned, white-haired high-cheek-boned man asked lowly.

"Creek."

"Nice people. Your daughter? Would you like to see her?"

"Can I?" Naomi asked with a smile as the family all gathered.

Obadiah looked the family over and said, "I'm sorry. I'm afraid too many people all at once will not be good. I only wanted to give you a full update and show you what we're up against. I'm sorry. I can't allow everyone at once."

"We'll wait, Naomi," Martha said lowly. "Let us know how she doing."

Naomi went in with the doctor and followed him down the hall towards Bena's room and the two stood outside of a large window which featured closed curtains. A nurse wearing a sterile suit and surgical mask walked up and Obadiah instructed her to pull the curtains back slowly.

"Why is she dressed like that?" Naomi asked as the nurse entered the room.

"These rooms are the most sterile rooms in the building, Naomi. Infection can set in with these kinds of injuries and I prefer to err on the side of caution. People often joke about eating off the floors in some places because they are so clean. Here in my unit? It is not just a statement," Obadiah said proudly as the curtains were slowly pulled back.

Naomi removed her hat and glasses, dropped them on the floor and gasped at the sight. Bena looked like a robot, not a human, not the once beautiful and vibrant child she had given birth to in July of 1985. She lay on her back naked, her head elevated, being held up by a neck brace that had straps attached to the ceiling. She was shaved bald and had a breathing tube inserted into her mouth. Her arms and legs were spread-eagle and slightly elevated by the slings holding them up. Her eyes were slightly swollen and shut and her skull was nearly the size of a small watermelon. Her side was cut open and a feeding tube was inserted into her stomach and tubes ran from her private area to drain urine. She looked nothing like herself and it pained Naomi to see her daughter in such a debilitating condition.

"It isn't as bad as it looks, Naomi." Obadiah said as five people dressed in business suits approached the two.

"How could it not be as bad as it looks? This is horrible," Naomi said as she covered the lower portion of her face.

"I'll admit, we're not out of the dark. We have a twenty percent chance things can go wrong, but I'm doubting that highly. We're monitoring Bena's brain closely to counteract a buildup of fluid, which is nonexistent, and the swelling is subsiding. It's retracting slowly, but it's subsiding."

"What is all the equipment here," Naomi asked as she eyed a panel of instruments before her and Obadiah.

"This here," Obadiah said happily as he pointed to the computerized panel situated outside of the window. "This is a state-of-the-art brain and heart monitor. Bena's cat-scan showed remarkable recovery only a day after her injury. So much so, scientists from MIT have come to study her progress. I hope you don't mind?"

"That has to be the best news I've heard since this ordeal began."

"Thank you. Bena was hit with a fragment of a bullet that pierced the skin of her skull on the right side and just barely penetrated her left temporal lobe. The temporal lobe affects memory and the comprehension of speech. Bena should not be able to recognize names or react to words, but she does. What has sparked our curiosity for study is Bena's response when the nurse told her Tiva was present. The heart monitors went ballistic and there was heavy brain activity. Other words, however, like dog, sunshine, happy birthday, any other word gets little response."

"What does that mean exactly?"

"My hypothesis is that Bena hasn't lost her memory. That means that there is little damage done to the brain, but her actions could also be attributed to the fact that it was her twin in her presence. Twins, especially identical twins, they have a very unique bond, even able to feel one another's pain in some cases."

"My sisters had that ability a while back."

"It comes and goes in some instances. What I want to do now, is announce your presence. See what kind of response we get. Would you mind? These people are engineers from MIT, by the way. They're the ones who've built this computerized system."

"I don't mind at all, Obadiah." Naomi said as she nodded at the staff. "Thank you for what you're doing."

"It is our pleasure," an older woman said lowly. "We wish you and your family all the best and a speedy recovery for Bena." she ended as she stepped back.

Naomi watched as Obadiah and the nurse used sign language to communicate. "I gave my nurse your name and relationship and told her to announce your presence. Here we go guys," Obadiah told the engineers as he gently grabbed Naomi's hand, soothing her nerves a little. "Let's see what happens, Naomi."

Naomi was on pens and needles. She knew not what to expect from this impromptu experiment on her oldest daughter. The nurse leaned forward and Naomi watched the lady, unable to hear her words, but clearly reading her lips as she mimicked the words: *Bena, your mother Naomi is here.*

The engineers gasped and Naomi let loose with a wide smile when the heart monitors began accelerating. The brain patterns on the computer screen intensified and for a brief second, Bena's eyes opened. Naomi and Obadiah both saw it; the wounded eighteen year-old had looked her mother square in the eyes for a couple of seconds before she closed her eyes once more. Through swollen eyes and in her wounded state, Bena still had the strength to pull her eyes open and see her mother. No one was certain if she'd even recognized her mother, but her actions were inspiring.

Naomi and the family would stay in town another two days before leaving for Oklahoma, leaving behind Tiva and Dawk, who'd been hiding out over to Malik's house in Maplewood during the family's visit.

Tiva and Junior, meanwhile, would set up in the waiting room and receive updates from Obadiah every three hours during his shift and would report back to Naomi, who was down on the ranch preparing for another round of sorrow amidst an on-going retaliatory move being conducted by various members of the family.

CHAPTER FORTY-ONE
EXPOSED

DeeDee sat in Naomi's old bedroom inside Kevin and Serena's old home back in Cicero sipping a cup of coffee. Naomi and the family had all made it back to the ranch earlier in the day and were preparing to bury his son as he sat alone watching the block as the sun set.

A lot was on DeeDee's mind. For one, he didn't like the way he had to move around ever since the day his son had been killed. Second, he wasn't sure if he was even going to make his son's funeral. And third, he felt as if the plan Naomi had put together was falling apart because he'd been waiting for days and hadn't encountered anyone. He'd suggested getting rid of everybody all at once, but Naomi felt her way would be better because the family could clean their own house, find out who was involved in Doss's shooting and exact revenge at a later date once the heat subsided.

Images of his son as a child filled DeeDee's mind. Doss was a fun-loving lad, but DeeDee had known early on that his son had it in him to be a gangster the whole time because he was a fearless youth who tried his best to imitate him at all times. When he was a kid, Doss loved wagons. It carried over into adulthood when he started his family. DeeDee laughed to himself as he reminisced over Doss pulling his children across the land in his flannel shirt shortly after he arrived on the ranch for the first time. He was a good father and husband, better than DeeDee could have ever hoped to be and had accomplished much more in life. The tears soon rolled down DeeDee's cheeks and he sat alone and wept aloud, missing his son tremendously, but having the understanding that what'd happened was a part of the business they were involved in.

"*It shoulda been me, son,*" DeeDee cried aloud as he bowed his head and heaved, finally able to release his grief alone and in silence.

Time ticked by slowly as DeeDee poured cup after cup of coffee, trying his best to stay awake. He'd stopped over to *Eastside Bar* and talked to his contact on the force earlier in the day. The man had given him a rolled up joint after DeeDee went into a long dialogue about his son's life. The officer told DeeDee that the weed would help him open up to himself. DeeDee laughed at the time, but he realized the officer was right because the weed had brought back long forgotten memories of his son's childhood, memories he would cherish the rest of his days. After several more tokes, DeeDee coughed aloud and covered his mouth as if someone could actually hear him.

DeeDee was going through an array of emotions as he reflected on the tragedy that had been thrust upon his family and what he would do with the remainder of his life once this last job was complete. The potent Mary Jane begin taking full affect as the seventy-five year-old sat calmly, his eyes focused on Serena's house directly across the street from where he sat in seclusion and just as Naomi had predicted, they'd arrived.

Three men pulled up in a dark brown cargo van and exited the vehicle and trotted down the side of the house towards the backyard. DeeDee got up from his seat at that moment and went and stood in the foyer just as two Cicero patrol cars pulled up to the home. He went and sat in Mendoza's Cadillac and watched as his contact and three other officers emerged from the side of the house with three men in handcuffs and escorted them to the waiting patrol cars.

When the officers left the scene, DeeDee headed over to *Eastside Bar* and waited for a couple of hours and an officer from the Cicero police department tapped on the door. The man was let in and while he and DeeDee shared a dry scotch, the officer handed DeeDee three photos along with the names of the men who'd tried to break into Serena's old home.

"Bahdoon 'Q-man' LuQman. Cesar 'Big Bounce' Guerrera, and Pancho 'Dead Eye' Vera," DeeDee said as he eyed the photos. "We've been looking for this Somali for some time now. Been had his picture, but we could never finger the guy."

"They said they were supposed to be going to a party when we busted them. Can you believe that shit? What a bunch of idiots," the officer laughed as he downed his drink.

"They'll be going to a party alright," DeeDee said as he slid the officer a satchel containing $50,000 dollars in cash. "What can you charge them with that will have them back on the streets say within a year or so?"

"Burglary. None of the guys have a jacket so I say sixteen months max? Maybe less for good behavior, but they won't be a problem until next summer at the earliest once my guys are done."

"It's been a pleasure, my man. This place is all yours now," DeeDee said as he escorted the officer out of the bar. He then locked up the place, handed the officer the keys to the establishment, and went and visited Bena before returning to the ranch two days later to attend his son's funeral.

The crew from Fox Park had played right into the Holland family's hands by sending men who were under the belief that they were going to kill two Asian men on this night, but they'd landed in the middle of a well-orchestrated trap set up by Naomi herself; and at the same time, the crew's mole was clearly exposed. The ducks were lining up for the family. DeeDee had done his part, the plan would now shift to Mendoza, who was already on the ranch with Francine readying for Doss's celebration with the rest of the family.

CHAPTER FORTY-TWO
THE DAY

Naomi stood on the front porch staring at Mary's refrigerated produce trailer, which was parked in the field to her right. The trailer was surrounded by a white fence and had yellow carnations resting on its top. Red carnations surrounded the bottom of the trailer inside the fence and a wooden stair case was placed at the rear leading up to the trailer doors.

Inside the trailer rested Doss's coffin. Morticians in Saint Louis had provided the services, supplying the family with a black marble casket with chrome handles and *Doss Dawkins* engraved in diamonds on the top. A black silk suit covered Doss's body and he wore a pair of black gator shoes. Naomi stood alone in her black all-in-one dress, eyeing the trailer sadly in silence as she reminisced about the good times she and Doss had shared throughout their storied relationship and past history.

Back inside the home, the family was preparing to walk out onto the patio and bring the cars around to the front of the home for the ride to Ne`Ne`s Hill where Doss would be buried on this sunny, but cool late September morning. The day was beautiful, there wasn't a cloud in the sky; but as the sun's radiant rays showered the land with its inviting warmth, the hearts of everyone on the ranch was carrying a heavy burden. Careful thought and planning had gone into Doss's funeral over the past week, now that the day had arrived, all many could do was try their best to hold back their tears and push on through the ceremony while leaning on one another for strength and support.

Mary and Martha walked out of the front door while the rest of the family exited onto the back patio. They greeted Naomi and stood on either side of her.

"Doss, Doss loved to pull the kids around in a wagon when they were babies," Naomi smiled through her tears. "I never thought I'd have to do the same for him. I wanted him to outlive me. I felt he deserved to given the life he was living. How foolish of me to believe this would end on a happy note."

"How and why it happened doesn't matter, Naomi," Mary said lovingly. "What matters is that the family loved him. Your kids loved him. We all loved Doss and the man he was here because that is the only man we ever knew."

"That's right," Martha chimed in. "Don't feel guilty because you're still here, sis. I'm sure if Doss had to choose he would choose to go first, but this isn't about that at all. It's about showing love to family, letting one another know how much we really care."

"Guilt isn't in my heart, Martha, nor do I regret anything. Me and Doss lived a wonderful life together. Call me selfish, but my bed is so lonely at night. I miss him holding me already. Even when he was alive and not around, I missed him, but I had the reassurance when I got that call that he was on his way home. He could hold me again. We could eat breakfast together and I'd tell him about the kids, who did what, who needed what—we were a family again—just a normal family. I'm never going to get that call again. I'm going to miss the kids' father forever," she cried lowly.

"Nothing about the way you feel over your loss is selfish, Naomi," Mary said, placing an arm around her sister's neck. "That's real love. You and Doss had something that's real and rare in today's world."

"We truly did," Naomi said as she began walking down the stairs towards a wooden wagon that had two Clydesdale horses attached to the front. The three sisters hopped into the wagon and Naomi guided the horses over to Mary's trailer, where DeeDee, Mendoza, Junior and Flacco were waiting by the staircase.

The family's three Suburbans pulled up along with Bena's car, which was driven by Walee, and everyone exited. The doors on the trailer were opened and a cool, cloudy mist escaped the insides and Doss's coffin came into view as DeeDee led the men and Naomi inside.

Walee, Tak, Udelle and Chablis climbed the stairs and a few minutes later, Walee, Tak, Udelle, Chablis, Mendoza, DeeDee, Flacco and Junior emerged with Doss's coffin.

Another hard-hitting moment was felt by the family as they watched the men walk down the stairs carrying Doss. Spoonie and Tyke grabbed their stomachs and screamed a painful scream that brought tears to everyone's eyes. "Daddyyyyy!" Tyke screamed. "Daddyyyyy!"

Family members began breaking down as Doss's casket was loaded onto the wagon. They all stood at the rear of the cart, huddled together and crying and hugging one another. DeeDee backed away and stood before the group. He looked over to the hill top where the canopy sat over Doss's grave and tears began to form in his eyes. He wasn't supposed to be around to see this day. He thought he'd die of old age surrounded by all of his family, including his beloved son. *"Foolish thinking,"* DeeDee said to himself as he bit his bottom lip and stared at Doss's coffin resting in the back of the wagon. "My son," he then cried. "My, my boy," he wept as he stepped forth and placed his hand on the casket. DeeDee then balled his fists and stood upright at the foot of his son's coffin, his body stiffened and his eyes poured tears as he moaned a loud and devastating moan before bending at the waist and grabbing his knees. "Forgive me, family," he moaned. "I just, it hurts. It hurts my *heart*!"

"There's nothing to forgive, il amico moi," Mendoza said through tears. "Let it go. You're with family."

Kimi, Koko, Spoonie and Tyke were all in line behind their

grandfather in a tight embrace, rocking side to side as tears streamed down their faces. Lips trembled, hugs were numerous, and moans spilled forth at random as the family eyed the coffin in a dreamlike state, still not able to believe that Doss Dawkins Junior was no more. The family all went and grabbed red carnations and after lingering for several minutes, they climbed into the cars.

Naomi was helped back into the wagon and DeeDee sat beside her while Mary and Martha sat on the second row of the carriage. Mendoza and Francine sat in the third row, Mendoza's eyes now covered with sunshades to hide his pain and Francine steadily dabbing her eyes with a silk scarf as she held onto several carnations.

"You ready, dad?" Naomi asked lowly.

DeeDee placed his left arm around Naomi, looked over to Ne'Ne's Hill and said, "Let's send him home, Naomi."

"Everybody ready?" Naomi asked aloud s she looked back.

Walee was driving Bena's pristine Lincoln. He was directly behind the wagon with Spoonie and Tyke in the front seat and Kimi and Koko in the backseat with Udelle and Chablis. "Y'all ready?" he leaned out the driver's side window and asked aloud.

Junior, Regina, Tak, Tacoma, Twiggy and Reynard were in a Suburban behind Walee. Tak leaned out the driver's side window and nodded. "Y'all ready?" he then asked as he looked to his rear.

Siloam was in a Suburban behind Bena's car with Jane Dow on her side and Flacco and several ranch hands in the backseat. She nodded and waved at the Suburban behind her, which held a host of ranch hands. "We're ready, Senorita Siloam," a ranch hand remarked from the driver's side as he blew his horn.

With the signal given, Naomi pulled the reigns and the Clydesdale horses began their walk across the land, strolling past Mary's field of pumpkins and onions, the cars following in a single file line. Halfway through the trek, Naomi heard those melodic strings, drums and the piano and the tears flowed heavily. Martha and Mary leaned into one another and Mendoza and Francine closed their eyes.

Inside Bena's car, Spoonie leaned into Walee and grabbed his right arm and placed it around her neck and grabbed his hand tightly. She needed her brother's strength for this journey as she listened to the music through her tears. Tyke laid her head on the passenger side door and cried openly as she held Spoonie's free hand tightly. Kimi leaned into Udelle and Chablis placed an arm around Koko and pulled her close as the song played on. None of the kids wanted to reveal the song they'd all agreed to play, but when it was heard, everybody felt it because it described to the fullest extent what Doss had done for his family throughout his life and in death even...

..."*So I have tried to...not be the one who'll...fall into that line...but what I feel inside...I think you should know...ohhh...and baby that's you, you, you....made life's hi-sto-ry...'cause you've brought some joy inside my tears...you have done...what no one...thought...could be...you've brought some joy inside my tears...*" Stevie Wonder's song *Joy Inside My Tears* rang out across the land from Bena's sound system, bringing tears to everyone's eyes as the family and friends reflected on Doss's life while caravanning in a single file line, following Naomi, who led the way.

The day she first met Doss in his slick, light grey out-fit, the first day they made love in Serena's home, the numerous times they'd made love in her office inside the Sears Tower, his joining her down in Oklahoma and the way he strengthened and supported her when Serena and Kevin were killed, his enthusiasm and support when she resumed her search for her sisters, his cooking abilities—all those memories and more encompassed Naomi as she guided the carriage across the land.

Yes, Doss Dawkins had given forty-eight year-old Naomi-Holland Dawkins joy beyond compare, he truly did bring joy to her tears as she reflected upon an awesome man she was fortunate to have met and loved. Wisdom, strength and courage. Gentleness, compassion and ohhh, the way he made her feel in bed. A good man had died if Naomi had to tell it. And he could never be replaced. If she had to live life all over again without him, and knowing of his existence once upon a time, there would never be another. There was only one Doss Dawkins Junior and Naomi had tasted the real thing. Its flavor was nothing short of sweet, loving and kind. That was her husband. That was Doss the man, the only man Naomi had ever loved in life and she would willingly endure a thousand deaths by God the Most High, if only to be able to spend just one more day with the man who'd been the love of her life...

..."*I feel that lasting...moments are coming...far and few between...so I should tell you all...the happiness that you bring...baby, baby, it's you, you, you,...made life's hi-sto-ry... ohh, baby...'cause you've brought some...joy inside my tears...baby, you have done...what no one... thought could be...you brought some joy...inside my tears...*"

The song played on and approached its crescendo as the family pulled up to the foot of Ne`Ne`s Hill where they all exited. Doss was carried up the hill, the family singing the chorus to Stevie Wonder's song, which was set to repeat, as they slowly ascended the hill where Doss's coffin was placed beneath the canopy beside his open grave.

Naomi stood before her husband's casket crying her heart out, her eyes closed and her body rocking side to side in a gentle manner as she reflected on what was a glorious life shared with the man of her life, her children's father. She would miss her husband something fierce and would always feel as if she was now half of a person because on this day, she was indeed letting go of half of her persona, half of her existence, the one thing in life that made her whole was no more.

Doss was sent home righteously by those who loved him. A ranch hand, who was an ordained minister, sent prayers up to God above as Doss's casket was draped with red carnations. The family then descended the hill and convened outside the guest house where the grill was fired up and food was prepared for Doss's celebration. His grave would be lowered and covered just before sunset.

****

"And Doss says to me, license or no license, I'm drivin' this rig back to Chicago! Naomi's threatening to leave my ass! And if I don't propose immediately I'm gonna have to stalk this woman the rest of my life," Mendoza said through laughter as he sat beside DeeDee, the two reminiscing about the events that led up to Doss and Naomi's marriage alongside Francine, Junior and Twiggy.

"Doss was the best at what he did, granddad. I'm gone miss the guy." Junior said as he bounced his daughter Malaysia on one knee.

"We all are, son." Mendoza replied as he scooped Malara up into his arms, taking her away from Francine. "So, when Tiva gets back you two gonna come to Montana and see the ranch me and your grandmother are putting together, right?"

"Wouldn't miss it for the world, granddad."

"Good, because I want to see my great grandkids set foot on their future inheritance while I'm still around. I have a new camera and all to take plenty pictures. We'll have to get there soon before the snow sets in. It gets cold there, you know?" Mendoza ended.

Naomi's five, meanwhile, were holding down the grills. Walee was master chef and he was taking his duties seriously. He'd watched and assisted his father on the grill for years and it was now his responsibility to prepare meat and vegetables for the family. He laid out three full slabs of ribs and sprinkled them with his father's secret rub recipe which he'd memorized and mastered to perfection before he closed the lid. He then turned to the other grill, where Spoonie and Tyke were waiting with two bowls fresh corn on the cob and cucumber and coated them with butter before spreading them out over the coals.

"Kimi, anybody heard from AquaNina?" Walee asked as he closed the lid and wiped his hands with a rag.

"We been calling and calling that girl. Me and Spoonie even went over to the condo back in town, but she wasn't there." Kimi answered as she sipped a glass of lemon tea.

"I talked to her a while ago. She at their house in Oklahoma

City," Koko said. "She ain't come to the funeral and hasn't even been to see Bay in Saint Louis."

"She might be devastated and scared," Walee said as he sat down in chair. "Everybody handle tragedy differently."

"We all devastated. And everybody scared for Bay, but we went there, Walee. Bay been nothing but good to 'Nina and this how she do?" Koko asked in disgust.

"We should go see how she doing tomorrow," Kimi said.

"Yeah. Yeah let's do that, family," Walee said. "Something up with AquaNina because it ain't like her to not be a part of all that's going on." he ended.

Naomi and Martha, meanwhile, sat out in back of the home beside the creek. "We'll head to Chicago the day Mendoza leaves out with Tiva and the babies," Naomi told Martha.

"What you gone need me to do, sis?" Martha asked as she rolled a joint.

"You're gonna smoke that?" Naomi asked.

"I sure as hell ain't gonna use it for fish bait," Martha quipped through light laughter.

"I have never smoked weed in my life."

Martha held the rolled out joint to Naomi, but she declined. "I know Kimi 'nem be toking, I wish they wouldn't."

"Why you don't say nothing?" Martha asked as she reflected on the night she herself had smoked with her neices.

"We actually have real good talks when they're buzzing, as crazy as it sounds. Kimi and Koko could be doing far worse, Martha. They're still virgins, you know?"

"Yeah. But for how long?"

Naomi smiled and said, "I was nineteen. Minus the weed and the murders I committed in Sylacauga, Kimi and Koko are me all over again. They seem to have things under control. Doing good in school, not man-hopping and they are book smart. They'll be just fine. Back to this Chicago business, though. All you'll have to do is drive. The guys we suspect are involved in

Doss's killing fell for what we put together and they're behind bars for now. All we have to do is fulfill our obligations to the Asians."

"What's gone be the deal in Chicago?"

"We're going to see an old friend, Martha. We'll visit an old friend." Naomi ended.

THE HOLLAND FAMILY SAGA

CHAPTER FORTY-THREE
CLEANING HOUSE

It was ten days after Doss's funeral, early October of 2006. Naomi's young five had indeed gone and seen about AquaNina down in Oklahoma City and what they saw when they got there was nothing short of a mess. AquaNina had trashed her and Bay's home and was doped up on sleeping pills. She didn't try to kill herself, however; she was just so distraught over the thought of losing Bay she'd entered into a bout of depression and all she wanted to do was sleep. Her parents were of no help, telling her to move on and find a man and to 'stop dealing with that thug family and their lesbian daughter'.

AquaNina felt alone. She had no one to turn to except the Holland-Dawkins family, but she felt like an outsider. Her feelings were unfounded, however, because she was well-liked by the family members. Kimi and Koko assured her that she was welcome to see Bay, and AquaNina had agreed.

Nearly two weeks later, however, she still hadn't visited Bay in Saint Louis. The young five were now furious with AquaNina at this point and time, especially Kimi and Koko, because they felt as if she'd bailed out on Bay in her most critical time of need. AquaNina had her reasons, though; but it would take a while for her actions to be understood fully. In the meantime, she would simply vanish, leaving the family wondering just how much she really did love Bay before she'd been shot in Saint Louis.

****

The wind whipped about tremendously on this cloudy late October day as snow flurries fell sparsely from the sky. Finland Xavier had been in court all day and was preparing to enjoy an evening dinner before heading home. For some time now, Finland had been off the scene as far as transporting cocaine was concerned. Ever since he'd learned that JunJie Maruyama had been shot and was in a coma, he'd backed away from the game entirely because his role in the business had become obsolete for the time being. Finland was actually contemplating retiring from the business because the Chicago Gang was finished in his eyes.

Feds were on to some of the organization's members, the crew's supplier was out of commission and many of its leaders were either dead or locked away. The business was defunct if Finland Xavier had to tell it. The long time counselor had just freshened himself up in the courthouse bathroom and headed out towards the exits where he knew his daily limousine was waiting. He trotted down the stairs happily underneath the snow flurries as the grey sky darkened, and he eyed a white BMW limousine with a tan-skinned woman wearing a black hat and sunshades, a short dress and three-quarter length black thin-wool coat holding a sign with last name Xavier on display.

Finland approached the chauffer as she opened the door and nodded. "Evening," he said politely. "I have reservations at Tru restaurant on North Saint Claire Street in forty-five minutes. Traffic is heavy so step on it," he added as he slid into the limousine.

"Don't worry, Mister Xavier. You won't be needing those reservations," the chauffer replied as she closed the door.

Finland looked out the window and realized that it was Martha Holland who'd welcomed him inside the limousine.

Martha stared at her own relfection, knowing all the while Finland was looking directly into her eyes through the mirror tint before she walked off.

"Good evening, Finland," a voice was heard.

Finland was so puzzled over the reasons why Martha was in town, let alone chauffeuring the limousine, he'd never noticed the three people sitting inside the car. He turned and made eye contact with Phillip Tran, Grover Kobayashi, and Naomi, his childhood friend.

"Phillip," Finland said surprised as Martha opened the door and slid into the front seat. "How's your father? I've been trying to—"

"They know everything, Finland," Naomi said calmly as she held onto a silencer-tipped Ruger .9mm with her right hand.

"Everything?" Finland asked. "Everything about what? All I know is that JunJie was shot and is in a coma, Naomi."

"Let's not play the 'find out what I know' game, okay, Finland?" Naomi said as she threw a stack of photos into Finland's lap as the car began moving forward

"Jarkowski has played both sides of the game, my friend," Phillip said as Finland eyed the photos, which showed him talking to an FBI agent by the name of Lisa Vanguard. "The son-of-a-bitch thought he'd killed my father, but he was able to hold on and give us the lowdown. Jarkowski is now dead. This agent, a Lisa Vangaurd, she blew his ass way in his office the day he shot my father."

"How did you get those?" Finland asked anxiously.

"Jarkowski was not our only contact, my friend," Phillip remarked stone-faced. "When Lisa showed Jarkowski those pictures, he went back a couple of days later to cover his tracks because he believed my father was going to give him up on indictment. We never thought Jarkowski would flip. Can't trust a mutherfucka in this game can you?"

"We also know you gave up one of our own, Finland," Grover said in calm manner.

"I gave up no one important! I gave up Asa Spade! Asa Spade? The man was a worthless ex-pimp who knew nothing about this business! Carmella kicked his ass and he was becoming a burden on the organization!"

"He was a stand-up guy, Finland!" Phillip yelled. "You gave up one of our own to save your own ass! Lisa had nothing on you, man! All you had to do was deny everything! Deny *everything*! But you panicked when she caught you coming out of Goddesses and asked you a few questions about my father! You gave up Asa Spade, and the date of the next shipment!"

Finland knew Phillip had him dead right. He'd committed all of those said acts of betrayal. He may have been a smart business mind and an excellent criminal defense attorney, but even his own knowledge of the law wasn't a strong enough deterrent when he was confronted by the federal government and questioned as to whether or not he and JunJie Maruyama, his main counterpart, were involved in criminal activities.

Lisa had asked him whether or not he knew if JunJie was involved in the hit on the Onishi brothers and he'd answered by saying he had no information regarding the hit.

"So you know JunJie Maruyama?" Lisa asked on that rainy day in July of 2006 as she followed Finland to his waiting limousine as he left Goddesses, his 'second home', over in Seattle.

"I know the man. We've done business."

"What kind of business?"

"A few real estate deals. Nothing more."

"And you're in town today because?"

"I love the night life."

"Your driver? The guy from Midwest Express? He says he's here to pick up a load of produce and take it back to Chicago in a couple of days. What if I were to say that he was unknowingly picking up a load of cocaine at the port? What if I was to say that if I find cocaine on your truck, I can bust your ass for distribution of cocaine and hit your ass with a thirty year sentence?"

"I'd say you're making a mistake."

"Am I now? Okay. This warrant will prove me wrong or right." Lisa said.

Finland thought back to that day and how he'd forged his own deal. He dropped Asa Spade's name on Lisa Vanguard to draw heat off himself and the Chicago Gang, believing he was making the right decision for all involved, but his actions had led to JunJie getting shot by Jarkowski in order for Jarkowski to cover his own tracks. Jarkowski had tipped JunJie off to the impending bust and JunJie was able to hide the container of cocaine the first go around, but Lisa was on to him by early August and salivating over his next shipment, where Laddy found 230 kilograms of cocaine.

JunJie was on his way to prison once healthy, but he'd held on long enough to let his son know there was a bug planted in his office the day he was shot. When Phillip and Grover went silent in the room that day, Lisa had no way of connecting Phillip and Grover to JunJie's business. They could easily deny that they knew anything and the case against them was weak. JunJie would bear the brunt of the federal indictment, but all roads led back to Finland Xavier, who by all accounts, had betrayed the crew and had basically sunk JunJie Maruyama and now had Asa Spade and his bunch in suspended animation.

"I can, I can reimburse the entire loss you guys took on the last shipment. One million eight hundred thousand dollars. I'll, I'll make it an even three million dollars. All my, all my savings," Finland pleaded as he eyed the three individuals.

Naomi, Phillip and Grover had cold, dead stares planted on their faces as the limousine rocked down Interstate-90 headed towards the Indiana state line. Naomi was crushed that her childhood friend had flipped and she was glad Finland didn't know of her whereabouts in Oklahoma.

"There was reason you weren't invited to my husband's funeral, Finland," Naomi said calmly. "Doss always had his reservations about you, but I didn't believe him. Oh, but how right he was."

"That's what you think, Naomi? You think I would've given up you and Doss? Well, I didn't! But Asa Spade? Asa Spade is a nobody! He's nobody! We can get past this!"

"I promised the Asians that I would take care of you for

giving up Asa Spade. My job is nearly done. You and I will forever be friends, Finland—we just can't do business because you have a big mouth." Naomi said as she racked her .9mm and waved it in Finland's direction.

Finland turned to Phillip and Grover and pleaded for mercy. "I'm sorry," he said. "Give me, give me a chance to make it right. Please."

The limousine slowed for traffic on the interstate and Finland tried to escape. The doors were locked from the outside, however, and Naomi wasted no time in pulling the trigger and shooting Finland in his upper leg. He leaned back and clutched his thigh and screamed aloud, banging on the window with his free hand, trying to get motorists attention, but it was in vain. The mirror tint shielded him and his plight from the rest of the outside world.

Seeing her friend in pain touched Naomi. She and Finland had over forty years of history, but she'd never imagined he would turn into the man he was on this day. "Please, Naomi," Finland cried. "Please, don't do this to me!"

"My family means the world to me, Finland. You've weakened us and the business we're involved in. There's no room left for you, il mio amico," Naomi said as she aimed the gun at Finland's head and let loose with three muzzled shots. Finland slumped back, gasped several times, coughed up blood and began trembling. A bullet to the heart seized his movements and Naomi, Phillip and Grover sat quietly as Martha guided the car through the dense traffic and made her way over to a car crusher in Gary, Indiana.

Ironically, it was the same car crusher where Finland's stepfather, Lester, had been disposed of by Mendoza and Lucky back in the late sixties. The old man who ran the business was mob-affiliated and had ties to Twenty-Third Street Mafia once upon a time. He received a $25,000 dollar disposal fee and the limousine was crushed before Naomi's eyes as she stood under the falling snow flurries, eyeing what would become her childhood friend's final resting place.

Eastside Bar had been sold already, Kevin and Serena's

homes, along with Lucky and Mildred's home and Mendoza and Francine's home back in Cicero were destined to be put on the market for sale in the near future through the upstart real estate company Naomi was planning to open down in Oklahoma City.

The old ways of the Italian Mafia based out of Cicero that'd once run the rackets for over eighty years had reached the end of the line in October of 2006. The Holland-Dawkins family was now in a position to run the business alongside the Asians, who by all accounts, were in a weakened state. The feds knew not of the Holland-Dawkins family's existence and their crew was still intact and going strong.

A new family was on the verge of seizing power in the Midwest, and they were more than capable of running the rackets as their skills were more adept to the fast-paced, cutthroat society that was becoming more and more prevalent on the streets of America's heartland. With that being said, the family still had unfinished business to clean up inside their own house before they could move forward with the rest of their plans.

****

"It done snowed already. It's only October and the ground here is covered with snow," Mendoza said as he walked out onto the porch with DeeDee, Junior and Flacco following close behind. It was all but a few hours after Naomi, Phillip and Grover had left the car crusher, and Mendoza and company were preparing to tour the land in full.

The Cernigliaros had bought a trek of land in Cut Bank, Montana. A town of around 3,000 citizens located 120 miles North West of the city of Great Falls, twenty-three miles west of Interstate-15 and only thirty miles south of the Canadian border. This part of the country was high and dry, but fertile.

During the day, when there were no snow or rain clouds, the sky was a pristine and clear light blue. Set against the flat span of land, Mendoza often joked that he could see Canada from his front porch. Big sky country was what the people here called it; but it was the night sky that ruled supreme in this most picturesque and serene part of the country that many knew only as a dot on a map if they ever knew of its existence at all.

From here, in the little town of Cut Bank, Montana, the aurora borealis, or 'northern lights', which were charged particles of atoms that lit up the night sky in all colors on the prism with hues of green, red, yellow and blue could be seen clearly with the naked eye along with countless stars that twinkled in the night sky. Mendoza and Francine had literally bought a front row seat to the rest of the universe as the night sky here was one of the most fascinating pieces of celestial artwork the human eye could ever witness on the planet.

Many of the people in this part of the state grew wheat fields. The Cernigliaros weren't agriculturists by a long shot, though. They were planning on breeding horses on the fertile land, which totaled fifty acres. Their home, a ranch-style four bedroom, two-story wooden structure, was nearly complete, save for an island kitchen counter, the bricking of the fireplace, and sinks and tubs inside three of the four bathrooms.

The Cut Bank Cottage, as the Cernigliaro's home would become known, was a smaller version of the guest house on the Holland Ranch, and would become another destination for the family as the town of Cut Bank was only forty miles or so from Glacier National Park, which lay to the west. It was the perfect getaway for friends, lovers and others to enjoy beautiful scenery in an atmosphere of piece.

Mendoza eyed the snow-covered land as the men left the front porch of the home, which faced north, and walked to their left where Mendoza had a kennel set up beside the home. "I went into town and was looking for a breed of dog to help out, to help out in the keeping of the horses Francine and I are going to purchase from Naomi, right?" Mendoza said as he led the men towards the kennel.

"What kind of dogs you bought, granddad?" Junior asked as he eyed the wide span of land, land that was barren in his eyes and flat beyond compare.

"I was thinking of bloodhounds like Naomi has, but they

were five hundred dollars apiece." Mendoza said as the men walked under the darkening grey-clouded skies. "So I went another route."

"Five hundred each ain't bad, Senor Mendoza," Flacco chimed in. "That is about the price Naomi paid for her animals years ago. You can breed your own from there like the family has been doing."

"You didn't know he was a cheapskate, Flacco?" Junior joked.

"I ain't a cheapskate, son. I'm just not paying five hundred dollars for some stupid animals that I have to feed everyday just to have them crap all over the place. I got a better deal anyway with the ones I got from this breeder I found in the papers. They're perfect for the land."

The men all walked over to the kennels Mendoza had set up where they eyed five Dachshunds—wiener dogs. DeeDee, Junior and Flacco were all silent as they stared at the miniature animals, trying to figure out what on God's green earth was Mendoza going to use these proton-sized creatures for on the ranch. What possible purpose could they serve in the aiding of the breeding of horses? They were useless in their eyes.

Flacco removed his ten gallon hat and scratched his head. "Is this going to be your alarm system, Senor Mendoza," he asked. "Because these low-bellied creatures can't do anything but alert you of an intruder."

DeeDee chuckled. "Can't even bite an ankle they so low to the ground. Reminds me of a sixty-four Chevy with them, umm, them—"

"Hydraulics," Junior said.

"Yeah," DeeDee said pathetically as he stared down at the hapless mammals. "Can't do shit with these...maybe they can tackle a chipmunk if they gang up and go hard."

"I'd put my money on the chipmunk, Senor Doss," Flacco said as he held onto his hat and looked down upon the dogs sadly. "Why do I feel like eating a hot dog all of a sudden?" he then asked. "Keep seeing foot-long buns running through my mind."

Mendoza chuckled and said, "I brought an ass, for this place, too. He's out by the woodshed to the north. Let's ride over there and take care of 'em, you guys."

"What are you going to do with a donkey?" Junior asked through laughter.

"I'm gonna take care of his ass, son. What you think? Come on. Let's ride over there, and I guarantee that this ass I got will be the most beautiful thing you've ever seen."

The men piled into Mendoza's Durango and rode up a dirt road that traversed the western edge of the property, Flacco driving and Junior sitting in the front passenger seat. DeeDee sat behind Junior and Mendoza sat behind Flacco.

Mendoza brushed the lint off his black silk sacks, pulled down on his fedora and placed a pair of sunshades over his eyes as he crossed his legs and stared out the window, scanning his glorious land and imaging in his mind the events that were about to unfold.

DeeDee coughed, choking back tears in a state of disbelief. He couldn't believe all the events that had led up to Doss's death. It was the ultimate act of betrayal in his eyes.

Flacco had been given a new position within the family. He was to be a bodygaurd when needed and this day was to be his test. His introduction into the life. Doss had shared a few things with Flacco from time to time, but never revealed his true self. All he told Flacco was that if he were to ever get killed, to look after his family. Flacco agreed and he was now holding true to his word. He understood the nature of the family business fully and had made up his mind that he would remain loyal to the people that had taken care of him and his family from day one. He drove across the land in silence as the intro to Pink Floyd's song *Shine on You Crazy Diamond Part One* played over the sound system with its bluesy drums and pounding bass line.

Francine and Tiva, meanwhile, were inside the home sitting at the kitchen table as Malaysia and Malara slept soundly on the C-sectional velvet sofas. Tears were running down Francine's cheeks. She'd co-signed to this day after learning of the tragedy surrounding Doss's death and the truth behind her illnesses after her mastectomy and plastic surgery, a time in which she was purportedly to be cancer-free. Francine's mafia loyalty was never in question. She would go along with Mendoza no matter the depth of the decisions her husband had to make. Still, the weight of the day held no consolation.

Tiva sat with her legs crossed, her bottom lip trembling as she looked over to her daughters while staring at the printed out message she held in her hands. *They're leaving now. I'm in the CLK. They'll be pulling out first in the Suburban.*

Tiva had grabbed Junior's phone to call her sister just seconds before Bay was shot and her father was killed. She'd held onto Junior's phone when she hopped out of the car to try and help Dawk protect her father and sister.

Junior was certain he'd deleted the text, but yet it remained. Tiva had stumbled upon the text while she was calling Martha and it was nothing for her to report back to Mendoza what she'd uncovered. By the time Naomi had met up with Phillip and Grover in Saint Louis, there was no doubt left as to the fact that Junior was in on Doss's hit. Purposely mentioning where Phillip and Grover would be staying in Cicero during the meeting in Saint Louis, and the appearance of Q-man, Dead Eye and Big Bounce at that address in Cicero, had only cemented the fact that Junior was indeed the mole inside the Holland-Dawkins family.

The thing that troubled Tiva was how could she marry the man who'd killed her father? A man she'd loved once upon a time and had given birth to his children. Their life was set in her eyes. Together, there was nothing she and Junior couldn't conquer. But the hard truth for Tiva was the fact that she'd married a snake. A man who'd attempted to annihilate those she loved the most. Her father was running the Chicago Gang, and she, Dawk and Bay were moving up in the ranks quickly.

Junior wouldn't go so far as to kill the mother of his kids, but he had it in for his wife's family. He'd tried to vanquish all three simultaneously in order to become Boss. If it weren't for her wanting to tell Bena about those jeans, and her battery being dead on her cell phone, Junior may have very well gotten away with his treachery and Tiva would've still been in love with the very man who'd killed her father. The thought was sickening to her stomach as she sat beside Francine, the two women now clutching one another's hands tightly and drawing off their individual strengths as they awaited the inevitable.

Mendoza, meanwhile, stared at his grandson with disappointment as Flacco drove slowly across the land. Eighty years of La Cosa Nostra. Eighty years and there had never been a mole inside Twenty-Third Street Mafia; never been a man who'd turned on his own family. It was bound to happen given the times because everybody was either talking to the feds or backstabbing the ones who trusted them the most. The crew DeeDee and Mendoza had constructed, however, was built for the day. Solid men, who through training and over a period of time, had only grown stronger despite a few blunders, which could be attributed to going up against a band of experienced and malicious cowboys and cowgirls—Carmella Lapiente` and her bunch.

Mendoza never thought his grandson would sink to the depths he'd traveled. He gave his grandson too much credit. Too much leeway while putting the plan together and it had cost Doss his life. For that, Mendoza knew he had to set matters straight for the family because it was on his end, that the gross act of betrayal had originated. It was a gut-wrenching decision. Mendoza could have taken the money and run off to Italy. Taken his family and disappearred. Honor would not allow that manuever, however; Mendoza would never be able to face the sun nor the moon knowing he had betrayed those who never waned in the business. He knew full well that what he was preparing to do on this day, was the right thing to do for the family and all invloved.

"For a while now I've been meaning to take care of this fuckin' ass," Mendoza said dryly as he eyed Junior.

"Where the hell is the fuckin' jackass you keep mentioning, granddad?" Junior asked as he looked towards the back of the jeep.

"I'm staring the son-of-a-bitch right in the eyes," Mendoza replied as he pulled out a .38 snub-nosed revolver, old school to the death of him he was.

Junior eyed his grandfather and right away he knew. He turned and looked straight ahead and said, "I have a family."

"That has been your problem ever since you lost your father —thinking about yourself. You know what? You're no more useful to us than them fuckin' puny ass dogs I got in the kennel beside the home. When you was staring and making fun of them mutts? You was looking yourself directly in the eyes you worthless piece of shit! They were euphemisms for what a weakling you've become, Faustino! But they'll be around! They'll be around long after you're dead and gone!" Mendoza yelled.

"Granddad? Let me live and I promise, I promise I'll stay here and no one will hear from me again," Junior said, still believing he could stop the inevitable. "I'm your grandson and you do this?"

"How did you get close to those Somalis?" Mendoza asked. "That is the only thing I have not figured out."

"Kathyrn Perez," Junior said lowly. "I paid somebody at the DMV in Missouri, got an address and matched it to a number through some phone company."

"You went through a lot to betray your own," Mendoza scoffed.

Junior said nothing. He merely stared out the windshield as she shook his head somberly. "Hey, look, if Toodie never answered, I would have done nothing, alright? I just got in over my head and was unable to back out." Junior blurted out in defense of himself.

"So that makes it, all right?" Mendoza asked rhetorically.

"It was the only way. What the fuck do you want from me?" Junior yelled as he turned and eyed Mendoza through watery eyes.

"I knew Doss Dawkins Junior long before you had the gumption to swim through your mother's womb, mutherfucka!

You beat out all the rest of 'em with your fortunate ass! Now look what you make me do!" Mendoza cried as he rocked back and forth in his seat and punched the roof of the jeep in frustration. "'Not my own I said' when your wife told me! 'Not my flesh and blood! He would never go against family'! But I was wrong! Dead damn wrong!"

"Tiva gave me up?" Junior asked in dismay.

"With ease. She did it with ease. That woman has more balls than you could ever hope to have! So I says, I says to myself, 'For as long as I am in the business—in this thing of ours—will I never respect the shit—my grandson has done—to *this* family'! That's what I told myself. I have to honor that, dammit!" Mendoza screamed as the jeep cruised across his land.

"*Mi si è fottuto, Mendoza! ERO da capo! Vi fate un mazzo di, negri prendere su di me? Fuck 'em!* (You fucked me over, Mendoza! I was to be boss! You let a bunch of niggers take the lead over me? Fuck 'em all!)

Tears ran down Mendoza's cheeks as he held the gun on Junior. "*STO Mendoza ora?*" (I'm Mendoza now?) he asked in a heartbroken manner. "*Le persone con cui abbiamo fatto affari con per decenni...questo è quello che sono nei vostri occhi si pezzo di merda?*" (The people we've done business with for decades are...that's what they are in your eyes you piece of shit?)

"*Ci siamo fermati in famiglia molto tempo fa. Mio e figlie è importante. Tiva ha i miei discendenti. Send me home old man!*" (We stopped being family a long time ago. My daughters is all that matters. Tiva has my offspring. Send me home old man!) Junior said coldly as Flacco brought the jeep to a halt on the most northern edge of the property where the horizon shielded them from sight.

"Get out!" Mendoza hissed towards Junior as the men all exited the vehicle.

"No matter how many years you have left, old man, you kill me here? I'll forever be a part of this land and this family! I did what was right in *my* eyes!" Junior screamed as he threw his fedora and scarf to the side. "Through my daughters I will live, mutherfucka!"

Mendoza spit at Junior's feet. "You're wrong, son," he said coldly. "Malaysia and Malara? They, they won't even know of your real existence. We'll, we'll make up stories about your life. Tell them what a great man you were. How much you cared about family. How you gave your life for those you love. And I'm sure your family in Saint Louis will tell those whom they love, just how much you loved them and how they loved you even more. See the big picture? Nobody that really matters in this big scheme of things will give a fuck about Junior no more. But, I'm sure you'll be remembered well by your so-called friends back in Fox Park. You fucked up! Fucked up big time by going against the family, dumb ass!"

Junior spat into the snow. "It's what's here," he said as he pounded his heart. "It's all in here. I die with honor today!"

"I bought those dogs for a reason you know? Thought you would read the play and spare me the agony of having to force your grandmother to live with the fact that she approved of me doing this job."

The look on Junior's was worth a million dollars to Mendoza. Junior was a hard ass. A man willing to die on his feet, but learning that his grandmother knew of his impending death was crushing. Junior had a last recant, however. "I should've used more arsenic on that bitch the day I sent the cops at Eddie," he said nonchalantly.

Mendoza said nothing as Flacco pushed Junior before a six foot hole dug into the ground. "Fuck all y'all!" were the last words Junior would ever speak. His voice echoed across the land, mixed in with one gunshot that'd slammed into his forehead.

Mendoza then went and stood over his grandson's corpse, which lay inside the hole in a crumpled heap, and emptied the five remaining bullets in the chamber into his skull. He then stood in silence for a moment staring down on Junior, imagining what could have been before he placed the gun inside his wool trench coat and turning towards DeeDee.

"Has my debt been paid, il mio amico?" he asked.

"In full," DeeDee responded lowly as he and Mendoza stared one another directly in the eyes and shook hands, thereby closing out the deal that would allow the family to move ahead into the next episode of their drama-filled lives. "The family believes he will turn himself in on a drug charge for now."

"Okay, Doss. Flacco," Mendoza then said wiht wet eyes, "burn his remains before you cover the body. Me and DeeDee, me and DeeDee will walk back to the home."

"See, Senor Mendoza," Flacco responded as he went to the back of the jeep and grabbed two four gallon plastic jugs of diesel fluid and two fifty pound sacks of lime in order to begin his task, his first job that would solidify his position within the family.

CHAPTER FORTY-FOUR
HOLDING POSITION

Three ambulances had just turned onto the family's ranch in early March of 2007, five months after Junior's execution in Montana.

Inside the first medical carriage was Bena Holland. She was now off life support and able to breathe on her own, but she was immobile for the time being and had no control over her bodily functions. She slept most of the time and also had to be fed because she had little control of her extremities. Bena's speech was slightly impaired, too, she could barely talk.

DeeDee and Mary believed it was too early to bring Bay home and Naomi did also. Obadiah Wickenstaff had reassured the family, however, that being home, around family would be of great benefit to Bena as she was in the clear as far as infections and complications were concerned. He did suggest that Naomi hire a full-time home healthcare staff along with a Nurse Practitioner so Bena's progress could be monitored properly and the family would have someone on hand to treat her should any complications arise, which were highly improbable to Obadiah. The bottom line was that Bena only needed rest and time in order to make a complete recovery. After receiving a referral from Obadiah, Naomi hired a medical staff, put a Nurse Practitioner on the payroll full time, and the family left Saint Louis and brought Bena home.

Fifteen year-olds Spoonie and Tyke were eagerly awaiting their sister's arrival along with Walee, Kimi and Koko. They all ran out the front doors of the home and waited while Bena was unloaded. She lay on a gurney, slightly woozy as she'd been awakened upon arrival. Her head was wrapped and her face was slightly swollen around her cheeks. She was heavier than her normal weight, but Obadiah said it was a good thing because that meant Bena's metabolism was returning to normal and she was able to sustain a regular dietary regiment.

The girls stood on the stairs as Walee went and helped Dawk and the medical staff carry Bena up the stairs. When Bena caught sight of her sisters before her, her weakened eyes perked up. She'd even managed to smile a little. "Hey," she whispered as she slowly placed her right hand onto the rail.

Kimi, Koko, Spoonie and Tyke's hearts melted and their eyes grew wet. Kimi reached out and rubbed Bay's hand before stepping aside and she and her sisters timidly followed the group inside the home, their hearts pounding with joy. Bena was wheeled into one of the downstairs bedrooms, which had been transformed into a recovery unit set up with medicines, gauzes, movable mattress, and a wall-mounted TV.

This was by far one of the happiest days the family had had in a long while. They were six months removed from losing Doss and the wounds were still fresh, but they were healing. Bena's arrival only served to uplift their spirits further. A dinner was prepared to celebrate Bay's return. Jane Dow was out on the patio playing and singing, but at a lower level than normal, and the family was in and out of the room taking turns sitting with Bay. It was a very exciting time for the family.

The next morning, Naomi, Martha, Dawk and Tiva were holding a meeting in Naomi's office. Naomi had wanted an update on the streets in Saint Louis.

"Me and Tiva keeping an eye on the club. Malik got it working, but it'll be at least another year and a half before we open up," Dawk said as he stood before his mother's desk.

"What about that other thing over in Fox Park?" Naomi asked, in reference to Toodie.

Tiva spoke up at that moment. "Malik say she been hiding out since Q-man and them boys been looked up in Cook County Jail. They gone resurface sooner or later, and when they do we'll get back at 'em."

Naomi sat behind her desk, crossed her legs and said, "The Asians were able to head down to Venezuela and talk to our supplier. They said he's willing to wait until we're back online."

"That's good," Dawk remarked. "It'll give us time to tie up some loose ends and establish new routes of revenue once we back in the business. Bay won't be well for another year or so, so we'll have time to find new markets."

"And I'm going to open an office in Oklahoma City and buy five more trucks. By the time Bena's well we'll have our own transportation from Laredo established is the plan."

"We can tap into more markets that way and be our own supplier here," Dawk said in a sure tone of voice. "I'm thinking Kansas City, Indianapolis and Cincinnati. And if we get rid of those Somalis, we can take the twin cities too. We set up business in those cities and we'll have more than enough buyers for our product."

"Good," Naomi replied as she wrote in her ledger, "we are all on the same page here so let's let sleeping dogs lie for now, recoup and get back at it."

"What if other clicks won't stand down?" Martha asked anxiously.

Dawk looked to the floor beneath his feet and thought deeply for a second. "They won't even see us coming, Auntie," he said. "If we're going to make this last run and I'm the one that's runnin' it? We goin' at it full force. We gone be on the offense this time."

"Dawk," Martha said as she placed her hands onto the desk and stared her nephew in the eyes, "you talking about taking over other people's businesses and moving in?"

"You have a problem with that, Martha?" Tiva asked. "We in this thing to be the ones on top and don't have room for anybody that's in our way. We gone own the Midwest."

"I'm gone be forty-eight years old this month, y'all. I said I'll help, but I'm not warring with these youngsters of the day."

"We'll be doing things much differently, Martha," Naomi chimed in. "I want you to take Finland's position in the family. Just set up a route, a couple of warehouses in Saint Louis, and me and the big three will handle the rest."

"You sure?"

"If I thought this move would get any of us locked up or hurt I wouldn't do it, Martha. Once we're back online, we will be the strongest organization west of the Mississippi. Just let us navigate the course. We have plenty of time to think it out, have powerful friends on our side, and the hiatus will do us all some good. We'll let those responsible for killing Doss cool off and we'll take care of them all." Naomi said.

"If you in, then I'm in, Naomi. I can do Finland's job without a doubt."

"Okay. And our crew on the street will handle the jobs that need doing when and if the time arises." Naomi ended as she stood up and escorted her family back downstairs.

CHAPTER FORTY-FIVE
LOVE ME WHILE I'M HERE

It was now May of 2007, two months after Bena's arrival and she was getting better and better by the day. So much so, that with a little assistance, she was able to walk the first floor of Ponderosa and even sit a spell. She and Tiva were up early this day and they were in the downstairs kitchen. Tiva was feeding Bay as she still would lose control of her movements at awkward moments. She scooped up some oatmeal and placed it to Bay's lips and she ate slowly, staring her twin in the eyes as she swallowed.

"All of them," Bay mumbled after swallowing her food.

"Hmm?" Tiva asked.

"Of them," Bay whispered.

"Say again, Bay?"

"All—all of—them. All of them!" Bay finally screamed.

Tiva needed no explanation. Although incapacitated and barely able to speak, she knew Bay was the same person on the inside. "We'll get 'em," Tiva said as she nodded her head up and down. "We gone get 'em back for what they did to you and daddy."

"Okay," Bena said lowly. "'Nina?"

Tiva sat the spoon down and grabbed Bena's hands.

"AquaNina is fine, Bay. Kimi and Koko 'nem talked to her right after New Year's, but that was on the phone. She back working at Pizza Hut in town, but she not answering nobody calls now. We, we just been here looking after you, Bay. 'Nina will come around, don't worry."

"Ugly," Bay said as she pointed at her bald head that was wrapped in a gauze.

"No, no," Tiva sang as she tightened her grip on Bena's hands. "Look at me, Bay. You still look like," tears filled Tiva's eyes. All of a sudden she could feel Bena's emotional pain. She broke down and had to stand up and back away. "You look like me, Bena," she said through her tears. "You're not an ugly person, and it's what's on the inside that matters anyway, sister."

Bay covered her lower face and just cried. She was heartbroken that AquaNina had never come to see her. Never bothered to send a card or relay a message. How could it just end was a question she was asking herself repeatedly. "Sleepy," Bay whispered as she pointed towards the hall that led to her bedroom.

Tiva walked Bay down the hall and sat with her sister the entire morning as she slept with tears flowing from her eyes. She helped Bay to the restroom, basically giving the medical staff the day off once they changed her head bandages. She fed her sister lunch and the two sat and talked. Later that night, after all the family had visited and gone to bed, Tiva sat before Bay and shaved her head entirely. Bay watched in amazement as her sister cleared her crown of hair completely.

"Now I look like you," Tiva said lowly as she got up and hugged her sister.

When Kimi and Koko returned home from college the following weekend, they were surprised to see that Tiva, Spoonie and Tyke, their mother, Mary, Siloam and Martha, had all shaved their heads in support of Bay, who'd come under the belief that AquaNina had left her because of her appearance. Kimi and Koko were sitting in the Great Room helping Spoonie and Tyke figure out who to work a newly purchased digital camera when Tiva walked in and nonchalantly handed the middle twins the shredders.

"What's this," eighteen year-old Kimi asked as she tucked in her chin and eyed the clippers.

"Clippers so y'all can shave y'all heads in support of Bay." Tiva said matter-of-factly.

"Ohhh," Koko sighed as she fumbled with the camera. "We talked about that and we don't think that would be a good look for us."

"A good look?" Tiva asked as she placed one hand on her hip, shifted and stared down at Kimi and Koko. "This isn't about you two, it's about supporting Bay."

"We are supporting Bay. We feeding her and help her bathe. Come on, Tiva why you asking us to do that?" Koko snapped.

"Okay," Tiva said. "I'm on my way to tell Bay how y'all really feel."

"Wait," Kimi and Koko said in unison. "How, how long we gone have to this?"

Tiva smiled, clicked on the clippers and said, "Just once to show support."

Kimi and Koko looked at one another. "Classes be over in two weeks. We be straight by summer I guess." Kimi reasoned.

Tiva was already in Koko's head before receiving an answer.

"Dang, T-top at least put a sheet down!"

"Nahh, you good. Kimi sit with your back to Koko while I do the damn thing."

When Tiva was done, she stepped back and looked at her sisters and burst into laughter. She'd made sure they didn't see one another until she was done. Kimi and Koko looked at one another and they—were—devastated. Tiva had sliced off all of their hair and their ears stuck out tremendously.

"What the hell did you do to us?" Koko screamed as she jumped up and charged at Tiva, who took off running while laughing aloud.

Spoonie and Tyke were rolling on the floor laughing. None of the family had anywhere to go no time soon, and Twiggy had refused to cut her hair completely because she knew her head was not made to be bald. Tiva merely wanted to shave her twins' hair for her and Bay's pleasure.

Kimi and Koko were furious with Tiva, but they didn't run after her. They finished helping Spoonie and Tyke and soon got the camera working and Spoonie and Tyke followed them around the house all day, recording reactions.

Walee was in the theater room playing the PlayStation game with his best friend, a young man named Kahlil Jamison, when Kimi and Koko walked in.

"Walee you saw Tiva?" Kimi asked aloud.

"Nahh. She might be over to the guest—" Walee paused when he caught sight of Kimi and Koko's bald heads. "She might be at the guest house," he finished.

"Aww, man," Kahlil said lowly.

"What?" Koko asked anxiously as she rubbed her head. "It's bad, Kahlil?"

"Nahhh. I was just caught off guard. Y'all straight." Kahlil responded kindly.

"Thank you," Koko said as she and Kimi left the theater room.

"Okay what y'all really think?" Spoonie asked as Tyke held the camera on Walee and Kahlil.

"They look like Dumbo the elephant with them big ass ears," Walee said as he dapped Kahlil. "Fuck they do that for?" he laughed aloud.

Kimi and Koko walked out onto the patio where DeeDee, Dawk and Naomi were sitting. "I got some designs on the bar for the club, momma," Dawk said as he slid his mother some blue prints.

Naomi picked the pictures up and eyed them. "These aren't bad, son. What kind of furniture—oh my!" she then said.

Dawk and DeeDee turned and eyed Kimi and Koko.

"What the hell happened to those two," DeeDee asked with a dropped jaw.

"Why they look like big-earred aliens?" Dawk chuckled.

"Shh. Don't, don't mention it." Naomi said lowly.

"Momma, you saw T-top?" Kimi asked.

Looking her daughters in the face was the hardest thing for Naomi to do without losing it. She put on a cough and patted her chest, her way of releasing the barrel of laughs she was suppressing in her gut. "I haven't seen her, baby," Naomi said as tears filled her eyes. She had to bend down and pretend she was picking something up off the ground to conceal her laughter.

Kimi and Koko eyed their grandfather and Dawk for a moment, wondering what they thought of their heads, but they didn't ask. Dawk had his hand over his mouth, heaving slightly and DeeDee was biting his lower lip, an obvious smile on his face as Spoonie and Tyke recorded the moment.

"Forget all three of y'all!" Kimi yelled as she and Koko walked off.

When Kimi and Koko left the patio, Naomi, Dawk and DeeDee cut loose before the camera. "Tiva said she was gone do it, DeeDee!" Naomi yelled through tears.

These were some happy times for the family. Tears that once derived from pain and sorrow, were now tears of joy and laughter. They were healing.

Bay was sitting up in her bed watching TV with Tiva, who'd been in the room the entire time Kimi and Koko were searching for her. The twins walked in with Spoonie and Tyke following and were about to confront Tiva when Bay gasped and spread her arms. Kimi and Koko iffed at Tiva as they strolled pass her and went and hugged Bay.

Bay patted their heads, raised her mattress completely and said, "Why you two shave your heads? Y'all got some meat heads."

Instead of getting mad or laughing, however, Kimi, Koko, Spoonie, Tyke, and Tiva grew wide-eyed and their hearts warmed. Today was the first day Bena had completed a sentence since the day she'd been shot. She was healing as well.

The sisters where all talking for a few minutes when a soft voice was heard out in the hall crooning. Spoonie and Tyke rushed to the door and yelled happily. Spoonie raised the camera and stood in the hall as Tyke ran back into the room.

"Watch this, Bay!" Tyke said happily as the voice was heard by all again, this time singing.

"*...I know you've got a little life in you left...I know you've got a lotta strength left...I know you've got a little life in you left...I know you've got a lotta strength...I should be crying but I just can't let it show...*"

Bay's favorite song, sung by a voice she knew all-too-well brought tears to her eyes. It was the sweetest voice she'd ever heard and she hoped that she would never have to go another day without it. Her baby, her love, was near. And she was making her presence known and professing her love to Bay before her family through song to let her know—she hadn't stopped loving her, she was there all along.

"I told you, she'd come around." Tiva said as she rubbed Bena's shoulder, AquaNina's voice still being heard in the hallway as she neared the room.

AquaNina continued singing as she stepped into the room, her head shaved completely and tears running down her face as she continued singing her version of Maxwell's song *This Woman's Work*..."*Of all the things we should've said that we never said...all the things we should have done but we never did...all the things you wanted from me...all the things that you wanted for me...*"

AquaNina, upon entering the room, broke down into tears and ran towards Bay, knelt at her side and grabbed her hand and kissed it softly before she leaned over and hugged her tightly, pouring her heart out. "I'm sorry!" she yelled. "Bay, I'm sorry!"

"It's okay. I forgive you. I forgive you," Bay mumbled as she hugged AquaNina and waved her hand, signaling Spoonie to stop recording as she held onto AquaNina and cried.

Bena's sisters and two medical aides that were in the room had all left to give Bena and AquaNina time to be alone. When the door closed, AquaNina lay beside Bena and looked her in the eyes.

"My mother showed me an article that described what happened to you," AquaNina said. "The paper from Saint Louis said where you got shot was an old mafia hangout. What kind of work do you do when you leave here?"

"Would it change how you feel about me?"

"No, Bena."

"Then I do what the paper says, 'Nina. I work where the paper says. That's all you need to know."

"Bay? I love you and I don't want anything else to happen to you. I would lose my mind if you were to…you know."

"Tomorrow isn't promised for what I do. Tomorrow is promised to no one. Love me while I'm here, 'Nina," Bay said softly. "Love me while I'm here."

"I have a lot of making up to do."

"We'll talk about it later. You're here now and that's what matters to me the most." Bay whispered.

"I, I don't care what you do, Bay. At the end of the day, though? I want us to be together." AquaNina said through her tears.

"You know me? You know who I am and you're okay with it?"

"You're like your father, and he was a good person. You're a good person. That's the Bena I know and love." AquaNina said as she laid her head in Bena's bosom, knowing full-well what she had in Bay. She loved her truly, and she was actually ashamed of herself for running out on Bay during her most vulnerable state. As she lay beside her love, AquaNina promised herself that she would never leave Bay again, no matter the circumstances. She was in it for the long haul. The word gangster was never said by neither of the two, but AquaNina knew that, that was the very person Bena Holland was; her eyes were open now, just like the rest of the family. And just as Bay's relatives had accepted her occupation, so would AquaNina.

"Will you still marry me?" AquaNina asked Bay.

"Thought you'd never ask," Bay responded lowly through a smile. "But you can never know what I do outside of Oklahoma."

"As long as it's you and I? What you do doesn't matter. But I trust you with my heart so that's not an issue."

Bay was more than ready to commit to the love of her life because she now understood AquaNina's emotions and actions fully. She'd learned that the woman she loved was a gangster and had grown scared, but Bay knew AquaNina couldn't stay away because she loved her too much. There were no ill-feelings from Bay towards AquaNina; after all, she'd lived a lie for some time and would've continued living that lie had she not been shot in Saint Louis.

AquaNina had never asked her why she'd lied. She didn't need to, if Bay had to tell it, because she knew the deal. AquaNina was perfect for Bay. She wasn't in the life, didn't dip into her business on the streets, and loved her for who she was; she was everything Bay could ask for and more. Bay would recover completely over the next year or so and would return to her normal self.

CHAPTER FORTY-SIX
A BLAST FROM THE PAST

"I don't wanna forget the present is a gift...and I don't wanna take for granted the time you may have here with me...'cause Lord only knows another day here is not really guaranteed...so every time you hold me...touch me like it's the last time...every time you kiss me...kiss me like you'll never see me again..."

Jane Dow's soft voice graced the ears of the family as she and her band did a cover version of *Never See Me Again* by Alicia Keys on warm sunny Saturday afternoon in May of 2008. At the top of the patio stairs were twenty-two year-olds Bena Holland and AquaNina Mishaan. Today was a double celebration. It was the day Bay and AquaNina were to become life partners and it was also Dawk's twenty-fourth birthday. Oklahoma didn't recognize same-sex marriages, but Bena and AquaNina wanted to unify their love before their family so they'd planned their own civil union and celebration. They'd bought rings for one another and had recited their own vows before the family. The family celebrated afterwards with a huge steak buffet and champagne.

A week later, sixteen year-olds Spoonie and Tyke were in search of a new DVD program. The family had taken many photos and Spoonie and Tyke had hours of video footage. Naomi's youngest wanted to put together a DVD complete with video footage and pictures, basically chronicling Bena's recovery up until the day she and AquaNina had their ceremony a week earlier. The programs on the home computers could not support the tasks the twins was trying to perform, however, so they had Walee chauffeuring them all over town in an attempt to find the program that had the right formatting features.

"Tyke," Walee yelled from the driver's seat of Bay's Lincoln, "we been to Best Buy, Walmart and three computer stores, we even been to the Home Depot! They don't have what y'all looking for here in the Ponc. We need to head down to Oklahoma City."

"You just tryna get at your girl over in Quail Mall," Kahlil said to Walee from the passenger seat.

"Already," Walee snapped. "That thing there got a tight…" Walee silenced himself, nearly forgetting about Spoonie and Tyke in the backseat.

"She got some friends, big dog?" Kahlil asked.

"Do she? Look, my sister Bay got a crib down there, ya' dig? And guess what?"

"She ain't there and you got the key." Kahlil said. Kahlil was a tall, slender-built seventeen year-old Albino with a head full of red hair that he kept braided and had green eyes. He'd known Walee since the two were younger hanging out at Kaw Lake Park where Spoonie and Tyke played softball. He and Walee loved to chase girls together and today was no different.

Walee was looking out for Spoonie and Tyke, but he was also aiming to get down to Oklahoma City to meet up with his girlfriend for a while and chill while Spoonie and Tyke shopped.

"Bay gone punish y'all if she know what y'all be doing in her place," Tyke said.

"Bet you gone run and tell that to, huh?" Walee asked.

"Not if you pay for our dvd program." Spoonie snapped.

"We got 'em again, girl." Tyke quipped as she high-fived

THE HOLLAND FAMILY SAGA

Spoonie.

Walee just shook his head. It never failed. Spoonie and Tyke would sit and listen, spy and sometimes coax Walee into a position where they were able to bribe him. They'd been bribing Walee for years now, and it was always over something they knew Walee really liked doing.

"We go half on it, home boy. I wanna see what your ole lady friends look like, ya' feel?"

"Cool," Walee said as he headed west out of town towards Interstate-35.

Kimi, Koko, Regina and Mary were following Walee and company as they headed out of town this sunny afternoon. Mary, wondering where Walee was headed, called his cell phone from the Maserati and he told Mary he was headed to Oklahoma City.

"That's an hour and a half away, Walee."

"Aww stop going soft, Auntie! We riders!" Walee said as Mary hung up the phone shaking her head.

The family made their way into the city and split up and did a little shopping. Tyke was quickly able to find the computer program she needed, but the family milled about the mall waiting on Walee and Kahlil. Several hours later, the family ate and were soon back on the road headed back to Ponca City.

Mary and Kimi chatted as Regina fumbled with the stereo from the back seat of the vehicle, using the remote control until she stumbled upon a radio station with an all-so familiar voice deriving from the Dee-Jay…

…"was on the bus next to Rosa Parks, right? And umm, I look over to her and say, 'sister, I don't know how you get to sit up front, but I'm glad you did 'cause my feet is aching! Where you work'? I then asked Rosa Parks," the Dee-jay stated as chuckles were heard in the background.

"Girl tell me that's not—"

"Shh! Shh!" Regina said as she cut Mary off and raised the volume.

The family members listened as the Dee-Jay continued telling her story…"When I asked her where she worked, girl she looked at me and told me to shut the you know what up!"

"Rose, Rosa Parks ain't cuss you out! Anyway you wasn't even around in the fifties!"

"Tracey, how come every time I relay adventures in my life you get ta' hatin'?"

"Nobody hatin'! You be exaggerating, Rolanda!"

"Well exaggerate this, I'm the oldest in this group, right or wrong?"

"You right." Tracey Fuller responded.

"And how old is we?" Rolanda Jones asked.

Tracey was thirty-eight, but she didn't want her age broadcast. "Go 'head with your little tall-tale," she said nonchalantly over the airwaves.

"That's what I thought! Now, after Sister Parks cussed me out, the bus driver got up and came over to our seat and told us to get up. I got up, but sister Parks stayed in her seat. So since Sister Parks ain't move—I sat back down! Eventually, John Law rolled up. Now, this Montgomery, Alabama *in the fifties* ya' heard me? We got arrested, tookeded to jail! Two Black women, tired from a hard day's work, trying ta' make it home—instead we rode downtown. I looked over to Sister Parks and said, 'these white folks meant what they said about not sitting in the front of the bus, huh'?"

"What happened," another Dee-Jay asked Rolanda through snickers.

"Dominique, let me tell ya', she squinted her eyes, and said to me, 'if it wasn't for you you little black heifer I woulda got away with the (bleep)'! Come to find out, Sister Parks been riding in the front seats of the buses for weeks! You know she was light-skinnddeded! She was doing fine! Gettin' away with it until my black ass showed up that day! So, go back and check your facts! If it wasn't for *Rolanda Jones*, the civil rights movement would have never started! And that's my Impact on History! I'm everywhere ya' heard? Now, we gone get off into this song Wifey by the group Next. And it's on level 'cause now we on wifey, hit us up at www, dot, fantasticfourshow, dot com, spell it out and listen on-line wherever you at in the world," Rolanda ended as the song was stopped and Dominique came on the air.

"Fool that's pronounced Wi-Fi! Y dash Fie!"

"Aww damn, we got technology and all this time I been— correction! We on Wi-Fi! That's Y-Fie! Log on to www,dot, fantasticshow, dot com and listen on-line," Rolanda ended as the song was started over.

"Regina this is the show you and Ne`Ne` used to listen to!" Mary said excitedly as she reached and turned up the volume. The family members listened to the show until they were out of range; but Regina would make sure to log on-line whenever she could to listen to a radio show that brought back so many memories from Ghost Town, little did they know, they were on the verge of a great discovery.

CHAPTER FORTY-SEVEN
TOGETHERWE WILL DO THIS

It was the second week of October 2008 and thirty-four year-old Ben Holland was enjoying a get together with old friends. Those old friends were the casts of the Fantastic Four Show. Ben and his wife Katrina, his aunt Henrietta and his sister Samantha Holland were into the second day of the get-together and Ben had been conversing with one of the Fantastic Show's members' husband, a thirty-seven year-old man buy the name of Calvin Huntley.

During their conversation, Calvin revealed a shocking revelation to Ben. Ben's friends, his aunt Henrietta, and sister heard the news as well. Ben Holland stepped back and looked at the crowd of people and replayed in his mind what he'd just heard come forth out of Calvin Huntley's mouth. *"She had a dimple in her chin, and a beauty mark under her left eye, just like you, Samantha. Y'all daddy had a dimple too remember? She had Sam's eyes too brer, she had Sam's brown eyes. On top of that she had a set of female twins riding with her in the backseat. She had female twins just like your daughters Samantha. You got more family out there Ben...Sam had people!"*

"So," Ben said as he rested his hands on his knees and smiled, "So you tellin' me my daddy had a sister?"

"Yeah man! I'm tellin' ya, brer, I ain't crazy man! Her name is Mary!"

There was a long silent pause, and then laughter, feelings of disbelief and also shock. For so long Ben Holland believed he was the only survivor, he and Henrietta. Henrietta reconnected with Ben, and together, they found Samantha. Ben and Henrietta both believed that Samantha was the lost member of the tribe, but it now seemed as if Ben and Samantha were the lost members all along.

"Oooh! This is huge! Ben, you wanna find them?" Rolanda asked excitedly.

"No doubt! No doubt Rolanda."

"Okay! Okay! I know what we're gonna do! Tomorrow we going back to Vegas, but before we leave, let's go on-line and see if we can find a Mary Holland!" Rolanda stated excitedly as the friends and family in Phoenix nodded their heads.

The search for Mary Holland produced two hundred and thirty-seven names on MySpace. USA Search had a multitude of names as well, but Calvin, who remembered how Mary looked, recognized no one on MySpace and the numbers of names on USA Search were enormous and they had no pictures. For the time being, MySpace, with nearly three hundred names and photos, was the best hope.

Ben and Calvin sat down at the computer and began looking for Mary Holland. Samantha used Katrina's laptop and she, Henrietta and Katrina began searching. JoAnne, Alicia and Dana went home to use their computer as the Dee-Jays rested for the drive back to Vegas.

The following Monday, Rolanda Jones, Dominique Huntley, Tracey Fuller and their friend, Brianna Stanford, entered Jazzy's office. Jazzy was the founding member of The Fantastic Four Show. She had given thirty-seven year-olds Rolanda Jones, Tracey Sanchez, and Dominique Huntley their start in the broadcasting back in September of 1991 and the show had blossomed into one of the hottest radio shows in the nation.

"Hey ladies, how was Arizona," fifty-two year-old Jazzy

asked with a bright smile.

"Jasmine, we found out that Ben had another aunt—Sam had a sister and she might've had two twins—we was thinking we could—"

Jazzy looked at the women in confusion. "Hey! Hey! Hey! One at a time! I got one set of ears over here!" she said as she interrupted the three women. "Now, one at a time, please."

"Okay," Rolanda spoke. "During our trip to Phoenix, Calvin, you know Calvin, right? Him and Dominique met back at Little Woods when we was like eleven years old at the time. I remember the first day they kissed and he—"

"Rolanda! Girl, you playin'." Dominique said through laughter. "Jazzy," she then said, taking over for her friend. "We learned that Sam Holland, remember Sam that was married to your friend Gabriella?"

"Yes. I remember Gabriella and her husband Sam." Jazzy said from behind her desk as she crossed her legs and eyed the women cautiously.

"Jazzy," Dominique responded through a wide, optimistic smile. "Sam Holland had a sister! We found that out down in Phoenix and we were thinking we could do a special show you know? To try and help Ben find his aunt that was looking for him back in the day?"

"We can't do that," Jazzy said matter-of-factly as she waved the girls off.

"Why?" Rolanda, Tracey and Dominique asked in a heartbroken tone.

"This is not a seek and find outfit, ladies. As much as I would love to help Ben in his endeavors? We just can't open up the lines up and search for anyone."

"She's wrong! There has to be a way for her to do this! She can do it if she wants to!" Brianna said through sign language.

"Don't' worry 'bout it, Bri!" Tracey said in a disgusted manner. "Gabriella was her friend back in the day and now her *son* needs help and she not even willing?"

"Tracey!" Jasmine yelled as she stood up from her chair. "You always get flip by the mouth with me! For the last time, you disrespect me again and you are fired!"

"I don't care, Jazzy! You always said you would *never* become Darius, but you do just what the people in Los Angeles tell *you* to do! You rule with an iron fist just like he tried to do! Just this one thing for us, man! We would *never* ask you for nothing like this unless it was really, really important and you know it!" Tracey screamed as tears of anger flooded the wells of her eyes.

Tracey was really pulling for Ben after learning all he had been through in life after losing his parents so tragically. All of the daughters were pulling for Ben, but they were now under the assumption that they had placed their hopes in the hands of the wrong person, albeit the only person, that could really help their childhood friend at least have a chance of finding his family.

"Get out! All four of you! Get out!" Jazzy screamed as she scooted from behind her desk and began ushering the women towards her office doors.

The four left the room and Jazzy slammed the door and went and sat behind her desk, but not before shoving all of her paperwork onto the floor. "I'm not like him!" Jazzy yelled out in anger inside the silent room.

The crew was scheduled to go on air in three hours, but Tracey had unknowingly struck a nerve with Jazzy. Darius was her former boss, a man she despised; and to hear Tracey make that comparison had stirred the woman. So much so, that she decided to call Calvin and get Ben Holland's phone number.

****

While Jazzy was over in Vegas trying to contact Calvin, Dawk, Bay and T-top, at the same exact time, had just entered their father's office inside Ponderosa, closing the door behind them. "We got a situation back in the Lou," Dawk said lowly.

Dawk was now leading the family into its next phase of the business. At the age of twenty-four, he was ready to take the lead position. He'd been trained by the best, was adaptable to his surroundings, and was a fierce competitor and an astute leader with killer instinct. Six-foot four inches of solid muscle, tan-skinned with a long ponytail, he was the epitome of a gangster and a leader in every sense of the word.

Bay and T-top were now co-captains of the new outfit. Their prowess, coupled with their courageous spirit made them a force to be reckoned with any and everywhere. The Holland family's reputation preceded them on the streets of the Midwest, and their resume' was unparalleled given their mafia roots. It was now understood by all, with Eddie serving ten years behind bars, Junior having vanished into thin air, and Doss being dead and buried, that The Big Three as they would become known by all, were now calling the shots.

"What's the problem," Tiva asked as she and Bay stood before Dawk, who sat in the same chair his father once sat when discussing business

"It's not a big problem yet, but Malik called me a few minutes ago and said Toodie and the Somalis done retooled and opened Ann Avenue again. Got a new crew and everything." Dawk responded.

"How long before we meet with Gacha and get the go ahead to start getting these people out the way for good? Because if they get stronger, we gone be right back in the same position we were in when Carmella was alive," Bay said as Tiva nodded in agreement.

"We scheduled to meet with the Asians in Cut Bank in a couple of weeks to see about setting up a meeting in the Margarita Islands. It'll be another three months at the earliest before we can meet with Gacha. I wanna be sure we will have a deal in place before we do anything, so I'm thinking we let Toodie and her crew be for now. I'm gone keep Malik out of Fox Park for now and give the family a few months before we get back to slinging iron. Tell me what you two think."

"It'll be good to hold off for now," Bay replied. "Let's talk to the Asians first and then plan our next move."

"I agree," Tiva chimed in. "Let Toodie 'nem relax for now

and we'll get back to 'em after we meet up with Gacha."

"That's what it is then," Dawk said. "Let's go find momma and everybody else and get ready for this chili Dimples no-cooking behind tryna fix," he joked.

"You is gone stop making fun of my cousin like that," Bay laughed as she and Tiva trailed Dawk out the room.

****

"Siloam just told me she got Jane Dow set to open for at a amphitheater in November over in Portland, Oregon y'all," Kimi told Walee, Koko and Walee's friend Kahlil happily as she sat a picture of warm tea and a bowl of cookies on the patio table and took a seat.

"Cool. Siloam 'nem gone be able to take pictures?" Walee asked Kimi.

"I don't know. Last time, last time they played a show in Tulsa a fight broke out and they never even got to perform let alone take pictures."

"Jane just need better gigs. Portland cool, though. A lotta bands played out there on Portland and they broke out big time." Kahlil said.

"Siloam said she used to play at that amphitheater," Koko chimed in. "Hootie and the Blowfish and that dude, umm, Kirk Romaine used to play out there."

"That's Kurt Cobain from Nirvana," Kahlil said, correcting Koko.

"How far y'all think Siloam gone take Jane 'nem?" Walee then asked.

"They always gone be an opening act until they come up with they won songs," Koko said. "They good though. It's a way for Jane to make a living, but they still have room for improvement."

"So when you and Udelle gettin' married, Kimi?" Kahlil asked.

"When you stop minding our business." Kimi replied, never

making eye contact with Kahlil.

"Come on y'all, it's getting a little chilly out. Let's go play cards in the library with momma 'nem." Koko said as the group got up and headed inside.

****

Regina, meanwhile, was over to the guest house trying her hand at making a homemade pot of chili for the family with the aide of Spoonie and Tyke. The counter was filled with onions, bell peppers, ground beef and numerous herbs and spices.

It was a warm atmosphere on the ranch. The family was mostly lounging around on this cloudy, cool October evening. Dimples had just poured a can of tomato sauce into a large pot. She licked her finger tips and rinsed her hands in the sink and saw the time on the clock. "Spoonie! Turn the lap top on so we can listen to the Fantastic Four Show!" she yelled from the kitchen.

Spoonie fired up the lap top, logged onto The Fantastic Four's website and the song *These Three Words* by Stevie Wonder was heard playing in the background. When the song ended, one of the Dee-Jays began speaking.

****

"Alright, friends, that was a classic from Stevie right there—umm, tonight—tonight we're going to talk to the son of a very special friend of mines." Jazzy said from the studio back over inside the Vegas studio as her girls looked up with wide eyes.

Jazzy handed Tracey a note that read, *"I'm sorry for my rudeness. Benjamin needs us and Gabriella was my friend. Together we will do this for the Holland family."*

Tracey passed the note around and the women grew happy. Rolanda blew kisses at Jazzy as Jazzy smiled while cueing up the line.

"Ben, you there?" Jazzy asked over the airwaves.

"Hello? Yeah, yeah I'm here Jazzy."

"Hey, Ben!" Rolanda, Dominique and Tracey yelled in unison.

"What's up ladies?"

"Rolanda? You wanna explain what it is we are doing tonight?" Jazzy asked.

Rolanda hadn't prepared anything so she had to wing it. "Well, earlier today, and I think I speak for my girls when I say what a great person Jazzy is, the world needs more people like her." Rolanda said as Tracey and Dominique agreed. "Now people, my buddy Ben, Ben, because this segment, well this night, is officially dedicated to family from this point forth, Ben has something he wants to say to his family. Am I right, Ben?" Rolanda asked.

This was the moment for Ben. Years, literally decades in the making, he hoped his friends could help him. "Yeah, umm, what I wanna say is that, I come up on the streets of New Orleans. Lost my father and my mother early on to a great tragedy not of their own doing. I thought my sister was dead, thought all I had left was myself. But my sister was alive the whole time and through God I found her."

****

"That's interesting," Regina said as she stirred the tomato sauce. "At least he found his sister after losing his parents, though."

"That's kinda like what happened with your momma and Auntie Martha and our momma," Tyke said as she fried ground beef in a large skillet.

"I know, huh?" Spoonie said. "People family be scattered all over the place, man. I'm glad he found his sister, too."

"They still talking," Regina said as she sipped a glass of wine, politely quieting down Spoonie and Tyke.

****

"That was a miracle in itself, Ben," Jazzy said back inside the Vegas studio. "I'm glad for you, baby. What do you want to really want to say, though? Because I know there is much more to your story, young man. Do you, do you have anything to say about the condition of the family in today's world given your experience?"

"Yeah. Sure do, Jazzy. If anybody has family that they care about, please, take nothing for granted. Let them know how much you love and care for them today. Love your family," Ben said in an emphatic tone. "Because for all we know? Tomorrow may never come and you may not get to say all that you wanted to say."

"That is so sweet, Ben," Jazzy said as she wiped her watery eyes, now understanding the depth and full scope of the situation at hand. A man had suffered a tragedy. And she was and her girls were the ones who could possibly right a wrong that had been in existence for over two decades."What else, what else can you tell us through your words of wisdom, Ben?" she asked. "What else do you have to say to the listeners. Speak your heart, baby. This is your platform."

"What I want to say tonight goes out to a lady by the name of Mary Holland, my father' sister. If she's listening, my name is Benjamin Holland and I'm looking for my aunt, Mary Holland."

"Ohhh, this is such a moment," Dominique said happily. "So Ben, Mary Holland, she's Sam's sister and your aunt, right?"

"Yeah. She my family. She came looking for us back in the day, but we were nowhere to be found. I hope she still looking because I want to know who she is. I know who I am—I'm Ben Holland, son of Samson Holland and Gabriella Holland—New Orleans, Louisiana."

"Okay, okay," Jazzy said lowly. "Now, Ben, you know the story about that day? What all happened?"

"Yes ma'am. From what I been told…"

"Wait a minute, Ben," Dominique chimed in. "We gone play a song and we'll talk off air. For everybody listening, again we're looking, we're looking for a Mary Holland. Mary Holland? If you're listening, and know of your brother Sam, give us a call at 8-0-0-3-2-6-3-6-8-7—that's eight hundred fan four for those listening—eight hundred fan four."

Dimples was out the door dialing the radio station's number the moment Dominique had given the station's number. She hopped into her husband's pick-up truck and sped over to Ponderosa while Spoonie and Tyke called members of the family.

****

The phones inside WKLV studios in Las Vegas were ringing incessantly. Callers were calling in from all over the country. People claiming to be Mary Holland were asking to speak to the Dee-Jays, eager to tell their stories. The show's producers knew what to ask, however, and none of the callers' stories fit either the description or the circumstances. Call after call was being rejected until one of the show's producers stood up and tapped on the plexi-glass window separating the producers from the studio.

Rolanda looked around and saw her producer pointing to her personal line so she picked up.

"There's a young woman on line seven saying her name is Dimples." the producer said in an excited tone.

"I don't know nobody named Dimples," Rolanda snapped.

The producer returned to the line and said, "I'm sorry, miss. Rolanda says she doesn't—"

"Tell her the name Ne`Ne`!" Regina said through tears. "Miss! Please don't hang up on me! I'm, I'm Ben cousin I swear! Tell, ask Rolanda if she remember the name Ne`Ne`, please! She used to call her show all the time from Jackson, Mississippi I swear on everything I love! Tell her! Ask her for me!"

The producer placed Regina on hold and said, "Rolanda? This lady Dimples on line seven said her sister Ne`Ne` used to call your show all the time from Jackson, Mississippi."

Rolanda had talked to literally thousands of callers over the years, but yet and still, she remembered one of her favorite callers from days long gone. Ne`Ne` had been dead for over eleven years now, but still, she was able to contribute to the family. Even in her time of rest, Ne`Ne`s life still held value years later. Regina's twin had not died in vain. Through her, hope was established.

"Is Ne`Ne` on the phone now," Rolanda asked with a smile.

"No, this is her sister Regina," the producer replied.

"Okay put her on," Rolanda said as she hung up her personal line and picked up on line seven. "Hello, caller?"

"Hello?"

"You're on with the Fantastic Four, baby, this is Misses Jones speaking."

"Misses Jones," Dimples said as her eyes filled with tears. She was running inside Ponderosa calling for her mother while she was on hold. "Please say you remember me and my sister. We called you all the time when we were teenagers in—"

"Ghost Town! I know, and I remember, sister! How you doing," Rolanda asked happily.

****

Back in Oklahoma, Bena and AquaNina was sitting on the patio having just finished wiping Bena's car down when they saw Martha and Twiggy's truck turn onto the ranch. The tractor trailer sped up the driveway. Bena had never seen Martha or Twiggy drive so fast. Worried something was wrong, she told AquaNina to call her mother. When 'Nina got up to enter the home, Martha began blowing the horn furiously. The truck came to a screeching halt and Martha exited the truck yelling for Mary.

"What's wrong?" Bena asked worriedly.

"We found, they got Sam son on the radio! Where Mary? He's looking for Mary!" Martha said as she, Bena and Twiggy ran into the house.

"Naomi! A man on the radio talking about he Sam son!" Martha screamed as she ran through the house. "Naomi!"

"In the library, Martha!" Naomi yelled aloud.

Martha and Twiggy ran into the library where Naomi met them with a face full of tears. Kimi, Koko and Walee were laughing aloud as Kahlil watched in appreciation.

"You're wrong, Martha!" Naomi screamed. "Sam had not a

child—but he had *children*!" she cried happily as she ran and hugged Martha. "He had *children* Martha!"

Martha saw Mary on the phone. She was laughing and talking loud, obviously thrilled over the situation at hand. There was a flurry of activity inside Ponderosa. DeeDee was smiling proudly at his family, Siloam was shedding tears, Dawk was amazed and excited, wondering what his uncle's son was like. Tiva couldn't wait to see her cousins for the first time.

Bay and AquaNina were in the kitchen with Spoonie and Tyke, who'd ran across the land from the guest house with Tacoma to share in the moment. They were listening on the lap top they'd toted with them.

Bay couldn't believe her ears. As far as she knew, everybody that was on the ranch was all there ever was in life. There were no more family members alive; but if her ears were correct, she had cousins somewhere out there in the world. Who were they? What were they like? She was giddy over all the possibilities as the Staple Singer's' song *Let's Do It Again* came to an end.

"Alright now friends, ohhh, this is epic, I don't think this has been done ever in the history of radio!" Rolanda stated excitedly. "Ben you there?"

"I'm here, Rolanda."

"Mary, you there?"

"Yes! Yes, I'm here, Rolanda!" Mary answered, her heart thumping with joy and anticipation.

"Okay, here's your question Mary—on the day you arrived looking for Sam Holland, where were you and what was the scene?"

"I was on Stony Brook Lane, or maybe it was drive," Mary responded immediately, recalling the day vividly in her mind. "I'm not sure if the street is correct, but I remember what happened like it was yesterday. I was in a white Chevy Caprice, me and my twin daughters, Ne`Ne` and Dimples, and their friend Sandy Duncan, a white girl. I remember I knocked on the door and this guy answered and it looked as if he was in an argument or something by the look on his face, but I asked anyway. I asked that guy did he know my brother Sam and he said—"

"Okay, okay," Dominique said through proud tears as she cut Mary off. "Ben?"

"Yeah, go ahead, Dominique."

"My husband is here in the studio with us, Ben, and the details this woman is giving, the people she described and what she is saying? It could have only been told had she actually been there—this—this is your Aunt Mary Holland, Benjamin," Dominique said, her voice cracking as The Spinners' song *Sade* began to play over the airwaves. "This is the Fantastic Four Show," Dominique said as tears of joy dripped down from her pointed chin. "We'll, we'll be back after these messages, everybody."

To be continued

THE HOLLAND FAMILY SAGA

Made in the USA
Monee, IL
02 December 2023